THE BRAVE WHITE FLAG

A novel about the fall of Hongkong

THE BRAVE WHITE FLAG

by

JAMES ALLAN FORD

With a Foreword by
Augustus Muir

London
HODDER AND STOUGHTON

The characters in this book are entirely imaginary and have no relation to any living person

*Printed in Great Britain
for Hodder & Stoughton Ltd., London
by Northumberland Press Ltd., Gateshead*

Author's Note

THIS is a story about the fall of Hongkong to the Japanese in December, 1941. It is dedicated to the memory of Captain Douglas Ford, G.C., who was executed by the Japanese at Big Wave Bay, Hongkong, on 18th December, 1943, and also to the memory of his comrades of the 2nd Battalion, The Royal Scots (The Royal Regiment), who were killed in the battle for the colony, who perished as prisoners-of-war, or who have died since their liberation in the late summer of 1945. This is not, however, their story. Their story has already been told by the regimental historian, Augustus Muir. This is a novel: all the persons appearing in it and all the actions ascribed to them are fictitious. It is only as regards the general course of events that the novel conforms with history.

Foreword

BY AUGUSTUS MUIR

JAMES ALLAN FORD, as a platoon commander in a battalion of The Royal Scots, fought in some of the toughest battles of the Hongkong campaign. To all who knew the facts, it was plain before a shot was fired that the Japanese would overwhelm the little Crown Colony. Winston Churchill, as Minister of Defence, wrote to his Chief of Staff:

"There is not the slightest chance of holding Hongkong or relieving it. Instead of increasing the garrison it should be reduced to a symbolical scale. We must avoid frittering away our resources on untenable positions."

It was to be a beastly, secluded and—it was hoped—a glorious little war of extermination.

With artillery of corps calibre, the advancing enemy fell first upon the Royal Scots (many of them sick with malaria) and got such a hammering that General Kitajima said afterwards the Japanese thought they had been at grips with a formation much larger than one infantry battalion supported by only a few howitzers. In the desperate battle of Golden Hill, Second-Lieutenant J. A. Ford was wounded but carried on; then he went into the critical counter-attack at the Wong-nei-chong Gap, was wounded again and continued to fight with a handful of survivors. In the end, he dropped in his tracks from loss of blood; most of his companions of that night were dead or very near to death. The Royal Scots, with officers and men of other regiments and of the Royal Navy, fought with a gallantry not often excelled in any theatre of war.

With sober brevity, the true story of the glories and muddles of the Hongkong campaign, which lasted only eighteen days, has been told in the Official History of the War; and now, in Ford's novel, we find the bitter taste of it—the blood and sweat and tears

7

of that hopeless death-struggle. James Allan Ford knew Hongkong, the luxurious safe-deposit of the wealth of the Orient, at the most dramatic moment of its history.

For years he rotted in prison camps in Hongkong and Japan— rotted in body, but kept his soul alive by a resolve never to succumb to the creeping corrosion of despair. It is remarkable that, from a nightmare world, he emerged with quiet self-control; for he had endured much more than the torment of captivity. To him was reported in detail what his brother suffered at the hands of the Japanese. Captain Douglas Ford, a fellow officer in The Royal Scots at Hongkong, had organised the smuggling into the prison camp at Sham Shui Po of medicines for sick men who were dying under the evil smiles of their guards. He was helping to plan a mass escape when a Chinese messenger betrayed him. Because he refused to disclose the names of his colleagues in the plan, he was tortured. He was tortured again and yet again. Even in the throes of the most sinister agonies that depraved minds could devise, he never broke. Holding his racked body upright, Douglas Ford went through the grim farce of a trial: he still refused to speak and was executed. Never was a George Cross more heroically earned.

The Brave White Flag was written under a poignant compulsion to tell what a bloody business war was for a group of young fellows who had the bad luck to fight in a campaign that was inevitably a lost cause. Between the lines we can read something of the ordeal of a young Edinburgh soldier who looks back, after nearly twenty years, on the days of his own testing with their memories that thrill and burn.

Contents

For maps see pages 12 and 200

A*

PART ONE

The River

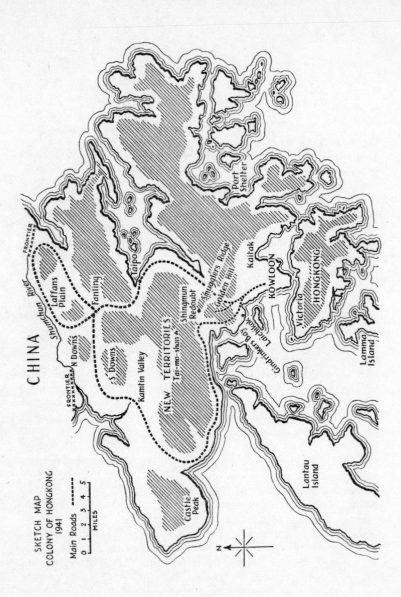

SKETCH MAP
COLONY OF HONGKONG
1941

Main Roads

0 1 2 3 4 5
MILES

CHINA

FRONTIER

Shum-chun River

Laffan's Plain

Fanling

N Downs

S Downs

Kam-tin Valley

Taipo

NEW TERRITORIES

Tai-mo-shun

Shingmun Redoubt

Smugglers Ridge

Golden Hill

Kaitak

KOWLOON

Gindrinker's Bay

Laichikok

Victoria

HONGKONG

Lamma Island

Lantau Island

Castle Peak

Port Shelter

N

Chapter One

CAUTIOUSLY but with stubborn determination, Second-Lieutenant John Morris picked his way through the coarse bleached grass and sun-blackened scrub towards the frontier of the colony, towards the Shumchun river.

The first time he looked back, he could still see his platoon of infantry. They were waiting where he had left them, strung out along the frontier-road: their steel helmets, battle harness and weapons incongruously, ominously obtrusive against a dusk-delicate background of rice-fields and mountains. They were watching his progress.

As he turned towards the river again, he wondered resentfully when he would be able to feel at ease with them. It was ten days since he had arrived in Hongkong, six days since he had been given command of 17 Platoon, D Company, in the Scottish infantry battalion which formed part of the colony garrison, and he still felt strange, unwelcome. His resentment was deep-rooted, for one of his few boasts was that he got on pretty well with people. Take his thirteen years at school, he could argue: although he had been too erratic a reader to make a scholar, too thinly overgrown and awkwardly handed to make much of a shape at rugby or cricket, he had found himself sought out and befriended by both swots and sweats. Take his year at Edinburgh University: although—lacking any particular ambition, reluctantly accepting his father's advice to study law—he had entered the Old Quad in a mood of distant, determined melancholy, he had found both men and women waiting to charm him out of his melancholy, to reconcile him to the study of law, and to give him, if not a definite ambition, at least a sense of direction. Take his year in the army, where he had found again—in the recruit squad, at O.C.T.U., in the officers' mess at the Regimental Depot, and on the troopship that had carried him east—that he did not have to thrust himself on strangers, that strangers made their way to him. It was true

13

that, until now, he had never been in a position of command. But he had appreciated that, on this occasion, he would have to take some initiative, and he had done his best to show his hand—a large, friendly hand—to 17 Platoon. And they had failed to meet him halfway. He knew little more about them now than he had been told six days ago by his predecessor, Lieutenant Williamson, and by the commander of D Company, the formidable Captain Craig.

"A good bunch," was how Lieutenant Williamson had described them, in handing the platoon over to Morris . . .

"A good bunch," he said, and screwed up his eyes and stretched out his mouth in a nervous spasm, and started to make left-handed adjustments to his generalisation. He was a small vigorous man of twenty-six, red and hairy. He made Morris feel too tall, too thinly languid, too pale, too smooth. "Most of them have been abroad a long time, of course," he said. "Most of them regulars, you see? Served in India before they came to Hongkong."

Morris offered him a cigarette.

"Never touch them." Williamson slapped his abdomen. "Spoil your wind."

One thing you could say in Williamson's favour: he was easy to understand. *Mens sana in corpore sano* summed him up, if you added a couple of glosses. 'Healthy mind', in Williamson's case, referred only to the rational faculties needed to pass examinations in accountancy and to memorise the infantry manuals. 'Healthy body' indicated both his fanatical zest for physical exercise and his morbid anxiety over prophylaxis.

"What difference does it make—being abroad a long time?"

Williamson clenched and unclenched his big-knuckled hairy fists. "Well, take your sergeant—'Smiler' Meechan, as the troops call him. You'll have to keep your eye on him. Lazy, you see? You'll have to make him toe the line."

Morris took a few nervous draws at his cigarette. He had already met Sergeant Meechan, M.M., a lean leathery man with the scar of an Afghan bullet furrowing his right cheek and distorting his dark face into a set, ironical smile. He stared bleakly at his cigarette and asked, "Any others I should perhaps keep my eye on?"

"The lot," said Williamson cheerfully. "Especially the regulars.

They've been a long time in the sun." Winking, he left it at that, as if his new responsibilities as second-in-command of D Company obliged him to be less than frank in his disclosures to the battalion's latest recruit and most junior officer . . .

Captain Hugh Craig, commander of D Company, had sounded frank, without disclosing anything . . .

Craig was anything but easy to understand. He was the most solitary as well as the most respected soldier in the battalion. Nobody seemed to know him well, but everybody spoke of him as if the field-marshal's baton had already started to protrude from his knapsack. In his middle twenties, with a Sandhurst and Poona training behind him, he was already the kind of commander whom Morris would have preferred to admire from a distance. His appearance was as formidable as his reputation. He was tall—no taller, perhaps, than Morris at full stretch, but his stronger build and erect carriage made him look twice the man that Morris felt himself to be. He had a small neat head and a pale brown, hard face; his fair hair was closely cut, and his blue eyes and thin lips were habitually narrowed. He walked with an odd, stiff-legged gait. With Williamson at his side, he looked like a young Prussian exercising his terrier.

"It's a well-trained platoon," he said. His voice still sounded surprisingly gentle to Morris. "But they're accustomed to regular officers," he added.

Morris was ready to blush in acknowledgement of his own temporary status, when his attention was distracted by Williamson, who was hitching his shoulders up and down in annoyance.

"I simply mean," said Craig mildly, "that they're accustomed to discipline."

Briskly readjusting his manner, Williamson grinned and blinked and nodded. "I've been telling him. He'll have to keep his eye on them, make them toe the line."

Craig was openly, disconcertingly, surveying Morris. "Did you command any troops at the Depot?"

"Not really," admitted Morris. He immediately regretted the vagueness of his reply and hurriedly tried to frame it with explanations. "I wasn't there for long. And I spent most of the time on courses—Signals and M.T." He paused, becoming aware that his manner was absurdly respectful. Shifting his stance a little, he said, hearing his harsh voice betray his nervousness rather than convey the intended casual air of camaraderie: "But I was a lance-corporal for three months before I went to O.C. T.U."

Craig responded with a movement of his lips that, though too slight to form a smile, was not unfriendly. "You'll shake down," he said. And then, with more conviction, he added: "Meechan will keep you right. He knows his job inside out. But don't let him think that you're leaning on him."

"I won't," promised Morris. And then, in an effort to tone down the earnest ring of his words he stretched out an uneasy smile . . .

Morris made his way towards the Shumchun, sweating through grass and scrub, worrying through the tangle of memories. Sergeant Meechan and the men were at his back, standing along the road, waiting, watching him. He swore at them—at their dark faces and critical eyes, and their polyglot slang and grotesque tattoo-marks. He swore at the mosquitoes whining round his head. He swore at the swiftly gathering darkness.

And then, with an anger-sharpened sense of his surroundings, he looked up, checked his pace, inhaled the cooling air, saw himself as a liberated law-student marching across China, and recovered his composure. When he turned his thoughts back to his present quandary, he tried to examine it dispassionately, to review the evidence from the impartial height of the Bench. It was simply a question of credibility of witnesses. Sergeant Meechan said one thing, and Captain McNaughton Smith said another. In considering which of these witnesses was to be trusted, Morris had to take evidence of character from other witnesses. He could not rely on his own judgement of character. Since his arrival in Hongkong ten days ago, he had met too many people to be able to sort them out with any confidence. Besides, other people's judgements of character usually struck him as being less tentative and therefore more comfortable than his own.

There was, for instance, clear-cut and corroborative evidence on Sergeant Meechan. *You'll have to keep your eye on him. Lazy, you see. Meechan will keep you right. But don't let him think that you're leaning on him.* There, in four concise statements, was an old soldier neatly pinned on a precognition-sheet.

The evidence on Captain McNaughton Smith was not so easy to sum up. Torrance and Anstey, the other two platoon commanders of D Company, had both offered testimony. Torrance, the curly-headed, yellow-eyed faun who shared a tent with Morris, had had most to say . . .

"Smith? One of the nobility, Johnny."

"Blue blood?" asked Morris, with a slight sneer.

Torrance interrupted his careful toilet to take a look at Morris. For a moment it was a long-faced look of frank curiosity; then it broadened into his customary look of comprehensive pleasure. He was a vivaciously, impudently handsome young man, who made Morris feel glumly dissatisfied with the plain, peering face he caught sight of in his own mirror. "I sometimes wonder," Torrance said, "whether Smith has any blood at all. Since he was thrown out of theological college his only psalm has been, 'The world's my oyster, I'll not want.'"

"Rich?" asked Morris. It was the end of his first week and he felt tired and timid.

"Rich as my granny's plum duff. It had everything in it except money."

"You mean," suggested Morris, with emphatic coarseness, "that he's all piss and wind?"

"Well," said Torrance reflectively, "I'd be inclined to agree, if you had said 'urine and flatulence'." He polished his pointed chin with a towel, wiped his smiling lips. "But don't underestimate him. He's the kind of chap who could talk the brigadier's wife into bed and keep the brigadier too busy discussing strategy to notice what was happening."

It seemed to Morris that he had learned as much about Torrance as about McNaughton Smith . . .

Anstey had been briefer, but quite as categorical. "McNaughton Smith is an ass," he had said, watching Morris with wide, searchingly blue eyes. "An ass and a sponger." And, as if expecting his opinion to be challenged, he had continued to stare at Morris with wide, wary eyes.

There was an earthy smell in the air now, an evening smell of freshening soil and moistened leaves. Morris wiped his brow and waved his handkerchief at the mosquitoes dancing dizzily before his face. He glanced round again and, finding that the platoon were out of sight, narrowed his shoulders and rested. Standing still, he heard for the first time the waters of the Shumchun. He assured himself that the flap of his holster was unfastened, and, in the instant of doing so, recognised that he was still preferring McNaughton Smith's word to Meechan's.

*

Captain McNaughton Smith happened to be the senior officer in camp that afternoon, when the message from the civil police at the frontier was received in the orderly-room tent. It was only six days since the battalion had moved from their barracks on the island of Hongkong to camp on the mainland of China; the companies had already started their programme of annual training in the hills overlooking the British frontier, but the battalion's headquarters were still in process of transfer from the island, and, for one afternoon at least, McNaughton Smith was in command. He was an impressively stout man with a deep, operatic voice. He did not speak; he flourished words.

"I sent for you, Morris, because I understand that yours is the duty platoon today—" He held up a large carefully-manicured hand to postpone Morris's ready acquiescence. "Under the generous provisions of standing orders, you will therefore have been excused training this afternoon in order to prepare for frontier patrol at dusk. I assume that your preparations are well advanced." He ended, not on an interrogatory note, but in a comforting, diminishing tone, as he might have done in pronouncing benediction; and then, as if springing a trap, he whisked up his eyebrows and stared in questioning silence.

Caught off balance, striving to adjust his trim, Morris wavered under the stare. This was his first exchange of words with McNaughton Smith since their formal introduction in the mess, and—his only finger-posts the contradictions of Torrance and Anstey—he found it hard to believe that he was expected to take the man's panache of language and gesture seriously. It was particularly hard to believe that McNaughton Smith sincerely assumed that the platoon were more or less ready to move off. Broad light still fell on the tent, packing the air with heat. Meechan and the men would be lying about in various states of undress, wallowing in the duty platoon's normal privilege of ease between patrols.

Instinctively, however, Morris knew that it would be unwise for him to answer honestly, and even unwiser to answer flippantly. He glanced at his shorts and said, trying to dissemble his cunning, "We haven't changed into slacks yet."

McNaughton Smith clamped his mouth and closed his eyes, as if he were mastering a spasm of pain. "You are new to the battalion, Morris, and I am ready to forgive you much. But you must learn that emergencies over-ride even anti-malarial precautions." He lifted a message-form from the table in front of him. "You have no time to change your trousers, my boy."

Uneasily Morris glanced at the orderly-room clerk's face in search of a smile. There was no smile there.

"I have been informed by Police-Sergeant Appleton that"— McNaughton Smith glanced at his watch—"seventeen and a half minutes ago he observed a party of twenty-three Japanese soldiers on the north bank of the Shumchun. They were armed, and appeared to be looking at possible crossing-places. Appleton kept them under observation as long as he could and then—four minutes ago—made his report by telephone." He beckoned Morris to the wall-map of the frontier, and Morris stepped out of his wariness and, wondering-eyed, moved obediently forward.

The police-station from which Appleton had reported stood on the south bank of the Shumchun, some miles east of the camp. The Japanese had approached the river from the east and had walked along the bank westwards out of Appleton's sight. There had been no reports from other look-outs.

"In brief, Morris, the Japanese have either completed a reconnaissance and withdrawn, or crossed the river unseen at some point west of the station. The only course for us is to assume that they have crossed the river." He was talking faster now, under the persuasive influence of his own appreciation of the situation. "You will take out your platoon as a fighting patrol to engage and capture or destroy any enemy south of the river."

There was no longer anything ludicrous about McNaughton Smith's manner. The occasion had swelled up to dangerous proportions, and the large manner now appeared to be drawn to scale. Emotionally confused, Morris had to make a conscious effort to fasten in his memory the detailed orders that McNaughton Smith was now issuing.

At last, like a brisk amen, came, "Any questions?"

Morris smiled. It was a small, uncertain smile—the only response he could immediately offer, inflated as he was with information, instructions, injunctions, and the strange, throat-filling sense of danger.

"For God's sake, boy," shouted McNaughton Smith, "don't stand there grinning like a ravished spinster. Jump to it."

*

The dust raised by the trucks as they skidded to an abrupt halt still hung in the air. Sergeant Meechan climbed down from the first truck and walked back to the second. "We can't take them any further," he said. And, falling from those twisted lips, the words sounded like a sardonic admission that he had seen to the erection of an obstacle.

Hunched beside the driver of the second truck, Morris frowned over his map. He had been tracing his progress from the battalion encampment on the eastern flank of the North Downs, across the old Kowloon-Canton railway lines, and round the Cheviots into Laffans Plain, where the thin blue line of the River Ganges trickled across the contours; and now, keeping his finger on the track where Meechan had called a halt, he frowned first on his chart of imperial nostalgia and then on the sergeant's helmet-shadowed face. "This isn't the place where Captain McNaughton Smith told us to de-bus."

"This is the closest we can get to it, sir," said Meechan quietly. "You can't take trucks over paddy."

Morris stood up and looked around. The only ways ahead were the single-file tracks along the paddy-bunds—the irrigation embankments that enclosed every rice-field, spreading a network of irregular mesh over part of the broad plain.

"The Shumchun's up there." Meechan pointed.

"I can read a map," muttered Morris.

The mistake over the de-bussing point irritated him. It did not matter, for the moment, whether it had given Meechan the impression that his draftie-wallah officer could not hold a map the right way up. It did not even matter whether McNaughton Smith had misread the grid or he himself had misheard the reading. What did matter was that, as soon as he had scribbled down McNaughton Smith's map reference for the de-bussing point, he had seen for himself on the wall-map that the point was not on any marked road or track and had made no demur. Instead, he had timidly suggested to himself that the map might be out-of-date and the cultivated area of the plain shrunken. To justify his craven silence he would have suggested any other absurdity that might have occurred to him. He had allowed himself to be over-awed, overwhelmed by McNaughton Smith.

"De-bus," he shouted, and jumped down.

As the men scrambled out of the three trucks, Meechan said: "You can see for yourself now, sir. We've got all that plain between us and the river. We'd have been better de-bussing on the top road—the frontier road. It's only a step from there to the river."

Morris stared at him. "You heard the orders, Sergeant. The idea's not just to get to the river but to comb all the ground from here to the river."

"Take us hours to do that, sir."

"You're a cool bugger," said Morris, with some astonishment. "You don't like walking?"

"We'll never be back in time for dusk patrol," Meechan argued quietly, almost casually, without looking at Morris.

But Morris was beginning to feel the swell of urgency again. "For heaven's sake, that's just routine."

Meechan twitched his scarred cheek. "So's this, sir," he said calmly. "Happens often enough. The Japs patrol their side of the river. We patrol ours. When one of their patrols is spotted, we sometimes run up to the frontier for a quick look-see. They don't come across."

Another voice—a hoarse voice—entered the conversation. Private Ripley, the platoon runner, a sharp-nosed, solemn-faced young man, had sidled up to Morris. "They won't come across 'ere, sir. They know better than 'ave a bash at us. They can't even shoot straight—slant eyes, like."

Meechan had built up an argument tall enough to cast a shadow of doubt over Morris, but Ripley's efforts to heighten the argument brought it tumbling down. "Come on," said Morris, rather pleased at the brusqueness of his voice. "We've wasted enough time."

*

In Number 4 Section, Private Jannelli was explaining how to escape from a strait-jacket and chains in a locked safe at the bottom of a river. Since the section was extended over a wide front, walking the bunds towards the Shumchun, he had to limit his audience to either the man on his right or the man on his left. The man on his right was Lance-Corporal Foggo, who had swung his arms carefully ever since he had sewn on his stripes. So Jannelli spoke to the man on his left.

"It's all in the bones," he said, bending and twisting his lithe little body to attract attention. "You've got to be double-jointed. See what I mean, Punchy?"

Private 'Punchy' McGuire had a battered face and a ready smile, an immense body and a simple mind.

"You couldn't do it, Punchy, strong as you are. Your bones aren't right, you see?"

McGuire nodded happily.

"Watch that Taliano, Punchy," shouted Private 'Pig' Fraser, on McGuire's left. He was a small, round-shouldered man with a snub nose, unhappy green eyes, and ears like wind-scoops. "He's tryin' to take a rise out of you."

"*Tik*," McGuire agreed complacently.

"I'm just keeping him cheery," Jannelli shouted angrily at Fraser.

"Shut your bastard mouth," ordered Foggo, the bow-legged tyrant. "And keep it shut."

Jannelli spat into the paddy and marched in restless silence, looking around, hungering after something new, something different, something strange. He began to count his steps. *By the time I get to a hundred, something will happen, something out of the ordinary, something queer . . .*

*

Morris had attached his headquarters to Number 5 Section, in the centre of the line. He marched with Corporal Barker, commander of the section, and set a fast pace. Ripley dogged his heels.

Smiler Meechan had fallen back to whip up the lagging flanks. "Come on, there, Sergeant Drummond. *Jildi*." His first shout cracked across Number 4 Section on the left. His next shout lashed the right flank. "Six Section, get your tails up."

Privates Paterson and Sime, the Bren gunners in the centre section, kept together. Paterson, a regular soldier, as tautly built as a whippet, carried the gun lightly on his shoulder. Sime, a short-legged shop-assistant with a round bespectacled face, sweated behind him, carrying the spare barrel and magazines and his own rifle.

"Smiler's all right," said Paterson. He tilted back his helmet and wiped his brow with the sleeve of his woollen shirt. Without regard to temperature or humidity he wore a woollen shirt and a cholera belt—articles of an old soldier's faith.

"He's not bad," agreed Sime reluctantly.

"But *him*!" Paterson glanced across at Morris. "Doesn't know his arse from a hole in the ground."

"He's just carrying out orders."

"Tips," conceded Paterson. "But who else in the whole British army would carry out old Double-Barrel Smith's orders?"

Sime nodded dubiously at Paterson's back.

"Bloody schoolboy, that's what he is."

"He's pretty young, all right," agreed Sime. "But," he added fairly, "he must be all of six feet."

"What difference does that make?" demanded Paterson. "You could stretch something with a wet navel to six feet—if you stretched it out as thin as Morris is."

"He's pretty thin," admitted Sime, and let the conversation lapse.

Dear Alice, he would write, *Sorry I'm later than usual writing. I left it for our duty day and then we were sent out sudden on a job.* He wondered whether Morris would censor letters as strictly as Williamson had done. It was a pity not to be able to tell Alice that he had taken part in a fighting patrol. *But don't you worry because we can look after ourselves all right and no mistake. Our new officer took us. His name is Mr. J. Morris and he comes from Edinburgh too and says he has been in the shop.* It was a pity not to be able to tell Alice that he liked Morris, but he did not want Morris to think he was a crawler. Whatever Paterson might say, crawlers didn't get promotion.

*

Corporal Macdonald, commander of Number 6 Section, took long deliberate paces, striking his iron-rimmed heels into the hard ground, as he thought of Poppy Wu.

*

Ninety-nine, a hundred. Jannelli swore at the ordinariness of everything around him. *By the time I count another hundred . . .*

*

They had set off in the strong light of late afternoon. As they marched northwards towards the frontier, the light failed—and with it Morris's sense of urgency. He tried to stay alert, expectant, tried to whet his suspicion on every peasant bowed in the fields, on every place ahead that might conceal a few soldiers; but— ineluctably as the lengthening of his shadow—his over-sharpened senses lost their temper, and the urgency of McNaughton Smith's orders lost its grip on him. In the grip of that urgency there had been no room for Meechan's arguments or his own doubts; but, after the grip had loosened, there was room enough.

Tentatively, he said to Corporal Barker: "Doesn't look as if we're going to see any Japs."

Barker was another regular, a sandy-haired, broad-faced, stockily built veteran waiting for his long-service medal and the pension that went with it—marking time for his *rooti gong*, as the troops would say. "Whiles we catch sight of them," he said quietly, "if we go ramstam up to the frontier the minute we hear they're on the prowl. But we'll not see them today, sir. They'll be back in their billets by this time."

"One of these days," Morris probed, "maybe they'll come ram-stam over the frontier instead of going back to their billets."

The corporal smiled. "They'll not come over the frontier till they're ready to come like a swarm of locusts, sir. And our Intelligence can't be that thick they'll not get to know when the swarm's gathering." His words echoed Meechan's. And, perhaps because he was a pleasant man, he made the words sound damnably reasonable.

To lull his doubts and starve his quick-growing resentment, Morris watched the men. He did not have to see them as a patrol dragging their feet in a prolonged yet perfunctory search under his command. He could look on them as strangers. He had become accustomed to the sight of them in their high khaki topees, but now that they were wearing steel helmets they seemed unfamiliar again, squatter and more powerful. In the long, low light of evening, the men on his left were dark against the west, and the men on his right were touched with the day's last radiance; name-less shadows and gilded heroes, the ghosts and graven images of war. For a few minutes, they were as comfortably remote as legends.

Meechan came up from the rear. "The frontier road's just ahead, sir," he said loudly.

Morris could glimpse the road and, from his memory of the map, knew that they were now only a short distance south of the Shumchun.

"I've got the trucks waiting round that bend to the left," said the sergeant. "Will we call it a day? The river's just the other side of the road, you know, sir."

"I know," said Morris coldly.

He bit hard on Meechan's question, suspecting that half the platoon had heard it and were waiting for his answer. It seemed to him, on the one hand, that ending the search at the road would be as bad as admitting that it should never have started, and, on the other hand, that pressing on to the very brink of the river would substantiate nothing except his dog-like capacity for carrying out orders. But he did not dwell on the dilemma. His decision was impulsive, instinctive.

"We'll halt on the road." He turned to look at Meechan—at the twisted mouth, blackened skin and sun-wary, sweat-washed eyes —and added pointedly, "I'll go up to the river and have a look around—on my own."

As he drew near the road, he blew his whistle and raised his right hand, signalling the blessing of rest. Without a word to anyone, he then set off alone for the frontier.

The first time he looked back, the platoon were still in sight, watching him. Self-consciously turning his face towards the river again, he thought of Meechan and McNaughton Smith and damned them both for thrusting him into such an awkward position. The second time he looked back, the platoon were out of sight behind the scrub. He narrowed his shoulders and relaxed his muscles, and suddenly stiffened again at the sound of running water.

The Shumchun was little more than a stream, a muddy swirling stream. But it was the frontier. Beyond it lay Japanese-occupied China. There were no Japanese to be seen. For that matter, there were no Chinese to be seen. But it was the frontier, and, the old urgency stirring in him again, Morris sank cautiously to his knees before taking a closer look, through his binoculars, at the enemy territory.

Beyond the river, the bare hills rolled northwards into Kwangtung province; and, beyond the hills, cumulus clouds piled dark pagodas into the sky. He could detect no sign of life but, just as he was about to rise to his feet again, he was startled by a sign of death. The swollen discoloured corpse of an infant floated past him, turning slowly in the current, as if to exhibit the different aspects of its horror. Morris watched it with loathing attention. More than anything else he had seen in the last ten days, it made him coldly and humbly aware of his strangeness at this end of the earth.

Meechan came up behind him so quickly that he was caught on his knees.

"I've sent Ripley along the road for the trucks," the sergeant said, casually looking up and down the river.

Morris rose to his feet, shamefaced. He felt obliged to make an effort to come to terms. "I'm sorry we haven't seen eye to eye today, Meechan." He pulled out his cigarettes and wondered what to say next. He could not imagine himself saying generously that there might have been faults on both sides; that he—through his inexperience—might have been over-cautious in carrying out McNaughton Smith's orders; and that Meechan—after long years of mock battle—might have become too unready to accept the possibility of the real thing. His mouth was not the right shape for that kind of flummery. The truth was that McNaughton Smith's orders had left no room for a subaltern or sergeant to exercise his own discretion. Strictly speaking, Meechan's objections had been—well, impertinent—bloody impertinent—grossly insubordinate, in fact. Suddenly irritated, Morris inhaled deeply. If he had made any mistake, it was only in failing to deal with Meechan according to the book. A man like Captain Craig would have had Meechan under escort by this time.

"Captain McNaughton Smith," said the sergeant, carefully responding to Morris's overture, "is a great one for making everything sound big."

Just as carefully, but in a colder tone, Morris asked, "What d'you mean by that?"

Meechan glanced sideways at him and grinned tentatively. "He doesn't really mean all he says."

"D'you tell me," asked Morris, with gathering anger, "that he gave me orders he didn't expect me to carry out?"

"In a way." Meechan stared across the river.

"What you're trying to say is that he was pulling my leg?"

"It's not for me to say anything like that."

Morris flung his cigarette into the muddy water. "I'm going to that police-station," he decided impulsively. "It's only about a mile or so along the road, isn't it? We'll see what Appleton says."

"I don't think he can help, sir," said Meechan quickly.

"I think he can. He can tell us whether he was sounding off an alarm or just making a routine report of the kind that nobody pays much attention to."

Meechan too was plainly angry now. "Mr. Morris, we'll both be up to the neck in trouble if you complain that Captain Mc-Naughton Smith made a great song and dance about nothing."

"Maybe he didn't," retorted Morris. "Maybe he was nearer the truth than you are. You'll come with me to the station. We'll take one of the trucks."

Meechan dropped his cigarette, trod on it, saluted, and strode back to the road.

*

The squat concrete police-station appeared to have been built to withstand siege. No sound came from it, no light. Meechan looked through the grille in the outer gate and shouted in Urdu. A torch was shone on his face. He shouted again, in an ugly, ill-tempered voice, and the gate was opened by a Sikh policeman, turbaned and bearded, impressively tall and silent.

In the duty-room Sergeant Appleton rose, grinning, to greet them. "Cup of *cha*, sir?"

Morris declined the offer and asked bluntly, "Did you keep a copy of the report you phoned in to our orderly-room this afternoon?"

Appleton drew in his smile and glanced apprehensively from Morris to Meechan. "Something wrong with it?"

"I'd just like to read it."

The nearer he had drawn to the police-station, the more certain Morris had become that he would find the report to be terse, matter-of-fact and as unalarming as the front page of *The Scotsman*. He had been right in all respects.

"Nothing wrong with it, is there?" Appleton's manner was now defensively quarrelsome. "Nobody's ever complained about my reports before. And, Lord knows, I've made out enough of them — just like that."

"Nobody's complaining now." Morris forced a smile. "We've been out looking for your Japs."

Appleton gasped. "You left it pretty late!" And then he remembered: "You'll be the chaps they're looking for."

"Who are 'they'?"

"We got a call from your orderly-room — oh, about an hour back — asking if we'd seen a patrol."

"Well, you've seen us now," said Morris.

Outside, in the dark, before they boarded the truck, he said uneasily to Meechan, "If Captain McNaughton Smith wasn't pulling my leg, Appleton must have read out that report to him hellish loud."

"Maybe a bit of both, sir," said Meechan vaguely.

It was too dark to see the expression on his face.

*

Morris drowsed beside the driver of the first truck, watching the road wind into the glare of the headlights, and the fire-flies fall away on either side like sparks; leaving the day behind him and ready to renew himself in the night, content that, whatever the platoon thought of him, he had done his duty as thoroughly as Craig himself could have demanded. A despatch-rider met the convoy near the railway and escorted it into camp. Tired and hungry, Morris saw no special significance in the escort until he marched into the orderly-room tent to report the return of his patrol.

The tent was crowded. Blinking shyly in the bright, smoke-acrid atmosphere, he immediately distinguished Craig and then the commanding officer, the adjutant, the signals officer and the motor transport officer. He saluted stiffly, the centre of attention in a sudden portentous silence.

Lieutenant-Colonel Henry Mair, M.B.E., Commanding Officer, demolished the silence with explosive anger. "Where the hell have you been? What the devil have you been up to? Do you realise the disorganisation you've caused? There's a search-party being mustered"—he swung round to the adjutant—"tell them to stand down, will you?" Short, square, as agitated as the moths around the hissing pressure-lamp, he turned on Morris again. "Did you get lost? How the hell *could* you get lost—with Meechan there? Answer, man. Don't just boggle."

Shaken, Morris tried to answer. "On Captain McNaughton Smith's orders, I took out a—"

"Damn you, we know what you were supposed to be doing. We want to know what you did."

"I carried out the orders, sir."

"Time, man, time!" Furiously, the C.O. slapped his wrist-watch. "How the hell could you take all this time—with Meechan there?"

The repeated reference to Meechan stung Morris. If he had relied on Meechan's instincts and disobeyed McNaughton Smith's explicit orders, might he not have laid himself open to a worse chewing than this? Did the C.O. know how explicit McNaughton Smith's orders had been? Morris glanced at Craig's face, and found no help in the chilly expression he saw there. "We had to search a lot of ground, sir."

The C.O. stared. His eyes were a startling blue. "You'll have to learn to get a bloody move on, Morris." No longer shouting, he was still packing his words with menace. "I've no time for scrim-shankers or dawdlers." He bent his head for a moment. "How much longer do I have to wait for your report?"

"No sign of any–any–enemy," Morris stuttered hastily, "in the area we patrolled—according to orders—or on the other side of the frontier, sir."

The C.O. stared again. "We were beginning to think, Morris, that you'd crossed the Shumchun to make certain you *would* see one of the Frogs."

It was not unkindly said, and outside the tent Morris took fresh heart and tried to offer Craig a fuller explanation, a complete vindication of D Company's honour. But Craig would not listen. Stiff-faced, flat-voiced, he said: "You've already made your case: you carried out the orders you got. And the C.O.'s made his case: you should have carried them out in half the time. On frontier guard, speed is more important than caution. You'd better see that your men get something to eat and take their quinine. You've kept them out in shorts after dusk."

Morris's throat ached with suppressed justifications. It was all so damned unfair.

*

"The first thing you've got to learn," said Torrance affably, reclining in mess kit on his bed, "is that there's no justice."

"Balls!" replied Morris, undressing while Ah Chan, the boy he shared with Torrance, filled his small canvas bath with hot water from a large kettle.

There was little elbow room in the tent. Immediately inside the flaps, between a varnished dressing-table and a warped chest-of-drawers, stood a card-table, the canvas bath and Ah Chan. At the other end of the tent, there were two iron bedsteads, heaped with mattresses and white linen, and veiled with peaked mosquito-nets like bridal palanquins. The centre of the floor was occupied by a stack of trunks and valises, on either side of which were a rattan chair and a grass mat. Morris was undressing on his mat, in the small space hemmed in by the central stack, the foot of his bed, the wall of the tent, and the canvas bath. It was only the clutter of the place—and his honest esteem of money—that reconciled him to accepting a field allowance of four shillings a day for lying hard.

"Look at it this way," persisted Torrance, laying aside his paper-back of Shanghai pornography. "First premise: only the weak look for justice—because, of course, the strong maintain their position by perpetrating injustices; second premise: there is no place in the army for weaklings; conclusion: there is no need for justice in the army."

Morris's attention was deflected by the boy, who was mildly reproaching him for having taken the trouble to roll up his shirts and shorts ready for the laundry. "Ah Chan fixee for wash-amah," the boy explained, stretching out a possessive hand for the soiled clothing. Morris yielded it up and started looking for his soap. With the kettle in one hand and the laundry-roll under the other arm, Ah Chan edged nimbly round the bath and lifted the soap-box from the chest-of-drawers. "He does everything except wipe my bottom," grumbled Morris.

"Trouble with you is you're too Scotch," decided Torrance. "Too independent, too conscientious, too serious-minded. That's why you got yourself into hot water this afternoon, and that's why—mucking up the routine for young Confucius here—you're keeping yourself out of hot water tonight." He picked up his book again and held it before his smiling face.

An odd chap, Torrance. An exciting chap, in some ways, with his passionate interest in words and women. But not the kind of chap Morris's parents would approve of. For one thing, he had come down in Honours English at the Varsity.

No sooner had Morris lowered himself into the little bath than the flaps of the tent were lifted and McNaughton Smith looked in, resplendent in white mess jacket and tartan cummerbund and trews. "This is indeed domestic bliss," he said loudly and jovially. "All as happy as pigs in ordure."

Looking over his bony knees, Morris reddened and said awkwardly, "There's a bit of a draught."

"I'm most frightfully sorry, old man. I was wondering whether you could lend me a clean handkerchief?"

Morris hesitated, clenching his fists under the water.

"Chinese laundering plays havoc with one's kit." McNaughton

THE RIVER 31

Smith beckoned to Ah Chan. "Boy, fetch two piecee handkerchief. You can spare two, Morris?"

Weakly, Morris nodded.

When the flaps had fallen again, Torrance said amusedly: "I hope you've plenty of hankies. You'll never see those two again."

"I should've told him to take a running jump at himself," said Morris bitterly.

"Why didn't you?"

Morris considered. "He had me at a disadvantage," he decided. "How the hell can you make a dignified speech when you're knotted up naked in a puddle of water?" Wearily he started to scrub his white skin, the steam swirling round him. "One thing," he consoled himself, "I know where I stand with McNaughton Smith now. And that's more than I can say of Craig."

"Craig treats us all alike," said Torrance, "with the contempt we deserve. He's a man of simple tastes, you know. He has no strong preference between one person and another or one thing and another—provided they're all perfect. His father manufactures chemicals, and he must be one of his old man's purest products—as immaculately conceived, as coldly regular as a crystal of . . . Chemistry wasn't your subject, was it?"

"Law."

"Lord," groaned Torrance, "I should have remembered that. It fits you like a french letter."

*

In the officers' mess, Anstey said peevishly: "It's all part and parcel of the mad scheme of things. Mair and Craig will keep you jumping around as if the Japs were going to attack at any minute. But all the propaganda from higher up will tell you there's nothing to worry about." It was the longest speech he had made to Morris, and he refused to be drawn any further.

Morris fled the mess as soon as he could and wrote a long letter home.

Chapter Two

If Craig's day had started badly it was Corporal Macdonald's fault, not Morris's. Until Macdonald had crossed his path, Morris hadn't put a foot wrong . . .

He rose at Ah Chan's first gentle touch and was standing outside the tent, clean and crisp as the hill air, happily conscious of bird-song over his head and of Torrance's reluctant splashing at his back, before the bugle had blown or the duty-piper inflated his bag for the rousing skirl, before the Chinese barbers had finished shaving their sleeping customers under the dew-bright canvas of the main camp at the mouth of the valley. He went down to the lines and walked around, tapping his ash stick against the toe of his boot and displaying interest in his platoon's preparations for the day. He remembered most of the men's names and noted that a few, like Lance-Corporal Foggo and Private Sime, were respectfully pleased by his recognition of them. He breakfasted well without wolfing in the officers' great rustling mess-marquee, repressing his greetings to senior officers until they had greeted him, and accepting all references to his fighting patrol with a modestly rueful smile. He inspected the platoon lines with Sergeant Meechan, commented on an untidily rolled mosquito-net (to demonstrate his alertness) and asked Private Jannelli to stand closer to his razor next time (to indicate his good-natured tolerance). Only once did he feel his foot slipping, when he learned that another man had reported sick with malaria, bringing the total of the platoon's absentees up to five (three malaria patients and one V.D. patient in hospital, and one convict serving a sentence in the civil prison at Stanley).

He asked Meechan, "D'you think he possibly got the bug last night—on the patrol?"

"He's had the bug for a long time, sir. Comes down with it quite often."

Morris felt that his foot was on firm ground again. And, to begin with, he thought that the case of Corporal Macdonald and the woman who signed herself Poppy Wu Macdonald was another matter beyond his control. On Craig's orders he conducted the corporal to D Company office immediately after roll-call and inspection.

Craig sat behind his table. It was only when he spoke—jerkily, impatiently—that he revealed his anger. "Your wife has written to the commanding officer," he informed Macdonald. "She says you're threatening her with violence. She doesn't try to explain what's behind it all, but she asks for protection."

Macdonald stood rigid and silent. He was a tall swarthy man with sombrely shining eyes.

"Have you anything to say?"

"Nothing, sir."

Morris saw their faces in profile, dark against the sun-struck canvas. They were looking at each other, eyes narrowed, as if Craig were searching for insolence and the corporal were carefully concealing it.

"I'm asking you again, Macdonald. Have you anything to say?"

"Nothing, sir."

As the silence lengthened and the hot canvas burned his eyes, Morris saw their faces blacken into silhouettes, silhouettes of striking similarity, and the similarity, suddenly revealed, frightened him more than the racked silence did.

"I warned you before your marriage that the Chinese have ways of their own. You won't get her to understand your ways by beating her."

Macdonald did not reply, and Morris began to share his reticence. The situation resembled a nightmare that Morris knew, when he was trapped by cruelly repetitive questions and tormenting silences, his throat thick with defensive explanations that he could not utter for fear of disclosing his true nakedness.

"You were a good soldier, Macdonald, until you met this woman Poppy Wu." The name sounded offensively absurd on Craig's dry lips. "I'll have to see that you stay away from her for a time."

Macdonald's dark eyes widened. "You can't do that. She's my wife."

"She's asking for protection, and you haven't denied that she needs it. The only way I can protect her—and keep you and the regiment out of the police court—is to confine you to camp when you're off duty."

B

The corporal's eyes were still wide with anger and grief when he marched out of the tent.

There had been no shouting, no swearing, none of the extravagant language or gestures that Morris had come to associate with military reprimand. And yet, even as an onlooker, he had felt his jaws become stiff and his breathing shallow.

"This kind of thing always makes me angry," admitted Craig. "It gives the C.O. a bad impression of the company. Are you listening, Morris?"

"Yes—I suppose it does look bad. But there doesn't seem to be much we can do to prevent it."

"On the contrary, Morris," said Craig sharply, "there's a great deal you can do and must do to influence the behaviour of your men on duty and off duty." He looked as if he were about to develop the topic; then he bent his cropped head and said, "Tell Torrance and Anstey I'm ready to start."

Morris saluted and obeyed.

He had wanted the day to start well. It was the last day of October and—according to Williamson, who frequently disclosed the accountant within the soldier by drawing neat double lines after terms and events—the end of the typhoon season. It was also the first day of D Company's annual rehearsal for war and, in consequence, the first day on which Morris would be at Craig's side for several hours at a stretch. He had hoped—he still hoped—they would get to know each other better.

When Craig and the three platoon commanders left camp in a truck, Williamson was mustering the company for a toughening route march including what Craig had called 'Legionnaire's breakfast'. Anstey had explained quietly to Morris that the 'breakfast' consisted of alternate spells of marching and doubling, and Morris had cautiously checked an impulse to mention that, as a Boy Scout, he had called the exercise, less colourfully, 'Scout's Pace'. He wasn't going to say or do anything on impulse until he returned to the privacy of his tent at night.

Craig sat with the driver, the three subalterns in the back of the truck.

Torrance looked restlessly around, as if searching for a way of escape. Then, turning his attention to his companions, he enquired after Anstey's health.

"Why do you ask?" demanded Anstey.

Torrance smiled impudently. "I thought you were looking a bit peaky."

"There's nothing wrong with me!"

"No need to bite my nose off. Wouldn't you say, Johnny, he looks a shade peely-wally this morning?"

Morris glanced from one to the other. They had little in common: the small, dark, secretive Anstey and the yellow-eyed, wide-mouthed, smiling Torrance. They seldom agreed, but there was something in the manner of their present disagreement that suggested rather a particular, hidden conflict than general incompatibility. "I don't know," he said carefully. "He looks much the same as usual."

Torrance was not yet ready to take life seriously. Anstey took life seriously and disliked the taste of it. It was, Morris supposed, all a question of background. Torrance was an only child whose divorced parents seemed to vie with each other in propping up his bank account. Anstey was at feud with his family and refused to speak of them . . . Morris found it easier to see the influence of background on other people than on himself. He could see his father in his sister; at sixteen she already had much of the practicality, energy and money-consciousness of the man who had worked his way up to a managerial post in a paper mill. And he could see his mother in his brother; for it was plainly she, a Highland woman, observing the hand of God in everything and keeping her home and everyone in it clean and ready for Judgment Day, who had given fourteen-year-old Davie his quick tears and furtive poetry. But he could see neither father nor mother in himself.

Aware of a twinge of home-sickness, he bent over his maps and started to think about the rehearsal, the tactical exercise.

*

The tactical exercise, the rehearsal of defeat.

Craig sat by the driver and wrestled with an old devil. This exercise provided the obvious opportunity for indoctrinating Morris and catechising Torrance and Anstey on the Military Situation in Hongkong. It was an opportunity that he was loath to grasp.

Torrance—was there anything more to him than a smiling face, a glib tongue and a sensitive palate and penis? And Anstey? Craig suspected that Anstey, who had been dragged by the scruff of the

neck from school into his father's corn-chandling business and
from there into the army, who now contained himself within layer
after layer of defensive attitudes, within a nest of Chinese boxes,
was at heart, in the innermost box, a coward. They seemed to have
only one character in common, Torrance and Anstey: they were
both reluctant soldiers. Morris, on the other hand, betrayed a
boyish eagerness to play the soldier. But he had still more of the
boy than the soldier in him and might yet resist the last stages of
the transformation.

The three subalterns were not men to whom Craig could confide
the heresy of commonsense. And he recoiled from the obligation to
teach them official dogma.

These were the articles of Brass-Hat faith . . .

*The indications are that Japan is reluctant to declare war on
the Allies, and the garrison of Hongkong are under orders to
avoid provocatory action.*

*If the Japanese do attack, the garrison will man the defences on
Hongkong island, with the object of denying the harbour to the
enemy, and will hold out until relieved.*

*The Japanese advantage in numbers will be offset by other
factors. They rely on rigid plans and stock methods and will be
confused by flexibility and originality. Their night-vision is poor.
Their light automatic weapons are poor. Their bombing is poor.*

Everywhere you turned in the colony, you could hear the
mumblings of the faithful . . .

Business men, like Roderick Gow, one of the *taipans*—the big
men—who had made fortunes during the boom years when Hongkong was supplying war materials to China. Gow said that the
Japanese were bluffing, that they would not risk war with the
British Empire.

Politically-minded people, like Gow's wife. She did not deny
that the Japanese might attack Hongkong, but—as a tireless
worker in organisations for the aid of war-distressed Chinese and
as an acquaintance of Madame Sun's—she was certain that, in the
event, Chiang Kai-shek or, at worst, the commander of the Com-
munist guerrillas in Kwangtung would despatch forces to take the
Japanese in the rear.

Soldiers, like Major Guthrie, second-in-command of the battalion,
who was inclined to think that war was imminent, and was certain
that the only Chinese to cross the frontier in either direction would

be those who hoped to fill their rice-bowls fuller on the other side, but was unable to consider the consequences in the same realistic manner. "Let the little Frogs come," he said. "We'll toss 'em into the ditches where they belong."

But Craig was not the only heretic. There were others, who had noted the weakness of the garrison, who had drawn his attention to the absence of battleships, combat aircraft and radar equipment; the shortage of transport, anti-aircraft guns, mortars and ammunition; the facilities for espionage and fifth-column organisation in a small colony overcrowded with hungry, homeless Chinese refugees; and the lack of reliable information about the Japanese, about the real nature of the threat to Hongkong . . .

Captain Walter Ballantyne, adjutant of the battalion. "Either the colony is strategically important or it isn't. If it is, we should prepare to defend it. If it isn't, we should evacuate it. But, being British, we muddle along the middle course, preparing a bow-and-arrow defence and evacuating most of our own women and children."

Lieutenant 'Breeches' Boyd, Royal Navy. "There were angels at Mons. There may, my dear chap, be cherubim and seraphim over Hongkong."

Craig tried to keep his own mouth shut, even at a time like this when G.H.Q. and Brigade, apparently choosing to discount all the presages of imminent disaster, kept the garrison footling around on unrealistic exercises. But he could not ignore the muddled thinking and arrogant assumptions that were condemning the garrison to a bitter, hopeless struggle. He could not ignore the certainty of defeat, for he did not want to be involved in defeat again. He knew the taste of defeat. It had never been out of his mouth until, released from school, released from the home which had always been loud with his father's hearty insincerities and crowded with his mother's fatuous guests, he had gone to Sandhurst and the purposeful action and orderly isolation of the army.

*

Morris studied his maps. He liked maps. On family outings in the old Austin (father with his hands firmly at ten to two on the wheel, mother craning her neck to look at other people's gardens, and he himself in the middle of the back seat to keep his sister and brother apart) he had always acted as navigator, taking more

interest in the maps on his knee than in the passing scene. At
O.C.T.U. he had emerged briefly from obscurity to take first place
in the map-reading examination.

The colony was all bits and pieces. There was a great ragged
peninsula hanging from the mainland of China, with a deeply
indented coastline and a mountainous surface, stretching for
twenty-odd miles from north to south—from the Shumchun river,
which almost severed the neck of the peninsula, to the streets and
wharves of Kowloon; there was the rocky island of Hongkong,
separated by a narrow channel from Kowloon; and there were
dozens of other islands, large and small, scattered around the
broken coasts. It was like a pattern of explosion.

It was like the pattern of an explosion that had not only
shattered the coastline but also buckled the surface. There were
only two sizable stretches of flat land: the area drained by the
Shumchun and its tributaries, which gave way to marsh around
the mouth of the river on the west coast; and, further south, the
broad Kamtin valley, which also opened on to the north-western
marshes. Elsewhere, the brown contours of hill and mountain
crowded the map, squeezing against narrow strips of cultivated
land and reservoirs, elbowing the circular road into shape, hemming
the sea.

Morris could have picked a better battleground.

*

"Pull into the side of the road," Craig told the driver. They had
reached the Kamtin valley.

Watching the subalterns jump down, Craig wondered how they
would react if he told them that they were now going to study
on the ground the opening moves in a military defeat. Torrance
would probably smile knowingly. Anstey would be silently suspicious. Morris would very likely blush as if it were all his fault.

*

Listening to Craig, Morris also listened to the shrill grating of
grasshoppers and the paper-thin voices of peasants in the fields,
until his scalp started to prickle, as if the heat-excited song of the
insects and the distant, high-pitched, twanging tones of the
Chinese were becoming palpable inside his head. He glanced
attentively at Craig's pale neat face and curiously at straw-hatted
women squatting to sickle the last of the rice-crop, and a man
turning stubble with a wooden plough drawn by a humped water-

buffalo. Seeing the smooth brown arms of the women, the man's bunched biceps and the wet, straining haunches of the beast, he was exultantly conscious of his own strength and energy. He pulled back his shoulders, stretched his arms downwards, squeezed his buttocks together and tightened his leg muscles in an impulsive concentration of physical pleasure. Relaxing the breathless tension, he gulped in warm, earth-smelling air.

"Are you listening, Morris?" Craig asked.

"Oh, yes."

"This is mainly for your benefit, this explanation of the background. Torrance and Anstey have heard it before. Have you any questions?"

"The plan is to defend the island." Morris recapitulated the explanation, while he searched for an intelligent question. "If the balloon goes up while we're camping at the frontier, Don Company fight a rearguard action over a prearranged course to give the battalion time to get back to the island. Why does the course start here instead of at the frontier?"

"Tactically, this is the best place to start offering resistance. The hills on the north of the valley would split up the enemy's advance. Anything else?"

Complacently, Morris shook his head.

"Right. We'll start looking at the defensive positions along the course."

The main road, which the truck had taken, came down the west coast between the South Downs and the marshes and ran across the mouth of the Kamtin valley. Morris's platoon, in the centre, were to cover the road at the point where it entered the valley; and Torrance's platoon, on the left, were to cover it at the point where it ran out of the valley, through a break in the wall of hills on the south. Anstey's platoon were to be far out on the right, up near the head of the valley, blocking the narrow pass that provided the eastern route round the South Downs.

Craig led his subalterns in single file along the bunds to Morris's starting position in the yard of a small farm near the road. Sway-backed pigs dragged their bellies in the dust between mud-walled buildings. Two tiny naked children fled into a hovel and, a few moments later, an old man appeared in the doorway, his withered hands clasped in front of his long brown gown, his face a mask of incurious attention.

"Not much of a position," confided Torrance, at Morris's back. "Too conspicuous, Johnny."

At Torrance's back, Anstey, who was always ready to point out defects, whispered, "Not much of a field of view either."

Morris nodded uncertainly. Leaning to one side to see past Craig, he found himself uneasily agreeing. He waited until Craig had shown him where he should place his three sections. Then, as off-handedly as he could, he suggested, "Wouldn't it possibly be better to have one or two of the sections outside the farm? It's pretty conspicuous."

"You won't be here long. By the time they get your range you'll be on your way back to your next position."

"I had in mind," said Morris, resourcefully changing his ground, "that outside the farm we might perhaps get a better view of the road."

"You'd have to sit right on the road to get a better view," said Craig patiently. "Anything else? We haven't much time but we might as well settle your doubts while we're here."

Morris hesitated, inwardly cursing his advisers and searching for a shrewd question of his own that would set Craig back on his heels. "One other thing," he said slowly. It was the only thing he could think of. "These mud walls won't give much protection. We should really dig weapon-pits—I suppose." He was beginning to see difficulties. "But maybe we'd better not muck up the farmyard?"

"The pigs would fall in," Torrance pointed out.

"Shut up," said Craig sharply. Then he turned on Morris, carrying forward his sudden anger. "I keep telling you—you won't have to hold this position for any length of time. Your job here will simply be to slow down the enemy by making them scatter off the road and chase after you. It'll be hit and run. There's to be no repetition of the kind of show you put on yesterday. If you get bogged down on this exercise—" His anger was expended. He left the threat unspoken and set off for the next position.

Red-faced, tight-lipped, Morris followed him.

They walked in single file along the paddy bunds and village paths, crossing the broad valley from north-west to south-east, and then climbed by mule tracks over the Tai-mo-shan range on the south. The air was heavy with humid heat, and Morris's cotton shirt and shorts clung to his wet skin. He kept his mouth shut, listened attentively when Craig was speaking, and allowed his

thoughts to wander at other times. There was a great deal more
to see and think about than the routes, landmarks and positions
that Craig pointed out.

They followed Morris's line of withdrawal up the valley . . .
At the gate of the walled village of Kamtin, men gambled cheerfully and noisily. Under a mango tree in Kut-hung, boys baited a
mongrel bitch.

On a wooded knoll near the head of the valley, Craig called a
halt. "I'll start from here with Company Headquarters and lead
the way over the hills. Anstey will watch your withdrawal, Morris,
and pull out ahead of you. You'll hold this knoll until he signals
that he's reached his next position . . ." Below the knoll, an
old man slept outside a dragon-roofed temple.

Up in Telegraph Pass, at the end of a long climb, they lay down
in coarse grass to rest and to eat their sandwiches. "Here," Craig
told Morris, "you will make a stand until dawn on the second
day . . ." A party of Hakka women, grass-cutters, shuffled softly
past, the black cotton fringes on their wide-brimmed hats fluttering
in the breeze and revealing their shy brown faces.

On a round-topped hill on the southern slopes of the range,
Craig said: "This is the last position. The two platoons will join
forces here and hold out until I signal that the rest of the battalion
are safely embarked for the island. Then you'll go hell-for-leather
down to the coast road."

Torrance grinned at Morris. "By the time you've finished prac-
tising this stunt, those long legs of yours will be worn down a
bit."

Morris nodded gloomily. "My backside will be wiping over my
footprints." He offered a rueful smile to Craig, who did not notice
it.

"We'll look at Torrance's positions on the way back to camp in
the truck. He'll withdraw along the main road." With a wave of
his hand, Craig indicated the swing of the road from the Kamtin
valley round the range on which they were standing. "We've got
exactly a week to perfect this exercise." He sounded resentful. "A
week tomorrow we start a two-day dress rehearsal, with the
Volunteers as the enemy, and with chaps from Brigade and G.H.Q.
watching every move we make."

It occurred to Morris that Craig was almost as secretive as
Anstey. He unfolded plans gradually and made tardy announce-

B*

ments about coming events, as if he were reluctant to share his knowledge.

They started to walk downhill. The light was already yellowing by the time they reached the coast road.

*

Walking from the truck up to the officers' lines to get ready for dinner, Morris wearied his tired and hungry fellow-subalterns by insistently talking about Craig.

"The trouble with Craig," said Anstey acidly, "is that he thinks he's too good for this backwater. He wants to get into a real war."

"The trouble with Craig," corrected Torrance sleepily, "is woman-trouble."

"Rubbish!" said Anstey, with sudden anger.

"What kind of woman-trouble?" asked Morris with interest.

"What kind d'you think?" retorted Torrance, freshening with hostility. "He wants to shag a bint called Mary Gow, but he's too starchy for her. So he shags us instead."

Morris sneered. "Anything Freud forgot, Torrance will fill in."

It had been a bloody awful day from start to finish.

Chapter Three

SATURDAY morning.

Mounted on an easy-going sad-faced horse, Captain Ballantyne inspected the battalion drawn up in parade order on the football pitch.

Morris had dressed himself for the occasion with great care and some confidence.

On disembarking from the China coaster that had carried him up from Singapore on the last leg of his long voyage east, he had landed a complete tropical outfit as recommended by the quartermaster at the Regimental Depot. It had been condemned on sight and in detail by the adjutant. His topee had merely lacked the embellishment of a tartan *puggree*. His small, officer's-pattern tam-o'-shanter could not, however, be modified and made acceptable; the officers of this battalion traditionally distinguished themselves from the officers of the other battalions of the regiment by wearing the large floppy pattern of tam-o'-shanter issued to all other ranks, and, consequently obliged to distinguish themselves from the other ranks of the battalion, they decorated it with a khaki ribbon stitched round the brim and dangling in two tails at the back. His khaki drill tunic had been written off as a 'bush shirt'. His cool cellular-cotton shirts had been dismissed on the grounds that they would not 'take starch and iron'. His 'bucket' shorts—with three-quarter legs which could be buttoned up during the heat of the day to expose his knees and let down and tucked into his stockings during the malarial hours of darkness—had been described by the adjutant as 'unsightly gadgets' and carefully examined by Torrance who, seeing that you buttoned up for exposure and unbuttoned for concealment, found in them 'an interesting reversal of the principle of french knickers'. His stockings had had to be discarded in compliance with the battalion's preference for hose-tops and socks, with puttees to cover the overlap. Left in his boots and underwear, he had ordered a new outfit from the Indian tailor attached to the battalion.

"How much will it cost?" he had asked Torrance.

"More than you can afford. But you don't pay for things *ek dum* out here, you know. The tailor can wait. All the shopkeepers and hotels wait. About the only thing you have to pay spot cash for is a whore."

The new outfit had not been completed in time for the first adjutant's parade after Morris's arrival, and he had been compelled to apologise and explain to Ballantyne—and to all the others, officers and bandsmen, straining to hear. But he had a complete outfit now and was as stiffly starched into shape as anyone else on parade.

After the companies had been inspected, the officers marched off to the right flank and fell in facing the band. Ballantyne, a regular officer with a deceptively sleepy expression on his sallow face, rode slowly down the line.

"Mr. Morris," he said in a clear, carrying voice, "pull your tam-o'-shanter a little to the right. Thank you. It looks less like a pancake now."

*

Saturday afternoon.

Williamson borrowed Torrance's car—a small, noisy, battered and unreliable open tourer hired from a Chinese garage in Kowloon and known throughout the battalion as the 'Mechanised Mess-Tin'. Like the adjutant's sad-faced horse and Major Guthrie's worn and crumpled glengarry bonnet, the car was an object of regimental pride and compassionate affection.

"Can't understand it," Williamson said, fussily trying to engage first gear.

"The controls are just like those on an ordinary car," Torrance assured him. "It's the Mess-Tin's response that's different."

"I don't mean the car. I mean you. A man of your age going to bed in the afternoon."

Torrance winked at Morris and Anstey in the back seat. "I calculate my pleasures, Willie. A lazy afternoon is the best preparation for a night of debauchery."

Williamson jerked his shoulders disapprovingly and turned his head to make a further comment. At the same time, however, he let out the clutch pedal and the car jolted forward, bouncing and shuddering.

"I thought you said you could drive," shouted Torrance indignantly.

"Faulty transmission," muttered Williamson, hastily correcting the steering to keep the car on the road. "Should be seen to."

Morris and Anstey held tight and kept quiet.

"Take my tip, Johnny. Don't make a habit of it—going out with young Torrance, I mean. You'll just spend more than you can afford and ruin your health. You all right now, Anstey?"

"I haven't had anything wrong with me," replied Anstey peevishly.

"No? Funny, that. Thought I heard Torrance asking you about your health. You can't be too careful in a place like this, you know."

"Oh, shut up," said Anstey.

Williamson took his hands off the wheel to crack his knuckles. "I'm looking forward to it," he said cheerfully. "Very decent of you, Morris."

He had borrowed the car to run across to Taipo on the east coast, where he was going to borrow a sailing-dinghy owned by one of his civilian acquaintances. Morris had made the journey possible by agreeing to drive the car back from Taipo while Torrance was having his siesta. Anstey had not figured in the original plan; he had turned up at the last minute to ask, rather sullenly, for a lift.

Williamson stopped the car abruptly in the fishing village, jumped nimbly out, rapped on the bonnet, blinked thoughtfully and said, "Hope you'll manage to get her back, Morris. Neglected, badly neglected. Needs a thorough overhaul and careful maintenance." He waved his hand and set off for the sea.

"If you're not going straight back," said Anstey slowly, "you can come with me. I'm going to take some photographs."

"Oh, I just want to have a quick look-see before I go back. I don't want to bother you."

"I'm meeting another chap."

Morris wondered how he was expected to respond. "Well, I'll see you back in camp tonight, maybe."

"You probably wouldn't want to meet him," said Anstey. His

manner was slightly resentful, his blue eyes wary. "He's Eurasian."

"What's wrong with Eurasians?"

They were facing each other, but not looking at each other.

"He'll be waiting. I'm late. I expected to get a lift from Welsh, but missed him. If you want to come . . ."

Morris nodded, bewildered by Anstey's behaviour, irritated at his own acquiescence.

"He's a professional photographer. And I'm very keen on photography, you know."

"You don't have to explain," said Morris, suddenly aware of his easy ascendancy. "I've nothing against Eurasians."

The Eurasian was waiting: a small round man with restless black eyes in a smooth plump face, Mr. Franco Mendes. He looked at least forty years old, and that, rather than his pigmented skin or his *chi-chi* accent, made him seem a strange companion for Anstey.

"Did you bring the filter?"

Mendes nodded with eager affability, his eyes alternately seeking and avoiding Morris's. " You are interested in photography, Mr. Morris?"

"I don't have a camera."

"I can get for you. Wholesale price to one of Charles's friends."

"Don't talk like a street pedlar," muttered Anstey. "How much is the filter?"

Mendes's mouth was slack with resentment. "It's a present."

"I asked for it," said Anstey touchily, "so I want to pay for it."

Mendes mumbled a price.

To cover his embarrassment, Morris lit a cigarette. Then, inwardly cursing his forgetfulness, he offered Mendes one. "I know Anstey—Charles—doesn't smoke and I . . ." The Eurasian accepted a cigarette and hastened to find his own matches.

Morris would have made his escape within a few minutes, had he not observed, when his prickly companions started to take photographs, a subtle change in their relationship. It was Mendes who chose the subjects: a conceited young man with a live pig in a wicker basket on the trailer of his bicycle; a shy girl with a face as shinily smooth as butter, as stupidly rounded as a pumpkin, wearing a fat pigtail in admission that she was still unmarried; oval-eyed shaven-headed children; a fisherman with his savings in his mouth, a row of gold teeth; sampans and small fishing boats; and a Pak Hoi junk heading out to sea, its brown butterfly sail flapping in the hesitant breeze. It was Mendes who chose the subjects, his black eyes brightly inquisitive, his plump face enlivened with confidence, as he searched the crowds and scanned the harbour; and it was he who chaffed and wheedled the models into their poses and found small coins in his gaping pockets for beggars and children who stood in the way of the cameras. Anstey followed this lead of his without question or challenge. It was only when Mendes turned aside from his professional activities and tried to entertain Morris by telling him about Taipo and the people who lived there that Anstey attempted to regain the lead. But Anstey's was a bookish knowledge, an intellectual interest. Mendes's was a wider knowledge, a warmer interest. It was Anstey who divided the colony's Chinese into Puntis, Hakkas, Tankas, Hoklos, and the polyglot masses of settlers and refugees from Kwangtung and other provinces who overcrowded the tenements of Kowloon and Hongkong. It was Mendes who saw the individual, the man distinguished by pride in his pig, the girl trembling under the gaze of three foreign devils.

Tiring of the emotional atmosphere, Morris announced, "I'd better be getting back."

Politely, the Eurasian tried to dissuade him.

"He's going to have more excitement elsewhere," said Anstey.

"I've really enjoyed the—" Morris could not bring himself to complete the courtesy. They were like a couple of sweaty-palmed girls, Anstey and Mendes. To bolster their self-esteem, you had to fill your mouth uncomfortably full with flattery.

"There's something in what Williamson says, you know." Anstey's voice was nervously loud. "The battalion's riddled with it. For that matter, the colony's riddled with it." And seeing Morris's bewildered frown, he added angrily, "Venereal disease."

It was not until he had found the Mess-Tin and chased the children off the bonnet, that Morris recovered from his irritation and recognised the germinating suspicion in his mind . . . Torrance's enquiries about Anstey's health. Anstey's assumption that Williamson, whose world was obviously thronged with all manner of germs, had been talking specifically about venereal disease . . .

*

Mrs. Gow had been describing the carnival that had been organised to raise funds for China and was to be opened by Madame Sun Yat-sen.

Her husband, Roderick, walked restively to and fro along the verandah, pausing at times to stare out over hills and sea, nodding his head occasionally as if to assure her that she held his interest. Craig, containing his own restiveness, sat where he could watch them both.

Even when they were together like this, they did not look like husband and wife. Roderick had the appearance of a fair-minded, liberal-principled man of considerable wealth, exuberant health and senatorial rank; while Mrs. Gow, with her sallow sun-worn complexion, neglected dun-brown hair and intense dark-eyed gaze, looked like a woman who had spent her life in bed-sitting-rooms. (It seemed characteristic that no one, in Craig's hearing, had ever addressed her or referred to her by her Christian name: Roderick called her 'my dear' or 'my wife'; Mary called her 'Mother'; everyone else called her 'Mrs. Gow'.) It was true that they had more in common than met the eye. They were both, in their own ways, world-makers. Roderick had created out of imports and exports a substantial commercial empire, while his wife attempted, through her activities in several political and charitable organisations, to remake the ancient world of China. But even in this respect they betrayed the differences of their natures: for Roderick was in and of his world, but Mrs. Gow was outside and alien to the world she had chosen. She was the kind of woman who liked to keep her world at arm's length; she abandoned the close-crowding problems of her home to husband, daughter and Chinese servants, and gave herself to the palliation of distant distress.

Craig saw himself as standing somewhere between them. He had to feel that he was in and of his world but he liked people to keep their distance. It was a sense of involvement in the events of the march, not the shoulder-rubbing with fellow-marchers, that gave him his pleasure. Mary, the woman unaccountably fashioned by the two people he was watching on the verandah, was the only person he did not wish to keep at arm's length. In his need of her, analysis and argument were futile, heart mocked at head, with a gentle mockery, which only deepened the excitement she could rouse in him with her immaculate beauty, and her grace of movement.

Craig glanced at his watch.

"My dear Hugh, she'll be here soon," reproved Mrs. Gow. "Talk to Roderick while I go and see why the boys haven't fetched our tea."

If she had wanted to spur on the boys, she would have asked Roderick to speak to them. She was, almost certainly, going to make surreptitious enquiries by telephone. *Is Mary there? Have you any idea where she is? Hugh Craig's been waiting here all afternoon for her.* It would not be the first time—Craig reminded himself uncomfortably—that she had tried to cope with this particular problem under her nose.

Roderick was standing against the balustrade of the verandah, looking down from the social heights of the Peak on the crowded business blocks and Chinese tements along the waterfront of Victoria, capital city of Hongkong, the pearl of the Orient. The view from the verandah was partially obscured by the palm trees and exotic shrubs in the garden. Oleander, hibiscus . . . Craig could not remember all their names.

Without turning, Roderick asked, "What d'you make of things now, Hugh?" He spoke chaffingly, as if to deny that he was worrying. "New governor, new general, new police commissioner, new puisne judge—we're turning over a clean sheet, eh?"

"It's just coincidence—all these appointments about the same time," Craig uttered the words quickly, dismissively. Oleander, hibiscus, hydrangea . . .

"True, true," said Gow. "But there's a smell of change in the air."

It was difficult to believe that a man like him—tall and erect, with a great, white-haired head and a handsome, kindly face— could be inwardly flawed. It was something that Craig did not want to believe.

"Not what it used to be, Hugh." Gow was looking out over Victoria, over the blue-water harbour, to the wharves and godowns of Kowloon. "First, the war in Europe cuts down supplies, knocks the bottom out of our business. Then the Government evacuate the British women and children and upset our whole way of life. And now, bless us, at the very time when we should all be trying to bolster our prestige in the Far East, there's this loose talk about bribery and corruption, this explosive nonsense of official inquiries . . ."

He hesitated, and Craig tried to head him off : "Why don't you clear out, all of you?" Immediately, he saw the dangerous implication of the question and added, with a touch of irritation to cover his embarrassment, "We won't have time to blow ourselves up here. The Japanese will see to that."

"I stay because I have to protect my business interests."

"But Mrs. Gow and Mary don't have to stay."

"They won't go. They wangled themselves into the nursing service when the Government tried to evacuate them, and, bless us, they'd wangle themselves into something else if I tried to ship them out. You see, we're not so sure as you are, Hugh, that the Japs will risk war with the Empire."

Two Chinese boys and a tea-trolley had appeared in the room off the verandah. A few moments later, Mrs. Gow returned to announce, "Mary's just phoned."

Her husband turned. "I didn't hear the phone."

Mrs. Gow looked steadily at Craig. "She's terribly sorry she had to keep you waiting. She'll explain when she arrives. Now, one lump, isn't it? — What have you been talking about?"

"I was asking why you and Mary don't leave Hongkong."

"You don't *want* us to leave, Hugh?"

"Yes. I'd miss you. But you'd be safer."

"But we're needed here."

"You could work for China elsewhere."

"But Roderick needs us too. This is a very trying time for him. All the malicious talk that's going on about Government contracts."

Craig could see Gow's hands clenched on the balustrade. "Tell me more about the carnival," he said.

*

Saturday evening.

Morris responded easily and happily to the crowded streets.

Torrance had left the over-heated Mess-Tin in Kowloon, and they had taken the Star Ferry across to Victoria. They had Ramsay with them, a second-lieutenant in McNaughton Smith's company. They were making for the 'Grips' — the Hongkong Hotel — and Torrance and Ramsay had agreed to walk a roundabout route on condition that Morris would not dawdle or hand out *cumshaw* and draw a swarm of beggars.

The main streets were crowded with vehicles—tram-cars, trucks, motor-cars, bicycles and rickshaws. The steep narrow side-streets were crowded with pedestrians, sedan-chairs, goods for sale overflowing from the shops, and industrious hawkers, barbers, cobblers, money-changers, scribes—there was never time to take in the whole scene. The pavements of the main streets, shaded by high arcades, were thronged with colourful people. The Chinese were out in mass and variety: girls in light pyjamas, girls in high-necked gowns slit to the knee, sometimes slit to the thigh, men in Western suits, men in cotton tunics and trousers, men in long drab gowns. It was a Chinese scene, but there were others, strangers in the crowd. Torrance pointed out a wealthy Portuguese, pretty Eurasian girls, a White Russian who led a dance band. And Morris distinguished for himself British, American and Indian faces, and beggars so wretched that they could not be said to belong to any nation.

There was no place where the eye could find rest from colour and movement. The buildings were plastered with gaudy advertisements, daubed with crude murals in the side-streets, crusted everywhere with signs in Roman letters and Chinese characters. Even the glimpse of sky was broken by the fluttering of flags, broad banners, dangling streamers and laundry.

There was no time for more than an impression of bigness and bustle, extravagant wealth and diseased poverty, laughter and the smell of spiced food, life and more life, red and gold. Morris wondered how he could describe it all in his letters home.

A procession was coming down the street. At its head, brandishing a drum-major's stick and clearing a way through the traffic, strutted a young Chinese girl in a brief uniform of blue and white. Behind her, several bands competed for attention, the brassy arrogance of Western marching music failing—even with the improvised support of motor-horns and bicycle bells—to overpower entirely the plaintive whine and rattle of Chinese stringed and percussion instruments. Behind the bands, there were banners and elaborately decorated palanquins.

"A wedding or a funeral," Torrance guessed. "You can never tell until nearly the end."

*

In the 'Grips', they took a table near the door and Torrance ordered gimlets. "Gin and lime," he explained curtly to Morris, "the standard tipple in these parts."

It was plain by now that he resented having to explain so much, to involve himself in Morris's ignorance of the particular conventions of the colony and lack of general urbanity. Morris would have been disturbed by the resentment, would have become more lumpish in conversation, more handless at table, had he not begun to see Torrance in a new light. The man who had seemed so impressively witty, so assuredly wanton, against a background of khaki, canvas and hills, now seemed younger, less assured.

Morris looked around. It was all very sedate and repressive after the gaiety of the streets.

"If you pass out tonight, Fatty," warned Torrance, "I'll ditch you, so help me."

Ramsay smiled sheepishly and nudged Morris. "Dickie's a great one for etiquette. He likes his debauches to be carried out with all decorum."

Morris nodded complaisantly and continued to survey the scene.

"And you, Johnny," said Torrance, signing the chit for the drinks, "—I was afraid you'd go around tonight looking as bashful as a pregnant nun, but it seems you're more likely to spend the night revolving your head like a model lighthouse."

"Sorry." Morris took his gimlet and, as he held it to his lips, noticed that a girl at the next table was glancing at him. Confused, she turned her eyes away. Choking, he laid the glass down and fumbled for his handkerchief.

"God!" muttered Torrance.

She wore a Western-style evening gown, and the young man with her wore a dinner-jacket, but they were both Chinese, remarkably alike—with luxuriant black hair and dark oval eyes, butter-golden skin, slender, neatly-made bodies. There was nothing particularly striking about her features. She might not even be really pretty. It was the gentleness in her face that drew Morris's attention. He watched her covertly, hoping that she would glance at him again.

"Look who's over in the corner," mumbled Ramsay. "Craig."

Morris turned away from the Chinese girl. "Is that Mary Gow with him?" he asked curiously.

Morris stared. She was pretty. Shining blonde hair and pale

skin. But her face was too expressive, too easily distorted when she spoke. And, somehow, she did not seem quite good enough for Craig.

*

"It's quiet tonight," said Mary arching her eyebrows as she looked around for familiar faces.

"It's early," Craig said. He rotated his sherry-glass precisely. He revolved unfinished thoughts.

"The evacuated matrons," said Mary mischievously, "would have paper fits if they could see these glamorous popsies."

Craig nodded. He had already noticed the exotic beauties escorted by some of the colony's bachelors and grass-widowers. The tangent of the conversation cut into one of his unfinished thoughts. "I was suggesting this afternoon that you and your mother should go too."

"You've found a popsy?"

He tried to smile.

"I'm sorry about this afternoon, Hugh."

"That's another thing that's been on my mind," he admitted. "You still haven't told me what kept you—"

"I was at the Braidwoods'," she said, staring across the floor, blushing slightly. "It was impossible to get away." Impulsively she touched his hand. "Forgiven?"

"Forgiven." But the thought was still unfinished, the sense of imperfection stronger.

"Three of your infant comrades-in-arms are eyeing us. Who are they?"

Craig glanced across. "The fat one's Ramsay. The other two are in my company: Torrance—that's the good-looking one; and Morris—the thin, awkward-looking one."

"Shouldn't you introduce me?"

"Mary, I've been waiting for a long time to see you alone."

She interrupted, frowning coquettishly: "But, bless us—as Father would say—you're so sober when we're alone."

His smile was forced, weary. "We're not going to be alone much longer. Here come 'Breeches' Boyd and McNaughton Smith."

Halfway across the floor, McNaughton Smith was already greeting her loudly. "My dear Mary, how enchanting you look in that new dress!"

Craig glanced at the dress. It *was* new: a pale blue dress

scattered with fine, dark, broken lines like flaws in the fabric. He
disliked it immediately.

*

"Time we had chow," decided Torrance. It was his party, "a
calculated introduction to the basic pleasures in a colony without
culture."

Morris rose last, moved slowly round the table. As if aware of
his hesitancy, the Chinese girl and her companion looked shyly
up at him.

"Good evening," he said breathlessly, and hurried after the
others.

They took rickshaws to a restaurant. As the lean coolies pulled
them along streets loud with oriental music and the clatter of
mah-jongg tiles, Torrance shouted to Morris: "They can do six
miles an hour, you know. Old China hands say—never look above
the ankles—the neat-jointed ones run best, even when they're
old."

Morris nodded complaisantly from a cloud of gin and gentleness.

Torrance seemed to be well-known in the restaurant. They were
ushered with great deference into a partitioned dining-room, led to
a vacant alcove and served by painted girls. The air was heavy
with odours of rich food, thin sharp wine and oily scent. The
dishes were too elaborate, too enigmatic for Morris's taste. It
seemed to him that they were all desperate inventions, frantically
unnatural combinations for perverted palates. He told Torrance so,
his tongue amusingly loath to tackle the polysyllables.

Torrance grinned. "You've got maggots in the head."

"A fitting phrase," murmured Morris happily.

There was too much to eat and drink. There were maggots in
his head, moving in circular procession. He sat very still, mastering
the creeping nausea. A girl twittered at his ear and wiped his
numb hands and prickling face with a hot damp towel. He could
not open his mouth to thank her. He sat still, watching Ramsay
clumsily pawing one of the other girls. It was impossible to read
her feelings from her painted face. Maybe that was why she wore
the paint. He shut his eyes.

When he opened them again, the girls were clearing away the
dishes, and Ramsay was fast asleep.

"I thought you were sleeping too," said Torrance. He looked
as contented as a purring cat. "We'll have to ditch him. We'll put

him in a rickshaw and tell the coolie to dump him at the Star Ferry."

Morris roused himself. "We can't do that."

"It's routine, Johnny. He'll revive in the night air, cross over to Kowloon, find the Mess-Tin and kip down in the back seat."

"Better make sure there's nothing of value in his pockets."

"Fatty doesn't own anything of value."

"And what do we do next?"

"I'll take you to meet some friends of mine."

"I've really had about enough. I could maybe see Fatty over to the car and wait for you there."

"You mean you don't want a woman?"

Morris lit a cigarette. He decided he did want a woman. He had been noticing women all day long, disturbed by their softness and strangeness.

"Have you ever had a woman?" asked Torrance.

"No." He was surprised how easy it was to be honest about it.

"Maybe you'd better go with Fatty."

Morris was again surprised—this time, by the other's gentleness. He looked across at him, embarrassed, defensive, grateful. "I'll go with you and meet your friends."

                    *

On the dark, dirty, narrow stair of a tenement in the Wanchai district of Victoria, Corporal Barker came face to face with a young Chinese.

"Hello!" he exclaimed. "You're Ah Chan, aren't you?—the boy who looks after Mr. Torrance and Mr. Morris?"

Ah Chan ducked his head politely.

"You live here?"

The boy ducked his head again, smiled nervously.

Barker slapped him on the shoulder, squeezed past him, climbed to the next landing and knocked on a door.

A Chinese girl opened it. "Hello, Backa."

"Hello, Mimi. Poppy in?"

Poppy Macdonald came to the door, a well-made Shanghai girl, her high cheek-bones warm with natural colour.

"Mac can't get away from camp to see you, so he asked me to give you this." Barker handed over a sealed envelope.

She tore it open, found some bank-notes and a letter, and glanced at the letter. "Tell him—I send answer to him by and by. You know?"

"Right," said Barker. "Goodnight."

"You not stay for drink?" invited Mimi.

"Some other time," promised Barker, with a friendly smile on his broad face.

*

Ah Chan had slipped back to the flat in which he rented two cubicles for all his dependants: wife, three children, senile father, consumptive sister, and brother. He stood behind the outer door until he heard Barker's heavy boots clatter out of the stairway. Then he turned to accuse his brother Chan Kin-kwok of destroying their peace of mind by his efforts to make money out of treachery.

His brother sneered. "He did not come to spy on me."

*

It was a long narrow room, rather a lobby than a room. The only light came from a single electric bulb hanging above the table and heavily draped with dusty red silk. Torrance and the old woman, at the end of the lobby, were almost lost in shadow; but sometimes the serving-tray she held by her side caught the edge of the light and returned a flash of gilt.

Morris sat at the table with the two girls, drinking cold beer. They were pleasant girls, but they were obviously tired. Their smiles were no more than practised arrangements of the lips, smiles stiff with fatigue; but they were soft-spoken, patient in their efforts to put him at his ease. They spoke to him about films, while the light burned down on his head, and the tray flashed in his eyes. He tried to rouse himself, take an interest in the conversation, help the two tired girls to fill the silence between strangers. "I like funny pictures," he said.

Torrance came back, picked up a glass of beer and stared down at him. "You look like something the cat brought home. If you want to clear out, I won't twit you about it."

Morris looked up, blinking against the light, recognising the other's sincerity again. Torrance wasn't, after all, an easy man to understand. But he was good. And the girls were good. They were all reaching out to him, touching him softly.

"I twitted Anstey, but I won't twit you."

"Anstey?" There was something he wanted to say about Anstey. What the devil was it?

"I was just trying to tease him out of his cage."

"I know what it was," said Morris, suddenly frowning. "He got a dose, didn't he? And it was your fault. And you had the gall to tease him about that too." He leaned forward pugnaciously. He felt that the mood suited him.

Torrance drained his glass and grinned. "Yes," he said, "I've worked hard to get Master Anstey out of his coffin."

One of the girls took Morris's arm. Still searching for an aggressive retort to put Torrance to shame, he allowed himself to be led into the adjoining room. It was a larger room, partially divided by hanging screens. The far end was furnished as a bedroom; the near end was bare except for a straw mat and two porcelain pillows. From the girl's hurried words and gestures, he gathered that he was being invited to choose occidental or oriental style. "I'll take the bed," he said roughly.

She followed him to the far end of the room and screened it off. A few moments later, he heard Torrance on the other side of the screen: "You dirty dog, Morris! You've left me on the bloody mat."

Morris started to laugh. He fell on the bed, unable to control his laughing. The girl knelt beside him and begged him to be quiet. But he laughed until the maggots renewed their procession round his head. Then, holding tight to the bed, he fell asleep.

*

Corporal Barker had just enough money for one beer in a Wanchai bar. The only people he recognised were Privates McGuire and Fraser of Lance-Sergeant Drummond's section. He read the sports pages of the evening paper.

*

Pig Fraser pulled out some crumpled dollar bills and tried to straighten them with sticky fingers. "Last one, eh, Punchy? It's late, see?"

"*Tik.*" McGuire had a drowsy smile on his battered face.

"I'll buy you *lacs* more another night. Any time you say. As long as we're muckers, see?" Fraser looked at his companion, with anxious green eyes. "And you'll look after me, eh? And I'll look after you. Nobody'll take a rise out of you when I'm around."

"Barker," said McGuire. "Over there."

They stared at the stocky little corporal.

"We'd better get movin'. That Barker's a great one for smilin'

and jokin', but he's a corporal just the same. You got to watch
him."

*

When Morris wakened, he was alone. Torrance called again
through the screen, "Hurry up, or we'll miss the last ferry."

The old woman had a taxi waiting. The streets were almost
empty, the pavements already strewn with homeless sleepers.

On the ferry, Torrance sought shelter while Morris went to the
rail to let the night breeze clear his head. A couple near-by turned,
and he recognised the girl and the young man who had sat at the
next table in the hotel.

"Good evening," he said.

They murmured politely.

He could not leave it at that. He was not, after all, speaking
Chinese. "I like the harbour at night," he said.

It was enough to start a conversation, to lead to introductions.
They were brother and sister, James and Anna Lin. They worked
in a newspaper office in Victoria and shared a flat in Kowloon.
They invited him to visit them at any time.

"Tomorrow evening?" he suggested boldly.

They were delighted. "I'll meet you," James offered. "Kowloon
is a confusing place for a stranger. I'll meet you and show you the
way to our place."

He shook hands with them carefully, looking down into their
small, gentle faces.

He drove the Mess-Tin back to camp. While Torrance and
Ramsay slept, he drove with his foot hard down on the accelerator
and his head high in the wind.

Chapter Four

DRUMHEAD service on Sunday morning. Captain Ewen, the
padre, dwarfed against the hills, almost inaudible under the open
blue sky. The hollow square of bareheaded soldiers in khaki drill.
The psalm of praise that echoed across the valley and set two of the
camp dogs barking. The commanding officer's dutiful mouthings.
McNaughton Smith's unctuous bellowing. Craig's compressed lips.
Torrance's melodious tenor. Anstey's occasional interpolations.
Meechan's gruff rearguard, a note or two behind, to see the band
and the singers safely through to the long amen.

Morris was inflated with a buoyant sense of gratitude for the
warmth of the sun, the smell of the hills, the comradeship of so
many men, the promise of the day.

*

Little Jannelli was seeking the friendship of Ripley, the platoon
runner, a man with a lively mind. They lay on the sun-dried grass.

"Well," concluded Jannelli, "the problem is—how did the
missionaries and the cannibals all get safely across the river?"

"'Ow did they?"

"You've got to work it out," urged Jannelli.

"It's too 'ot."

Jannelli turned away, disappointed. He was beginning to think
that he was the only man left in the world with a taste for puzzles
and queer things.

"Look at that Bible-puncher," muttered Ripley hoarsely. Corporal
Macdonald lay between two tents, reading his Bible. "'E's 'aving
trouble with his bint—his squaw, like."

But Jannelli did not want to gossip about people, ordinary
people.

*

Morris had cornered Anstey at last.

"Look here, Charles, if you've caught a packet from one of
Torrance's friends, you shouldn't try to hide it. You should tell
Craig and get treatment right away."

59

Anstey was explosively angry. "Craig's the last man on earth I'd tell anything like that. I'd sooner tell the C.O. or the brigadier."

"So long as you tell somebody."

"There's nothing to tell, you ass. I didn't touch the woman." He spoke with loathing. "I went into a bedroom with her just to shut Torrance's stupid mouth."

"Sorry, Anstey. I won't tell him."

Anstey looked away, his blue eyes dark with hostility. "Leave me alone."

*

George Sime dabbed at his moist round face with a handkerchief and said thoughtfully, "There's a man I just don't understand." Lance-Corporal Foggo walking past perkily on his bow legs, fingering his little moustache, looking for trouble to report, looking for another stripe.

Paterson glanced up. "Bastard Foggo? Nothing to understand." He lay back again on the grass. "How about me, Georgie? Understand me?"

Sime hesitated and took off his spectacles to wipe them. "Not really, Pat," he confessed reluctantly. When he replaced his spectacles and stole a glance at Paterson, he was surprised and gratified to see a smile on his companion's dark, lined face. A smile made Paterson look like a different man.

*

Ah Chan presented his accounts. Written in a round hand in a small notebook, they detailed Morris's indebtedness for:

Wash
1 tooth pase
1 soap
1 bomb

*

It turned out that the 'bomb' was an electric torch bulb.

"A bomb," Morris explained patiently with words and hands, "is something that goes off with a BANG."

Ah Chan blinked nervously and, as soon as he had received payment, hurriedly withdrew. He was as timid as a wild bird.

In the middle of the afternoon, Craig looked into the tent, where Torrance was resting and Morris was starting a diary.

"The C.O. has decided to dine in the mess tonight," he said quietly. "I'll expect you both to be there."

Morris looked up in dismay. "Will we be able to leave after the meal?"

"I'm afraid not. The C.O. will make a night of it."

"But I've arranged to meet some friends," protested Morris, hearing the creaking of the bed as Torrance sat up to listen.

"Sorry about that. This kind of thing doesn't happen often, but when it does, our private arrangements go by the board. You'd better phone up your friends and explain."

"I don't know their phone number," retorted Morris, reddening.

"But you know their address?"

"No, I don't," said Morris angrily.

Craig regarded him steadily.

"Telepathy's been known to work," said Torrance.

Craig quitted the tent.

"You're a dark horse, eh?" observed Torrance happily.

"You don't know the people," Morris said. He swore, abandoned his diary, lit a cigarette.

*

It was the first time that the C.O. had dined in the mess since Morris's arrival.

According to Torrance, Mair was a man of limited intelligence and unlimited nervous energy. The rank and file called him 'Old Horse' or 'Old War-Horse.' Craig occasionally commented on points of practice: "The C.O. doesn't like this sort of thing . . . The C.O. sets great store by . . ." But these comments amounted to no more than an index of Mair's attachments to the traditional forms of military etiquette and the official texts on infantry tactics.

Morris knew even less about many other officers of the battalion. He had few opportunities to meet them, except in the mess. And, in the mess, he always felt that he had only small beer to offer at a party where the air was already intoxicatingly heavy with the richness of other men's offerings: old 'Daddy' Guthrie's crusty ale; McNaughton Smith's abundant dessert wine; the dry sherry of the two Oxonians, Farquhar and Holt; the stolid port uncorked by Major Ingham and gravely passed around by young men, like Welsh, who were still rinsing the taste of mother's milk and ginger beer from their mouths; the neat spirit, in temperate tots, of soldiers like Ballantyne and Craig.

It was a grudging humility that Morris felt. It left a sore spot, aggravated by the petty injustices he had to suffer and the disabilities he inflicted on himself.

One of these disabilities was the lack of mess kit. Under war-time regulations, mess kit was no longer part of an officer's prescribed wardrobe. Indeed, at the Regimental Depot, the high-necked blue uniform had been worn only by aged senior officers and had been derisively regarded by the junior mess as symbolic of the old order that had given way to new. Here, in Hongkong, however, commanders like Mair had cocked a soldierly snook at the emergency regulations. He could not compel his officers to provide themselves with 'blues'; he could not compel them even to dress for dinner; but, by the Lord Harry, he would set them an ostentatious example.

Under the rustling canvas and the hissing pressure lamps, the line of trestle tables was bravely dressed in crisp white linen. Seated around the line of tables on wooden benches, which were carefully wedged underneath to prevent them from rocking on the uneven ground, the officers wore their best: regimental blues, dinner suits, white mess-jackets with tartan cummerbunds and trews, or service dress. Only seven young second-lieutenants, including Morris, wore service dress—barathea tunics and tartan trews. Two or three out of that seven also wore self-conscious expressions and fiddled with their khaki collars and ties. They would probably appear in mess-jackets—the cheapest style of conformity—when the C.O. next dined in mess. Morris sneered at his soup. *Let them buy monkey-jackets, bum-freezers. And cummerbunds, belly-bands, too. I'm damned if I will, come hell or high water.*

It was not his usual mood. Usually he was too ready to run at any man's bidding. It was only under great provocation that he could dig his heels in and risk attracting attention to himself. And Anstey had provided that provocation, just before dinner. "Craig expects us to dress, when the Old Man dines in mess," he had pointed out primly. Morris had leaned over him and muttered, "You're a po-et and don't know it, as Paul said to Peter, when he burned his bum on the gas meter." Anstey had retorted, "You'll come to heel soon enough when Craig whistles." Morris had assured him fiercely: "Craig won't get me into fancy dress unless he pays for it and stuffs me into it." Anstey had smiled offensively: "If it's a question of money, I can let you have—" Morris had restrained an impulse to blacken one of Anstey's wide blue eyes and turned away.

Only once during the evening was he taken from under his stone and examined. They had left table and were drinking in groups in the ante-room.

"Morris," said the C.O. genially, "the rugger season has started again. You'll have to get some togs and put in a bit of practice. You've got the build of a three-quarter."

It was well meant. Morris could see that. But he felt obliged to be truthful. "I'm afraid I'm not much good, sir."

"You'll soon run the rust off."

"I never was much good, sir."

"You mean—you don't want to play?"

"I'd rather not, sir."

The C.O. raised his eyebrows and moved on.

Morris emptied his glass quickly and looked at his watch. The Lins would be saying: "He didn't really mean to come. He was drunk last night."

"How many newspapers are there?" he asked his neighbour, Welsh of A Company.

"Lord, there must be hundreds of thousands."

"I mean here—in Hongkong."

"Counting the rags in Chinese as well?" asked Welsh, pompously giving the matter his attention.

"Ye-es, I suppose so."

"I don't know," admitted Welsh.

Morris reflected that, in any case, the only telephone was in the orderly-room. If he used it, the whole camp would soon know of his absurd pursuit of chance acquaintances.

"Boy!" He spoke more loudly than usual. "Gimlet, please."

'Daddy' Guthrie glanced across, gave him a crumpled smile, winked at him, one drinking-man to another. Behind Guthrie, Craig was watching, with an expression that Morris interpreted as: "Down, Rover, down!"

Chapter Five

CRAIG wore his Prussian mask, criticised in a soft, scarring voice. Williamson—copious sweat rolling down his red smiling face and hairy forearms and legs—went from platoon to platoon, forcing the pace, setting himself at the hills with aggressive confidence in his strength and energy. "Too much beer," he shouted to the laggards. "Too much smoking."

D Company practised the rearguard action from the Kamtin valley, through the Tai-mo-shan range to the Castle Peak road. Morris tried hard to please Craig. He began to appreciate that his sergeant and his section commanders knew their jobs, and tried to learn from them. He also began to sort out the men, trying to improve his command over them.

Most of them were ordinary, understandable, likeable swaddies: who swore and laughed and grumbled and bragged their way across the valley and over the hills; who told each other that D Company was worse than the Glasshouse, but—before the rest of the battalion—wore their sweat and dirt like the distinguishing badges of chosen men. There were only a few of the men—a few of the regular soldiers—who stayed outside Morris's comprehension: dark-faced, taciturn men with watchful, inexpressive eyes, who worked efficiently but apparently without thinking or feeling, who seemed to be nothing more than mobile extensions of short Lee-Enfields and Chinese Brens. He reacted to them as he reacted to the taste of water from a bottle at the end of a long hot day, to the smell of sweat-soaked woollen shirts: he could not wholly like them but—since they formed a distinctive part of the pattern of coarse, vigorous living that had freed the lusting man within the law student—he could not wholly dislike them.

As he sorted out the men, he found it easier to get on with them . . .

On the way up to Telegraph Pass, one humid afternoon, he heard Paterson, the Bren-gunner in Barker's section, shouting from the rear: *"Man-man! Tairo!"* And he halted, before Paterson, having tried Chinese and Urdu, was compelled to resort to English.

Sime, the second man on the gun, had collapsed. His round face streaming, his spectacles slipping down his nose, his wide mouth convulsively gulping air, he seemed to be in a bad way.

"Winded," diagnosed Paterson curtly. "A *tori* breather and he'll be all right, sir."

Sime nodded eagerly. As soon as he had recovered control of his breathing, he was anxious to start moving, to demonstrate his hardness. Morris, however, made him strip off his equipment, and, seeing that Paterson was ready to shoulder it, said self-consciously: *"Maskee.* I'll take it. You'd better give him a hand up to the Pass."

Paterson was the only one in the section who appeared to be unimpressed. He was one of the dark-faced watchful men . . .

McGuire and Fraser, a curiously matched but inseparable pair, wanted to drum up.

"The M. and V. doesn't agree with my stomach unless I melt the gippo," Fraser explained to Lance-Sergeant Drummond, with one unhappy green eye on Morris.

"Go ahead," said Morris. "Make it snappy."

Fraser was kept busy pulling puny handfuls of coarse bleached grass for big McGuire, who sat in contented concentration, tending a small smoky fire and heating their tin of meat-and-vegetable stew. Jannelli, a restless little man, was anxious to help, but Fraser was anxious to slave alone. There was a squabble.

"Less bobbery," warned Lance-Corporal Foggo, the real tyrant of Drummond's section.

"Jannelli," said Morris. "They tell me you're a great hand at puzzles. See if you can stump me."

Jannelli grinned and came forward . . .

Corporal Macdonald, the Bible-puncher, the squaw-man, fell into step with Morris.

"Sir," he said, "I hope I'm not speaking out of turn, but I'd like to know whether my wife has written in again."

"Not that I know of. I don't expect she will," added Morris, intending to offer comfort.

"I've asked her to write," said the corporal dourly. "I want her to tell Captain Craig that he doesn't have to confine me to camp."

C

Morris tried to make light of the matter. "We're all confined to camp these days." Then, sensing the depth of Macdonald's feelings, he added: "I'll find out whether she's written. If she doesn't write, you should have a word with Captain Craig in private and tell him your side of the story."

Macdonald smiled sourly. He was another of the dark-faced men, but he was distinguished from the others by his intelligence and by the sombre light in his eyes.

*

Across the valley and over the hills, sometimes by day, sometimes by night, until they could run the course without thinking, until they were harder muscled and longer winded, until they became acquainted with some of the people of the valley—like the cross-eyed boy who herded ducks with the aid of a long bamboo cane, the three girls who, with their trousers rolled up on their plump thighs, made liquid manure from open cesspools and fed their vegetables, the old man who sat outside the temple near the knoll.

Morris learned to sling the bat. He took the words on trust from the squaw-men, the men with long-haired dictionaries to take to bed with them. "Ding-hao!" he greeted the cross-eyed boy, and the boy grinned and said something not dissimilar in sound. "Fai-ti-ah!" he urged the girls and, although they did not work any faster, they seemed to understand that he was giving them jocular encouragement.

Across the friendly valley and into the lonely hills, where a few Hakka women cut grass for fuel, and the hawks hovered, like ragged scraps of dark paper, and the dead were buried . . .

Sergeant Meechan lifted the lid off one of the earthenware urns that were grouped here and there on the lower slopes of the hills. Morris bent over and saw a skull and thigh bones inside.

"First, they bury the corpse shallow," said Meechan dryly. "Then they dig up the bones, and stuff them in a *chatty* pot. Then, so help me, they bury the bones again."

Further up the slope, they came upon one of the final burial places, a concrete niche in the hill. On the floor of it, a piece of rock held down a bundle of thin paper slips. Meechan extracted a few of the slips and handed them to Morris.

"That," he said, "is the kind of money you spend in Hell."

"Thanks," said Morris, stuffing the blank paper into his shirt pocket. "I'll buy you a beer there."

*

The platoons practised separately for the first two days of the week, learning their positions and their lines of withdrawal. Then they practised together as a company for three days, learning to synchronise their movements.

"Get a grip of it," Williamson urged the platoon commanders. "The Volunteers are out for our blood. I happen to know, see?" He screwed up his eyes cheerfully. "Week-end soldiers. Beer-drinkers. That's them. If you let them score any points off us, the Skipper'll strangle you with your own guts. O.K.?"

In their few hours off duty, they were restricted to camp.

"Rhythm of training," explained Williamson.

"Rhythm of the old oxometer," said Torrance.

"We maybe need the rest anyway," said Morris, mediator.

*

Craig watched the pattern neatly drawn on his map being untidily extended across the earthy-smelling valley and over the windy hills. He saw how keen Morris was to please him, and how the keenness accelerated the blunders.

In the newspapers, he read the reports on the inquiry into Government contracts. He did not see Gow's name in print, but he could still see Gow's hands on the balustrade.

He wrote to Mary and received no reply.

He was badly bitten by mosquitoes one night in the valley, and Lumsden, the medical officer, gave him half-a-mugful of quinine to drink.

"All the best," he said.

Lumsden watched him drink. "The best is good enough for me."

He acknowledged the thrust with a smile. He was too tired to argue, but he knew that for Lumsden, as for everybody else, the best would never be good enough.

Chapter Six

As they drew near the Kamtin valley, Morris's three trucks passed a platoon of the enemy, the Hongkong Volunteer Defence Corps, standing beside the road, waiting for the exercise to begin.

One of the Volunteers shouted, "You're late."

Some of 17 Platoon yelled from the trucks: "Tips! We're giving you a start, see? — You're the boys that want to get a bend on. It's in the bag, soldiers."

Morris smiled, glanced at his watch. Eight-twenty-nine. He would be in position at the farm by eight-fifty, and would be ready to meet the Volunteers, the Japanese or the whirling dervishes by nine, when the exercise started.

Craig was waiting beside his pick-up vehicle. As the platoon jumped down from the trucks, Morris reported to him.

"We're in good time," said Craig quietly. "Torrance and Anstey should have reached their positions now. H.Q. is already established on the knoll. Before I go along there—any questions?"

"I think we've got it taped."

"Right. Zero minus twenty-one."

Morris adjusted his watch.

"I'll see you up at Telegraph Pass. We can compare notes there, after dark." Craig offered an anxious smile. "For heaven's sake keep your wits about you, Johnny."

Morris nodded cheerfully. It was the first time Craig had called him by his Christian name. "See you at the Pass," he said.

*

They doubled from the road to the farm.

Smiling and sweating, Sime lowered himself into the crackling grass. "Ten minutes in hand," he said contentedly.

"This boy Morris wants to leave us to Smiler," grumbled Paterson. "Smiler doesn't lose any more sweat than he has to."

"It's certainly flipping hot," Sime conceded pleasantly.

Paterson spat at and missed a hovering dragon-fly.

*

Morris adjusted his binoculars and searched for signs of move-ment, although he was ready to bet a sterling pound to a Chinese penny that the Volunteers would not trudge far from the coast road on a day as hot as this. Indeed, if they were going to play their part realistically, they would advance cautiously down the road until they bumped opposition.

He would provide the opposition. His Bren-gunners carried heavy wooden rattles to simulate fire for the umpires' benefit.

*

"Where's the umpire?" asked Sime.

Paterson made a coarse suggestion.

Sime sat up and looked to the rear. There were women working in the fields, two ragged boys lashing a water-buffalo along a track, and an old man in felt hat and long gown standing on the main road. But there was no white-arm-banded umpire. And without an umpire there could be no official casualties. And without casualties there would be no opportunity for Sime to step forward and take command.

*

"Mr Morris," called Sergeant Meechan. "Some jiggery-pokery going on behind us." He pointed to an old Chinese in felt hat and long gown. "He's watching them."

Morris turned and stared to the rear. "Watching who?" he asked apprehensively.

"It must be *them*—squatting behind a bund or standing in a ditch."

Morris blinked rapidly and peered into the sun-shrunken dis-tance. "What the hell's all the mystery about? Who's *them*?"

"The Volunteers, sir."

"The Volunteers!" He glanced at his watch, shook it. "It's only three minutes past nine—zero plus three."

"There," said Meechan, pointing again.

Not far from the old man, a few reed-like rifle barrels sprouted jerkily from behind an embankment.

"But they can't have out-flanked us in three minutes," objected Morris in a sudden panic.

Meechan spat contempt. "They've jumped the gun. They were planted there before we arrived."

"We should call for an umpire," said Morris indignantly. "He'd see that they couldn't have got that distance from their starting-line in three minutes."

"Better argue the toss later, sir. If we don't get out of here fast they'll cut us off."

Morris nodded quickly, his mind racing. "You take one section along the bunds—fast. If the Volunteers open fire, get down, and keep them off. I'll follow with the other two sections under cover."

He kneeled beside Corporal Barker's section and watched Meechan's party withdraw. They ran well—like an unco-ordinated caterpillar jerking rapidly along narrow tracks. Suddenly a hand-rattle ripped up his hopes. The caterpillar disintegrated into spiky segments falling on either side of a bund.

"That's the enemy firing," said Barker uncomfortably.

Paterson swung his rattle in vigorous counter-fire.

"Pack it in," shouted Barker. "What are you firing at? You can't see them from here."

"What does that matter?" asked Paterson. "They don't know we can't see them, do they?"

"Shut up," said Morris bleakly. Why had Meechan's party scattered to both sides of the bund? Had they lost their heads—or had they bumped a party of Volunteers right across their path? "Come on," he said. "Follow me. Keep your heads down and your mouths shut." He made the two sections sweat along the edges of muddy fields and along irrigation ditches.

*

"We couldn't do it any other way," argued Sime breathlessly, rolling from side to side of the ditch as he dragged his short legs through the water.

Paterson swore. "We could get up on the bund and fight it out!"

Sime's shining face widened with pleasure as he was seduced into visualising a brisk fight on the bund, with rifle-bolts clicking and rattles raucous, and Barker expiring on the umpire's word, and Private George Sime raising his arm and shouting, "Follow me, lads!" Then his heel struck a slimy stone and he slipped and fell backwards, clawing with short fingers at the brittle grass on the embankment.

Paterson helped him to his feet and complacently told him, "Your arse is all wet."

He hitched his rifle-strap on to his shoulder again and, with

both hands, explored the extent of his dampness. While he was
doing so, the Volunteers appeared on the bund. They leapt into
view and stood—larger than life against the sky—looking down on
the section, grinning. Paterson gave his rattle a last desperate
swing. "You're dead," one of the Volunteers told him. George Sime
clutched his wet backside and stared at his captors and tried to
understand what had happened.

*

Tight-lipped, breathing hard, Morris marched into Kamtin and
approached a group of three officers laughing and talking in the
shade—an elderly staff-major with bulging blue eyes and white
feathery hair, and a captain and second-lieutenant of the Volunteers. He saluted the major and thrust forward his explanation.
"Morris is my name, commanding the centre defence platoon." He
hesitated, sniffing the atmosphere. The major wore an expression
of amiable surprise. The other two were grinning. "I bumped a
party of Volunteers. The sergeant in charge of them claims to have
killed or captured my whole platoon."

"How did it happen?" asked the major. He had stepped forward
and was now standing uncomfortably close, staring and smiling
and nodding. His companions were jerking with suppressed
laughter.

"Are you an umpire, sir?" asked Morris stoutly.

"Yes. Indeed I am, old chap. I haven't got my arm-band up yet."
He pulled it from his shirt pocket and said apologetically, "It's early
in the day yet, you know." The two Volunteers could no longer
suppress their laughter. "Sober up, gentlemen," begged the major.
"Let Mr.—ah—this young man tell us how it happened."

"They were right across my line of withdrawal," said Morris, his
voice shaking with anger. "They must have been behind my first
position before zero hour."

The major nodded eagerly and patted his arm. "You're perfectly
right, old man. I give you full marks for sizing up the situation.
Pity you let them knock spots off you, though. I'll have to count
that against you, I'm afraid."

Morris was choked with indignation.

"But don't worry, old fellow. I'm going to resurrect you and
your men. Let me see." He rubbed his chin and blinked, in cheerful
consideration. "You know, I think you should go straight to the
knoll and explain the situation to Captain Craig. Tell him you

spoke to me. And tell him we'll hold up the war for—ah—half-an-hour, shall we say? That should give you nice time to get back to the knoll without rushing."

"We'll fight the next round according to the text-books," promised the captain, with a sneer. He had an absurd ginger moustache.

*

Taking full advantage of the truce, Morris marched at ease, sullenly smoking.

"I'm not going to take it lying down," he assured Meechan at his back. "I'm going to make a full report in writing."

*

Over his shoulder, Jannelli tried to pass the message to McGuire. "Got it, Punchy? They started hours before we did. It was a kind of a joke, see?" He drew a wide grin on his face to illustrate the words.

"*Tik hai*." The big man nodded and smiled.

"Well, tell Piggy," urged Jannelli for the second time. "And tell him to pass it on."

"I heard you," said Fraser, trying to see round McGuire's broad back. I could've heard you up at the Shumchun. Call it a joke, do you? You want to watch yourself, boy. There's nothin' funny about the Volunteers takin' the piss out of us, is there, Punchy?"

"I should've tangled with them," said McGuire. And he bunched his fists and scowled at Jannelli.

*

"He's not fit to be a lance-jack," decided Paterson. "A squint-eyed bandsman with a bag over his head could've seen we'd never be able to slip past."

Wet shorts chafing his legs and constantly claiming part of his attention, Sime was tempted to agree for peace's sake.

"If I could've let a few of them feel the weight of my rattle, Georgie, they wouldn't be so bloody chipper."

Wet shorts or dry, Sime was no rebel. "If it was the real thing, we'd maybe be glad Morris didn't stick us up like targets."

*

Morris was in a better frame of mind already. He was beginning to see his way out of the humiliation of defeat. On the knoll, he would give Craig a brief explanation, as the umpire had suggested. It would be little more than a blunt allegation of duplicity and a plea for judgement to be reserved. Craig would, of course, accept the explanation with the natural restraint of a man who had asked for an egg and been handed a scorpion. But, immediately after the exercise had ended, Morris would write a full report that would not only justify his presentation of a scorpion but also ensure that the Volunteers suffered its final sting.

Mock battle, he would point out, is a conventional exercise for testing military skills. If the test is to be valid, the conventions must equally restrict both of the combatants.

That had a fine, full-mouthed ring about it. And it was logical. If anyone chose to dispute the logic, he could soon silence him with a *reductio ad absurdum* —

If one of the combatants is permitted to anticipate the conventional start of an exercise, the other combatant should be allowed to continue the exercise after its conventional close and score points by waving rattles at the enemy forces on their way home.

To answer the criticism that he could go to hell with his logic, that he had been faced with an unforeseen challenge and had failed to meet it, he would put in a bit about realism —

If the Attack were on this occasion allowed to over-ride a convention for the purpose of testing the Defence's reaction to unexpected developments, they should at least have been obliged to play their part consistently. Having started the exercise before zero-hour, they should have continued the exercise. The platoon waiting north of Kamtin area should have fired on 17 Platoon's trucks going south. The party already in position in the valley should have fired on 17 Platoon as they debussed. The only justification for departing from convention is to provide a greater element of realism. An exercise in which neither the agreed conventions nor the realistic probabilities are respected cannot result in any conclusion of military significance.

It might need a little polishing to bring it up to professional standards, but it already had a sting in its tail.

*

It was Meechan who first noticed that Anstey's platoon were withdrawing according to plan. Strung out across the head of the valley, they were running smartly towards the knoll in order to lead the way into the hills. Morris grinned. When Anstey heard about the truce, he would be spitting angry that he had sweated it out.

c*

For Morris, walking at an easy pace, the heat was tonic. The first shout from the knoll bounced off his consciousness, leaving no deeper an impression than the shrill song of grasshoppers or the thin voices of women working in the fields. He breathed deeply and spread his fingers to comb the air—air palpable yet light as sunstruck water flowing around him as he walked—fathomless air flooding the great valley. The second shout harpooned his attention. Someone was standing on the knoll, waving a stick and yelling.

"It looks like the C.O.," said Meechan apprehensively.

Morris's pulse quickened. He turned his head and called out, "Smarten up there."

"I'll chase them up in the rear," offered Meechan.

The C.O.—if it was the C.O.—did not seem to be satisfied with the platoon's response. He continued to wave his stick and yell. Morris quickened the pace and leaned forward as he marched, straining to catch the shouted orders before they fell short of him.

" 'E's telling us to double," said Ripley huskily.

Morris gave the order and, as he led the way and set the breakneck pace, kept his ears cocked and his sweat-stung eyes turned towards the figure on the knoll, and took note of the omens: a brandished stick, index of agitation; the tag-ends of words conveying nothing but the shouter's impatience; glimpses of a tiny, blood-suffused face; and, at last, five distinct words that killed his lingering hope that Meechan might have been mistaken—five words that summed up a whole way of life—"Get a bloody move on !"

He sprinted forward, his chest crammed with labouring heart and his mouth full of explanations. As he scrambled up the knoll, he shouted, "We were—captured."

Mair threshed a stunted tree with his stick. "No bloody wonder you were captured ! Dragging your backsides across country like a string of buffalo."

"The Volunteers—jumped the gun, sir."

"I'm glad somebody can still jump," the C.O. interrupted.

At Mair's back, red-haired Farquhar, the assistant adjutant, shook his head slowly and decisively. Morris took the hint, swallowed his explanations in one hard indigestible lump, and shouted to the sections as they scattered hotfoot over the knoll: "Into your positions."

"What the hell," demanded Mair, "do you think they're already doing—hiding from you? Get your teeth into the job, man."

"Yes, sir," said Morris hoarsely. Glimpsing a bolt-hole, he turned and ran across the knoll to join Meechan. Urgently he asked, "Everything all right?"

The sergeant twitched his mouth. "I think," he said, "I'm going to have a bout of malaria."

Morris stared at him, wordless. Then, observing Private Sime's bespectacled face turned towards him, he yelled, "Look to your front, man."

*

Sime looked to his front.

"Told you," said Paterson. "Proper bastard, he is."

"He's rattled," said Sime charitably. "Can you blame him? Listen to this."

The Old Horse's voice again, thick with fury, but close enough now for his words to carry. He had followed young Morris across the knoll.

"Mr. Morris," he was saying, "when you've finished scampering about after your men, perhaps you'll tell me what you're going to do next?"

"Company headquarters and 16 Platoon have withdrawn according to plan," said Morris hurriedly, "so I've simply got to keep the enemy at long range until I get a signal from Mr. Anstey."

"Aren't you going to send a message to your company commander?"

"Yes, sir."

Sime took a quick glance round. Morris's face was red. Meechan's face was twitching badly. The assistant adjutant's face was dead stiff, as if he was frightened somebody might notice him. The Old Horse's face—Christopher!

"What are you going to tell him, Mr. Morris?"

"I'd like to give him a brief explanation, sir, of how we came to be captured and—"

"You're at war, man," bellowed the C.O. "Your company commander doesn't want explanations. He wants the facts of the situation. Where are the enemy?"

"There they are," said Paterson softly. He nudged Sime and pointed out a section of the Volunteers advancing across the paddies in extended line. "Morris'll never spot them from where he's standing," he muttered, with sly pleasure.

Raising himself from the ground—and maybe from the ranks too—Sime thrust a shaking finger towards the approaching section and shouted his platoon commander's salvation: "Enemy advancing, sir."

The Old Horse glared down at him. "Who the hell," he asked, "is that hysterical ass?"

*

Night was a new flood, flowing from the east, filling the valleys and lapping up the mountains, extinguishing the sunset flames on their barren, eroded crests: a quiet, cool tide that washed away the sweat and dust of the day. Then the wind rose, beating the warmth out of the body, sucking at nose and ears.

Morris lay in Telegraph Pass, waiting for Craig.

As he waited, someone stumbled across to him. It was Meechan, shivering and bowed. "Sorry, sir. It's the b-bug."

"Better go down."

Meechan saluted limply and shuffled away.

*

In the Peninsula Hotel, Kowloon, Captain Finlayson of the Volunteers wiped tears of laughter from his eyes and smoothed his ginger moustache.

"It's not really funny," said the dark girl.

"Nell has a passion for young boys," explained the blonde to the captain, "and this Morris sounds perfectly infantile."

"It's not that," said the dark girl, blushing. "I mean—what would happen to us all if the Japs did attack?"

"Fortunately," the captain reassured her, "the Japs don't know Morris is here. If we can keep his existence dark, I don't think they'll risk crossing the frontier."

*

Once every hour Morris went round the sentry posts.

"Perishin' cold," whined Fraser. It was the first time Morris had seen him apart from McGuire. "What's the budji, sir?"

"Almost three. You'll soon be relieved."

Morris lay and listened to the wind, the howl of a pye-dog, and the dead note of a gong from some distant temple. Like Fraser, he was cold and tired and lonely.

Although he did not now expect the Volunteers to attack before dawn, or Craig to make good his promise and come up to the Pass, he could not relax to sleep. He was sorry that the Volunteers had not tried to force the Pass under cover of darkness and given him a chance to demonstrate his alertness. And he was wounded by Craig's failure to turn up, which could mean only that Craig had accepted the C.O.'s version of the action in the valley and did not wish to hear any other version.

When the Volunteers attacked, just before dawn, 17 Platoon were already standing to arms, shivering, complaining of hunger, rubbing the sleep from their stiff-lidded eyes and slack jaws, breaking wind, clearing their noses and throats. Morris directed the swinging of rattles until an umpire recalled the enemy.

"We've wiped out that bunch, sir," said Corporal Macdonald with savage pleasure.

Elated, Morris led the platoon quickly down to the round-topped hill where he and Anstey were to make a last stand. There was no time to greet Anstey or look for Craig. The Volunteers had followed him through Telegraph Pass and were already extended across the slopes overlooking the round hill. He gave Ripley a message for company headquarters, announcing his arrival and the enemy's advance, and waited for an umpire—some Atropos in khaki—to respond to his platoon's gallant rattling and thin out the enemy lines.

"Mr. Morris,"—it was the C.O. again, rested, fed, washed, shaved, freshly dressed, briskly interested—"have you given a fire order?"

Morris started to scramble to his feet.

"Stay where you are, man. You're fighting a battle."

"I've instructed the section commanders to control the fire at present, sir."

"You know how to give a fire order?" asked Mair dryly.

"Yes, sir."

"Well, give one."

"17 Platoon!" shouted Morris. He looked at the Volunteers again, blinked rapidly, tried to estimate the range with sleepless eyes and agitated mind. "Three hundred—"

"Three hundred?" roared Mair. "Where the hell's your target? Point me out any enemy as close as three hundred yards."

"Four hundred—" shouted Morris.

"Five hundred," roared Mair, beating his stick against the sides of Morris's boots.

*

"To some extent, Craig, I sympathise with you," the C.O. said. "At the same time, I can't accept you've done all you could to knock him into shape."

Craig accepted the reproof in silence.

"It's just as well," continued the C.O., "that Morris will never have to run this course in earnest."

"I don't understand, sir."

Mair sagged a little and shook head and stick in bewilderment. "I'll be telling company commanders tonight. Change of plans, Hugh. A big change. A bloody queer change."

For a moment, Craig wondered whether the battalion had been recalled. Then he realised that a sun-weary veteran like Mair would not describe recall as 'a bloody queer change'. It was their retention in this lost garrison that was queer. Under the mulish hide of him, Mair knew that.

"It means starting all over again. There isn't much time either, I suspect. We'll have to get a bloody move on."

*

Torrance came into the tent, slightly drunk, his curly hair disordered, his yellow eyes gleaming with amiability.

"What the devil have you been doing all night, dear old Morris?"

Reluctantly, Morris admitted, "I'm writing a report on the exercise."

"Wasting your time. It's dead."

"There's still the *post-mortem*." Morris had no patience for drunks unless he was drunk himself.

"There won't be a *post-mortem*. There are greater things in store for us, Johnny. All your sins will be forgotten if not forgiven before anyone has time to read your report."

His oracular manner made Morris pause. "What's up?"

Torrance grinned. "Blessed if I really know."

Morris turned back to his work.

"But there's something in the wind, Johnny. The Old Horse is neighing to all company commanders. And Farquhar let slip that we might be moving very soon."

"Where?"

"Who cares? Anything for a change!"

Morris continued writing. The prospect of change excited him, but, being sober, he was unwilling to betray his feelings.

"Tear it up, Johnny. You'd never get it past Craig anyway."

"It's for Craig I'm writing it," admitted Morris sourly. He was still smarting from Craig's few, sharp, dismissive words of reprimand.

"Wasting your time. Craig doesn't love us. Craig will never love us. Because, poor man, he doesn't love himself."

Torrance stumbled across to his bed and, swearing softly, tangled with the mosquito-net. After he had freed himself and stretched out on top of the covers, he seemed to remember that he was fully dressed, for he sat up again, whistling between his teeth, and removed his shoes, socks and tunic. Tiring then, he left the rest of his clothes on and lay down. Just before he went to sleep, he murmured comfortably: "Even the weariest river winds somewhere safe to sea."

PART TWO

The Wind

Chapter One

"GOOD!" said Williamson, rubbing his hairy hands in enjoyment of another neat conclusion.

Company-Sergeant-Major Duncan and Company-Quartermaster-Sergeant Silver kept their hands behind their backs and their views to themselves. Duncan, a single man who had invested a good deal of money in volumes of universal knowledge and courses in modern business practice, always resented changes in routine that disturbed his time-table of studies. Silver, in contrast, had already achieved his ambition and was content to rest on his laurels as the most capacious beer-drinker in the battalion; it was simply the prospect of hard labour that made him resentful; lesser men might have to work up a thirst, but Silver's was a happy accident of nature, a lily that he was always loath to gild with the sweat of his brow.

"Of course, we'll suspend annual training for the time being," Craig added dryly.

Silver was the only one who responded to the humour. "And waste the whole night sleeping, sir?"

Duncan frowned. "We'll have to know more about it before we can draw up a roster for work-parties."

"Quite right. We'll go over the ground carefully before we attempt any spade-work." Craig nodded approvingly. Duncan always needed a good deal of encouragement. "That's all, thank you. Mr. Williamson, send in the platoon commanders."

Alone, he sat back in his chair and looked out of the tent at the sunlit canvas stretching up the valley. For a moment, he was content to sit, aware of the lightness of the morning, of the lightness of his mood. Then he found himself trying to explain his lightness of mood. If it was a reaction to the change of defence plan announced by the C.O. last night, it was certainly not a rational reaction. Although the immediate consequences of the change were, first, the abandonment of the footling exercise which young

Morris had unwittingly exposed as a farce, and, second, the employment of the battalion on more realistic preparations for war, the changed plan nevertheless struck Craig too as 'bloody queer'. It might be, of course, that it was the very air of desperation about the change that was exciting.

Morris entered the tent and asked, "Can I have a word with you before the others arrive?"

Craig nodded. Morris would never know how narrowly he had escaped a clash that might well have echoed between them for the rest of their service together. It was only the C.O.'s hint of the change of plan that had deflected Craig's anger and made him once again postpone the reckoning with Morris. But was it only that? Was there not something about Morris himself that deflected anger and impeded bitter reckonings?

"Two things," said Morris. "First, I've written a report on the exercise." He laid it on the table.

Would Morris ever know what he was up against? Would he ever see that failure could only be expiated, not explained away? Then Craig noticed that Morris was watching him with wary grey eyes, trying to understand him, as he himself had just been trying to understand the brass-hats who had changed the defence plan, as the brass-hats were presumably trying to understand the Japanese across the frontier. Morris was not the only one who did not know what he was up against.

"The old defence plan is dead," he said quietly. "The garrison is being split—the three infantry battalions on the mainland, the rest on the island. Our job on the mainland will be to man the old Inner Line, a string of pillboxes across ten and a half miles of rough terrain. We'll have two thousand men trying to do the work of twenty thousand. We won't be risking a whole company in preliminaries in front of the Line."

"I'd still like you to read the report," said Morris stubbornly.

Craig nodded. He saw that an announcement of Armageddon itself would not reconcile Morris to rough justice.

"The other thing," said Morris hurriedly, "is this trouble over Corporal Macdonald. He's a good man, and I was wondering whether you might let him see his wife and try to patch up their differences."

"You'll answer for his good conduct?"

"Yes."

"All right. Fetch Torrance and Anstey now."

Alone again, Craig glanced through the report. Morris seemed to be able to match his actions to his beliefs. His actions were awkward because his beliefs were still crude, but he was in a happier position than a man who always felt like two men.

For the moment, however, there was still a kind of happiness in Craig, a happiness that might be no more than the feeling that quickened the ranks when, the tedium of waiting over, orders were shouted and muscles responded and the tramp of marching feet filled the hollow of the mind again.

*

It was an easy day, an empty day. The Old Horse had taken away all the company commanders to look over the Inner Line, and Don Company were getting to rest up, after their week-end on the exercise, before the work on the Inner Line started. Jannelli searched for someone who could talk about things out of the ordinary.

There was a man in Corporal Macdonald's section who had lived in South America. He was called Rudolph Richardson, and he spoke like a bird—with neat quick movements of his lips— because he was accustomed to speaking Spanish. He liked to talk about the time when he was a lancer in a revolution, and about the kinds of brothels he had visited. He could tell of some strange things done in brothels—things that made you want to see the faces of the women who could do them and of the men who enjoyed watching them.

Jannelli had settled down beside Richardson and was waiting for him to finish his afternoon siesta, when Elastic-Legs Williamson started to muster the whole company for wiring practice. The practice dragged on for two solid hours, until Williamson tore a finger on a good sharp barb and went away at the double to get himself disinfected and bandaged. The three other officers —Torrance, Anstey and Morris—had a quick word together, and Torrance told the company to collect the gear together and then fall out.

Jannelli went to look for the bird-man again.

*

In the early evening, before the senior officers had returned, the Mess-Tin rattled out of camp, with Torrance at the wheel, Morris in the broken bucket-seat by his side, and Sergeant Wade of Torrance's platoon and Corporal Macdonald of Morris's in the back. With only one halt on the way, to repair a break in the petrol feed, they reached Kowloon and, at the bottom of Nathan Road, parked the car and separated: Wade and Macdonald to the Star Ferry pier, the two subalterns to the Peninsula Hotel.

Torrance was now in high spirits. When the rumoured move from the frontier camp had translated itself into a change of defence plan—involving no more than the cleansing of old pill-boxes, the digging and wiring of holes in the ground, and the playing of the mock-battle game on a new board—he had been unusually dejected. He had not worn an honest smile from the time that Craig had announced the change until the time that Williamson had torn his finger on the barbed wire. But he was a new man now.

Over a glass of canned Milwaukee beer, he spoke with antici-patory relish of the different ways in which they might spend the evening, while Morris thought of ways in which he might try to renew acquaintance with the Lins.

"Which is it to be?" Torrance asked generously.

Morris hesitated.

"I was forgetting—" Torrance sat forward, suddenly curious. "There are those friends of yours—"

"That's just a duty call." Morris took a mouthful of beer to sharpen his tongue for falsehood. "A cousin of my father's—I promised to visit him."

Torrance grinned.

"It's true. Skinner's his name." That much was true. But on his second day in the colony Morris had discovered that Skinner had gone down to Singapore on business for a month or two.

"He might stand us a dinner."

Morris shook his head. "He's a Fifer."

They had another beer.

"There's a girl I know," said Torrance, nodding his head vaguely. "Joan Aitchison. She has some kind of a Government job. We might go across, eh?"

Joan Aitchison was a horror: with a boyish crop of blonde hair, a lean-hipped figure like a scrawny fashion model's, a sharp voice and a thrusting manner. There was another girl with her—Nell Griffiths—dark, full-bodied and quiet, but with a slight moustache and an oppressive habit of staring. A couple of lemons.

"I'm sorry," Nell apologised, in a soft husky voice, "I didn't catch your name."

"John Morris."

Nell's eyes widened and her red lips parted.

"Morris?" screeched Joan, breaking off her loud conversation with Torrance. "Then you're—" She started to giggle.

Morris clasped his knees and tried not to blush.

"But we know all about you," she explained, thrusting herself towards him, with inquisitive eyes and ingratiating smile. "We heard all about you on Saturday night—from one of the Volunteers who had been fighting you."

Morris did blush.

"Did you win?" asked Nell encouragingly.

"We haven't exactly decided yet," he said.

"How odd!" Joan exclaimed. "You decide *afterwards*?"

Torrance intervened. "They didn't actually shoot at each other, you see."

"Next time," promised Morris, "we will."

When Joan recovered from another fit of giggles, she told him, "I think I'm going to like you."

"I'm sure I am," murmured Nell.

*

The Peninsula Hotel was soon too large to contain them. It had been built to house an empire. Its vast lobby was a refuge from the intimidating masses in the streets outside, with their cryptic tongues and secret purposes and constant shadows of disease and poverty, vice and subversion—an echoing sanctuary in which colonists could grow larger than life, inflate their sense of mission, expand their enjoyment of profits, spread large their dream of benevolent autocracy . . . Morris waited for an opportunity to make the point. In the meantime, he could see that the place was certainly too large for the hilarious occasion that Torrance and Joan were trying to contrive. Their witticisms were too quickly absorbed into the murmuring silence, and their laughter sounded flat. He could also see that it was too large for Nell, who was working hard to project the illusion that only he and she had survived some catastrophe, the memory of which still constrained her to speak in whispers. In the spaciously cool lobby, the intimate warmth of her efforts leaked rapidly away; under the bright electric stars of the colonial heaven, her illusion shone pale.

Torrance was the first to suggest a move. "Where do we go from here?"

Where do *we* go? Quickly Morris tried to toe his brother-officer's shins under the table and succeeded only in rubbing his leg against Nell's knees. He recoiled hastily.

He could not believe that Torrance really wanted to spend a whole evening with Joan—all mouth and hands. He himself certainly did not want to spend much longer with Nell—all eyes and bosom. Her proximity had revived his interest in an entirely different girl—a girl with timid eyes and unobtrusive breasts . . .

He was often, in his single bed, a comprehensive lover of women, pursuing all kinds of female shadows. Yet now, in the hours before girls became ghosts, he was ready to exchange the certain pleasures offered by Nell for the uncertainty of finding Anna and the impossibility of achieving more than an exchange of words and a touching of hands. What had happened to the Don Juan of the dark? Had the light—even the light of electric stars—bleached him beyond recognition? That was bloody absurd, beerily absurd.

All right. What was wrong with Nell? Moustache. But it was no more than a faint shadow. And wasn't it supposed to be an unmistakable indication of sexual fervour? Sexual fervour, though. Wasn't that, in real life, a little intimidating? She disclosed the narrow pit before she had taken time to glaze his eyes? But that was not the whole reason for his reluctance. Searching for a reason, he glanced at her. Nell the nubile, with lustrous dark eyes, full red underlip, smooth neck, round breasts, and everything else under the table. Imagining her nakedness, he thought of his own nakedness, the nakedness under his skin. To get a ghost-girl or a tired whore he had to uncover only his body. But, to get a woman who was not a mere extension of his own will, he would have to uncover more of himself. Surely to heaven that was not the reason for his reluctance?

"All right with you two?" asked Torrance. "The White Russian place?"

Nell glanced at Morris.

Her hesitancy pleased him. "Fine," he said. "Suits us."

On the steps outside, she told him, "You didn't sound very keen."

At a loss for words, he tried to look surprised.

"Maybe you had better fish to fry?" she asked.

There were always better fish somewhere in the sea . . . "As a matter of fact, Nell," he said, and it sounded like someone else speaking, "I had half-promised to look up some friends."

She was hurt.

Quickly he assured her, "I can see them some other time . . ." A fish in the hand . . . the outstretched hand, still reaching for the better fish.

Torrance and the blonde had disappeared.

"D'you know where the White Russian place is?" he asked uneasily.

"No. We'll just follow—" She looked up and down the road. Her surprise might have been genuine.

"That's that." Nervously hefting the burden of his new responsibility, he asked, "What do we do now?"

*

Corporal Macdonald closed the door, slipped the key into his pocket, walked quietly along the lobby and entered the room in which he rented a cubicle. Poppy was not at home.

Mr. Ng was eating a small bowlful of rice with a few wafers of dried fish as relish, before starting his night-shift at the docks. He had not seen Poppy.

Mrs. Cheung, wife of a salesman in the Joyful Prosperity hardware store, rolled her fifth child into his bedding and reluctantly admitted that Poppy had gone out with Mimi Pak, the taxi-dancer.

Back in his own cubicle, Macdonald decided to wait. If he went to the taxi-dance hall, he might lose his temper. If he lost his temper, anything might happen. And he didn't want to get young Morris into trouble with the Skipper.

Lying down on the straw mat that covered the wooden bunk, he noticed that Kwan Yin was back. On the partition at the end of the bunk hung a gimcrack shrine of matchwood and red paper to the goddess of compassion. He knew the meaning of compassion better than any unconverted Chinese did, better than most converts did. 'Finally, be ye all of one mind, having compassion one of another . . .' First Epistle General of Peter, three, eight.

He took the shrine to the communal kitchen and burned it in a clay stove. When he had gone back to his cubicle, Mrs. Bun, wife of an ivory-carver, watched the wisp of smoke from the matchwood curl upwards in front of the red and gold tablet of Tso Kwan, god of the kitchen.

*

"Those friends of yours," said Nell. "Would I know them?"

They were sauntering up Nathan Road.

"I don't think so." Morris took greater interest in a display of leather goods on the other side of the road.

"It's a small world, Hongkong."

"They're Chinese."

"I know lots of Chinese."

"James and Anna Lin," he said submissively.

"Really? They live quite close to us—Joan and me. We know them quite well."

"I wonder," he said casually, "if you could let me have their address. I'm not sure that I've got it right."

"You haven't visited them yet?"

"I haven't had much time and—"

"Let's go there now."

He grinned happily, frowned. How could he renew such a slender acquaintance, explain all that had to be explained, achieve all that he wanted to achieve, with Nell by his side, nubile Nell?

"They're always glad to have company," she assured him. "We'll buy a bottle of sweet wine. They like that."

*

In the taxi, Morris sat on the edge of the seat, answering in monosyllables, taking careful note of the route. Nell lay back, told him how happy she was, asked him how—in a world so small—she had not met him before. He glanced at her once. He had heard of it happening in a taxi, but had not considered before how awkward it would be.

It was James who answered Nell's knock on the door. He was wearing spectacles and a jacket of crimson silk. He smiled at Nell, glanced at Morris without recognition, and looked back at Nell again.

"We're not disturbing you?" she asked, rather nervously.

He murmured politely and stood aside, inviting them to enter.

"It was terribly funny," she explained quickly. "I've been meaning for ages to come along, and tonight I find that Johnny's in the same boat."

Morris met James's politely-trying-to-remember scrutiny with a small, reassuring smile. "Not the boat that we met in last time," he said significantly.

"Isn't Anna in?" Nell interrupted.

"She's working late."

"We brought some wine," said Nell.

Morris saw that she was fanning a tiny spark of friendship. She did not know the Lins much better than he did. For her, this visit was simply one way of keeping him on her hook. "I just wanted to say hello," he assured James.

"You'll stay to taste the wine, I hope."

"I know Anna likes it," said Nell. She was moving some of James's books and papers to make room for herself on the sofa, although there were several empty chairs in the room. Women were the bloody limit.

Impulsively, Morris followed James into the kitchen. "I'm sorry about this," he told him softly. "You can't possibly remember me. I met you and your sister about a fortnight ago. We arranged to meet—"

James nodded delightedly. "I remember. We were to meet the next night?"

"I couldn't get out of camp and couldn't get in touch with you. You didn't tell me your address." In a happy confusion of apologies and laughter, they found each other again. "Let me help you with the glasses," offered Morris, seizing two of the three that James held. "Nell said she was an old friend of yours, so I took the chance —maybe she's not really an old friend but—"

"She lives quite near here," said James politely.

Morris felt obliged to explain, "I hardly know her—"

"Wine shortens the distance between strangers," James said slyly. "And perhaps, later, you will both excuse me while I finish an article I'm writing? I can work in another room, you see."

"No. I didn't mean—" But James had gone.

Over the first glass of wine, Nell commanded the conversation. James appeared to enjoy her gossip. Morris did not understand it. He dangled his glass between his legs and cast about for some way of correcting James's misconstruction of his broken explanation in the kitchen. It was a farcical situation, and he found that he could think only in terms of farce. Once, for instance, he saw an opening in the conversation when he could have said: "If we ever run into each other again, Nell, I hope you'll let me know the outcome."

Later it occurred to him that he could either demonstrate his lack of interest in Nell (perhaps by starting to call her Miss Griffiths) or reveal his interest in Anna.

"Will Anna be very late?" he asked.

James did not know.

"We can't stay very late," said Nell, with the seductive accent of one who knew better places for frying fish.

Cheerfully, James winked at Morris.

*

Macdonald lay on the wooden bunk, waiting.

If he went down to the dance-hall, he would lose his temper without shifting his doubts. But if he waited here and she came back with a man . . .

*

Morris wondered how many reflections of Anna there were in the room. The style of furnishing could be described as eclectic with a bias towards the oriental, or Chinese with concessions to comfort; the West provided the seating and the electric fire and fan, the East the blackwood tables, lacquered screen and cabinet, carved camphor-wood chest and blue and white porcelain. All the books and newspapers that he could see were, however, in English.

He also wondered in how many ways Anna resembled James. James was a nice chap, but he was so widely read, so well informed, that he made Morris feel uncomfortable.

"I envy you your knowledge of affairs," he admitted.

"The part of me that was educated in England," said James, "believes that only knowledge—greater and greater knowledge of ourselves and our world—can solve problems like war and poverty. The part of me that grew up in China believes that too much knowledge—like too much of anything else—is itself an evil."

"I must be Chinese," murmured Nell. Since James had started to trot out his string of leader-writer's hobby-horses, she had been nursing her empty glass in dreamy silence.

"If we live in a volcanic world," James asked, "is it wise to know everything about volcanoes?"

Morris grinned. "If you learn the habits of volcanoes, you'll know when to run for cover."

James smiled weakly and rose to fetch the bottle. "We've ranged round the globe tonight, Johnny, but we haven't reached Hongkong yet." There was a sharper edge on his words now. "What do you think of the situation here?"

"Not that," protested Nell. "That's getting on my nerves. Everybody seems to be talking about The Situation."

Morris tried to formulate a wise opinion. "I think," he said, "I think there might be trouble." It was the minimal estimate of a soldier. If he wrote off all risk, he wrote off his own utility.

"Sometimes I wish I'd gone with the other women," Nell confessed.

"Why not go still?" asked James. There was something troubling him.

She frowned. "You really think there's going to be trouble?"

James took off his spectacles. "Anna and I are going away."

"Going away?"

"Yes, Johnny." He handed them replenished glasses, without looking at their faces. "We're going to join our mother and elder brother in Singapore. They are making arrangements for us all to travel to America." He sat down and sipped his wine. "You know our proverb?—Of all the thirty-six alternatives, running away is the best."

Dejected and embarrassed, Morris asked, "You're going soon?"

"Pretty soon."

"I'm sorry. For my sake, I mean."

"For my sake," said Nell, "drop the subject."

There was a long uneasy silence. Then she spoke again: "Good heavens, is that the time?" And they all rose to their feet.

One last regret delayed Morris. He was wishing that he had seen Anna in this room and been able—even for a few minutes—to substantiate his dream of a small but perfect place of gentleness and quiet.

Impatiently, Nell opened the door.

*

Wide-eyed, slack-jawed, she stood in the entrance to the cubicle. She was rigid with surprise and fear. She was alone.

Without taking his eyes from her, Macdonald swung his legs off the bunk. "Come in," he said quietly, aware of the hush that had fallen over the other cubicles. "Come in, Poppy." She took one hesitant pace towards him. He held out a hand, hating to see her like this, like a frightened animal. "Come and sit down." He grasped her arm and made her sit at his side.

"Where have you been?" he whispered. She was wearing her best gown, a high-necked, sleeveless sheath of silk slit from hem to thigh. Her mouth was painted and her hair was perfumed. "Where have you been?" Her skin was as smooth as the silk she wore—miraculously hairless, poreless, Chinese skin. The sight of her high-boned face and the touch of her arm stirred in him like another anger.

"You don't tell me you come," she said sulkily.

He squeezed her arm. "Why didn't you write, Poppy? I know you got my letter. Barker handed it to you. He saw you read it. You knew they might not let me out of camp if you didn't write. Maybe you didn't want them to let me out?"

She shuddered slightly. Then, jerking her head up, she asked loudly and harshly, "You got cigarette?"

"Why didn't you write?" he whispered savagely.

"You say you beat me."

"I said I'd beat you if you were bad again. You don't have to be frightened if you're good—good, you understand?"

She nodded casually. "You got cigarette?"

"Do you understand what I'm saying?" he pleaded desperately, his temples throbbing painfully, his whisper hoarsely strained. It was always like this. She would neither fight back nor totally submit. Her resistance was merely a kind of misunderstanding. "Listen, Poppy. You've been bad again. I know where you've been. You've been hiring yourself out at the dance-hall."

"No dance, no money."

He let go her arm and punched it—hard. "I give you almost every penny I get," he said, choking with rage.

She sat still for a moment, her mouth trembling; then, with quick nervous hands, rummaged in her handbag until she found a cigarette. When she lifted it to her lips, he seized it and crushed it to shreds between his shaking fingers. She watched him, with the simple fear of a soulless animal. It was only as an animal she would ever learn. He would never teach her with words. And he had to teach her. He had taken her out of the dance-hall, and he didn't want her to go back. He took off his belt and stood over her.

Misunderstanding again, she started to undress. His anger hurt his head and throat. It was a swelling, sickening anger against the flawless armour of her ignorance, against the dumb resistance of

evil, against the frustration of his will, against the insolent
resurrection of flesh. He squeezed the buckle of his belt until the
metal tongue pierced his skin.

*

Mr. Cheung heard the belt falling on the floor. He continued to
trim his toe-nails and listen.

His wife was mending a shirt. Four of his children were asleep.
The fifth—the eldest—was awake and sweating. Every night he
sweated and sometimes he spat blood, but he was earning enough
to pay for his own medicine. Mr. Cheung, husband of a diligent
wife, father of three sons, first assistant in the Joyful Prosperity
hardware store, sole tenant of a cubicle as large as the foreign
soldier's, could afford to take interest in other people's troubles.

When he heard the bunk in the next cubicle rhythmically creaking, he pricked his wife's leg with his nail-scissors, grinned and
made a coarse gesture.

*

Nell walked out, leaving the door open. Morris turned away
from James, hearing a soft confusion of voices and laughter on the
stairs, a little explosion of other people's greetings that echoed in
his emptiness. "It's Anna," he said.

Suddenly, still talking and laughing, she came from the lighted
landing into the dark hallway and almost bumped into him. "Oh!"
she said, looking up at him, her lips parted, her eyes wide with
surprise.

He grinned exultantly. If they had been alone, he could have
taken her in his arms. There might never be another time when he
would feel so sure of himself, so sure of her.

"Mr. Morris," she remembered, and stepped back and looked
around, unbalanced by shyness.

"I came to see you," he said. "This was the first chance I've had
since . . ." There was no need for explanation.

Nell switched on the light. Women—some women—were the
bloody limit. Anna and he were unable to look at each other now.

"I've done my best to entertain—" James started to justify
himself.

"We've had a grand time," Nell assured everybody. "But we'll
have to go now. Next time we come, we'll make sure you're both
going to be in."

Morris damned her to hell and glanced at Anna. He had forgotten how perfect she was. In a high-necked Chinese gown, she looked smaller, more delicate, more graceful, than in Western evening dress. Her face was heart-shaped, her eyes set wide apart —dark, shining, timorous eyes.

"I hope you *will* come," said James, watching Morris with fresh curiosity.

"Yes," said Morris. "I don't know exactly when I'll be able to get away."

There was a moment of awkward silence until Nell once again made to open the door, which had swung shut. James hurried to forestall her this time, and Morris, desperately bold, seized the chance to touch Anna's arm and whisper, "Saturday?"

She looked up, nodded breathlessly, and turned towards the door.

*

Outside, he felt slightly drunk and began to sing with solemn emphasis:

> " 'Ye Highlands and ye Lawlands,
>   Oh! where hae ye been?
> They hae slain the Earl of Moray,
>   And hae laid him on the green.' "

Nell tried to join in, but had to confess her ignorance of the song.

"It's a sad song," he said happily.

"I can offer you a better one."

With a generous flourish of his hand, he gave her leave to begin.

"On the gramophone," she explained.

He cooled. "No time tonight, Nell."

"But you've got to have something to eat before you go back. You must be famished. I am. I'll make you something while you listen to the gramophone. It'll be quicker than going to a restaurant."

He became aware of his hunger. Recklessly, he grasped her arm. "You're a good girl, Nell."

*

An Italian tenor. When he sang his words into the winding groove of the record, he must have looked absurd, making elastic shapes with his mouth and spreading gestures with his hands. But the record gave back only the disembodied song, and Morris could forget the animal absurdity of its creation. The notes stretched across the dark room and touched him, prickling his head as the touch of Anna's arm had done, and moving in his full belly.

Sitting beside him on the sofa, Nell laid her hand on his knee. "What a hard knee you've got!" she murmured.

"Yes," he admitted. Vaguely, he wondered whether he was now expected to touch her knees and comment on them. It would be pleasant enough to touch them, but it would be difficult to describe them in terms adequate to the occasion. They were round. He would have to say that they were as round as—something. He couldn't think of anything particularly round and romantic. So, in default, he turned his attention back to his own knees. "They're knobbly," he said frankly.

Warmly, she asked for an ash-tray. The only one that he could discern in the darkness sat on an occasional table on her other side. While he leaned over her legs to reach it, she laid a caressing hand on the back of his head. Loath to risk hurting her feelings by displacing the hand, he kept his head bent and passed the ash-tray to her through the narrow space between her legs and his shamed face. She stubbed her cigarette and, gingerly, he replaced the ash-tray on the table.

"Johnny," she murmured, clasping his head in both hands now and gently bringing it to rest on her bosom.

He slipped his arms around her. Because the room was dark and she was gentle. Because his mind was full of sleepy thoughts of Anna. Larger than ever before, life opened in front of him. And, for once, he felt as large as life.

Aware that her heart was beating as loudly as his, he shaped his hand around a breast, around a thigh, marvelling—without self-mystification this time—at the softness and strangeness. With clumsy, impatient, insolent fingers—fingers that had fumbled through all the lonely dreams to this certain, other flesh—he unbuttoned the neck of her frock.

The tenor's last exultant note reached across the room and touched his sensitive scalp, withered abruptly into the scratching searching of the needle in the empty groove, and clicked into silence.

"Hell's teeth!" gasped Nell. "I hear them coming."

Torrance and Joan. Their brittle laughter outside.

D

Morris groaned, desperately kissed Nell on the mouth and ran his hands over her lost body.

"Switch on the light," she whispered urgently, hurriedly buttoning.

When the other two boisterously entered the room, Nell and Morris were sitting far apart, warm, tremulous, avoiding each other's darkened eyes, speaking in hollow voices.

"What's been going on here?" demanded Torrance happily.

"Had a good time?" asked Joan, her eyes hard with suspicion, her mouth exaggerating her friendliness.

Yes, a good time. But not so good as it might have been.

Chapter Two

TUESDAY, 11th November.

Captain Craig, accompanied by his second-in-command, Lieutenant Williamson, his warrant officers, C.S.M. Duncan and C.Q.M.S. Silver, and his three platoon commanders, Second-Lieutenants Anstey, Morris and Torrance, inspected D Company's positions in the Inner Line.

The battalion were to hold the left sector of the Line, from the west coast, across the Castle Peak road, up to an imposing system of concrete defence-works, called Shingmun Redoubt, built into the narrow north-west end of Smugglers Ridge. To the right of Smugglers Ridge, a Punjabi battalion and a Rajput battalion were to hold the remainder of the ten-and-a-half-miles-long Line, across to Port Shelter on the east coast, blocking all the other land approaches to Kowloon. There was not time to walk the length of the battalion's front line or to inspect the imposing Redoubt which, although dwarfed by the height and mass of Tai-mo-shan to the north, stood high enough to dominate the sector. But Craig indicated, with a swing of his ash stick, the disposition of the forward companies—C, B and A—from the sea up to Shingmun; and, in order to leave the subalterns in no doubt as to their responsibilities in the reserve company, he drew attention to the length of the front line and emphasised his point by telling them that Shingmun Redoubt, which had been designed for defence by at least three platoons, would be held by only one platoon of A Company.

D Company were to hold the reserve line, about a mile behind the front line, stretching from Gindrinkers Bay, across the Castle Peak road, and across the forward slopes of Golden Hill, almost as far as the south end of Smugglers Ridge.

Lunch, for Craig and his subordinates, consisted of sandwiches (corned beef) and water (chlorinated). Conversation limped along safely and insincerely until Anstey decided to speak.

"What puzzles me," he said irritably, "is why we should suddenly change our defence plan. There must be a reason, and it seems absurd that we should be kept in the dark."

"Security," explained Williamson, jerkily hitching his shorts up. "Ours not to reason why. You see?"

"Actually," said Torrance, "it's just a military device—like scrubbing clean floors—to keep us all from getting fat and lazy."

"How long," asked Morris, as if he had wakened from a daydream, "how long have we got to put the Line into order?"

"Not long," said Craig. "We haven't been given a deadline, but we've been told to get cracking."

"Why the urgency?" demanded Anstey, blue eyes wide in his small dark face.

Williamson explained, "Don't want to be caught with our trousers down."

"Only six shopping weeks till Christmas," added Torrance.

Anstey turned angrily away.

Craig stood up. Work, as Williamson might have said, as Williamson might yet say, was the best remedy for a troubled mind. Work carried out in the spirit in which a man pulled his trousers up, without reasoning why . . .

Captain Craig, in accordance with orders, completed his reconnaissance by 1700 hours and returned with his party, by truck, to the frontier camp.

*

Wednesday, 12th November.

Second-Lieutenant Morris, closely followed by Lance-Sergeant Drummond, acting as his platoon sergeant in Meechan's absence, Private Ripley, his runner, and the three section commanders, Lance-Corporal Foggo, who had temporarily taken Drummond's place in Number 4 Section, Corporal Barker of Number 5 Section, and Corporal Macdonald of Number 6 Section, walked around 17 Platoon's positions and tried to plan the work of completion.

17 Platoon were to form the left flank of D Company, straddling the Castle Peak road. Torrance in the centre and Anstey on the right were both on the forward slopes of Golden Hill.

"We've got the most important position," observed Foggo, forefinger and thumb brushing up the ends of his little moustache.

Morris gave a casual nod. He did not feel obliged to point out that company H.Q. were to be on the left flank and that Craig had obviously decided to position 17 Platoon there so that he could keep a close eye on them.

To begin with, Morris ensured that his subordinates knew the lie of the land. The ability to read a map and appreciate ground was, he felt, one of the basic attributes of a good infantryman.

Even on the map, Tai-mo-shan, head-in-the-clouds mountain, three thousand, one hundred and thirty feet high, dominated the ragged, rumpled spread of the New Territories, commanded the granite barrier that ranged across the peninsula from the Taipo road on the east coast to the Castle Peak road on the west. North of this mountain barrier lay the only part of the colony that Morris knew well—the Kamtin valley, the low hills beyond, the valley where the battalion were encamped, and the Shumchun river. South of the barrier stretched the Inner Line.

"It's terribly shut in," said Lance-Sergeant Drummond, looking around him. "With the hills, I mean."

Tai-mo-shan in front of them, overlooking the whole sector; Smugglers Ridge on their right; Golden Hill at their backs. It was only when they looked westwards, across the island-scattered water, that they could see the sky without raising their eyes. That would not have worried Meechan. Drummond—large, dark, womanish eyes, a tilted nose and a full lower lip—was less helpful than Meechan had been. He was too respectful, too sensitive.

Morris stood in need of help. The Inner Line was no Maginot Line; its widely spaced pillboxes provided no more than a skeleton system of defence; to complete the system a great deal of digging and wiring had yet to be done. And Morris's knowledge of the principles of static defence was as slender as his legs. By the time he had joined the army, the Maginot-Line principle had seemed as out-dated as the principle of the hollow square. He had been taught to fight on the run, more often backwards than forwards, the Dunkirk drill.

Brooding over the siting of all the earthworks and barbed-wire fences needed to complete the defences of his area, and over his reluctance to turn to Craig for advice, Morris started to allocate the pillboxes. There were three in his platoon area: one on either side of the Castle Peak road and one down by Gindrinkers Bay. The two flanking the road were built into rocky slopes, presenting inconspicuous faces of concrete, smoother and paler than the natural outcrop, with shadowed slits for eyes and guns. The one on the verge of the salt-marsh had been constructed in the shape of a cottage—a severely rectangular cottage with blind windows. From the outside, these pillboxes looked comfortably compact, re-assuringly solid. Inside the first, on the right of the road, Morris was reminded of the stairs of an Edinburgh tenement in winter, of dank stone and plaster and clinging air.

"It's all yours," he told Foggo, his voice vibrating in his own ears. Nobody else spoke.

Inside the centre box, Morris noticed the damp moulds on the walls, the dispiriting dirt.

"I'll get it scrubbed out and aired," said Barker mildly.

Inside Macdonald's cottage, Morris began to feel angry.

"Terribly shut in," said Drummond.

Macdonald assured everybody : "They'll look better in a day or two, after we've mucked them out."

They might be made to look better, but they would still feel like burial vaults. Leading his party outside, Morris changed the sub-ject. "Platoon headquarters and company headquarters will be in the hollow behind the centre pillbox."

"In the open, sir?" asked Foggo. His manner was half-obsequious, half-resentful.

Morris replied obliquely : "You'll have positions in the open, too. To finish the Line, we've got to dig and wire a lot of weapon-pits and listening posts. We're supposed to site them today and start the spadework tomorrow."

"Spadework !" exclaimed Ripley, the runner. "It's gelignite and pumps we'll 'ave to use, sir."

Living rock and salt-marsh.

"All we can do is pick the likeliest sites, and ask Captain Craig to vet them tomorrow morning," Morris decided weakly.

Conscious of his weakness, he kept himself and his N.C.O.s at the picking of sites until the light began to fail and the whining of mosquitoes reminded him of Craig's warning that this was the worst malarial corner of the colony. In the truck, on the way back to camp, he passed round his cigarettes in an effort to make amends.

*

Thursday, 13th November.

Fraser was pretty sure he was being victimised.

As soon as the Skipper and the Boy had made up their minds where they wanted the first pits dug, Foggo started throwing his weight about. He told off Jannelli and the little bum-boy, Wait, to clean out the P.B., and split the rest of the section into two gangs—Fraser, McGuire and a Durham miner as one of the gangs.

"Two weapon-pits, I want," said Foggo, "and see that they're good."

"How come Jannelli's gettin' the soft job?" demanded Fraser.

"I don't want none of your bastard buck," said Foggo, sharp as a razor. "Get digging, *chullo*."

"It's a funny thing how Jannelli always—"

"Look, Fraser. Just get digging, or I'll put you on a bastard fizzer, see?"

Foggo meant it, all right. He'd put you on a charge quick as spit. He thought he was a real *burra sahib* with his one dog-leg, marking time for promotion now that he'd got command of a section. There were plenty of Foggos going around. But they'd better watch their step. Fraser had been on his own before. Now, he had the strongest man in the battalion for his mucker.

It was a bad place for working—behind the P.B., on top of the ridge, where everybody could see you. But there was only one pick. Fraser took a shovel and waited for McGuire to break the surface of the ridge. The miner, Feltham, sat on his hunkers and lit a cigarette.

The Skipper was no better than the Boy when it came to looking for places to dig pits. The rock wasn't just on the top.

"*Man-man!*" said Feltham. "Let the pick do the work, Punchy. Here, I'll show you."

"Leave him alone," warned Fraser, "or he'll split your head open—understand?"

"He's going to snap the haft. That's rock—solid rock—he's hitting there."

"All right, so it's rock. That's not worryin' Punchy. You just watch him."

They watched him.

*

From the side of Golden Hill, Morris and Torrance looked glumly down.

"Battalion headquarters one side of the road, company headquarters the other side," said Morris.

Battalion headquarters were to lie immediately behind Foggo's section. The signals officer, the intelligence officer, and the assistant adjutant were already exploring the concrete shelters built into the back of the ridge.

"It would be easier to slip between Siamese twins," said Torrance bleakly. "If we ever have to move into these positions, we'll have a fat chance of getting a night out on the quiet."

McNaughton Smith appeared below, walking along the ridge, apparently surveying the reserve line. He caught sight of them and climbed up to join them.

"Your men, Morris?" he asked, waving his stick over his shoulder.

Even as he admitted that they were, Morris noticed that only one of the three men visible on the ridge was working, and waited for reproof.

"Ugly," said McNaughton Smith. "All three of them. A single ugly man is always interesting. A group of ugly men is an affront." He stared solemnly at Morris, as if he were waiting for an explanation or apology.

Torrance came to the rescue. "These men of Morris's," he said pompously, "were hand-picked to defend battalion headquarters. Their faces are their fortifications."

McNaughton Smith looked around, head back, breathing deeply as he surveyed the reserve line again. "This may well be the last ditch," he said. Then he slapped his stick against his fat leg, wished them a good morning, and started to climb towards Anstey's position, on the right of the company's line.

Torrance grinned. "You understand, my old? They shall not pass. Here we fight to the death. It is for the France."

Without a drink, Morris could not clown.

*

Friday, 14th Nov. 1941.

Dear Alice,

  We are having a bit of a change just now and it means a lot of hard work for us, but yours truly is taking it with a smile as per usual. Of course I can not tell you all about this change and even if I could I do not think you would know what I was talking about. It does not make much difference to things any way. Sometimes I wish I was home again, after all I did not join to be a navy. I am glad to hear your mother is getting extra coal and tell Auntie Bella these things I sent her were table mats not for hanging up. No promotion yet, so I hope

*you are managing on the money. Look after yourself, I wish
you were not so far away.*

Your loving husband,

George.

Morris frowned over the letter. Sime shouldn't really have mentioned the change at all. But, if the references to the change were
deleted, there would be little left for Alice to read. And, if he
asked Sime to rewrite the letter, what the devil could the poor
chap find to say? Morris added a 'v' to 'navy', and initialled the
envelope. Passed by censor.

It was time to wash and change for dinner. Torrance had already
gone down to the mess to whet his appetite on pale sherry. Ah
Chan was waiting, as unobtrusive as another piece of furniture in
the crowded tent, merged in the pattern of light and shadow
around the sibilant centre of the pressure lamp, the pattern that
already seemed comfortably familiar. The boy's cheek caught the
light, round and smooth as a girl's, as a Chinese girl's. It might
have been Anna standing there.

Morris roused himself from his paraffin dream, broke up the
familiar pattern into its unfamiliar parts. "Sorry I've kept you
waiting," he muttered.

As he undressed, he wondered why he had made so little effort
to get to know Ah Chan. Guiltily, he tried to make conversation.
"I wish I knew you better."

Chan gave him a puzzled, uneasy look.

"Where do you live? Where your home?—No, I know where
your tent is. I mean—where do you stay at other times? Where
your family? Kowloon, Hongkong?"

"Hongkong side," admitted the boy nervously.

Morris smiled encouragement. "Wife Hongkong side?"

"Wife wash-amah."

"In camp here? Good. And children? Small pieces?" he added
in an effort at pidgin.

Chan held up three trembling fingers.

"Good man! In Hongkong, I suppose? But who looks after
them? You have someone else in house—mother, sister, brother?"

The boy's face was ugly with fear.

"*Maskee*," said Morris. "Fetch hot water now."

He was disappointed and puzzled. But he had done his best and,

D*

already cleansed of some of his guilt, he started to wash off the sweat and dirt of the day's work on the Line.

*

After dinner, Craig sat with his empty hands on his knees.

There was nothing in the mess to read. He had leafed through the morning papers before dinner, he had long since seen all that he wanted to see of the old British magazines, and he could not —without provoking a chorus of tiresome chaffing—look into the other magazines, which were brought to the mess by Birse, the motor transport officer, and seemed—from the comments they excited—to contain little but photographs of women in underwear. How his puritanical reputation had started he could not remember —unless it had grown out of his small appetite for alcohol—but it was now as traditional as Guthrie's crumpled glengarry bonnet. And as Guthrie could not inoffensively buy a new bonnet, so Craig—to avoid running the gauntlet of ridicule—had to keep a straight face at dirty stories and did not dare open Birse's magazines.

There was nobody to talk to. Walter Ballantyne, old Ingham and Kenny Kerr—the only men whose conversation he enjoyed— were absent. On his right, Guthrie and Young, the lieutenant-quartermaster, were recalling the giants of yesteryear, knitting together memories and make-believe, defiant, self-justifying, like old women knitting socks for nobody in particular. Like all dead-beats they found their solace in drinking and disparaging the wounding present by boasting of the invulnerable past. They could not credibly boast of their own soldierly feats; wisely, they boasted of the men they had served with, in Flanders and India, and especially of the dead men, the long-dead men, the men who were buried deeper every time Guthrie and Young told their stories. Craig had more in common with the group on his left, a school of subalterns talking shop, Torrance leading a mutinous minority in criticism of the new defence plan, and Welsh—spokesman for the contented or careless majority—sipping port and offering generous assurances of the competence of everyone in command. Although he knew that his conversation had a depressive effect on most subalterns, Craig would gladly have joined in the discussion but for two considerations: he could not explain the plan without disclosing the reason for the change; and he could not evaluate the plan without damaging the morale of men like Anstey.

He knew—but the subalterns did not yet know—that a ship carrying two Canadian battalions was steaming westwards to reinforce the garrison. And now that he knew the reason for the change in the defence plan, he had lost his pleasure in it. So long as he had looked on the change as a bold move forward by the main force of the garrison, in order to meet defeat in the hills of the mainland instead of on the crowded island, he had been excited out of his routine discontent, his garrison-sickness. But now, knowing that the brigade on the mainland was merely to be a delaying force which would ultimately withdraw to join forces with another full brigade on the island, he returned to his vomit.

It was difficult to play General-Officer-Commanding British troops in China on the information supplied to an infantry company commander, but it was impossible to resist the attractions of the game. To get it started, you had to set aside all political arguments and all the grand considerations of strategy. The reinforcement of the garrison indicated that the old men in Westminster and Whitehall still considered that the colony could and should be held against attack. Damn them to hell for their proud eyes, their paper flesh—but you had to accept their distant view. The board for the game consisted of a mountainous peninsula, crossed by an unfinished line of pillboxes; and, a mile from the tip of the peninsula, a rocky island ringed with pillboxes. The pieces for the game now comprised five instead of three infantry battalions, and one machine-gun battalion, with a reserve of local volunteers and the support of artillery and engineers. Your method of playing depended on your valuation of that line of pillboxes north of Kowloon, the Inner Line, or the Gindrinkers Line—as Guthrie preferred to call it.

In 1937, presumably on the assumption that, since a large force would be needed to defend Hongkong against Japanese aggression, a large garrison would be stationed in the colony, the construction of the Inner Line had been ambitiously started. A year later, after the Japanese had moved menacingly close to the British frontier, and presumably after Whitehall had made a more realistic reckoning of Britain's armed strength, the unfinished Line had been abandoned, and a stop-gap garrison of four battalions trained to hold the island until relieved by stronger forces. Now, in 1941, with the Japanese hard against the frontier, and the armed strength of Britain massed at the other end of the world, you had to decide whether, with six instead of four battalions on the board, you should patch up and man the Inner Line.

Craig was all for starting the fight as far forward as possible, but he had no faith in the Line. Even if the whole garrison manned the Line, there would still not be enough men to hold the pillboxes, to cover the wide gaps between them with fire, and to form a reserve sufficient to prevent a break in the front line becoming an enemy breakthrough to Kowloon. The Line had been built for twenty thousand men, and the whole garrison—clerks and cooks and all—could not amount to more than ten thousand.

The only comfort he could find for the moment was that the secrecy about the reinforcements from Canada had been well preserved. He doubted whether even Mrs. Gow would have caught a straw in the wind this time.

Chapter Three

MRS. GOW gave him a brave, exemplary smile. "We didn't expect you this Saturday, Hugh. Mary's out. I don't know whether I'll be able to contact—"

"It was you I came to see." Words like a quick coat of varnish over peeling paint.

"How wise you are!" She spoke nervously, extending the falsehood into the dimensions of mere gallantry. "Like the Chinese sages, you choose the lesser happiness."

"That," Craig said, stiffly seating himself, "was an un-Chinese remark. You force me to say either that you are the lesser happiness or that you're no judge of character. You make me lose face."

She laughed, looked at him with an intense, dark-eyed gaze. "You have a very thin face just now, Hugh. You worry too much."

He allowed her to continue.

"Thank heavens," she said, "Roderick seems to be getting over his worries."

Evasively, Craig looked at the carriage clock on the table at her elbow.

"You're in a hurry?" she suggested.

He checked his denial, suddenly aware that she wanted him to agree.

"I hope you can stay for half an hour," she said helpfully, "and keep me company till I go out. A committee meeting." She leaned towards him, with a penitent smile on her sallow face. "I haven't had my sun-downer yet."

He rose and poured drinks.

"We're having a China Ball at the Peninsula on the sixth of December. Will you come?"

"Hardly in my line, is it?"

"You'll have to buy a ticket, whether or not you come. If you don't help the Chinese, you can't expect them to help you. And none of your scathing comments about the Chinese army! Incidentally, does all this Japanese activity mean anything?"

"What activity?"

"That's the first thing I've said tonight that's made you prick up your ears. You don't mix with the right people, with the Chinese. They know more than your intelligence officers do. I hear of Japanese troop movements in the Canton area, Japanese shipping in the Pearl River."

"I hadn't heard," he admitted. "Probably for some fresh move against the Chinese." But he was remembering what Ballantyne had told him in the morning—that some of the Indian troops were already moving into their sectors of the Inner Line. He finished his gimlet.

"We've time for another one," said Mrs. Gow.

*

Morris took a taxi. "As quick as you can. Savvy? *Chop-chop! Fai-ti-ah!* More one dollar you makee go fast." Moist and flustered, he lit a cigarette, fingered the ugly swellings from mosquito bites on his forehead, and revolved his grudges and qualms as the driver made a reckless bid for the bonus.

Torrance had overloaded the Mess Tin. Anstey, Fatty Ramsay and Holt, the intelligence officer, had been crammed into the back, while Morris had balanced on the broken bucket-seat. As predictably as Torrance's reaction to a smiling woman, as Ramsay's to a bowl of chow, the machine had broken down. That was the first grudge.

It had broken down at Laichikok, about halfway between Morris's positions in the Inner Line and the outskirts of Kowloon. Morris had wanted to walk the rest of the way, but had been persuaded to wait while Torrance and Holt collaborated with greasy fingers under the bonnet, demonstrating their patience and incompetence. That was the second grudge.

In the end, a Chinese lorry-driver had towed them into Kowloon. It should have been easy for Morris to detach himself at the garage. He had been bitching long enough to make himself unpopular. But Torrance had refused to let him go until they had looked for reconciliation through the bottoms of beer glasses. That was the third grudge. But maybe that wasn't a grudge. Torrance was a good chap.

Two grudges then, and two qualms. First, there was the risk of meeting Joan or Nell. His attitude towards Joan was one of simple dislike. His attitude towards Nell was difficult to define. Oddly enough, he could visualise her more clearly than he could Anna. And he took pleasure in visualising her. She was a broad target but, now that he was flustered, the ease of approaching her made her all the more comfortable a prospect. It was, however, Anna he was going to see, and that gave him his other qualm.

An amah opened the door. Anna came to meet him. They looked at each other quickly, and could not look at each other again for a long time.

"James isn't home yet," she said breathlessly.

"I meant to be here sooner," he said. "We had trouble with the car."

"He works too hard."

"We've been hard at it too. I wasn't too sure I'd be able to get away tonight."

She sat down and looked at her hands. He had time to observe and to be disappointed that she was wearing Western dress —a plain frock, blue with white spots. And then it occurred to him that she might have chosen the foreign style in his honour.

"I didn't have time to get flowers—or anything."

She smiled.

Morris looked at his own hands. He had known it would be like this. They were strangers. This was the most audacious of all his encounters with girls.

"I thought we might go out and get a meal, but maybe you want to wait for James—or maybe you've already had your meal? I'm so late."

"It isn't late."

"Where will we go? A quiet place. A little place. Some place where I won't see any uniforms." He observed her guarded smile, her averted eyes, those oval, Chinese eyes. And suddenly, shamefully, he became aware of the ambiguity of his words. "But maybe," he said hurriedly, "maybe you'd rather go to the Peninsula—or the 'Grips'—or the—"

"I like little places."

"Good." He looked at her carefully. In her own way, she could be as inexpressive as Craig. To make certain that he had wiped out the ambiguity, he added, "We'll have a drink at the Peninsula first."

*

Craig saw them enter.

He had sipped his way slowly through two Tom Collinses. He could not face a third and could not see any other way through the hours of waking darkness. He had tried to leave after the first drink, after the second, and, when he saw Morris and the Chinese girl enter, he tried again to leave. He did not want to have anyone looking at him.

But he hesitated at his table, taking brief comfort from his surprise. Morris and a Chinese girl. Somehow or other, Morris would look out of place with *any* girl—except, perhaps, a long-legged, bony-hipped, flat-chested innocent who could play filly to his colt. Certainly, with a small shapely Chinese girl, he looked too long and thin and seemed to have too many arms and legs.

That was cruel? Amen, that was cruel. It was also honest. There was too much falsehood in the name of compassion, in the name of brotherly love. How could you love a man unless you understood him, recognised yourself in him? Love without understanding was merely the offer of a mental vacancy, as a whore's love was merely the offer of a physical vacancy. Words confused people. All men were *not* brothers.

Angrily, he saw that Morris had noticed him. The embarrassed subaltern spoke to the girl, and the girl glanced across the lobby. It was time to leave.

*

"Does he often spend his evenings alone?" Anna asked.

Morris had to admit that he did not know.

"He looks like a lonely man."

The continuing solicitude for other men was beginning to rankle. "That's just because he's alone."

"No. He has a lonely man's face."

"It's the blankest face I've ever seen. I can never tell anything from his face. I think you're just feeling sorry for him. You don't need to feel sorry for Craig. If he's on his own, it's because he wants to be on his own. He knows far more people than I do."

Laughing, she said, "Now I am feeling sorry for you."

It was the first slackening of the tension between them.

"I've nothing against Craig, you know," he said, suddenly generous. "Far from it."

"But you don't smile at each other. You don't nod your head or wave your hand as other soldiers do when they see a comrade."

The dread that had prompted Morris to insist on drinking in the Peninsula, in full public view, now prompted him to make another gesture. "Will we go across and join him?" Although certain of her response, he was surprised at his temerity.

"Perhaps he doesn't want company?"

"Maybe not. I'll introduce him some other time, so that you can see what he's really like."

"Thank you."

In his uneasy state, Morris thought that he could detect an ironic inflection. "I was forgetting," he said quickly, roughly. "You and James are going away. There may not be another time. You'd better meet him now."

She seemed a little afraid, and that pleased and strengthened him.

*

It was not often that he fell into such a mood. Few men paid their debts of pride to society so promptly, met the obligations of responsible existence so fully, as he did in all the other seasons of his temperament. Craig felt that he, if anyone, should be granted an occasional moratorium for despair.

When he saw Morris and the Chinese girl approaching, his first impulse was to pretend that he had not noticed them, to leave the hotel as fast as he could, but he paused to consider Morris's red face and aggressively staring eyes, the girl's careful walk—and his own self-betraying, self-destroying mood. He was falling back into a way that he had once known too well, the way of bitter acquiescence in failure. As a boy, he had felt that he was the victim of circumstances. Now, he knew that circumstances were always of his own making. He could, with a record like his, have long since wangled his escape from the condemned garrison into some other unit. He could still escape from his hopeless entanglement with Mary Gow. He could—at this moment—start to reach a reckoning with Morris, the very symbol of his other self-betraying, self-destroying involvements, the embodied cry for help, the spendthrift heart.

"Good evening," said Morris guiltily.

Craig rose, looking at the girl, to lessen the embarrassment of the ritual. She was rather plain. All Chinese seemed plain to him. Her best features were her diffident eyes, her flawless golden skin.

"I'd like you to meet—Captain Craig, Miss Lin. Miss Lin and her brother work on one of the local newspapers."

When this obviously prepared statement of introduction and extenuation had been delivered, Craig invited them to join him, invited them to drink. "I didn't know you were interested in the Fourth Estate," he said to Morris, remembering to smile, giving the bald assumption a gloss of *bonhomie*.

The subaltern moved about in his chair. "I read the papers every day. Sometimes I even believe them."

"Do you believe them?" Craig asked the girl, his voice sounding like someone else's.

"It's easy to believe the bits I write—lists of guests at social functions, for example." She glanced at him, bright-eyed. "Miss Gow, wearing a gown of green satin, was escorted by Captain Craig." She laughed. "I remembered—all of a sudden. The last Governor's Ball."

Craig looked at her more carefully.

"I should have remembered sooner," she said. "Mrs. Gow has been a kind friend to my brother and myself."

"You're on one of her committees?"

"No, not that. I am what James calls a non-political animal. He is a political animal, but his politics are not the same as anyone else's, so he can't join any committees either."

Morris laughed, plainly as proud and happy as a dog with two tails.

"You're interested in politics?" she suggested to Craig.

"Not really."

"Of course, that wasn't a fair question to put to a soldier—a British soldier."

It was a point that Mrs. Gow seldom took into account. He smiled, and wet his upper lip in the third Tom Collins.

*

Morris, anxious to sustain the conversation, which had been surprisingly brisk and affable so far, asked Craig, "Have you eaten yet?"

"I'm not particularly hungry. But don't let me keep you from your meal."

Anna might be right. Craig seemed to be at a loose end, and loose ends were always lonely. "If you'd like to to join us—" Morris glanced at Anna for confirmation. She looked up at him, smiling. He wondered why the hell he was trying to drag Craig into the party.

"Thanks, but I should really be going." Craig made a slight bow to Anna as he rose from his chair. "I hope you'll excuse me."

Afterwards, Morris said, "He lives according to a time-table, and it doesn't allow much time for drinking."

"He didn't touch his drink."

Morris shook his head over the waste. "Well, he paid for it himself." He laughed with her, grateful to Craig for the empty place at the table, the easiness in the atmosphere. "You handled him very well. He's a bit of a dry stick."

"Dry stick?"

"Stiff. Serious."

She started to laugh again.

"He *is*. He's always like that."

She bent forward to hide her laughter.

"Well, what did *you* think of him?"

"I thought, Johnny—I thought he was very like you."

After the first shock of the comparison, he was rather pleased.

*

Corporal Barker sat outside the dance-floor area and drank his second and last beer. He had loaned money to Drummond and left himself short. Even if Drummond hadn't tapped him, he might still have been short. He could spend his pay in a night. When he drank beer he liked to fill his mouth with it. There was no taste in a sip.

His heels marking the beat of the band, he watched the men with money taking their pick of the taxi-dancers. Rudolph Richardson, from Macdonald's section, liked the bold-looking bints. He had danced with a strongly-made, red-cheeked Shanghai girl like Poppy Wu, a Portuguese with thick lips and cow's eyes, and a long-legged *chi-chi* with paper flowers in her hair. It was easy enough to guess all the other pieces Rudolph had his eye on. Paterson was different. He looked as tough as mule-hide, as hard as his Bren gun, but he had spent all his tickets on two moon-faced dolls who didn't stand much higher than his navel, the kind that, in the ordinary run of things, had to wait for Chinese boys to hire them. George Sime had picked a big-breasted White Russian, danced twice with her, and sat tight after that, waiting for Paterson to come back to the table between dances.

After swallowing his last mouthful of beer, Barker counted his money and decided to have a dance. The cashier seemed to think one ticket wasn't enough. Barker grinned. "Why not? They come out of the machine one at a time, don't they?" He got his ticket and went inside the barrier.

"Hello, Backa!" It was Mimi Pak.

He didn't want to dance with Mimi. She was too thin. "How are you? How's Poppy?"

"She O.K. Mac go see."

"Uhuh. I came over with him. She's a good girl now?"

Mimi giggled.

"Don't you bring her down here any more. Mac doesn't like it."

"O.K., Backa. Tickets now?"

"Blackmail?" He smiled happily and gave her his ticket.

"More," she said sullenly.

"You've got the wrong man, Mimi. Old Backa's on his beam-end. But watch his footwork."

They had hardly made a round of the floor when a clash of cymbals ended the dance. It cost a lot of money to buy time at a taxi-dance. Barker went to get some of the tickets he had seen in the nervous clutch of George Sime's hand.

*

"But James will be disappointed if you don't come up."

"Next time," promised Morris. "Dick Torrance will be waiting for me."

A woman's high-pitched singing undulated across the dark street. There was a spicy smell of cooking in the clean air.

"Thank you very much, Johnny."

"Before you go, Anna—when can I see you again? The trouble is I don't know exactly when I'll be able to get away." Thought of the obstacles that lay between them weakened him. "When will you and James be—leaving? Soon?"

"I leave it to James. He has not decided."

"Would you be free next Saturday?"

"I think so."

He wanted to kiss her, but she stood with her hands demurely or defensively clasped in front of her, and her head slightly averted.

There would be no meeting halfway. It would either be a one-sided seal on the evening—or assault. "Well, I'll see you next Saturday."

"And thank you, Johnny."

She looked up and smiled, and impulsively he bent down and kissed her, on the side of the mouth. She stepped back, wide-eyed, breathing hard, but uncomplaining. "Good night," she said, and turned and ran.

He stood still for a few moments, grinning boldly at the empty doorway.

Chapter Four

THE air was holding everything together. Moist and warm, it lay in the hollow behind Barker's knoll, between the Castle Peak road and Gindrinkers Bay, weighting the canvas of the tents that housed the medical officer's post and the headquarters of D Company and 17 Platoon. Still and dense, it hung over the entire sector, clamping sound to its source, pushing the mountains closer around the battalion. It intensified Morris's feeling that the battalion's move from the frontier camp to the Inner Line had been a move from freedom to prison.

He stood outside his tent, smoking a limp cigarette, waiting. He was waiting for a wind to peel the clammy pressure off his flesh, to needle some vigour into his bloodstream, to polish his tired eyes, and to blow clear a space for him to stand and think in. He was waiting for Ah Chan to bring water so that he could wash off the sour smells of damp concrete and of soil shovelled suddenly out of the shallow, centuries-deep weapon-pits into the light, the burnt smell of pick-split rock and the cruel smell of new barbed wire. He was waiting to ask Craig for a night off.

It was Friday evening. But only by clock and calendar. There was none of the usual Friday signs of rediscovery of lost interest and spent energy: no spitting or polishing for Adjutant's Parade on Saturday morning; no enthusiastic arranging of strenuous sports for Saturday afternoon; no arguing about week-end passes. The hollow was almost deserted. The three sections of 17 Platoon were in their own positions, washing in cold water or waiting around the pillboxes for the evening meal, killing time in the interval between one nameless work-day and the next, cursing the Inner Line, cursing the brass-hats who had first conceived it and the brass-hats who had now ordered it to be manned and made complete. The N.C.O.'s and men of company and platoon headquarters were still on fatigue, carrying wire up to Anstey's positions on the forward slopes of Golden Hill. Only four people were in sight: C.Q.M.S. Silver was drinking beer, sitting to sea-ward of his tent, where he could not be observed from the road; C.S.M. Duncan was stooping in and out of the tent, packing and unpacking a tin trunk on the grass, plainly trying to make up his mind which of his books to keep beside him and which to send down to Kowloon for storage; at a trestle-table in front of his post, Captain Lumsden, the medical officer, was checking an inventory and turning a deaf ear to his self-appointed deputy, Williamson.

Denied a hearing at the medical post, Williamson approached Morris. Sweat darkened his shirt, shone on his red face and glistened in his thick hair. He clapped a mosquito against his cheek and said, "Malaria."

"They don't all carry the bug," muttered Morris.

Williamson puckered his face impatiently. "Numbers, man. Any more casualties?"

"Lumsden's got the score, hasn't he?"

"I'm asking you."

"O.K. One casualty in 17 Platoon today."

"Another one, eh? Not on Lumsden's list, either," said Williamson, blinking aggressively.

"Not on his malaria list. It's a case of syph." Morris smiled malevolently.

"Nothing funny about syphilis, is there? Who is it?

"Feltham."

"Man should be put down." Williamson clapped another mosquito to death. "Fifth dose he's had, isn't it?"

"I've lost count, but," Morris added with vicious satisfaction, "last time, so the story goes, the Skin Man said to him, 'I'd cut it off and give you a wooden one if I didn't know you'd get termites in it within a month.'"

Williamson was angry. "Wrong way to look at things," he said ambiguously. "At a time like this, too."

A time like this. A time when circumstances fitted like a strait-jacket.

Last Sunday, the day after Anna, two Canadian battalions had arrived out of the blue sea. When the news of reinforcement had reached the frontier camp, Morris had been one of the least sur-prised and least jubilant subalterns, had been cheerfully prepared to accept it merely as further evidence of the flowing tide of his fortune . . .

"Do you realise," Welsh asked reprovingly, "that a reinforcement of two battalions makes all the difference?"

Morris straightened his face, made his voice sound hollow. "You think the Japs could have licked us?"

Welsh held tight to his port as he changed direction. "It would have been a long, hard fight," he said . . .

The tide had turned while Morris was looking the other, inward way. He had heard the sucking of ebb-water and had not listened . . .

"No bloody transport," said Birse incredulously, on Monday night. "They arrived without a single bloody wheel-barrow."

"Obviously a mistake," muttered Major Ingham charitably.

"I met some of them today," said Major Guthrie. "Nice chaps, but sadly in want of training. Some of them haven't fired a live round yet . . ."

Only on Tuesday had Morris noticed that he was standing high and uncomfortably dry. That morning, some of the battalion's most experienced N.C.O.'s had been detached for duty as instructors to the Canadians. Morris had lost Barker and Macdonald, his main props in the platoon since Meechan had contracted malaria. And before the day had ended he had been made to feel the measure of his loss. The battalion had been ordered to leave the frontier camp and occupy their sector of the Inner Line . . .

"Does this mean war?" Anstey asked bluntly, his small dark face stiff and expressionless.

"We've got to be ready for war," answered Craig.

Anstey was not satisfied. "Is this move the result of what the papers would call 'a deterioration in the situation'?"

Williamson nodded vigorously. Either he was impatient to draw a line under Peace and start a fresh column for War, or he was simply happy to hear a literary quotation he could recognise.

"Not so far as I know," said Craig. "The idea is to speed up the work on the Line. We've a lot to do yet. We're not getting on very quickly, ferrying work-parties back and forward."

"You dig a hole faster," Torrance explained to Anstey, "when you've got your bedding in it as well as your pick and shovel" . . .

Anstey had gone away suspecting that Craig was concealing the truth. But there seemed to be no grounds for his suspicion.

Although the whole of the Inner Line had been manned, the entire Mainland Brigade deployed in war stations, nothing else had happened to suggest an emergency. The Island Brigade were still dispersed: the English battalion were carrying on with their normal garrison duties; and the two Canadian battalions were brushing up their basic infantry training. And, whatever the military fraction were doing or thinking, more than a million and a half civilians were—so far as one could judge from the newspapers—still unalarmed, still taken up with the hazards of peace. That was exactly how Morris felt. Things were bad enough without a war.

He went inside and started to undress, throwing his shirt on his camp bed and his singlet on the ground. They made his end of the tent look demonstratively untidy, and, cursing Craig's Teutonic orderliness, he picked them up and rolled them into a bundle, which he laid on his camp chair.

Camp bed, camp chair, Craig. The hard work might have been tolerable if it had led at the end of each long day to the absurdly luxurious tent near the frontier and the easy company of Dick Torrance, instead of to this spartan tent and the cold company of Craig. This tent was no more than the place where he and Craig dressed and slept. They went to the mess for food and company—separate plates, separate companions. Morris had put his best foot forward, but Craig had become even more forbidding in manner and sparing of speech than he had been at the frontier.

It was some comfort that the frontier camp had not been struck. The plain inference was that the battalion would be going back there as soon as they had dug and wired the Line into shape and played a game or two of defending it. Roll on, prayed Morris, roll on.

When Craig arrived, Morris had his question ready. "Any chance of getting a couple of hours off tomorrow night?" He had decided that his manner should be easy (so that he could meet any shirtiness on Craig's part with a broader smile, a plainer indication that he was not in earnest, that he was—in the troops' phrase—coming the bag) but not so easy as to seem casual (and encourage Craig to give an equally casual refusal).

"At a time like this," said Craig, "we can't look for any privileges that the men don't get."

At a time like this. Morris started to feel angry.

"If we're to get the work done," Craig said, irritably scratching his short fair hair, "we've got to give them a sense of urgency."

"We're all working pretty hard."

"Not hard enough. We're nowhere near ready for war."

"You'll need more than holes in the ground if a war starts," said Morris, breathless with suppressed anger. "You'll need men in the holes fit enough to fight. At the rate we're going, the men'll be too flaked to fight."

A mosquito whined inside the tent.

"Where's Ah Chan?" asked Craig. "We'll be late for dinner." He sat on his bed and started to unlace his boots.

The troops, Morris reflected bitterly, would be lying on grass or concrete, sharing out lukewarm tea and broken-meat stew from the dixies. His compassion for them made him all the angrier that he had been denied another privilege.

*

A white villa, set on a rise and surrounded with shrubs and trees, had been selected for the officers' mess. It was much more comfortable than the marquee up at the frontier and stood conveniently between the front and reserve lines.

"We'll sit here tomorrow night eating and drinking," Morris argued. "What difference would it make to the troops if we sat eating and drinking three miles down the road, in Kowloon?"

Anstey stared at him. "Craig's the only company commander who isn't giving passes. He's the only one who wants a war, and he seems to think he can bring it nearer by getting ready for it. If I were you, I'd take French leave tomorrow night. He couldn't do anything about it. You'd call his bluff."

"Listen to who's talking," scoffed Torrance.

"I don't give a damn for Craig."

"You don't like him, you mean. You jump when he cracks the whip."

"Only when he has a right to crack it. He has no right to keep us all in the lines without a break, when the other companies are getting passes."

"So you're going to call his bluff?" pressed Torrance.

"It's Morris who wants to go, not me."

"You're a wriggler, Anstey."

"Wrap up," said Morris.

Anstey was not a likable fellow, with his dark hurt face and his staring blue eyes, but Torrance rode him unfairly.

"I'll tell you something else you can get ready to protest about," Torrance said to Anstey. "Craig's been talking to Williamson about working on into the dark by the light of hurricane lamps. The only thing that holds him back is the risk of doubling the number of malaria cases."

"You're a liar," said Anstey, his voice fading as he glanced over Morris's shoulder.

"Here he is," said Kerr, the signals officer, at Morris's back.

"You will not," said McNaughton Smith, at Kerr's side, "be unaware, Morris, of the significance of the last day of this month?"

Morris waited until he saw that McNaughton Smith was also prepared to wait. "We've got to get the digging finished by the end of the month," he mumbled.

McNaughton Smith grasped Kerr's arm in mock astonishment. "The boy's wits are on the turn!"

Kerr winked at Morris. "You'll be able to celebrate the end of the digging with Atholl brose on St. Andrew's night."

Gratefully accepting the prompt, Morris said, "Good."

"Better than you think," McNaughton Smith assured him. "As junior subaltern, Morris, you will have the privilege of proposing the health of His Majesty."

"Good," said Morris, without enthusiasm.

" 'Gentlemen, the King,' " said Kerr helpfully. "That's all there is to it."

"Don't," warned McNaughton Smith, "don't—for mercy's sake, Morris—make it sound apologetic."

*

On Saturday morning, Morris arranged for Ah Chan to carry a letter. He scribbled it before following Craig up to the white house for breakfast.

Dear Anna,

       I won't be able to see you tonight. We're confined to our lines just now. As soon as I get a chance I'll look in at the flat in the hope of seeing you. Don't go away without telling me.

                          Yours,

                             Johnny.

It struck him, on second reading, as the kind of note he might send to an aunt. He searched for some simple way of telling Anna how his world had shrunk around her.

P.S. I can't say how sorry I am that I have to break our appointment.

A lawyer could say as much to a client. Defeated, Morris swore to himself and slipped the letter into an envelope.

*

The air freshened over the week-end. On Monday evening cirrus clouds furrowed the sky.

"It might blow," Craig guessed.

"Won't come to much," said Williamson confidently. "Typhoon season's over." They were descending the hill from Anstey's position on the right flank. "Weak link, Anstey," added Williamson.

Weak chain, amended Craig.

Torrance waved to them. He was still working, supervising the erection of a barbed-wire fence. Ten to one he would pack in as soon as they were out of sight.

Battalion headquarters area was deserted except for a few clerks. They parted company there. Williamson was sharing a tent with the assistant adjutant.

"Never finish digging and wiring by the end of the month, Skipper. Only six days left."

Digging, wiring, exercises in defence, exercises in withdrawal, mortar practice—if ammunition could be spared. "We'll see."

Craig crossed the road, jolted down into the hollow and made for his tent. He was glad to find it empty. In his own quiet, self-conscious way, Morris was obtrusive company.

There was a letter from Mrs. Gow, with a note from Mary enclosed. He read the note.

D/H

Do I have to ask you to take me to the China Ball? Why don't I see you? Why don't you write? I languish. Must I look for a tall Canadian?

Love,

Mary.

She'd have looked already.

He started to undress, suddenly feeling more cheerful. The air was clean and invigorating now. The men would be brisker about their work tomorrow.

*

Sergeant Meechan returned to duty on Tuesday. For a few minutes, he was a lean, dark, wry-mouthed stranger.

"Meechan!" Reddening with pleasure, Morris shook hands.

"Bit of a change, sir," said the sergeant, looking around the hollow.

Morris nodded, trying to take the measure of the man again.

"It's Smiler," shouted a man on top of Barker's knoll to his comrades on the forward slope.

"Get on with your work," roared Meechan. "No discipline in this platoon, sir," he added dryly.

"Maybe not. You can knock us into shape again."

Smiler smiled.

"We can't be doing too badly," said Morris cheerfully. "Captain Craig told us this morning that some of us would get leave this week-end."

"Squaw-men?"

"I suppose they'll get preference." Why shouldn't they? He was almost a squaw-man himself.

"Come on," he said. "I'll show you the posts. It's grand weather for working today." A fine fresh wind.

*

The wind rose.

On Thursday afternoon, it was chilling sweat-patched khaki against skin, tearing shouted words apart, sucking at mouth and ears. Dust from the diggings blew across the sector, peppering eyes and nose, rattling on drumming canvas.

"If you don't put your backs into it," warned Morris, exasperated, "we'll be losing our night out."

"It's not so easy—in a wind like this." Shouting, Lance-Sergeant Drummond sounded bolder than usual.

"We'll make it all right, sir." Lance-Corporal Foggo was deferential again, now that Drummond had resumed command of Number 4 Section.

"We'd better make it."

Craig had not said that the issue of passes would depend on the progress of the work. In his usual manner, he had announced his decision without explanation. But Morris did not have to cast about for an explanation. He could immediately dismiss the improbability suggested by Anstey—that Craig himself wanted a night out and, at a time like this, felt obliged to extend the privilege to a few of his subordinates. Nor was Morris tempted to believe that his own angry outburst on Friday night had influenced Craig to relax pressure on the tiring company. It was safer to assume that the passes were dangling carrots which would be withheld unless the donkeys of Don Company spent their last energies and dragged themselves to the deadline in Craig's neat time-table. And, although that assumption heightened Morris's rebellious mood, he drove his men. He drove them, although he knew that he was cracking the whip only because his own night out was at stake. He would have to spend Sunday night, St. Andrew's night, in the mess. (Gentlemen, the King. Officers below field rank did not enjoy the privilege of being able to add, God bless him.) But Craig—God damn him—would not, could not, refuse to let him off the leash on Saturday night.

The wind rose and the glass fell. On Friday, typhoon signals were hoisted.

Sergeant Meechan's mouth twitched. "That's all we need now. A pukka typhoon to blow down all the bloody wire."

"Might blow a bit," shouted Williamson. "Too late in the year for a real typhoon." He scowled at the signal on a hillside south of the company's area. "Not even gale force yet."

Morris said nothing. This was already a wind that could clear a wider world around him. It howled in his ears, clutched at him, held him. It made him slightly afraid—not of falling short of Craig's deadline—but of the unimaginable fury of the approaching wind, the big wind, typhoon.

On Saturday morning, the signal was changed. The wind had reached gale force.

Morris was called by the company runner from his efforts to keep his men moving towards night, digging for his pass, wiring off the space in which he would meet Anna. Craig and Ballantyne were waiting for him on the road. Three empty trucks stood behind them, headed north. His apprehensions were quickly resolved. 17 Platoon were ordered to strike the frontier camp.

"Now?" he asked.

The adjutant nodded, a sympathetic smile on his sallow face.

Craig said: "Wear battle order. Take a box of ammunition and iron rations for two days."

"Two days?"

"You don't think you can do it in less?"

"Depends on the wind," said Ballantyne comfortingly. "You might finish by nightfall tomorrow. But we'll make the deadline Monday noon."

The wind swirled round them, struck Morris in the face and brought cold tears to his eyes. He tried to stretch his mouth into a wry smile.

"I'll see if I can keep some Atholl brose for you," promised Ballantyne.

Morris nodded, grateful for the adjutant's sympathy, sorely aware of Craig's lack of sympathy. It was easy enough to see through Craig this time. He could have sent Anstey or Torrance to strike camp, but then he would not have had his tent to himself for a couple of nights. *All right, Craig, the pleasure is mutual. Stuff that in your bloody brose.* But the wind that was blowing Craig away, blowing St. Andrew away, blowing the King away— God bless him, God grant him a full, field-officer's blessing—was also blowing Anna away. His face numb under the pummelling of the wind, Morris turned and bawled for Meechan.

*

Major Guthrie, who was in command of the small party left to maintain and guard the frontier camp, kept to his tent. Morris stood around and watched.

"Cast off the guys," shouted Meechan. He had struck camp often enough before. He would not stop to think that the canvas was falling over another finished part of his life. "You can't knock the bloody tent down as long as it's tied to the ground. Use your *malum.*" When the sun-bleached canvas collapsed, the men knocked the wind out of it, extracted the pole-bones and bundled it up.

"Get it down, Richardson," shouted Meechan. The South American and another man had placed themselves on the leeward side of the tent they were handling. Stubbornly, they were trying to topple it over against the wind. "If it was wearing knickers, you'd knock it over fast enough." Meechan was the kind of man who used women. He left them at the barracks gate, the end of the camp road. He would carry no photographs, no letters, no ache.

Morris watched his own tent fall and stared at the patch of smothered pallid grass that remained to mark his and Torrance's place.

He lent a hand in the roaring, cursing struggle to flatten the officers' mess marquee. McGuire balanced one of the main poles on each shoulder and, wide-eyed, thick-necked, carried them down the road. Empty-handed, Fraser followed him, screaming like a startled crow, "Look at him! Look at Punchy!"

Poles and bundled canvas were borne in single, slow, wind-checked file down to the trucks, which carried them across to the chain of open wagons on the railway line. Guthrie's party had already loaded most of the furniture and heavy baggage and had already sent livestock—dogs, cats, hens and a monkey—down to Kowloon.

Morris wandered about, dazed by the noise of the wind, the shouting and the cracking of loose canvas. He looked into a few tents and examined with melancholy curiosity some of the jetsam inside. One or two fragments seemed portentous: in one tent, a broken tin whistle; in another tent, an unfinished drawing of a girl and a botched crayon sketch of the river. Sadness, he decided suddenly, was a kind of strength. "Come wind, come wrack!" he said loudly. When he looked out of the tent to see whether anyone could have heard him, he observed that the men had stopped work and crowded around the fallen orderly-room marquee. He hurried across and found that Jannelli had been knocked down by one of the heavy poles. White-faced and trembling, the little man lay on the ground.

"He'll be all right in a minute. Nothing broken," said Meechan. "What I want to know is how the hell it happened."

"It was his own blame," said Fraser, defensively sharp. "He got in the road, see? I had to let go my end. It was the wind."

"You could have killed him," said Morris indignantly.

"It was the wind, sir. And he was standin' right in the road of it."

Morris looked at the men around him. He was certain that Fraser was lying and he could see an uneasiness that might be corroboration in some of the men's faces.

"Take Jannelli down to the guard tent and get him a mug of *cha* with plenty of sugar in it," Meechan told Lance-Corporal Foggo. "The rest of you, back to your work, *chullo*!"

For the next half-hour, Morris kept an eye on Fraser, partly to see that he pulled his weight and partly to show him that he was under suspicion.

The work became tedious. Hands fumbled and tempers frayed. By dusk, the camp was no more than a collection of tents that had still to be struck. When Morris called a halt and the platoon closed in, black-clad Chinese moved down from the hills and started scavenging around the bleached patches on the grass.

Daddy Guthrie emerged from his tent to see to the mounting of the guard. A crumpled glengarry and an aura of whisky. But he carried himself as if he were mounting guard at Balmoral. "Not that the Frogs are likely to move by night," he assured Morris. "Their night-vision is very poor. You'll dine with me? — Come round as soon as you've cleaned yourself up."

*

The bulk of the heavy luggage and the only livestock left in camp were crammed into Guthrie's bell tent. "I like to have my things around me," he explained grudgingly. Within a tight barricade formed of trunks, boxes, valise and camp-bed, defying the combined threats of wind and 17 Platoon, he stood beside a card-table jammed against the central pole. His old Boxer — a dog that seldom took the air — sat, at the opposite side of the pole, on a chest stencilled 'DEOLALI'. Above their heads, moths and other insects clouded around the hanging pressure-lamp.

"Makes it very cosy," said Morris.

"Sherry?" Guthrie poured one sherry and one whisky. "Sherry interferes with my digestion."

They drank standing, as if they were in the ante-room of the mess.

"The wind's slackening now, sir."

"The typhoon's moving in to the north. We're well to the flank of it. Appleton brings me the news from the police-station. Nice chap."

"Yes, sir. I met him once." Morris decided not to tell the story of their meeting. Guthrie was not himself. Daddy Guthrie had become Major Guthrie, and might not see anything funny in a captain's irresponsibility or a subaltern's credulous bungling.

E

Maybe the wind was getting on his nerves. Maybe the solitude had saddened him.

A batman announced that dinner was ready.

"You didn't keep a boy, sir?"

"Not at a time like this, Morris. The Chinese don't have much spunk, you know."

The crack in the record—a time like this, a time like this. "D'you really think we're on the verge of war?"

Guthrie frowned, finished his whisky and took his place behind the table. "Dinner," he said.

Morris sat opposite the dog. The batman was waiting in the entrance of the tent, holding two plates of soup. Ravenously hungry, Morris lifted his spoon and then—as unobtrusively as possible—replaced it on the table while Guthrie asked God's blessing on the meal. With his head slightly bowed, Morris noticed that the Boxer was watching him.

As the meal progressed—tinned soup, tinned meat and vegetable stew, tinned pineapple chunks—Morris became grateful for the formality of the occasion. It was another part of the barricade. Secure from each other, he and Guthrie ate their food without complaint, removed the shrivelled insects that fell on the table, and discussed with some delicacy the breeding of Boxers. He was particularly taken with Guthrie's description of a fine bitch he had kept in India, although he knew from the outset that the major was still talking about Boxers. The meal ended with hard biscuits and whisky.

"My last dinner here for some time," said Guthrie, with a rueful smile. "I leave at noon tomorrow. You'll be in command then, Morris."

"I'm sorry you're going, sir."

Guthrie nodded vaguely. "You can spend tomorrow evening with your lads. There's no better way of getting to understand them. But I'm sorry you'll miss St. Andrew's night in the mess. And you the junior subaltern. Tell you what, m'boy," he added cheerfully. "You'll propose the loyal toast tonight, eh?"

Morris grinned. "Do I say, 'Sir, the King'?"

"No, no. Willie's a gentleman too, and a damn loyal one."

So Morris rose to his feet and said—as grandly as McNaughton Smith could have wished—"Gentlemen, the King!"

And Guthrie rose and said, "The King, God bless him!"

But, two whiskies later, Guthrie was solemn again. "My last dinner here." He broke a biscuit, dipped a fragment in his whisky and gave it to Willie the Boxer. "Another thing, Morris. This is the last camp that some of your lads will strike. Don't forget that, when you're sitting with them tomorrow night."

"It's difficult to believe we're on the verge of war."

"It's always difficult to believe that, especially difficult for soldiers to believe. But it's only a matter of weeks now, maybe only a matter of days."

"I haven't been told very much."

"There isn't much to tell. But you don't imagine, now, that we're striking camp because of the wind?"

"The gale signal went up this morning."

"The signals I'm thinking of went up a long time ago."

Morris felt restless, impatient. He believed, for the first time, that war was not only inevitable but also imminent. And he wanted to get out and walk around. He wanted to think in the dark about himself and Anna.

"Appleton keeps me posted," said Guthrie. "Plenty of straws in the wind now. Ocean-going steamers diverted to Singapore. Harbour closed at night. Supernumeraries advised to go while the going's good."

Morris stiffened attentively. "Supernumeraries?"

"Everybody who isn't enrolled for defence work of one kind or another."

"Advised to go where?"

"Any damn place they can get to. There are still ships in the harbour, still civil planes coming in to Kaitak."

The tent shuddered under a swirling gust. Morris accepted another whisky, drank it quickly and tried to get the pole between him and Willie's watching eyes. Guthrie started to recall the giants of the past.

When at last Morris escaped from the tent—the strength washed out of his sadness by whisky, his self-esteem trampled by the giants—the wind sucked his breath away. He stood leaning against it and felt it blow the darkness through him. It dropped for a moment and, deprived of support, he stumbled forward. Then it struck again, thumping canvas, knocking over a bin of empty food-cans and scattering them across his path.

It was blowing itself out. And it was blowing a world apart.

PART THREE
The Hill

Chapter One

GOLDEN HILL came into view when the trucks turned the western flank of the Tai-mo-shan range. Its broken scrub-patched slopes were still dark with morning shadow, but its bald crest was already bright under a pale clear sky.

The two trucks ran swiftly down the Castle Peak road, winding along the ragged coast, skirting the calmly radiant sea. Morris sat in the back of the second truck among Macdonald's section and joined in the chorus led by Richardson:

> " 'I took my girl for a ramble, a ramble,
> Down by a sha-a-dy lane,
> She caught her foot in a bramble, a bramble . . .' "

The singing had started the night before. With Craig behind him, Morris could have loaded the last of the canvas and gear by the light of headlamps and led his men back to the Inner Line for a late, cold supper. But, with Meechan beside him, he had chosen to call a halt before dusk, while there were still a few tents standing. After posting sentries, he had seen to the building of a fire and helped to cook an enormous meal from their own rations and from other supplies that had come to light during the day's clearance. He had shared with Meechan the finger or two of sherry that Guthrie had left behind, and made the rest of the platoon draw lots for the six cans of beer that George Sime had discovered. At the sing-song after the meal, he had, under pressure, given them "The Bonny Earl of Moray", solo and—to begin with—almost *sotto voce*. Later, much later, he had fallen asleep still watching a spiral of sparks and song rise into the darkness.

Now, the last tent stowed away and Drummond's section left to guard the wagons until an engine arrived, the rest of the platoon were singing again as the trucks carried them back on Monday morning to their concrete vaults and their holes in the ground.

" 'Singing hey jig-a-jig,
    Stuff a little pig,
    Follow the band . . .' "

It was the kind of morning that seemed to hold vague but pleasurable promises. Everything conduced to optimism: sunlight and sparkling water, the speed of the trucks, Richardson's inconsequential song, a rested body, and a good report to render, hours before the deadline.

"By rights," said one of the men, lapsing from a flight of song, "we should get passes tonight." He winked impudently at his mates. "We missed out at the week-end, didn't we?"

The song fell to bits.

Morris grinned. "We're a couple of days behind with our work."

"*Maskee,*" said Richardson. "Fair's fair, sir."

*

The last light of that Monday was burning on the crest of Golden Hill when Morris and his men, washed of their work and jubilant, abandoned their positions again and took the road south to Kowloon. Fair might be fair, but they did not linger to flaunt their rights.

"*Chullo!*" Paterson shouted to Sime, "before they change their minds."

Morris left in the last truck, which was almost empty. Round the first bend, Torrance stepped into the road, signalled the driver to halt, and jumped aboard. He winked at Morris and told the driver to put his foot down.

"You've got a nerve," said Morris cautiously.

Torrance laughed and looked around happily. "I've been on that hill long enough."

"Ever since Saturday night," said Morris sarcastically.

"It's a long time since we had a night out together."

"I've got a date."

"We could have a drink together first."

Morris was loath to be ungracious. "There isn't much time, Dick. We've got to be back by eleven. And Craig means eleven. He wouldn't have let us off at all, if Ballantyne hadn't been there when I asked." They sat close together, silent. Torrance was still smiling, still looking hungrily around at the darkening hills and the gathering of lights across the peninsula, the harbour and the island. "We could have one drink," said Morris, repentantly.

Torrance nodded. "I asked Anstey to come along too."

"You didn't have to do that!" Morris was glad to find an outlet for his feelings. "You knew bloody well he wouldn't dare cross Craig. Why can't you leave him alone?"

"I really wanted him to come this time."

The sincerity of the words was unmistakable, but Morris was unready to acknowledge it. "Like hell you did. Why do you keep riding him?"

"Just this afternoon I thought of the answer to that." Torrance pulled off his tammy and let the wind tangle his hair. "I sat on the side of the hill and entered into a state of enlightenment." He pressed the heels of his hands together, shaping the open lotus, like an irreverent Buddha. "I ride Anstey because I want to remake him after my own image. I want him to be like me. I want everybody to be like me. Just as you want everybody to be like you."

Morris took time to consider. "I don't want everybody to be like me."

"You do. You'll be forced to admit it, if you don't let your legalistic mind push the point to an absurd extreme."

"Coming from a man who takes so much advantage of the differences between male and female—"

"The absurd extreme. Nobody's got anything against the old ball-and-socket principle." He rubbed his hands briskly together. "Which leads me to the entirely unconnected question of your date. Who is it? Nell Griffiths?"

"My father's cousin. Skinner."

Torrance nodded amiably. "The phantom Fifer."

*

On the way to the Lins' flat, Morris began to have fresh qualms. "I don't know why I'm doing this."

"You're not suggesting, Johnny, that I deliberately drowned your judgement in gin?"

"Maybe I am."

"You're forgetting," Torrance said cheerfully. "The whole plan hinges on your pleasure. If the birds haven't flown, I'll slip away after I've been introduced. If they have flown, we'll go on a monumental batter to obliterate their memory."

Morris palmed his temples. "It's not that I don't want you to come, Dick," he said confusedly.

E*

"I knew that. I'd never force myself on you."

A moment or two later, Morris grinned. "You're a bloody liar."

*

"It was really Anna who made the decision," James insisted. "I was all ready to leave. 'Earth has no feasts that don't break up', I told her, as I packed my bag. And she started to unpack it and told me, 'Any soil will do to bury in'."

"D'you always argue in proverbs?" asked Torrance.

"Only when we're angry," said James happily.

Anna glanced sideways at Morris. "He made up his mind to leave the colony when people were hinting that it was cowardly to run away. But, when the Government advised us to leave, he was very angry and made up his mind to stay."

James joined in the laughter. "And now Anna argues that, if I stay, I must make myself useful—volunteer for some kind of defence service. This is woman's logic, isn't it? She doesn't grasp the liberal principle involved."

Torrance was watching Anna. "Are you volunteering?"

"As a nurse. I have started my training."

Morris nodded approvingly.

"And what would you like me to do?" James asked disputatiously.

"A.R.P.," suggested Anna primly.

"Why a merely passive part?" he demanded. "There is another Chinese proverb," he told Torrance. "A very old one. A very Chinese one. 'If you bow, bow low.' If I must defend, why should I not become a soldier?"

"You don't rate us very highly?" asked Torrance.

"It is a traditional attitude. 'Good iron is not made into nails, good men are not made into soldiers.' But I am ready to change tradition." He was in a gay, boastful mood. "You could train me, Dick. You are a skilled soldier."

Torrance's eyes brightened. He recited:

> " 'My soul, there is a country,
>   Far beyond the stars,
>   Where stands a wingèd sentry
>   All skilful in the wars.' "

James smiled delightedly. "There are no skilful soldiers this side of the stars?"

Winking at Morris, Torrance replied, "Only one to my certain knowledge. Our company commander."

"I'm not sure," added Morris, "that he's on this side of the stars."

"This is good talk," James decided. "I will recite some Chinese poems. But we must drink wine at the same time."

Embarrassed, Anna told him that there was no wine left to offer.

"Then I'll go out and get some."

James's movement stimulated Torrance to say, "I should really be going."

James was disappointed.

"But I'll walk down the road with you, and you can recite all the way."

"It's better with wine."

"Everything's better with wine." Torrance glanced from Morris to Anna, his yellow eyes bright with amusement. "If you can wait a little for your wine, James and I will have a drink somewhere and exchange a few wild verses."

*

"He's my best friend," claimed Morris.

Anna smiled carefully.

"You liked him?"

"I think I was a little afraid of him." She laughed then, as if exorcizing her fear. "He is so full of life!"

Morris was puzzled. "He was on his best behaviour tonight."

"I mean—he's so intense."

Morris nodded doubtfully.

She was sitting beyond his reach and, while they chattered about nursing and the China Ball, he was always conscious of the ambivalent distance, short enough to tempt him to the edge of his chair, long enough to make accidental contact impossible. They did not move until, giving up James and the wine for lost in a wilderness of poetry, she decided to make tea. Then, resolutely, he followed her into the kitchen.

Filling a kettle, she looked up at him attentively and said, "Foreign devil."

He was briefly shocked out of speech and movement. Numbly, and without complete understanding, he saw that his reaction had surprised and embarrassed her. The kettle overflowed and cold water splashed on them. Hastily, she dropped the kettle into the sink, turned off the tap, snatched up a hand-towel and dabbed at the damp spots on his tunic.

"That was very silly," she said breathlessly.

He smiled narrowly, colder still than the water.

Resting the towel on his arm, she looked up, her eyes dark and her mouth trembling as she spoke. "It was just silliness. I'm sorry."

"Chinese men," he said quickly, warming as he chased a sudden glimmer of explanation, "don't help in the kitchen?"

"James does, but he can't think Chinese any longer."

"Scotsmen don't often help in the kitchen," he boasted carefully. He knew that he had not found the full explanation. But, just as she lifted the towel and tried to turn away, he put his arms round her and bent down and kissed her mouth. Then, without releasing her, but entering into his happiness cautiously, he asked, "You don't think of me as foreign?"

Her answer was a long time coming and, tormenting himself out of pleasure in her closeness and warmth and fragrance, he compelled himself to recognise the absurdity of his question. Did she think of him as foreign? Of course, she did. Every time she heard his Scots tongue or looked at his coarse-textured, brown and red patched face.

She gave him an answer. "I wondered how much you thought about the difference."

"You were testing me, you devil?" He kissed the top of her head.

"Your friend thinks about it."

"Dick?"

She laughed softly, and tried to free herself. "I was going to make tea. Please, Johnny."

"Promise you'll never call me a foreign devil again. But, no, that's not the point. Tell me, instead, whether you—whether you mind having a foreign devil as a friend." *Friend?* Why was he still so west-of-Suez cautious?

"I don't mind," she said quietly.

"Anna," he announced grimly, hoarsely, "I think I've fallen in love with you." She did not look up. He let her go, so that he could see her face. She was smiling, her eyes averted. "Don't you believe me?"

"It is not a question to ask me so soon." She backed away from him, her smile now impudent, and lifted the kettle.

"But I'm not asking you to say how *you* feel about *me*! Even if you loathe the sight of me, you can see that I'm—but you're not going to answer, are you?"

He sat on the edge of the table and watched her make tea. He was content to watch. He felt sure that they were separated now only by the length of the room.

"I'll come to the China Ball," he decided.

"No. I'll be busy."

"You will be. I'll see to it." he boasted happily.

*

He met Torrance at the truck.

"Good time, Johnny?"

"Not the way you mean!"

They smiled sleepily at each other.

"Well," demanded Morris, "what's the verdict?"

Torrance answered obliquely: "Better keep her under your hat. The Old Horse would send you home in disgrace."

Morris reddened. "Craig's met her."

"It's the old guard you'll have to watch—Mair, Guthrie, Ingham, Young. They'll send you home or castrate you."

Angrily, Morris exaggerated: "I'm taking her to the China Ball, and I hope some of the old guard are there to see us."

Torrance began to grin. "I hope so too. Time something took their minds off this bloody war."

*

Next day, Tuesday, 2nd December, the battalion were ordered to hold themselves ready to stand to their war stations at short notice.

"How short is short?" McNaughton Smith demanded of the adjutant. "Or, to put it more concretely, how long is a piece of string?"

"From here to the Shumchun," said Ballantyne, with a sleepy smile.

Craig intervened. "We can take it we're confined to the Line from now on?"

"More or less." The flippant vagueness was obviously meant to counter McNaughton Smith's argumentative insistence on explicit detail. Verbal fencing of this kind always irritated Craig. "It needn't bar your night out on Saturday, Hugh. We'll know where you are, and we can phone you if anything blows up."

Craig shook his head.

"War," said McNaughton Smith, "is only one kind of social activity. There are other more important kinds. Wellington danced before Waterloo, and I see no reason—apart from the natural stiffness of your gait—why you shouldn't dance before this battle."

"Wellington was ready." Craig spoke jocularly, but he was glad to find an occasion to communicate even a hint of his anxieties. "We won't be ready for weeks yet. We're going to be caught with our slacks down."

"There's nothing definite in the intelligence reports," said Ballantyne coolly. Over the past week or two, he had become distantly defensive on such questions, as if to give warning that he would not listen to criticism of the last-minute upheaval of the garrison. "We may get all the time we need—for serviceable rough and ready, if not perfect. You may have to keep your slacks up with McNaughton Smith's piece of string."

Craig felt estranged. Ballantyne had stepped behind the censor, effaced himself in the solidarity of the old guard. He tried not to sound bitter. "We'll need more than holes in the ground before we're ready. We haven't started serious training."

"Idle bugger," said Ballantyne pleasantly.

McNaughton Smith stared glumly at the adjutant's feet.

On his way back to the hollow, Craig revised his plans. The first essential was to stock the pillboxes with ammunition; the second, to train the company in defence and withdrawal, to make them ready.

Rough and ready. The thought recurred to him next day. If he could not rid his mind of perfect standards, it was not because he still respected the false standards of perfection that had led him to choose a military career: the standards that had seemed inherent in the final certitude of the sword, in the orderly structure and self-regarding discipline of the soldier's isolated world. The idea of perfection lingered in his mind, without specific reference, simply because he could see so damnably far into things. They had been ordered to make themselves ready for war. And he could not prevent himself from thinking of all that a state of readiness implied.

How did you make men ready for war? There were boys in his company to whom the Chinese were as strange as the Japanese, boys who would find it hard to stand their ground and die on Golden Hill, at the other end of the earth from the hills they called their own. And there were old sweats who had lived so long in the East that they had lost not only the immediate sense of home but also some of the ways they had learned at home. One old sweat had *Maskee* tattooed across his chest; all the old sweats had the word lodged in their heads. *Maskee . . . Never mind! . . . What does it matter?* Men who had learned to think like Chinese could be expected to fight like Chinese—loathly, with a shrewd earthy preference for the thirty-sixth alternative.

The defence of Hongkong called for the kind of battle that only men blinded by emotion could fight, men who could not or would not see that the flag they were following was the white flag of surrender. To make men ready for such a battle you would have to remake them.

Men like Sime there, leading a mule. Reluctant leader. Reluctant led.

*

Number 5 Section, under Lance-Corporal Arkison in Barker's absence, were helping to carry small-arms ammunition up to the pillboxes in Anstey's and Torrance's areas. Craig had borrowed a mule for the day from the Indians, and Arkison, nudged forward by Paterson, had nominated George Sime as muleteer.

"It's as easy as talking to yourself," Paterson urged Sime.

Nervously, Sime looked at the loaded mule.

"If it won't budge, leather it with the reins and shout, '*Jildi*.' If it starts to run away from you, shout, '*Tairo*.' When you want it to stop, shout, '*Bus*.'"

"They should have sent a sepoy along with the mule," said Sime defensively. He did not want to seem ungrateful. He knew, as well as Paterson did, that he was not strong enough to carry a full box of ammunition up the hill, journey after journey till nightfall.

"I'll stick behind you," promised Paterson. He heaved a box on to his shoulder. "Get a grip of the reins." He slapped the beast's rump and yelled, first at it and then at Sime: "Giddup! *Chullo!* Whatever happens, don't let go of the reins or we'll never see the brute again."

The mule plodded forward at a reluctant pace that suited Sime's short legs. With the leading rein tightly wrapped round his hand, he led the beast up through the battalion headquarters area, acknowledging with a set smile and an occasional nod of his head the encouragement and abuse showered on him by clerks, signallers, drivers and some of Drummond's section.

"Ride him, cowboy!"

"Get off your knees, Sime." Pig Fraser's nagging voice from the top of Drummond's ridge. "Punchy could carry that load on his own back."

"Tips!" bawled Paterson in the rear. "Only difference is McGuire doesn't have a tail."

As they approached the rise at the end of the headquarters area, Paterson warned: "Step out a bit, George. They go faster uphill."

The mule took the rise quickly, as Paterson had foretold. On top of the rise, however, it halted. "*Jildi*," said Sime. "Come on, *jildi! Chop-chop!*"

Paterson's dark sweating face appeared over the rise. "It doesn't talk Chinese, George." He punched its rump and yelled until it started to move again.

The path round the flank of the hill skirted some patches of cultivated land and a few mud-walled hovels, and then climbed steeply towards Torrance's area. Quickening his pace to keep ahead of the mule, Sime panted up the narrow track. He heard Paterson's warning cry and, in the same instant, felt the wet muzzle against his right arm. Instinctively he recoiled towards the left, and the beast, thrusting past him, pushed him off his feet.

"Hold on, George!"

Sime held on and was dragged alongside the track, out of a dry paddy-field, over a bund and into a cesspool. Gasping and sobbing with terror and disgust, he struggled to keep his head above the green scum, and clenched his fist desperately on the rein. Jerkily, the mule dragged him through and, at length, out of the stinking filth. He shouted, "*Tairo! Bus!*" in a voice hoarse with anguish, until the mule came to a halt.

Keeping well distant from Sime, Paterson climbed hastily ahead. "Let the brute go. Let it come up to me. And you—get down to the M.O. *ek dum*—you'll need to be fumigated."

Wide-eyed, trembling, Sime went down the hill. He kept his face to the front and tried not to see the men scattering from his path, tried not to hear the screaming laughter and angry railing.

The M.O. made him stand in the hollow, well away from the tents, and strip off all his clothes. Orderlies ran up to him, flung

bucketsful of water over him, and hastily withdrew. It was like
a fire. Naked except for a pair of dripping spectacles, Sime stood
his ground. When he had been well doused, he was made to wash
himself several times from head to foot. Then, disinfectant stinging
his flesh and pricking in his nostrils and eyes, he was given some
pills to swallow, jagged with a hypodermic needle, and told to lie
down for a while.

When he lay down, he wondered whether he would ever rise
again.

*

When Morris lay down on Friday night, Craig sharply reminded him to rise and visit his night-sentries at least twice before
dawn on Saturday.

It was a night for sleeping. It was a cool night, a blanket night.
Mosquitoes and crickets were chilled to silence. Clouds curtained
the moon and stars, and darkness lay heavy on eyelids.

"Twelve o'clock and two o'clock," Morris reminded himself.
"Concentrate on twelve. Twelve. Twelve. I will arise and go then
and go to—bloody hell." Rebelliously, he turned his mind from
auto-suggestion to Torrance's suggestion. Lying within arm's reach
of Craig, he relished the memory of his mutinous conversation with
Torrance that afternoon.

French leave. Torrance could pronounce the words as seduc-
tively as Eve must have mouthed *apple*. It was both liberty and
licence he held at offer. "You've got all the argument you need,"
he had said, coiling his assurance round Morris's effort to discuss
the *pro* and *contra*. "A perfectly plausible, well-rounded argument,
reaching as high as your manly chest when she stands on tip-toes."

"Seriously, Dick, we'd be running an awful risk."

"I got away with it on Monday night, didn't I?"

"We weren't on short notice then."

"Which brings us back to where we started: Craig's leaving
the Line tomorrow night."

"It's hard to believe. He hasn't mentioned it yet."

"I heard them myself. Ballantyne and Craig. Then the Old
Horse himself chipped in and told Craig not to be a stubborn mule,
to stop worrying about things that couldn't be helped, to get
away from the Line for one night. Short notice doesn't mean you
have to stand with your finger on the trigger. Later on, I heard
Ballantyne warning McNaughton Smith to leave a phone number

tomorrow night. That's all that short notice amounts to."

Morris stretched his tired limbs on the camp-bed and listened to Craig's soft breathing. It was always dark before Craig fell asleep. He gave nobody the chance to look at his slackened face.

"The fact is," Torrance had argued warmly, "we in Don Company are beginning to think like Craig. We're beginning to look for war. But nobody else seems to think that this emergency will come to anything."

Morris reviewed the evidence.

On Wednesday, Craig had conveyed a standing order that, from that night forward, each section should guard its area with double sentries from dusk till dawn. (Before Morris could expand his sympathy for the hard-worked and malaria-depleted sections, Craig had characteristically underlined the order by instructing his three platoon commanders to make at least two rounds of their sentry-posts each night. Morris had gone to sleep indignantly on Wednesday and had wakened, refreshed but shamefaced, on Thursday to admit that he had slept the whole night through and to submit to Craig's soft-voiced, sharp-edged rating.)

When Corporals Barker and Macdonald, released by the Canadians, had returned to the platoon that morning, they had reported a slackening of tension in Kowloon, a rumour that the Japanese forces were withdrawing from the frontier area. They had also sheepishly boasted that they had been getting out of barracks every night. (Don Company, by way of contrast, had spent Thursday night and the first hours of Friday morning in confused tactical exercises, responding sleepily to Craig's commands and Williamson's criticism of their health and strength.)

And today, Friday, there had been another piece of evidence. An aeroplane had passed high overhead, and Morris and his platoon had looked up at it, curious but unconcerned. Craig had stormed amongst them, shouting at them to take cover and keep their heads down.

"Is it a Jap?" Morris had asked from the ground.

"Of course it is! We've nothing but a few training-planes. It's a Jap on reconnaissance. And you were standing around giving away your positions."

In the mess, however, there had been a clash of opinion on the omens to be read from the flight. And it seemed to Morris that, if a vote had been taken, the majority would have been found to

favour one or other of the two comforting views: namely, either
that the pilot had been off course, or that the Japanese would not
have reconnoitred so openly if they had been planning an early
attack on the colony.

Drowsily, Morris looked at his watch. He could no longer see
how he had hoped to progress from the evidence of Craig's mis-
reading of the omens to a justification of French leave.

*

"Just for an hour or two," Morris stipulated, raising his voice
above the drumming of the pick-up and the rattling of bones in
the ancestral cupboards of his mind. "We've got to be back before
Craig."

Holt, at the wheel, sharply handsome, understandably dignified,
said, "I'm staying for one hour only." Ear to the ground, lips
closed, intelligence officer.

"Good Lord!" Torrance exclaimed. "What can you do in an
hour?"

"I just want to see some people I promised to meet."

"Same here," said Morris with interest and affection. He felt
that the blessing Major Ingham had given to Holt's request for
leave now gilded his own departure, made his offence a merely
technical one. He lit a cigarette and casually exposed his last
anxiety. "There isn't likely to be anybody else from the battalion
at the China Ball?"

"Might be a few there," said Holt. "But you'll be able to keep
out of sight in the crowd."

"That wasn't really our intention," said Torrance. "We were
going to flaunt ourselves a bit."

"You'll be stretching my neck too," Holt said composedly.

Morris hurriedly offered assurance. "We won't be stretching any
necks. Not tonight."

Torrance started to sing, and Morris joined in. While they sang,
he wondered why Torrance chose to tag along, why Torrance, the
man who wanted to remake his fellows after his own cat-faced
goat-footed image, was content to let someone else shape modest
pleasures for him.

> " 'Singing hey jig-a-jig,
>   Stuff a little pig,
> Follow the band, follow the band, oh, follow the band!' "

In the Peninsula Hotel, the persuasive music of the dance-band and the shuffling and murmuring of persuaded couples guided the subalterns up the broad staircase to the ballroom. The air was opulently, provocatively tainted with perfumes and the redolences of food, drink and tobacco. At the head of the stairs, the subalterns twitched at tunics and ties, smiled at each other, and made for the crowded doorway. His eyes still unaccustomed to the brilliant light, Morris felt slightly giddy as he watched the spinning orbits of the dance, male and female turning on their own axis as they progressed with all the other couples round and round the floor, faces and fine clothes churning past him in a gay galactic stream.

Holt caught sight of his friends and excused himself.

"We'd better have a stiff drink," decided Torrance.

"Wait!" Peering incredulously across the room, Morris seized his companion's arm. "Isn't that Craig over there?"

Torrance moved his head about, trying to see between dancers. "You're right," he decided. "Sitting down, with that thorny rose of his, Mary Gow."

They drew back from the doorway and looked at each other.

"Craig!" Torrance swayed between laughter and indignation. "I never thought I'd live to see old Stork-Legs dancing."

"He's not dancing," Morris pointed out bleakly.

"That bint of his won't let him sit out every dance for the next hour."

"We can't hang around here for an hour." The word was more decisive than the thought. He was looking at a light, and as he looked he saw the ring of darkness round it. "We'd better wait for Holt downstairs." The music was falling to pieces before it could reach him, brittle fragments jangling against his ears.

"And Anna?"

Morris swore. "We'll have to get her out here." He swore again. He had swallowed his plummy self-pity and was spitting out the four-letter stone-hard word left in his mouth. "We'll get a boy to page her."

Torrance, who was facing the doorway, grinned. "Here's your boy coming. Single-track-minded and double-breasted."

It was Nell Griffiths. Red-faced, Morris greeted her, and was surprised and heartened to find that she was neither embarrassed by the memory of his explorations nor resentful that he had failed to make a second expedition.

"I didn't dream you'd be here," she said throatily.

"We're not," said Torrance. "You're dreaming. And shame on you for dreaming a dream with us dogs in it!"

"We're on French leave," Morris explained.

"And," added Torrance, "we find that our uncle is not in the garden as we expected."

"Our company commander's here," Morris explained. "We'll have to go away again."

Nell looked up at him. "We could call Joan out and all go some place else."

"We don't have much time, Nell."

"Moreover," said Torrance, "we promised to see Anna Lin here." Nell narrowed her painted mouth. "We're studying Cantonese," he continued, "to get interpreter badges to wear on our sleeves."

"You want me to bring her out here?"

Impulsively Morris touched her arm. "And then we'll all have a drink together downstairs."

She returned to the ballroom. Morris lit a cigarette. Torrance leaned against the wall and surveyed him with impudent yellow eyes. "Two women at your beck and call, and your hour is fast running out. It is the life, is it not, my old?"

"It is the life." Morris felt rather pleased with himself for the moment.

Nell and Anna came out together. Smiling, they detached themselves from the fringe of people in the doorway and walked slowly towards him. It was like a wisp of a dream in which scattered things were gathered together in an impossible confusion of delight and dismay.

"Nell," said Torrance, "if you dare to be seen with a man of my reputation—" He held out his arms and shuffled his feet with exaggerated impatience.

"But your uncle—"

"We'll dance here."

It was so obvious a manœuvre that Morris felt ashamed.

Anna stood in front of him, a reproving smile on her mouth, her dark eyes diffidently restless. "Nell has told me. You shouldn't be here."

"I just came to explain—to see you."

"Why can Captain Craig come?"

Morris surprised himself by answering immediately, "He hasn't had a break for a long time."

"He looks tired."

"We always seem to talk about other people."

She looked away. "Because we know about each other."

"Anna!" He wanted to seize this chance. "I may not be able to see you again for a long time. It really looks as if there's going to be a war." And then, noticing the quickening of her breathing, the shimmer of silk across her bosom, he added, "I mean that, even if the scare eventually blows over, it's going to be a long time before I'll be allowed to leave the Line to see you." She was still nervous. Gently, unobtrusively, he touched her bare arm. She was wearing a sleeveless Chinese gown. "I like you best in Chinese dress."

She looked up guiltily, smiled.

"Listen, Anna—even if there's a war—after the war—"

The music had ended.

"We'll have that drink now," called Torrance. "Down below!"

Hell! There was never time to say enough. The best words were always left to grow cold in the mouth.

While they were still on the stairs, Holt caught up with them. "We'll have to go," he said urgently. "There's some talk of officers being recalled. Boyd of the Navy says that it's only staff officers, but we can't take a chance on that." A drum-roll sounded down the stairs. "They'll be making an announcement," Holt guessed. "Come on."

They ran out of the hotel. While Holt, followed by Torrance, clattered down the steps to fetch the pick-up, Morris turned to the girls. "See you soon," he promised hastily.

"Don't we get a kiss?" asked Nell.

Torrance turned and called out, "Kisses are for free tonight." He bounded up the steps to kiss first Nell, then Anna.

Morris followed. Nell's mouth was wide and warm. Anna's was cool, but she put her hands on his arms and held him tight for a moment.

"Don't forget me," he said lightly to them both, and started to descend.

"God bless you, Johnny," called Nell softly.

He turned, and saw them against the light from the hotel. Nell waved her hand. Anna stood perfectly still, as he had left her. He lifted his hand in a brief gesture of farewell and ran down the dark steps.

He sat in the back of the pick-up, empty of emotion.

"This must be it," decided Holt.

"What?"

"This is the war, my old," said Torrance patiently.

"I'm too tired."

They parted company on the Castle Peak road. Holt took the pick-up to the M.T. lines. The other two stood for a few minutes, taking in the silence.

"False alarm," grumbled Morris.

"Nothing to drink in your tent?"

"Nothing but paraffin. I'm going to bed." Wearily, he stumbled down into the hollow. Then, suddenly ashamed of his ungraciousness, he halted and looked back. Torrance was already out of sight, on his way up Golden Hill. "Goodnight, Dick. See there aren't any spinsters under your bed."

" 'Night, Johnny!" The voice came strangely from the darkness of the hill under the star-blackened sky. "God bless!"

Lonely now, Morris decided to visit his night-sentries before he lay down.

Chapter Two

'O God, our help in ages past,
Our hope for years to come,
Our shelter from the stormy blast,
And our eternal home!'

Mouthing the words of the hymn chosen by Padre Ewen, Craig wondered whether anyone else in the crowded room could detect an ironic ring in this last-minute reference of responsibility to God.

'Sufficient is Thine arm alone,
And our defence is sure.'

Covertly he looked around at the men who, with or without God's help, would command the defence of the western sector of the Inner Line. They had breakfasted together for the last time, Mair having decided that the company officers should in future take their meals at their posts. They had been gathered from the breakfast table by Ewen, who, pulling his dog-collar forward and stretching his neck, as if reaching for his usual Sunday stature, had suggested a brief service of dedication.

Grimly impatient, Mair now chanted a few scattered words of the hymn, lending occasional, reluctant authority to the praise. Daddy Guthrie stood next to him, second-in-command to him, and second to Ewen in aggravating his impatience. Guthrie—who was under orders to scout up the Castle Peak road with the Bren-gun carriers—had insisted on waiting for the service, but now sang monotonously, without his usual punctilious pleasure, and stared moodily into a purgatorial distance between Bren-gun carriers and his eternal home. It was likely that he was still pondering the problem he had raised at the breakfast-table—the problem of safe-guarding Willie the Boxer. Ingham, the only one who had had the

152

temerity to suggest that the dog should be put down, stood on Mair's other side, stolid, ready, confident of the efficiency of the carrier crews, mortarmen, signallers, drivers and other specialists of Headquarters Company.

Wilson, commander of A Company, had gone straight back to Shingmun Redoubt after breakfast, carrying the responsibility for the defence of the key-position of the Inner Line, without benefit of clergy, without even his C.O.'s blessing. The Old Horse, patently preparing the way for a bold benediction, had asked him encouragingly, "How d'you feel about it?" Wilson had answered casually, "I could do with less concrete and more men." And, stiffly, Mair had let him go away, unseasonably honest and unblessed.

McNaughton Smith, to whom B Company would look for leadership, was at the moment contending with Ewen for command of the choir. Ignoring the padre's appealing glances, he was singing loudly, fervently, and always at least half a bar behind, and inciting others to follow his leisurely, reverent example by nodding his head occasionally to draw attention to his timing.

Ketchen, commanding C Company, had a tremulous bass that went well with his drooping forelock and his broken nose. He sang in much the same manner as he marched, head down and hands clenched, pushing pugnaciously forward to the next halting-place.

Amen.

Clasping his hands together, Ewen started to pray. Craig bowed his head slightly, withdrawing his attention, feeling—as he had felt since childhood—uneasy in the presence of a man speaking to a god. But there was a finality about the prayer that touched everything else to which he turned his attention. Through the open window came a smell of burning grass. Willie sat by Guthrie's right leg, blinking against the sunlight, helplessly dangling his tongue. On the floor behind the dog lay the morning paper with the news of Roosevelt's personal plea to the Emperor of Japan and an account of the China Ball. Amen. Mary would still be in bed. Amen. Let her lie there. For ever and ever.

*

"For God's sake," blustered Roderick, "face the facts! This is your last chance, my dear."

To Mrs. Gow's relief, Mary shuffled into the room. "Last chance to do what, Father?"

He tried to rescue his argument by standing up and looking down at them. "All the ships in the harbour," he said deliberately, "are clearing for Singapore today."

"You want us to go away?" guessed Mary, drowsily tightening the sash of her dressing-gown.

"It isn't too late. I can wangle it."

"I promised to see Maud Granger this afternoon."

Roderick strode angrily out to the verandah, and Mary took his chair.

"The coffee will be cold," said Mrs. Gow faintly. "When did you come home last night?"

"I wasn't late. The Ball was a wash-out. Some senior officers were recalled to their posts, and Hugh—Hugh left with them."

"And you came home then?"

"No, I didn't," said Mary with a nervous burst of anger. "You may as well know—he ditched me—for good. I think it was for good. I don't honestly know. He's so—so damned wordless!" Suddenly on the point of weeping, she appealed to her mother: "What's wrong with him? Why does he keep himself shut up?"

"There they go," said Roderick from the verandah. "Some of them heading out now."

"And why has he ditched me?" asked Mary, distraught. "Because I went out once in a while with other men? Because I wanted sometimes to be with ordinary men, talkative men, gay men? He must know that he's the only—" She burst into tears.

Hurriedly, frowning, Mrs. Gow rose from the table, touched Mary's hard young shoulder, and went to dress. She had promised to help with the arrangements for Madame Sun's departure from the colony.

*

Private Cratchley stood in the sunlight, his fair hair cropped close, his empty blue eyes blinking nervously, his flesh strange with prison-pallor.

"It took a war to get you out, eh?" gibed Sergeant Meechan. "Maybe you'd rather have stayed in choky?"

"No," said Cratchley. He spoke softly, as if he were unaccustomed to the sound of his voice in the open air. "Glad to be out, sergeant."

"Glad to have you," said Morris encouragingly. "We're pretty short-handed. Bad place for malaria, this. As a matter of fact," he continued, intent on relieving Cratchley's constraint, "over a hundred of the battalion are down with malaria right now."

"Macdonald's section?" suggested Meechan. "Might as well go back to his old section."

Morris hesitated. "Unless—maybe you'd rather change your section?"

"No, sir. Thank you, sir. I'd like to go back to Corporal Macdonald."

Morris watched the convict walk neatly down to Macdonald's cottage. "What was he in for?"

Meechan spat. "Rape."

The air was tremulous with the chirring of grasshoppers.

*

In the cinema the darkness quivered with the light and sound of the dream drawn large on the great screen. It was a darkness that clasped like the arms of a man.

"If the Japs get their hands on you," whispered Joan urgently, "you know what they'll do to you."

Joan could never surrender herself to the clasp of the silvery dark. She chattered away the charm of every film.

"Don't talk about it just now," begged Nell sleepily.

"You always say that! You keep putting it off. You'll put it off till it's too late. This is definitely the last night I spend in that flat. I'm moving over to the island tomorrow. I'll stay with the Greshams. Well, why don't you say something?"

"Look," said Nell.

The dream had been wiped off the screen. In its place, a crudely scratched message ordered all servicemen to return to their units.

"Heavens!" gasped Joan. "We'd better move tonight."

She dragged Nell outside. There, the darkness was cumbered with rain clouds.

*

The pattering of rain on canvas wakened Morris. Immediately he fumbled under the pillow for his watch and tried to remember whether he had already visited his night-sentries. Then, in one glad instant, he recalled his conversation with Jannelli about re-incarnation on his first round of the posts, and decided that it was still too early to make his second round. He lay and listened to the rain on the thin canvas—wondering why his awareness of the uncertainty of his protection should heighten his pleasure in listening—until he fell asleep.

It was almost five o'clock on Monday, 8th December, before he wakened again. He rose, tucked his rumpled shirt inside his slacks, put on his boots and battle order and, taking care not to waken Craig, groped his way out of the tent. The air was cold and fresh after the rain, and a few stars were visible. He stumbled over a guy-rope, worried about his vision, and started his second round of the scattered sentry-posts.

He liked to hear the old challenge in the dark: "Halt! Who goes there?" It was one of the few things that made this army seem as real as the armies of the past. He could not readily visualise men like Jannelli and himself holding a trench on the Somme, advancing in scarlet tunics against the Boers, charging the Old Guard at Waterloo, falling before American muskets or under English pikes, marching as mercenaries in the army of Gus-tavus Adolphus. Soldiers, he concluded, were dignified by death. History dealt mainly with the uniforms they left behind. It was, he considered, a neat conclusion, for the time of morning, and he completed his round in an indulgent dream of Anna.

As he walked up from Macdonald's area, making for his tent, he became aware of movement in the dark hollow.

"That you, Mr. Morris?" It was Ripley, his runner.

He smartened his pace. "What's up?"

"Balloon's up, I think, sir. Skipper wants to see you."

Craig spoke to his subalterns beside Torrance's bivouac, in the centre of the company line. He had come straight from battalion headquarters. The war with Japan had started. Every man in the company was to stand to arms till dawn.

Williamson jerked his shoulders up and down and rubbed his hands together, closing another account. Anstey stuck his fists into his greatcoat pockets and shivered. Torrance was shivering too, as he sloughed his sleep. "They might have waited till after breakfast-time," he said.

The sense of unreality seized Morris again and held him until, as he lay on top of Barker's knoll watching the first light taint the darkness, he heard a murmur of distant explosion. "Demolition," explained Ripley hoarsely. "Our own sappers." Morris watched the light gather. Craig had said that patrols drawn from the forward companies would advance into the hills in the earliest light and observe and delay Japanese movements across country, while Major Guthrie's force of carriers offered resistance on the Castle Peak road. Morris lay still, thinking of the patrols, until Sergeant Meechan asked his permission to let the platoon stand down.

After a dispiriting breakfast of tepid tea, bread and margarine, Craig set the company to work on wiring and other routine tasks, and the memory of explosion and patrols started to dissolve in sweat. But, at eight o'clock, Japanese bombers escorted by fighters flew over the Inner Line, scattering leaflets, heading south. Cockled clouds and falling paper. "They need special planes, the Japs," said Ripley scornfully. "Short legs, like." The sudden belly-heaving crunch of bursting bombs. "Kaitak," guessed Ripley. "They're after our planes. Silly twerps. Even if they 'it them it won't make any difference to us."

The certainties of war began to accumulate as the platoon laboured quietly over final tasks. Craig relayed a message that the Japanese had crossed the Shumchun river in strength. Groups of Chinese villagers filed down the road to Kowloon, silent, unhurried, laden with possessions. The tents in the hollow were struck.

Ah Chan helped Morris to sort out his belongings and put away everything except what seemed to them essential for a campaign. Mildly disagreeing—Ah Chan taking thought for his master's comfort, and Morris anxious to avoid seeming sybaritic— they wrapped up his camp-kit in his valise and packed a trunk with military and civilian dress and a surprisingly varied and strangely irrelevant collection of things he had brought as souvenirs of home or gathered as trophies of the long voyage east. After the trunk and the valise were ready for transport to Kowloon, Morris swithered over the bundle of necessaries that was left—a change of underwear, an extra shirt, a pair of slacks and a jersey to wear between dusk and dawn, two pairs of socks, six handkerchiefs, razor, shaving brush, shaving soap, tooth-brush, tooth-paste, toilet soap, towel, brush and comb, nail-scissors, steel mirror, talcum powder to ward off prickly heat and foot rot, and the notebook in which he had once before attempted to start a diary. Finally, he packed them all into a canvas bag, except two handkerchiefs, shaving-soap, tooth-paste, hair-brush and talcum powder, which he presented to Ah Chan.

The packing was Ah Chan's last service. He and the other Chinese boys had been instructed to return to their homes. Sincerely, Morris thanked the young man. "I hope we'll meet again soon," he said, and held out his hand. Ah Chan was stricken with embarrassment. His fingers were limp and cold. He went away without saying anything coherent.

"I'll do batman for you," promised Ripley.

Later, Morris saw the boys leaving, laden like the other refugees streaming down the road towards Kowloon, but clearly distinguishable in their white mess-jackets.

"Queer," suggested Ripley in his husky, portentous voice. "They're the ones should be fighting. Not us."

*

When James Lin returned to the newspaper office, Sammy King was still sprawling lazily over a desk, cracking melon seeds with his teeth, smoking a cigarette. His moon face was as inexpressive as his narrow-brimmed, high-crowned felt hat. A sports writer ready to wait the war out.

"Did you get through?" asked James sharply. In the past it had always been possible to look on Sammy's bulging sloth with an indulgent eye. But during the last six hours this swivel-chair sportsman, this American-trained critic of useless activities, had become the easy target for frustrated anger.

Reflectively Sammy said: "I got through. Matron's office. She says none of her staff skip back to the island till she gets the okay from the director."

"What use can Anna be?" demanded James. "She's just started her training." He took off his jacket. "Kowloon's the first objective. They should start evacuating it now."

"Put any more people on this island, brother, and it's liable to sink."

Wearily, James sat down and put on his spectacles. "I'm going to get Anna out of Kowloon—even if I have to use high explosives to do it." As he reached for the telephone, the air-raid sirens wailed again, and out of habit he took a note of the time—1.40 p.m.

Sammy stood up and pulled his hat over his forehead. "Anybody wants me," he said, "I'll be in the basement—like the newspapers told us."

*

Next morning, Morris was ordered to lead out a fighting patrol.

The enemy were advancing slowly down the Castle Peak road, moving forward gradually as their flank columns won through the hills to the sea. They were now within two miles of the Inner Line. Their flank columns had already driven most of the patrols from the forward companies down from the hills, and might at any moment attempt to cut the road behind the sappers who, covered by Guthrie's force of Bren-gun carriers, were blowing up the road-bridges. The carriers, which had no room for effective manœuvre on the narrow coast-road, were to be relieved by Morris.

Craig gave the orders in the presence of the C.O. and the adjutant.

"Don't go looking for trouble," Mair warned Morris, a reminiscent light in his eye. "Don't go hunting the Frogs, d'you understand?" He struck the ground with his ash stick. "Just push back any of them that look like interfering with the sappers' work. Is that clear?"

"Yes, sir." Released from the dragging uncertainty that had stretched out the previous twenty-four hours, Morris felt an accession of strength and energy. Then he saw that they were all staring at him—Mair aggressive, Ballantyne sleepily aloof, Craig tautly attentive—all looking into him, probing for his weaknesses.

Morris saluted and ran down into the hollow to muster the platoon. Before he marched them up to the road, he carried out a brief inspection, walking smartly along the ranks, looking at equipment, sometimes—with a curious flicker of recognition—catching sight of a face. Steel helmets, respirators corded against chests, packs on backs, water-bottles and bayonets hanging from belts, ammunition in pouches, bandoliers and haversacks: this, he assured himself excitedly, was the disguise of war; this was the way in which men like Jannelli and he concealed themselves and yet made bulky shadows on the pages of history.

Leaving Sergeant Meechan to see to the men, as they filed out of the hollow, removed all papers from their pockets and deposited them with C.Q.M.S. Silver, Morris went up to the road with Ripley at his heels. Mair had gone. Beside Ballantyne and Craig stood Williamson, in battle order. Before anyone spoke, Morris knew what had happened.

"You'll take your orders from Williamson," Craig said. "I've put him in the picture."

To consummate the transfer of command, Williamson, the branky boy, started to shout: "Look lively, there! At the double!"

Morris climbed up beside the driver of the first truck, with orders from Williamson to halt the convoy as soon as he sighted the sappers. Glad to turn his back on Williamson's hairy energy and twitching tyranny, he lowered himself stiffly into the seat. He had been weighed and found wanting. It was Williamson, wrapped in full flannel, who had tipped the scale. *Maskee.* Keeping his eyes to the front, Morris started to whistle self-consciously. There was a rumble of guns in the air as the convoy started off, like a roll of drums to give the Japanese fair warning of Williamson's personal intervention in the battle.

At the front line, where the road ran between the promontory occupied by C Company and the ridge, occupied by B Company, running up to Shingmun Redoubt, a party of men pulled aside hurdles of wood and wire, and waved 17 Platoon forward.

The road ran between the rock-broken sea and the steep hills. A gunboat, H.M.S. *Cicala*, was steaming off-shore. A clatter of carriers came down the road, already withdrawing. Morris nodded to the commander, Captain Niven, and urged his own driver to get a bend on.

Major Guthrie and the sappers were still working on a bridge, covered by the guns of one remaining carrier. Morris left his truck at the side of the road, led Lance-Sergeant Drummond's section forward to the bridge, saluted Guthrie and announced, "17 Platoon to relieve you, sir."

The major waved his hand impatiently. "Tell the carrier to withdraw. But keep your men this side of the bridge. This is the last demolition and we're almost ready to blow."

Morris hesitated, balancing the apparent folly of trying to protect the sappers by hiding behind them against the certain folly of contradicting a field-officer.

"Get a move on." Guthrie was in a snappy mood.

Leaving Drummond to take up position behind the bridge, Morris went forward to the carrier. He was watching it slew round, when a sudden movement on the hillside made his heart leap and his legs stiffen. It was one of the patrols returning. Unshaven, dirty, breathless, a corporal and three men slithered down to the road.

"They're not far behind us, sir," panted the corporal.

"Any casualties?" asked Morris, slightly ashamed of his interest.

"Not in our lot, sir. But we met Corporal Strachan's patrol earlier this morning, and he told us he had just sent Smith '23 back. Sword-wound on his arm."

"*Sword*-wound?" *Sword* was the twist of the knurl that brought the surrounding dangers into alarmingly sharp focus. *Sword* was an even older sound than the challenge of the night-sentry, a colder sound.

"They've got Chinese bints guiding them," complained one of the privates.

Morris accompanied the patrol down to the bridge. The rest of the convoy had arrived, and Guthrie and Williamson confronted each other, red-faced, thick-necked. Morris kept at a safe distance until Guthrie had disengaged his anger and carried it back to the sappers. Then he reported to Williamson, smooth Jacob to hairy Esau. "We've relieved the last carrier and taken up position."

"Position?" repeated Williamson furiously. "Call that a position?"

"Guthrie's orders."

"Nothing to do with Guthrie! Been relieved, hasn't he?" Williamson screwed up his face. "I'm in command."

Carefully cool and correct, Morris asked, "You want me to cross the bridge?"

"You'll do what you're told to do," said Williamson with menacing ambiguity. "Niven warned me, you know. Guthrie pulled them out too quick at the last bridge. Saboteur ran in and cut the fuses. Chinese. And got away without a scratch. Better get the trucks turned round," he ordered. "If we're caught with our slacks down, Guthrie's the one who'll carry the can."

F

Morris memorised the mixed metaphors. Torrance would make great play with them.

By the time the drivers had turned the three trucks on the narrow road, Guthrie was giving orders for the withdrawal. Williamson was to leave immediately with two trucks and run slowly back to the Line, making sure that the road and the lower slopes were free of Japanese.

Williamson saluted. "I'll report to Captain Craig," he said, blinking rapidly.

Guthrie nodded, apparently missing the implied threat. "You, Morris, stand by for my order to follow Williamson." He eased the steel helmet off his forehead and tried to smile. "Nothing like a glengarry for comfort," he said.

When Morris was ordered to withdraw, he wondered whether the sappers were thinking that old Daddy's main concern was to shelter his own comrades. He withdrew very slowly, until a heartening explosion shook the air, and the sappers' truck roared into view, with Guthrie standing up in it and signalling full speed.

*

"Funny sort of war, this," ventured George Sime that evening, when Number 5 Section had gathered in their pillbox for supper.

"What's wrong with it?" asked Corporal Barker, smiling. "You been in any better wars, George?"

"Two days," Sime pointed out, "and nothing's happened."

"Nothing's happened to us," corrected Lance-Corporal Arkison, scraping the bottom of the dixie to gather the last of the gravy. "Somebody else must have felt the weight of all those bombs and shells."

"That's the very point that George is trying to make," said Barker. "Why don't the Japs share them out better?"

Encouraged by the corporal's bantering manner and the appreciative sniggering of other men, Monkey Jackson, centre-half in the battalion's football team, said: "Growin' fast into a real soldier, our George, since he was dipped in the shit."

Barker looked round. "If that's the case, Monkey, I should've dipped you a long time ago."

Sime stared bleakly at his congealing stew.

"Who's for more gippo?" mumbled Arkison, with his own plate ready.

"Me," said Paterson. "Me and George. The key men in this section. The rest of you just carry ammo for our gun."

Barker checked that the sentries' portions had been laid aside. "Cut the cards," he ordered. "Highest card gets the gash gippo. Lowest card takes the dixies back to the cookhouse."

Sime took the dixies.

Paterson swore. "Never fails," he muttered wonderingly. "You must keep all the low cards up your sleeve."

*

Craig was already awake, wrapped in his greatcoat, hunched on his valise, when the runner trotted down into the hollow to summon him to battalion headquarters. The luminous hands of his watch marked seven minutes after midnight. He stood up and, listening to the crackle of distant small-arms fire that had wakened him, followed the runner across the road.

In one of the small concrete shelters built into the rear of Lance-Sergeant Drummond's ridge, in an atmosphere thick with heat and tobacco smoke, Mair scowled at a wall-map of the battalion's sector, Ballantyne tapped a pencil on the war-diary, and a frightened clerk sat by the telephone.

"They're attacking Shingmun." Mair shook his head angrily. "We got a message from Wilson before midnight, and the Japs were already right up at the Redoubt."

Ballantyne said calmly, "They seem to have come down from Tai-mo-shan, crossed the pass, and climbed to the perimeter wire of the Redoubt before they were spotted."

Craig was not surprised. He knew that Wilson would not be surprised. Three or four nights ago, one of Wilson's subalterns had carried out a dummy attack and, under cover of darkness, had led his platoon right into the Redoubt. There were too few men at Shingmun, and, because of a brigade order requiring him to send out strong patrols, not only to search his own front but also to maintain contact with the Indians on his right, Wilson had not even had the chance to deploy his few men to maximum advantage. "And now?" Craig asked.

"That's just what I want to know," said Mair. He swung round on the clerk. "Get a move on, man. Get through to A Company."

Ballantyne looked up at Craig. "The intelligence reports gave us to understand that the Japanese were poor at night-work."

"You can set a match to all those bloody reports." The C.O.

switched his indignation from the nervous clerk. "They told us the Japs were poor at bombing, too. But, in their first raid, the little beggars wiped out our grounded air force."

"It remains to be seen whether they're good at night-work," said Ballantyne coolly. "With those rubber sneakers on their feet, and renegade-Chinese guides in front of them, they've reached Shingmun. But they've still to fight for the Redoubt. And it's a dark night."

Craig wondered why they were taking so long to come to the point. He unbuttoned the neck of his greatcoat and stepped away from the heat of the hissing pressure-lamp.

"Sit down," said Mair considerately. He had suddenly relaxed. He was filling his pipe. "They've gone straight for our key position." He stared at his pipe. "They know what they're doing. No question about that. They know that command of the Redoubt would give them command of this whole sector. And they'll hammer at that lump of concrete till—"

The telephone bell interrupted him. He snatched the receiver from the clerk. "Wilson? . . . Mair here . . . I understand that. Get on with it, man!" He sat perfectly still, his bright blue eyes staring into space, his mouth open. "Is that all? . . . What am I to make of a report like that, eh? . . . All right, all right, Wilson. But for God's sake keep us informed. And—Wilson— good luck." He handed the receiver back to the clerk and picked up his pipe again. "He doesn't know what's happening. That's the sum and substance of the report. He's lost contact with the two platoons outside the Redoubt, and the platoon inside the Redoubt with him are stymied. The gun-slits are too shallow. The gun-muzzles can't be depressed far enough to bring fire to bear on the approach slopes." He looked from Ballantyne to Craig, a bitter smile on his mouth. "The Redoubt was designed for long-range defence only. Comic, isn't it?"

Craig tried to force the point. "Shouldn't I warn my company to stand by to counter-attack?"

"Eh?" Mair seemed to resent the suggestion. "It's too early to commit my whole reserve, man. The situation's too—too confused. I've spoken to the Brigadier. He agrees."

Craig looked at Ballantyne, hoping for a fuller discussion of the tactics. But the adjutant was carefully reading the war-diary, frowning, tapping his pencil.

"Wait, man, wait," urged Mair. "Wait till we get Wilson's next report."

They waited. The clerk was relieved at one o'clock on Wednesday morning. The relieving clerk had cold air clinging to his uniform, a smell of wet grass on his boots, and Craig's belly stirred as if with hunger. They waited in silence. With nothing to listen to but the hissing of the lamp, it was difficult to recall the urgent crackle of distant firing. With nothing to look at but a paper map and the cramped figures in the oily-yellow smoke-shot light, it was difficult to visualise the sharp outlines of men and rocks against the muzzle-flash of small-arms.

When the telephone rang, Mair took the receiver again. The line was bad. He raised his voice. "You hope to hold out till dawn?" He glanced at Ballantyne, his face stiff. "I don't want brave words, Wilson. I want the facts . . . Enemy in great strength . . . Listen, Wilson, I can't put in a counter-attack until daylight." Craig sat forward, opened his mouth in protest. Staring coldly at him, the C.O. continued: "I can't risk my whole reserve. You understand? . . . Good man, Wilson. Keep us in touch . . . I know, I know. I don't hold it against you . . . Right. Good luck, old man!" He handed the empty receiver to the clerk. "He'll hold out as long as he can. It won't be long."

"If I'm going to have a crack at the Japs up there," said Craig tensely, "I'd rather do it now—before they've a chance to consolidate."

"Talk sense, man," said Mair hoarsely. "You're no longer my reserve. Now that the Japs are up on the north end of Smugglers Ridge, I need Don Company on the south end to block the way through the hills to Kowloon. I don't want you further forward. I want you further to the right. The easiest thing to do is to switch Morris from left flank to right. Tell him that—whatever the cost—he has to stop the Japs advancing from the Redoubt along the Ridge." He nodded to the clerk. "Get me Brigade."

Craig told Morris more. He told him to hold himself ready to counter-attack along the Ridge just before dawn.

When he returned to headquarters, he found Ballantyne standing outside the shelter, refreshing himself in the cold air.

"The line to the Redoubt is dead."

"I expected that," said Craig. "It's all quiet again."

"Poor old Wilson."

"What did Brigade say?"

Ballantyne shivered. "Counter-attack at first light. They agree with Mair that D Company should stay in the rear, blocking the Ridge and the Castle Peak road, and that the only company he can now throw against Shingmun is C. But they don't agree with him that C hasn't the strength for the job. Ketchen has fewer than forty men left, you know. Malaria."

Craig considered quickly. "I'll have a word with the Old Man."

"He'll tell you what he told me—we haven't reached the stage of desperation yet."

*

"I suppose," said Meechan out of the darkness, "we'll be going in first?"

"The Skipper didn't say." Morris tensed his muscles, trying to squeeze the chilly tremor out of his voice. "But we're nearest the Ridge now."

"We'll be going along the top of the Ridge?"

Morris looked to the right. Near as it was, Smugglers Ridge was lost in darkness. "He'll tell us which way to go."

They lay together, with Corporal Barker's section, in the centre of the platoon. Lance-Sergeant Drummond was on their right, up in the pass between the Ridge and Golden Hill. Corporal Macdonald was on their left, linking with Anstey's platoon. They lay still, searching the cold silence for sounds of movement, waiting for the light.

When Morris heard the first faint cry from the Ridge, it was rather the responsive stirring of the men around him than the cry itself that roused him from his chilly torpor.

"Pye-dog," said Paterson dismissively.

There was a murmur of disagreement.

Morris stared in the direction of the Ridge, as if his eyes might help him to hear. The second cry, when it came at last, startled him. "It can't be one of Drummond's men. It's too far forward," he decided. "It must be one of A Company—trying to get back from the Redoubt."

"Might be a trick," warned Meechan. "Might be a Jap scout."

After the third cry, Barker said: "Sounded like a cry for help. One of A Company—wounded, maybe?"

Morris, resenting this complication, glanced at his sergeant.

"Let him shout," advised Meechan harshly.

"We can't lie here listening to him all night," objected Morris. "He'll give us the willies."

Meechan was dour. "If we start horsing around in the dark, how are the rest of the company to listen for Japs?"

"Two men could handle this. Two volunteers." Stubbornly, Morris turned to Barker's section. "I want two volunteers to go up there quickly and quietly and bring that man down. I'll warn the rest of the company not to fire on the Ridge."

After a cold, dark moment, George Sime spoke: "I'll go, sir."

"You!" muttered Paterson savagely. "Flaming lot of good you'd be! You'd have to be carried down too."

"Anybody else?" asked Morris.

"You can't take Sime," Paterson protested.

"He's as good a man as any. In fact, it looks as if he's a better man than most. I'm still waiting for another volunteer."

Barker said, "I'll go up with Sime, sir."

"Not you. You're needed here." Morris rose to his knees. "If I don't get a volunteer, I'll have to detail somebody." His voice shook. He was no longer sure that he was doing the right thing.

At his back, Meechan spoke: "You'd better go, Paterson."

"Why me?"

"You're Sime's mucker. Leave your Bren. Take a rifle."

After a moment, Paterson swore softly and viciously. He rose to his feet, accepted a rifle and, without speaking to anyone, started to walk down into the valley between Golden Hill and the steep side of the Ridge. Sime followed him.

Soon afterwards, the British artillery started to shell the Redoubt. One of the first shells fell short, exploding on the side of the Ridge, and a few fragments of shattered rock dropped among Barker's section.

"God help Paterson and Sime!" Meechan muttered.

"The gunners are just ranging," replied Morris angrily. "That won't happen again."

He sent Ripley down to warn Macdonald of the mercy mission

and, unable to lie still any longer, he himself carried the message up to Drummond in the pass.

*

When his challenge was answered, Jannelli announced to the section, "It's Morris."

"We should've taken the chance," grumbled Fraser, "and shot him."

Lance-Corporal Foggo spat. "Watch it, boy! You ever heard of a field court-martial?"

Jannelli winced as another salvo of shells burst on the far end of the Ridge. "He's all right—Morris."

Morris came up the hill and stumbled amongst them. "How's tricks?" he asked.

Jannelli sat up and smiled in the dark.

"All quiet, sir," reported Drummond. "Except for the shell-fire, I mean. I've got a couple of men down the other side of the Ridge to keep contact with the Punjabis."

"What's goin' to happen to all our kit?" interrupted Fraser.

"It'll be all right," Morris promised.

"Looks to me," said Fraser brassily, "like we should've dug our holes up here." He was losing his nerve, little Piggy.

"We'll maybe dig some more up here. Anything else?"

"Aye. When do we get some chow. McGuire's starvin' hungry."

"He'll have to wait." Morris turned away from Fraser, and told Drummond that two of Barker's men were climbing up the side of the Ridge to rescue one of the wounded survivors of A Company. "They'll maybe not find him." Morris sounded worried. "He seems to have stopped shouting now. But maybe his voice doesn't carry in this direction. Did you hear him earlier?"

"No," said Drummond hoarsely.

Liar. Liar and coward. Jannelli lay down again, ashamed.

*

Morris returned to his post in the centre of the platoon. The shelling of the Redoubt had ceased, the way along the Ridge was once again open to the enemy, and Paterson and Sime were still somewhere on the Ridge. He wondered whether they were still groping about for the man who had shouted, the man who might no longer be a man. He tortured himself with the thought of their sweating towards the bare satisfaction of looking on a dead face and finding a name for an unknown soldier.

Lying beside Meechan, he waited until a new anxiety pricked him. The hours of darkness were unwinding, and Craig had still to issue detailed orders for the counter-attack. Rousing Ripley, who had been curled in sleep like a dog, he stumbled round the hill to Macdonald's post. From there he sent Ripley down in search of news.

"Long night, sir," said Macdonald.

"Almost over now." Morris looked round. "Who's that shivering?"

"Cratchley, sir."

"Malaria?"

"No, sir." Macdonald sneered. "He's just not used to the open air. Been in a snug cell too long."

Morris glanced at the corporal and said tentatively, "Struck me as a quiet, dependable sort of chap."

"He raped a Chinese girl."

"So I heard."

"You can't depend on a man who's done a thing like that."

Morris submitted to the reproof. But, as he lay there, he thought about rape. And he felt, for the first time in his waking life, that he was capable of ravishing a woman. Even the thought of the violence of the act seemed to answer the unquiet promptings of his mind, the tremulous urges in his belly.

As the light ran in from the east, the day before Morris began to take shape.

Paterson and Sime came round the hill, carrying a wounded man on a stretcher made with their rifles and a greatcoat. Rescued from one of his anxieties, buoyant with gratitude, Morris ran to meet them.

"Jamieson of A Company," said Paterson abruptly.

"He's still alive, sir," Sime smiled wearily, proudly.

Morris nodded, clapped Sime's shoulder. "Bloody good," he said, hoarse and excited. "Bloody good."

"He spoke to us a bit," continued Sime. "He was in Mr. Welsh's platoon. Mr. Welsh was killed."

Morris nodded. Welsh, pompous little Welsh. He would think about him later.

F*

"Get yourselves something to eat before you come back," he told them. "I'll see that Captain Craig"—he caught sight of Paterson's hard dark face and tried to make his voice sound less shrill—"I'll see he hears about this."

Paterson had the last word. "I don't want anybody to think I volunteered," he said harshly. "Come on, George, *jildi*!"

Morris stood on the open hillside, watching them march in broken step down into the streaky obscurity of lingering shadow and chalk-blue morning mist. His head ached. Jamieson alive and Welsh dead. Sime's loyalty and Paterson's contempt. The rapid spreading of light across the Ridge; the weight of all the sleepless hours on his shoulders, the rumbling of his empty stomach; the impossibility of his leading a counter-attack. He was looking for a place to lie down alone, when he saw Craig and Ripley climbing towards him.

*

Morris looked like a stranger, a shabby, frightened stranger, with a pale face and stupid sleepless eyes.

"You should be further up the hill," Craig told him curtly. "You can't control your platoon from here." He hesitated, guiltily aware of his punitive reluctance to relieve the subaltern's anxiety. "The C.O. has decided not to counter-attack."

Morris stared. "Why?" he asked, suspicious, resisting. He had spent the night with the succubus of counter-attack, and the demon-arms were still around his neck.

Impatiently, Craig explained: "He doesn't consider he can muster a reserve strong enough to retake Shingmun."

Slowly, Morris stretched his reprieve across his face in a wide grin.

"We've to sit tight in our present positions and stop the enemy from advancing along the Ridge." Craig hesitated again, struck by the sudden hardening of his dislike of Morris. "Sit tight, you understand? Don't disclose your positions. Keep your heads down and don't move about."

"What about kit? We had to leave in a hurry last night, and we don't have much with us."

"It's too late to collect anything now."

"And what about rations?"

"You've had breakfast?"

"No."

Craig checked his anger. "Silver's fault," he said. "You'll have to make the best of it now. Eat your iron rations."

"Can I send some men down after dark to collect warm clothing and rations?" asked Morris resentfully.

"If we're still here. We may be forced to withdraw before night."

Morris's face slackened with surprise.

On his way down, Craig judged his subalterns. Morris—the one who had seemed to have something of a soldier in him—was taking too long to find his feet. Anstey and Torrance, the civilians, had already—each in his own way—assimilated the fact of war. Anstey had drawn further away from his platoon, and Torrance, deprived of other company, had drawn closer to his. Anstey had become the junior commander in the military manuals, practised the disciplines that appeared to diminish the individual responsibility for killing, that dignified death by ritual. For Torrance, however, there was no such easy way. He would look, not at the finger that applied the correct pressure to the trigger, but at the distant man who met the bullet. He would suffer through all his acute senses until they were blunted by battle.

He was sitting now against a grassy slope, eating an orange with delicate relish. He would be able to find manna in a desert.

"Anything new?" he asked.

"Nothing yet," said Craig, halting.

"Slow war, this."

Craig smiled.

"But somebody must be making progress," said Torrance. "Last night we were waiting to go forward. Now we're waiting to go back. It makes me feel I'm taking part in the show."

Undoubtedly an asset. It would soon be only his own discomfort and pain that afflicted him. He would quickly learn to endure—to ignore—the sufferings of others.

Pity withered fast in war. Although it was only a few hours since Shingmun had been captured, the name was now important, not because men had died there, but because the loss of the Redoubt had inflicted humiliation on the battalion and threatened the security of the rest of the Inner Line. If any people still spared a thought for the corpses under the shattered concrete, it was because the full significance of the disaster was obscured by the failure of the Japanese to press their advantage and by the delay in withdrawing the battalion.

Withdrawal was inevitable, with the enemy on the north end of Smugglers Ridge, overlooking the whole sector. The battalion would have to fall back on the Golden Hill line, which was well-defined on the map, stretching from the south end of the Ridge along the crest of the Golden Hill range and down across the Castle Peak road to the sea, but was sketchily drawn on the ground, with some scattered and eroded weapon-pits and a few broken stretches of rusting barbed wire.

While he waited for orders, Craig became impressed by his company's isolation and preservation. Bombers flew over, heading towards Kowloon and Hongkong island. Off-shore, the gunboat *Cicala* was hit. The forward companies were shelled. But there was only one attack on D Company. A Japanese biplane on leisurely reconnaissance suddenly dived on Morris's centre section and fired a few bursts from a machine-gun. It was almost a playful performance, and Morris reported that it had caused no casualties.

The orders did not come till the late afternoon. The battalion were to withdraw after dusk: D Company to occupy the top of Golden Hill; the rest of the battalion to block the Castle Peak road.

Craig conveyed the orders to Torrance first. "Any questions?" he ended.

Torrance nodded. "Will I never get off this bloody hill?"

*

Lying up in the pass with Drummond's section, Morris neither saw nor heard the withdrawal of the rest of the battalion. As the hours of darkness passed, the men beside him became restive.

"It sticks out a mile," asserted Fraser. "They've forgotten about us."

Morris looked at his watch again. According to the plan that Craig had conveyed to him, battalion H.Q. and Headquarters Company should have moved back immediately after dusk; then the forward companies should have retired to their new positions astride the road; then Craig should have led Anstey's and Torrance's platoons up the face of Golden Hill and, as soon as he had disposed them along the crest, sent word by runner to Morris.

"Maybe," Drummond ventured softly, "the runner can't find us in the dark."

"Give him time," said Morris. "It's not midnight yet."

He began, however, to think of some of the accidents that might befall Craig's runner. And, from the apprehension that Craig might fail to make contact with him, it was only a heart-leap to the problem of his own consequential responsibility. How soon could he safely assume Craig's failure? If he withdrew his platoon before the rest of the battalion were ready to meet the enemy, he would be accused of disobedience and, perhaps, of cowardice. If he delayed until his platoon were cut off by the enemy, he would be posthumously accused of lack of imagination and initiative. He decided to wait till one o'clock in the morning—or, perhaps, two o'clock.

Having pushed his resolution so far forward, he was surprised when the runner appeared before midnight and panted out the order to withdraw.

The platoon closed in on Macdonald's post. Meechan and the runner led the way up the hill, and Morris brought up the rear. It was a long, difficult ascent in the moonless dark. The strain was as much on mind as on muscle. The platoon were extended up the precipitous hill-face like flies on a window, with the enemy somewhere at their backs. Every time a dislodged stone clattered down, or a steel-tipped boot struck sparks on rock, or a man stumbled and fell with a rattle of helmet and harness, there was a nervous murmur of cautioning and cursing. Whenever Morris had to halt to allow the men ahead to overcome an obstacle, he turned and peered anxiously down into the dark. But there was never sight or sound of life below.

Craig was waiting for them. He gave them the right flank position, on the bald top of Golden Hill. C.Q.M.S. Silver was also waiting, with a dixie of gravy and six loaves of bread.

After he had inspected the section positions and the night-sentry posts, Morris joined Macdonald in a shallow pit, where they ate their bread and gravy in thankful silence.

"Better get a few hours' sleep," Morris advised.

"Yes, sir."

They pressed close to the ground for warmth. Macdonald mumbled.

"What did you say?" Morris asked.

The corporal made no answer, and Morris guessed that he was praying. He was tempted to say a prayer himself, but while he was still thinking of the strange fitness of prayer spoken in the dark on top of a hill, he fell asleep.

Chapter Three

STRETCHING out of the shelter of the shallow pit, out of the light of his dream, Morris found the coldness and darkness of early morning. Shivering, he heard again the voice that had wakened him.

"You could kip on top of a flagpole." It was Sergeant Meechan, brutally alert.

Morris saw that Macdonald was no longer beside him and peered at his watch.

"It'll be an hour, anyway, before the light comes up. I've got the sections standing-to." The sergeant put a stone flagon into his hands. "Breakfast. Silver's doing us proud."

It was rum. "Is this all?"

The sergeant swore. "That's Navy rum neat."

"I mean—is there nothing solid?"

"That's the kind of rum you have to chew."

Morris choked on his first mouthful.

"See? You forgot to chew."

Morris took another, smaller mouthful and returned the flagon. Ungrateful for the warmth that strengthened his limbs, he stood up and pulled his equipment straight. "You should have given me a shake before this," he grumbled. "And you can tell Silver I don't think much of his breakfast."

Meechan lowered the flagon from his mouth. "We don't want to dishearten him," he said cheerfully, as he turned to climb back to the crest.

Now that he was warm, Morris was uncomfortably aware of his grubbiness. He pulled out a handkerchief, rubbed the corners of his eyes and blew his nose. He walked a few steps further down the back of the hill and urinated. While he was standing there, relieving some of his discomfort and promising himself the pleasure of a surreptitious smoke, he had a sudden attack of heartburn. Cursing Silver, he walked slowly along the back of the hill, breathing deeply, swallowing convulsively, in an effort to master the spasms.

"Are you there, Mr. Morris?" It was a hoarse summons from Ripley, the dog waiting to be taken for his morning walk.

Together they visited the sections. Drummond was again on the right flank, Barker in the centre and Macdonald on the left. Unable to find even shallow pits, most of the men were lying in the open. But in or out of pits they were all flushed with West Indian courage. Fraser was the only one who lodged a complaint: McGuire was hungry again.

Morris took up position with Macdonald on the left, hoping to make contact with Anstey at first light. As he waited with the silent men, he strained for sight or sound of movement, scanning the dark precipitous slopes below him, listening to the combing of wind through the scrub. Occasionally his attention returned to the pungent uprush in his throat. Occasionally his attention wandered to the pack-humped figures of his men sprawling along the crest in a single, scattered line. He envied them their comradeship, wished that he could have Torrance by his side.

It was someone else who came to his side: creeping up from the rear, triumphantly and scathingly announcing his un-challenged arrival, demanding from the nearest man the where-abouts of the platoon commander, bouncing along the line, tramp-ing on men lying in his way, the personification of cold comfort, the poor man's comrade, Williamson.

"Caught you napping. Might have been a Jap," he pointed out severely. "All-round defence is what we need here."

Morris swallowed his rum again and said thickly: "Don't talk rot. We can barely cover the front."

Williamson sniffed. "Been drinking rum?"

"It was all we got for breakfast." He could not keep a querulous note out of his voice. "It's given me devilish heartburn."

"Serves you right. I've spoken to Craig about it. I don't hold with it. Dutch courage."

"There was nothing else to swallow, to warm us up."

"I had a drink of water and did a few jerks."

"Good for you," said Morris. *Good for you, Williamson!* he added to himself, improving the sarcastic inflection. *Good for you, you branky boy!*

They watched the light find the hills and slowly give them shape.

"Who's on the right flank?"

"Drummond."

Williamson blinked nervously and shook his head. "He's not sound."

"I've put Meechan with him. I'm waiting on this flank to contact Anstey."

Again Williamson shook his head. "Quite a gap between you and Anstey." And later, when the darkness fell from the heights, he pointed out Anstey's positions on the saddle below, and Torrance's positions on the shoulder of the hill beyond. "The rest of the battalion are somewhere on the other side of that hill, McNaughton Smith on the high ground, Ketchen down on the road."

Morris stared down the steep scrub-and-rock-strewn slopes below him. "It looks to me as if Don Company's been put on ice again. The Japs won't waste time mountaineering. They'll throw all their weight against the companies straddling the road."

Williamson squirmed on the ground and clenched his hairy fists. "Tactics—" he said, announcing his next topic.

But a movement on the left distracted Morris's attention. Looking over Williamson's bobbing helmet, he saw six men scrambling up out of the haze in front of Torrance's positions and guessed that they were returning from patrol. He was wondering whether he too should have sent forward a patrol to search the slopes below his area, when he was startled by a rattle of small-arms fire. "They've cut it too fine," he exclaimed to Williamson, who had jerked round to investigate the interruption of his review of tactics. "They've got the Japs on their heels." They were falling, poor devils.

"They *are* Japs!" retorted Williamson excitedly.

Morris peered. With a chilly sensation at the base of his spine that made him cinch his buttocks, he discerned the pudding-bowl helmets. He had imagined that there would be more difference than that: he had assumed that—even at a distance—there would be an unmistakably alien air about them, visible marks of enmity.

"First blood," said Williamson hoarsely.

"Watch your front," Morris shouted to his men. And, because the effort of shouting heaved the tremor out of his stomach, he gave another order: "Safety catches off and a round up the spout. Fire by sections."

"Sloppy order, that," commented Williamson.

Anstey's platoon were firing now.

"An attack all along the line," guessed Morris. He wriggled further forward and looked down into the drifting haze for targets.

Macdonald crawled alongside him and said with grim satisfaction, "Our turn next." A moment later he pointed: "There they are. *Lacs* of them. All on the left," he added in surprise. Like rows of sunken buoys rising and swaying in the undertow of milky water, the enemy climbed slowly against Anstey and Torrance.

On the corporal's order, Richardson came forward with his Bren and opened enfilading fire on the enemy on the left. With the impatient stuttering of the gun in his ears, Morris divided his attention between the buckling lines of buoys and the empty mist below his own positions. He moved back to Williamson. "We're right out of the picture here. The fight's all on the left."

"Your job's to watch the right flank. You should be up there yourself. Drummond's not sound."

"Right. Will you keep an eye on this end?"

"Eh?" Williamson gaped indignantly. "I've got my own work to do. Communications in the rear." As he rose to leave, a bullet whistled overhead, and without straightening himself he bounded across the scarred red earth and leapt nimbly down the back of the hill. His years of strenuous training were beginning to pay off.

As Morris wormed his way forward to tell Macdonald he was moving to the right flank, he caught sight of a Japanese no more than thirty yards downhill from him. Covered with a net sprouting tufts of dry grass and leafy twigs, the man stood motionless among the scrub. The camouflage and the stillness were so deceptive that Morris's instant recognition of his enemy faltered for a few pulse-beats towards doubt before he reached to his holster and shouted, "Look out! A Jap right below you!" Before he could draw his revolver, before Macdonald or Richardson had time to swing round, someone behind him fired, and the Japanese jerked violently and tumbled backwards, his net dragging out of the scrub and his feet kicking into the air.

"Any more of them?" asked Macdonald savagely, turning head and gun slowly as he searched for a victim.

"He seems to have been on his own—sent up to knock out the

Bren," guessed Morris. "Who fired that shot?" he asked, looking round at the section.

"Me, sir," admitted Cratchley, the convict, with a thin smile.

"Good work."

Macdonald was less satisfied. "You had to get your target pointed out to you. You're supposed to keep your own eyes open."

When, with Ripley at his heels, Morris reached the right flank, he lay down and reflected on the restraint of his men. In Number 6 Section, only Macdonald, who had steadied himself by shouting, and Richardson, who had felt the shudder of the Bren, had been able to speak and act freely. Number 5 Section had turned their heads as he had passed them, but only Barker had found words to respond to his greeting, and the words had been hoarsely uttered. The same tense silence held Drummond and his men. Fraser was without complaint, Foggo without occasion to call any-one to order. It was a bad sign.

Then, far out on the left, there was an exchange of small-arms fire that echoed around the hills like Chinese crackers. Some Japanese had almost gained the crest, and, through his binoculars, Morris watched Torrance's platoon rise and run forward to repulse them. The glinting of bayonets flashed excitement from the left flank to the right. Drummond's men started to talk.

"It's the Skipper up in front," cried sharp-eyed Jannelli.

Craig was leading the charge. As he jerked forward, stiff-legged, he swung his arm. The noise of the bursting grenades and a faint tremor of shouting carried up to Morris's ears.

"They've done it," shouted Jannelli happily.

Morris relaxed, breathing deeply, craving a smoke. He felt reassured. He and his men needed only movement and noise to liberate them from the constrictions of fear. Movement and noise. He remembered the butcher's assistant in the recruit squad at the Depot, who—alone and unembarrassed—had enlivened the charges on empty trenches and sheep-grazed hills with his throat-swelling, eyes-starting bellow of "Scotland for ever!" Although the butcher-boy had been pitied and scorned by Morris and the other recruits, he had reached to the heart of the matter. He had heard the guns around him; he had seen his enemy waiting for him; and he had roared loud enough to fill all the bullet-swept space between them. But, at the end of his recruit-training, he had been labelled simple-minded and transferred to the Pioneers

There was a lull in the battle. Morris lit a cigarette and realised that he had got rid of his heartburn.

*

A very queer battle, thought George Sime. He felt that he was outside it, that it could not touch him. The little men on the distant, sunlit hillside and the far-off firing in the still, hot air had seemed out of place, out of reality. He had a clear idea of what a real battle looked and sounded like. He had only to close his eyes and he could hear the anger of the guns and see the bulky, sky-tall infantrymen moving forward in extended line, with rifles at the high port, through a haze of smoke. It was impossible to stay outside that kind of battle; it was possible to die in that kind of battle. Since the firing had stopped, the grasshoppers had started to chirp again. And that seemed to Sime to sum up all that he was trying to tell himself.

"They're withdrawing, the Japs," muttered Paterson. "They're going right down the hill."

"They give in pretty easy," said Sime. "It's only about two hours since the battle started."

"Listen to the big man!" scoffed Monkey Jackson. "Look at the medal on his chest already!"

Sime reddened. "I don't see—"

"Well, polish your bloody spectacles."

"I don't want to quarrel with you, Monkey."

"Too true, you don't. You know what'd happen to—"

With a twist like a startled lizard, Paterson swung away from his gun and drove his fist into Jackson's astonished face.

"Cut out the bobbery," shouted Barker.

Dazed and bleeding from the mouth, Jackson continued to stare at Paterson. There was a singing in Sime's head, as if he had taken some of the impact of the blow. The singing became a swishing sound that grew louder and louder, making him feel dizzy.

"Take cover," yelled Barker.

Sime was engulfed in a great explosion that flung him forward on his face. The noise battered at his head again and again, gradually losing its first violence. He felt sick at the stomach and tasted the red earth on his mouth.

"All right, George?"

He struggled to his side, gasping, "What happened?"

"Mortars," said Paterson grimly. "They're going to mortar some holes in our line before they attack again."

Sime sat up, adjusting his helmet and spectacles and rubbing the earth from his lips. He saw Jackson lying doggo and—feeling some guilt for the blow that the centre-half had suffered—he asked, "All right, Monkey?"

"Monkey's dead," said Paterson, and he spat down the hill. "The only one that copped it."

"Move back a bit," shouted Barker. "They've got our range here."

They moved back and left Jackson lying alone. As he crawled away, Sime looked incredulously at the corpse. It was unfair that it had to be Jackson.

*

Morris shouted another warning, and Jannelli held his face close to the ground. In the shadow of his helmeted head, he saw a small white sea-shell. The second shower of mortar bombs hissed down the still air and slapped against the crest of the hill, bursting in a fury of noise and vibration. Tears of sweat dropped from his face. It was funny—it was a funny place to find a sea-shell.

"Missed us again," cried Feltham. He reached out and touched Jannelli. "The Boy's got the right idea this time. If we keep moving about, they'll never get our range, will they?"

Jannelli raised his head slowly, listening to a new murmur in the air.

"It's a spotter plane," announced Wait. He looked up thin-faced at the sky and clenched his fingers round his thumbs. "They'll get our range now."

But the next bombs fell short again, blasting the dust from the bare crest. Piggy Fraser shouted at Morris and Drummond: "What's the sense of lyin' here waitin' to be killed? We're doin' no fightin' up here, are we?"

"Shut your mouth," yelled Drummond wildly.

"And keep it shut, you bastard," added Foggo.

Jannelli searched for another shell and wondered whether the ground that he was lying on had buckled up out of the sea in a primeval fury of thunder and earthquake against which bursting mortar bombs would have sounded like pricked soap bubbles. He wondered too whether he was the first member of the human race to touch this little white skeleton.

The fourth shower of bombs slapped down behind them, and, through the roaring waves that lashed up over them, Jannelli heard a long-drawn scream. It tore across his mind and made him distort his face as if he too were screaming. It was Feltham who had been hit. His back was a ragged mess of broken flesh and shattered bone. Even after the scream had rattled out in his distended throat, his body continued to jerk and twitch.

"Back to the crest," shouted Morris. He looked up at the circling biplane. "We'll have to keep moving."

Jannelli started to crawl up the hill, watching Fraser. Fraser was staring with fascinated horror at the dead Durham miner. McGuire scrambled away from him, leaving him unsheltered, and he did not seem to have the strength to follow. He clawed weakly at the ground and stared at the twitching corpse as if he could not separate himself from it, as if he had fallen heir to the agony.

*

Craig block-lettered a message to battalion headquarters, reporting that his company had repulsed the enemy's frontal assault, inflicting heavy casualties; that they were now standing fast under accurate air-directed mortar fire, suffering heavy casualties; and that stretcher-parties from H.Q. were urgently required. The angular words, the conventional phrases, did not give a true indication of the precariousness of the company's position. Mair knew well enough that they had no ammunition for their three two-inch mortars and could do nothing under bombardment but take punishment. But did he know yet that they were in danger of being outflanked? In a few cramped words, Craig reported that he was trying to renew contact with B Company, who had apparently fallen back to evade the mortar bombardment.

Soon after Craig had despatched the message by runner, Torrance reported hastily that there was no sign of B Company on the far side of the hill, that B Company's positions were already being occupied by the enemy. Even as Torrance spoke, Japanese machine-guns opened fire on his platoon from the top of the hill. Craig cursed McNaughton Smith and sent for Williamson.

"If we're going to cover both the flanks and the front," he told Williamson, "we'll have to get back there." He pointed to a knoll that lay behind them in a shallow depression at the mouth of the little valley between Torrance's hill and Morris's hill. "Take Anstey's platoon and two of Morris's sections back there immediately. Tell Morris to stay on top of the hill with one section—to keep an eye on the front and the right flank and give us early warning of any Jap moves. I'll stay here with Torrance's platoon and cover you till you're in position on the knoll. Got it?"

Williamson made a face like a pig and, although he was lying on the ground, contrived to salute. "Won't take me long," he promised. He sprang to his feet and sprinted across to the saddle between the hills, zig-zagging as if he had a rugby ball under his arm and a scattered defence between him and the goal-line.

Craig ran along the slope to join Torrance.

"They're coming down," Torrance reported. "We can't stop them. Too much cover up there."

The Japanese were darting from boulder to boulder, working their way downhill under cover of bursts of fire.

"When they get a bit closer, we can use grenades on them."

"No grenades left," said Torrance. He was looking tired. "You used most of them yourself."

A man on their left was hit.

"They've got the bulge on us here," shouted Sergeant Wade. "Can we pull back a bit?"

Craig looked round and saw below him a gully that had been eroded by heavy rains washing down into the basin which held the knoll. "Take a couple of sections down there," he told Torrance. "I'll cover you with the other section. Make it fast."

The subaltern smiled. "Going this way, even Williamson couldn't pass me." He shouted orders and led his party downhill.

Craig called for rapid fire from the covering section. But the heavy automatics above continued their thunderous stuttering. There were cries at Craig's back that made him wince. He glanced round and saw the casualties scattered down the slope and the survivors flinging themselves into the gully.

"We'll move back slowly," he told the covering section. "Keep on your bellies and don't panic. Take your time from me." He started to worm backwards and downwards.

On his way down he came upon Torrance. There were wounds in the subaltern's back. His helmet had fallen off, and his sweat-dampened hair and face were powdered with red dust.

Torrance opened his eyes. They were darker than usual. "Not quite fast enough," he said carefully.

"I'll have to drag you. It's not far."

"Don't leave Wade. He stopped to help me—got hit."

The wounded were dragged downhill, under fire, under torture. Torrance suffered in silence most of the way. It was only over the last few yards, when Craig had to move quickly over the lip of the gully, that the subaltern pleaded hoarsely, "For God's sake—leave me!"

In the gully, Craig took command of the platoon. He had the severely wounded—Torrance, Sergeant Wade and two privates—placed in cover, and he stood close to them to direct the platoon's fire. He felt vaguely, hurriedly, that, hearing his orders and encouragement to the firing line, they might be distracted from their pain.

He heard Torrance say to Wade, "We didn't get off this—bloody hill—after all."

Wade, whose legs were shattered, answered with trembling lips, "Ach, we got over the back of it, anyway."

They had disengaged themselves from the action and seemed ready to disengage themselves from life. There was nothing more Craig could do for them. It was for a man like Lumsden to assess their chances of survival, or for a man like Padre Ewen to bless the chance that they might not survive. There was nothing Craig could say to them, in the way of comfort. The only thing he had to say was that it would be impossible to move them down to the knoll, under fire. And it was too early to tell them that.

It was Sergeant Wade who noticed the signal from the knoll. "Mr. Williamson in position, sir," he reported.

Again, Craig sent two sections in advance. They reached the knoll without a casualty. Relieved, he lingered in the gully until a light mortar bomb exploded on the slope above. "Ranging shot," he said. "We'd better get out." He knelt down beside Torrance. "When they see us leave, they'll switch the mortars on to the knoll. You'll be all right here. I'll send up stretchers as soon as I can."

"Right," said Torrance. His face was pallid and strained, his yellow eyes discoloured.

Acting on impulse, Craig drew the subaltern's revolver from his holster and placed it in his right hand. Torrance looked at him and tried to smile. He understood. But he would not pull the trigger. He would cling to life till the last agonising moment.

Stiffly, Craig stood up and signalled to the covering section to withdraw.

"Best of luck, sir," muttered Wade.

Craig nodded, tight-lipped, and leapt out of the gully.

*

Morris watched the withdrawal to the knoll and, isolated on Golden Hill with Drummond's section, envied Craig, Williamson, Torrance and Anstey their comfortable proximity below.

"Keep your eyes open for a signal," he said hopefully to his runner. "They might be pulling us back soon now."

Williamson, when he had come to claim two sections, had told Morris that he was to keep the front and the right flank under observation, and it was not until the branky lieutenant had gone off with the best of the platoon that Morris had started to question the purpose of this observation. To secure the rest of the company against surprise—Undoubtedly. But for how long? Until they were in position on the knoll? Or until Craig decided that there was no longer any danger of surprise? There was room for doubt. And even assuming that Craig had intended him to stay on the hill till ordered to withdraw, Morris could still see room for doubt. The situation had radically changed since Craig had last been on the crest: the Japanese had disappeared from the front; the only movement in the last hour or two had been a leisurely withdrawal by a small party of Punjabis on the right flank: there was no shadow of threat from front or right flank to the men on the knoll. But the Japanese mortars were still trained on the crest. Feltham lay dead, and Wait had gone down to the knoll, nursing a broken arm.

Morris decided to take a last careful look around. If all was quiet, he would exercise his right of discretion as the commander on the spot and rejoin the rest of the company. He crawled over the crest and, while he was scanning the empty slopes below, he heard the swish of mortar bombs in the air and shouted warning.

Drummond's thigh was slashed open. He lay staring wildly away from the wound while Foggo applied a tourniquet. Trembling with fear and anger, Fraser turned to Morris: "It was your fault. They seen you movin' about."

Heart-sick of the whole section, Morris ordered them to withdraw. Foggo and McGuire carried Drummond. Ripley, Fraser and

Jannelli jolted wearily behind. It was a long descent, a glum procession.

Craig met them. "What's the matter?" he asked sharply.

Morris began to have misgivings. "It's all quiet. Except that they're still mortaring us."

"You were the only men in the battalion in a position to spot enemy preparations in front," Craig said cuttingly. "You'd better get back up there fast." Then he beckoned Morris aside and asked angrily, "You got my orders from Williamson?"

"I wasn't sure—"

"You can be sure this time. You wait for my order to withdraw. You realise this might be looked on as cowardice?"

"Is that the way *you* look on it?" asked Morris indignantly.

"I'm accepting your explanation," said Craig harshly.

With Ripley and the section of four men Morris climbed back to the bald top, golden-red under the high sun. He climbed in chastened silence, hating the hill, the steep hill with ugly eroded flanks that gave it a hungry look, the hard hill that did not yield underfoot or cushion falling hands and knees, the dry hill with no cover deep enough to absorb the heat, with only a scurf of brittle grass and a crawling and chirring of insects. He climbed as if he were climbing the sheer slope of noon, thighs and calves trembling with fatigue, heart pounding, blood hammering at his temples, throat and nose achingly dry, flesh bathed in sweat, chafed by damp clothes and heavy harness. His movements lost all precision and when a sniper opened fire from the left, it was all he could do to change his step and move over to the right.

*

Craig conveyed to Williamson the orders and information brought by runner from battalion headquarters. His voice sounded oddly loud in his own ears, now that the Japanese had lifted their bombardment of the knoll.

As he had guessed, the battalion had suffered a reverse on the left. Ketchen had been killed and McNaughton Smith wounded, and their companies had been driven back against the reserve line held by the survivors of A Company and a draft from Headquarters Company. A new line had been stabilised about half a mile north of Laichikok on the outskirts of Kowloon. There was no immediate danger of an enemy break-through, but the G.O.C. had decided to withdraw the Mainland Brigade to the island. The Scots and the

Punjabis were to be ferried across after dark. The Rajputs were to delay the Japanese for another day or two.

"Well," said Williamson, "that's that."

It was the end of more than Williamson could understand. It was the battalion, not the Mainland Brigade, that had been defeated, and the debit of that defeat could not be balanced by a credit of casualties. Compassion did not enter into the accountancy of battle.

"When do we start to withdraw?"

Bitterly, Craig ignored the complacent question until he had scribbled a message and dismissed the runner. "We've to fall back gradually," he said then. "First, we'll send the walking wounded down."

"Better the stretcher-cases first, eh?"

"There are no stretchers. All the bandsmen, cooks and clerks are manning a last-ditch position under Guthrie in front of Kowloon."

Williamson jerked up and down uneasily. "Make our own stretchers? Shirts and rifles."

With an impatient gesture Craig said, "We'll need our rifles."

"You can't carry stomach-wounds and chest-wounds over your shoulder."

"We'll have to leave them."

Williamson flushed with indignation.

"It's a long road back," said Craig harshly. "A hard road. We'd just torture them to death."

C.Q.M.S. Silver led out the first party of walking wounded, six men. C.S.M. Duncan led out the second party, five men. Anstey, wide-eyed and silent, led out his platoon, escaping a burst of machine-gun fire from the enemy up on the left flank. Williamson started to lead out Torrance's platoon and was caught by another burst of fire from the left. Two men fell and were left behind: a private splayed out in death; a wounded lieutenant. Williamson was close enough for Craig to see the shocked expression on his face as he twisted cautiously round to examine the injury to his carefully nourished and strenuously exercised body. He was predictable enough for Craig to guess at the torment he was suffering while he tried to classify himself as walking wounded or severely wounded. There was a confusion of pity and contempt in Craig as he watched. For once, at least, he did not try to explain his feelings. For once, he did not feel ashamed of his streak of cruelty.

Then Williamson gathered his limbs in to his body, sprang up and ran after his men. From his bloody slacks, it seemed that he had been hit in the buttocks. And that was that.

Craig was left with two sections of Morris's platoon and six severely wounded men on the knoll; four severely wounded—including Torrance—in the gully up on the left; and Morris and one section up on Golden Hill in front.

*

It was the first heavy mortar bombardment since the forenoon. As soon as he could emerge from the shock, Morris called to each of the scattered members of his party. On the right, Ripley, Foggo and Jannelli replied. On the left, McGuire and Fraser were silent. Crouching, he ran along the crest in search of them. Fraser was lying on his back, sobbing under restraint, unable to give full vent to his feelings for fear of aggravating the pain in his wounded belly.

"Steady," said Morris nervously, slipping one arm under the private's raised knees and easing the other under his back. "I'll try not to hurt you."

"Get Punchy, will you?" pleaded the little man. "Mr. Morris, get Punchy to carry me. You're hurtin' me. Oh, watch it! Oh!"

Morris lowered his burden and shouted for McGuire. There was no answer. "I'll look for him after I get you down the back of the hill. I can't leave you here. They might mortar us again." Looking away from the ugly distorted face, clenching his teeth against the anguished complaints and tormented cries, he carried Fraser down to a patch of shadow. From there, he saw McGuire sheltering further along the back of the hill, and called him across. "Didn't you hear me shouting before?" he demanded.

McGuire stared stolidly past him.

"Punchy," croaked Fraser.

Jannelli appeared above, shouting and pointing. Morris turned round and saw someone on the knoll giving him the signal to withdraw. He heaved a deep breath.

"Right." He grinned at Fraser. "Punchy can carry you down now."

McGuire scowled.

"Pick him up," ordered Morris, "and carry him down slowly." They started the long descent.

"I don't want to see this hill again," said Jannelli, smiling, excited.

"Me neither," muttered Ripley hoarsely.

"Save your breath," ordered Foggo.

At the knoll they were welcomed by Barker's and Macdonald's sections. But before Morris had time to greet Meechan and relax in the atmosphere of platoon loyalty, Craig took him aside and gave him orders for the withdrawal.

"I'll take your other two sections back. You can wait here and get your wind. You'd better hang on for half an hour to make sure the Japs don't follow too close on our heels."

Morris accepted the task of rearguard with one qualification: "Could you take McGuire and Fraser and leave me two other men?"

Although Craig's expression did not alter, it was possible to sense the sudden gathering of anger in him. "Fraser's done for. No point in carrying him any further."

And Morris noticed then, with sick apprehension, badly wounded men from the other platoons, lying near by.

*

Mrs. Gow insisted on everyone retreating to the cellar.

"We have seventy-five per cent protection here," she argued. "Three sides out of four are bomb-proof," she added for the benefit of old Willox, who had raised his heavy white eyebrows. As the house was built on a steep slope of the Peak, only three walls of the cellar were subterranean, the fourth concrete wall being weakened by the windows overlooking the harbour.

"You've forgotten the ceiling and the floor," Willox suggested sourly. Then the first bombs fell, and he transferred his ill-will to his wife, who was moaning nervously. "Put something over your face," he advised. "There are children present."

The three children were sitting together in a corner, conversing in fierce whispers, while their mother—Jenny Brewster—leaned close to young Peter Deveaux for comfort.

"It's time Singapore sent us some fighter planes," he muttered to her.

"You think they've got defences to spare?" demanded Willox. "After losing the *Prince of Wales* and the *Repulse*?"

"Don't forget the children," quavered his wife vindictively.

Mrs. Gow wondered what on earth had possessed her to allow

these people refuge in her house. "We're not very well liked," old Willox had admitted. "Not many places we can show our faces in, and we've got to find some place safer than our own." And Tim Brewster had earnestly assured her: "Roderick insisted. I said I didn't want to inflict three children—not to mention Jenny—on you. But you know what he's like." And Mrs. Deveaux, the massive, hard-drinking widow, had led in her crippled son of twenty-five and announced: "I've got to know Peter's safe while I'm working at the hospital. I won't bother you much myself. Bed-and-breakfast sort of thing will do for me. And then of course there was Maud . . .

Mary and Maud were sitting on either side of a window, staring out. They had come home early from the hospital, complaining that there were too many auxiliary nurses. They were both rather peaky-looking. Maud, too, had a young man over on the mainland.

Mrs. Gow longed for Roderick to return and help her to cope.

Jenny was whispering to Peter, "But didn't I hear Tim saying that the Scotch battalion had been pushed back?"

"I don't like that kind of gossip," said Mrs. Gow, surprising herself with her firmness.

Peter withdrew his hand from Jenny's plump arm. Eager to conciliate, he stammered, "The c-communique today said that the situation was well in hand."

Reddening with anger, old Willox kicked the paint off a chair-leg.

*

It was time to leave. Morris stood up and looked around. All quiet. The quiet hills, the quiet dead scattered like litter, the quiet wounded lying on the knoll. Quiet himself, he gathered the four survivors of his party and started to lead them out.

Jannelli caught up with him. "What about Fraser, sir?"

Morris did not halt. "Fraser and all the others are too badly wounded to move."

Then there was a scream from Fraser. "Don't leave me, Punchy."

"I'll help to carry him," offered Jannelli.

"It's not that," explained Morris angrily, stopping and turning when Fraser screamed again. "He wouldn't last it out."

Lance-Corporal Foggo stared back at the knoll. "That bastard's making it worse for the others."

"Get him," decided Morris. "Go back and get him. Quick, McGuire, before he screams again."

McGuire muttered that he was tired.

"Give him a hand, Jannelli."

As the two men walked back to the knoll, Ripley commented: "'Ell of a man, McGuire. Not much of a mucker, like."

Morris nodded. Not much of a comrade.

*

"They're pulling out," said Torrance. "The last of them. Can you see who they are?"

Wade did not answer.

Torrance lifted his head carefully and saw that the sergeant was dead. They were dying in order of rank in the gully. The two privates had died first.

He found a smooth, cool stone by his side and held it until it felt as warm as his hand . . . until it felt warmer than his hand.

*

His high-crowned narrow-brimmed hat like an elongation of his head, Sammy King might have passed for Lao Sze-shin, god of longevity. Instead of an almond, he was holding melon seeds.

James Lin stared at him, closed the door, and walked across to the window. "The police are quitting Kowloon," he announced. "Rioting and looting have started already. Wang Ching-wei renegades are in uniform and carrying arms."

"Everybody," said Sammy, "gives a kick to a tumbling wall."

"I've left it too late." James looked down into the bannered street. "I should have gone this morning." Business was booming for the fortune-teller across the way. Instead of digging trenches or building barricades or searching for weapons, people were paying for glimpses into a fabulous future. "We're a shiftless race, Sammy."

"Speak for yourself, boy. I got no call to go to Kowloon."

James put on his spectacles. "We talk too much. We don't do enough."

"That's the way we like it."

"We laugh too readily. We submit too often."

Sammy cracked a seed between his teeth.

"We are too wise, and not clever enough."

James sat down. Would it still be possible to reach Anna? Could she be persuaded to change her mind and leave with him? Could she be escorted through the streets without injury? Would she really be safer on the island than in Kowloon? . . .

*

Forcing their way through dense scrub that tore their khaki drill and scratched their flesh, they came upon a concrete nullah.

"Catchment," panted Ripley. "For the reservoir, like."

"It'll take us down to the road, sir," said Foggo, leaning against a tree to rest his bow legs.

McGuire grumbled, "Time somebody else took a turn with Piggy." His heavy face dripped sweat.

"Jannelli's not complaining," said Morris.

McGuire licked his upper lip and looked down at Fraser's unconscious body.

"I'll spell you," offered Morris contemptuously.

They followed the winding nullah down the steep slope and found a road. While Foggo scouted up the road, Morris consulted his map. "We're on this road here." He pointed for Ripley's benefit. "Runs from Smugglers Pass down to the Taipo road." He looked around, searching the descending road and the hills—glazed with the yellow light of late afternoon—for the rest of the company. "The Skipper must have meant the Taipo road. He forgets I don't know this place from the Garden of Eden." He whistled for Foggo and went to help Jannelli lift Fraser again. Weakly conscious, the little man opened his putty-coloured lips and asked for McGuire.

"We're giving him a spell," said Jannelli.

"Punchy!" called Fraser, gathering his strength.

Morris turned to McGuire, who was sitting a few yards away. "Over here," he ordered.

"Punchy!"

"He's coming," said Jannelli.

"Punchy!" Fraser shut his frightened green eyes and opened his mouth wide in a last spasm of pain. By the time McGuire had shambled up to his side, he was dead. They stood round him in silence.

"All right," said Morris angrily. "Let's go." It was easier to leave corpses sprawling over a battlefield than to leave Fraser lying neatly at the side of the road. "Come on, *jildi*."

At the bottom of the road, Kerr—the signals officer—was waiting, neat and friendly, beside his motor-cycle. "I'll take your chaps to the company position, round the corner, on the Taipo road.

The Old Man wants to see you." He pointed to a summer-house sheltered by tall trees, and clapped him on the shoulder. "No raspberries this time, Johnny."

As Morris approached the summer-house, Mair appeared on the verandah and came briskly down the steps. "All right, eh?" he asked with an awkward smile. "None the worse, eh?"

"I'm all right, sir, thanks."

"Good, good. Come in and have a seat and tell me about it." Uncomfortably Morris followed him into a cool room, where redhaired Farquhar sat at a table covered with books and maps. "Get Morris a drink. Sit down. Sit down, old man. Any difficulty disengaging from the enemy?"

It was tempting to lie, to fabricate a story worthy of the occasion. "They had withdrawn from Golden Hill, I think, sir. At least, they didn't harass us."

"I should think not," said Mair approvingly. "They'd had enough, eh?"

"I suppose so, sir."

Mair nodded. His smile became a reflective frown. "Have a drink," he urged. "I'll be back in a minute."

As the C.O. strode outside again, Farquhar held out a very large whisky. "The day hasn't gone too well for the battalion," he explained, when Morris scowled in bewilderment at the hero's draught. "Don Company put up the best show by far."

"So that's it. Well, I didn't have much to do with it."

Farquhar shrugged his shoulders. "I don't discriminate. The Old Horse picks the heroes. I just pour the drinks. First for Anstey, then for Craig, now for you."

Morris looked up from his whisky. "What about Torrance and Williamson? Are they not back yet?"

The assistant adjutant stared blankly, and withdrew to his chair. "Williamson went straight down to the rear—wounded in the buttocks. Torrance—you haven't heard?" He stared again.

"Heard what?" asked Morris harshly.

"He was left behind," Farquhar said. "He was badly wounded." Morris stood up slowly.

"They couldn't move him."

Morris leaned against the table.

"There were others too," said Farquhar nervously. "I've marked them all *Died of wounds*, but, somehow, it doesn't seem right. I

G

mean—they may not be dead yet. I'm not denying, of course, that it was more merciful to let them lie."

"But Torrance—"

"Drink up," pleaded Farquhar.

Morris gulped down the whisky. It caught fire in his empty stomach, and the flames rose, twisting giddily, to his head. He found the chair and sat down.

"Craig told you about Torrance?"

"Yes. I'd better get your casualties listed too."

"Where was he hit?"

"I don't know."

"Was he conscious?"

"I don't know. Now, let's get your casualties down."

Morris tried to remember, but he could not see past Torrance, and he was sliding away from Farquhar.

*

It was Roderick who brought the news that the garrison was evacuating the mainland. Flustered, he blurted out the few details he had heard.

Willox said sourly: "Well? We always knew the men on the mainland were only there to delay the Japs."

"Delay?" Roderick was more surprised than indignant. "From Monday till Thursday—you call that delay? Bless us, there hasn't been time to bring all the supplies across or to blow up the installations."

"Maybe the folks that are left Kowloon-side will need some supplies and installations," said Willox, raising his voice.

"What's wrong?" asked Jenny Brewster from the doorway.

Since both the men remained silent, Mrs. Gow broke the news.

"What's happening to the civilians?" asked Peter, appearing at Jenny's back.

"The ferry's still operating," muttered Roderick.

"The auxiliary nurses—" Peter limped into the room. "They'll get across all right?"

Roderick turned his back on Willox. "I don't know," he said irritably.

Tim Brewster, when he arrived later, knew. "They've been told to stay at their posts." Peter, with a stricken look on his face, left the room. "He has too many girl-friends," said Mrs. Willox.

Later still, after the evening meal, Jenny made the remark that

Mrs. Gow had been waiting for. "It wasn't the Indians who gave way. It was the Scotch battalion. Tim heard this afternoon." Now it was Mary's turn to leave the room. Jenny raised a hand, as if to stop her, and, after the door had slammed, opened her eyes and mouth wide to assure everyone, "I didn't mean to hurt her feelings."

"True, true." Roderick indicated, by shaking his head and his glass of whisky, that no harm had been done. "She must face facts, like the rest of us." And with a tolerant smile, he explained unnecessarily, "She's known Hugh Craig of the Scots for a long time."

But she hadn't known herself for very long . . . Mrs. Gow sat still, feeling helpless.

*

Farquhar touched Morris to life again. The room was dark, the table was bare, and the assistant adjutant was harnessed for the march.

"Time to go, old man. Your platoon's waiting outside."

"What!" Morris struggled to his feet. "Why didn't you waken me before?" His head ached, his mouth was sour, and his stomach was sickeningly empty.

"C.O.'s orders."

Shivering, Morris stumbled outside.

A voice spoke harshly in the dark: "Get your fingers out. On to the road, *chullo*." It was Sergeant Meechan. He approached smartly, thrust his face close, and stared quizzically. "I told you. You could kip on a flagpole."

"Growing lads need their sleep," said Morris, grateful for the sergeant's presence.

"You grow any more and you'll turn into a flag-pole."

They smiled uneasily and drew apart. While Meechan gave the platoon the order to march, Farquhar told Morris: "The Japs don't seem to be following up, but we'd better move fast. Go straight down the road till you meet Birse with the transport to take you down to the ferry. Anstey's ahead of you. Craig will follow with Torrance's platoon."

Torrance.

Morris caught up with the rear section of the platoon, Barker's section, and fell into step. The men were marching with the jerky, stiff-legged gait of fatigue. Angrily he told them to get their heads up. Only one man in the section responded by squaring his shoulders; and a distinction of moonlight blanched his uplifted round face and shone on his spectacles. From the front came Meechan's impassive descant, "Keep in to the side of the road."

Morris marched on, thinking of Torrance dead. No more bare legs in bed for Torrance: his legs would soon be bare to the bone.

The wooded hills on the west fell away, and a breeze blew in from the sea, clean and cold and smelling of tangle. From the hills on the east came a faint challenge, which Meechan answered.

"Major Guthrie's party," explained Ripley, suddenly appearing. "Last ditch, like."

Some of Guthrie's men rose out of the dark scrub and waved pale hands. "Good old Don!" they shouted.

Barker's section responded, raising their heads at last and murmuring among themselves. "Good old Major Guthrie!" shouted Sime.

"Shut up," said Morris savagely.

A few minutes later, the platoon reached their transport. Birse —looking, in his helmet, greatcoat and equipment, unlike the man who had brought dirty magazines into the mess—directed them to commandeered buses. "Keep your heads well down," he advised. "There are fifth-column snipers in Kowloon."

Morris wondered about Anna. Disregarding Birse's warning, he kept his face close to the bus window. At the mouth of the street leading towards the district where Anna lived, a crowd were jostling around a bonfire. It was the brightest light he saw on the journey, and he was tempted to regard it as an omen, and thought confusedly of the destroying flame, the glimmer of hope.

Aboard the crowded ferry Craig sought him out. "Well done, Johnny," he said quietly.

"Whatever I did," said Morris bitterly, "I didn't do well."

Craig looked at him in silence for a moment, and turned away.

There were scattered, flickering lights in Kowloon that, seen from mid-channel, gave the old city the appearance of having already been sacked. But Hongkong island—the backbone of steep hills and the city of Victoria cramped along the narrow north shore —was in disciplined darkness. The men on the ferry stood close together and silent.

On the dark island the company marched by platoons from the

Naval Dockyard to Murray Barracks, where they were fed with bread and tea and allowed to rest for a few hours. When he shut his eyes, Morris tried to think of Anna, tried to forget Torrance.

*

On the hill, the stone and the hand that held it were both cold now.

PART FOUR

The Island

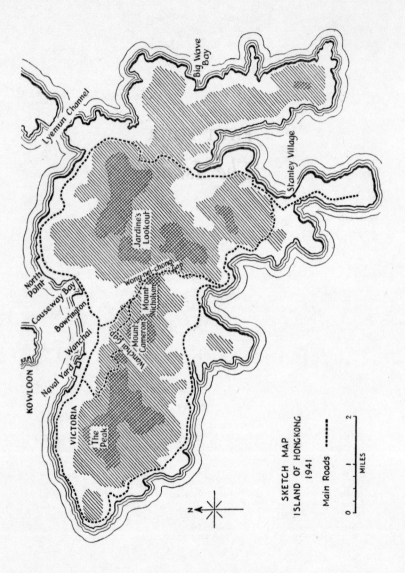

Big Wave Bay

Lyemun Channel

Stanley Village

Jardine's Lookout

Wong-nei-chong Gap

North Point

Causeway Bay

Bowrington

KOWLOON

Naval Yard

Wanchai

Mount Cameron

Mount Nicholson

Wanchai Gap

VICTORIA

The Peak

N

SKETCH MAP
ISLAND OF HONGKONG
1941

Main Roads -------

0   1   2
MILES

Chapter One

"Now," said Craig, "we make a fresh start."

He walked into the main ground-floor room of the abandoned house in which he had been ordered to set up his headquarters, lifted the only table large enough to serve as a desk—a blackwood table with a bowl of languid flowers on it—and carried it into the light from the window. The flowers shed their sickly petals, and some discoloured water spilled out of the bowl, and he had to restrain an impulse to dash table, bowl and flowers against the wall.

It was the kind of occasion that searched out his inadequacies. His three companions—C.S.M. Duncan, C.Q.M.S. Silver and Lieutenant Holt, his new second-in-command—stood silent at the door. It would take more than brisk talk of a fresh start and clumsy movement of furniture to inspirit them. Holt was still the intelligence officer, with a displaced look on his sharp face; and the warrant officers had not yet had time to wear their memories of Golden Hill thin enough to see through. It was an occasion that called for the wounded McNaughton Smith's panache, or the missing Wilson's poker-faced wit, or the dead Ketchen's barrack-room familiarity.

The battalion had suffered a humiliating defeat. They had been defeated by men they had held in scorn, by the Frogs with slant eyes, bow legs and cloven-toed canvas-and-rubber boots, by orientals. West had been defeated by East, the traditionally active, thrusting West by the traditionally passive, submitting East.

The extravagant praise that had been lavished on D Company, for standing fast on the right of the line, did not deceive Craig. A simple measure of the extravagance was that Morris had suddenly become widely known throughout the battalion as the man who had stayed on top of Golden Hill. Morris, who had been driven back to his post, who had done nothing but take punishment. Morris, who himself had a taint of the East, with his unassertive manner and his Chinese girl-friend. The extravagance of the praise was, Craig recognised, a simple measure of the battalion's humiliation, the humiliation that had now to be wiped out in a fresh start.

"Get something to clean up this mess with, Silver," he said quietly, falling back on the only tactics that came easily to him. "Open the window, Duncan. It smells musty in here." He beckoned to Holt. "Pull up a chair. We've a lot to do."

Before dawn, the battalion had moved in trucks from Murray Barracks, in the heart of Victoria, eastwards along the main north-shore road, to take over the defence of the north-east coast. It was a temporary assignment, pending the evacuation of the Rajputs from the mainland; and the responsibility of the role was comparatively slight, since the sector commanded the stretch of sea-channel that was already covered by the Rajputs in their last-ditch positions on the mainland. The intention of the G.O.C. was that the shaken battalion should seize the opportunity to refit and reorganise.

Craig had already reorganised his company into two platoons, making up Morris's complement with the survivors of Torrance's platoon, and Anstey's complement with clerks, drivers, bandsmen and convalescent malaria patients. He had posted Morris in front, to man three pillboxes along Causeway Bay, and Anstey on open ground in the rear.

"First," he instructed Holt, "a list of weapons and ammunition, including the Vickers guns Morris has inherited with the pillboxes."

"Does Morris know anything about Vickers guns?"

"No, but Meechan does."

"And Anstey?"

Craig detected the critical tone, but answered patiently, "He's not quite so ignorant as Morris is."

"Then why put Morris in front? After all, he suffered heavier casualties than Anstey did."

"Morris," said Craig reluctantly, "is probably sounder than Anstey. Does that answer you?"

"Perfectly," said Holt, with great composure. "I entirely agree."

Weapons and ammunition, wrote Craig.

He might be wrong about Morris, Chinese Morris. It was on the ferry that he had glimpsed once again the potential soldier in

Morris. What was it Morris had said?—No matter. It was the spirit behind the words that had impressed.

"That's the siren," announced Duncan.

Fire tasks and firing policy

Lyon light policy

Very light signals

He might be wrong about Morris. He might be wrong about Anstey. He did not know them as he knew Torrance now.

"Air-raid," said Silver gloomily, as he came in to wipe the table.

Double sentries

Challenges in Chinese

Tools for shallow trench latrines

Bedding and clothing

Bombs fell in the distance.

"Nothing to stop them," said Duncan bitterly, from the window. "Not enough ack-ack to scatter the hawks."

Foot inspection

"Come over here," ordered Craig. "There's work to be done. You can start to list the wounded on duty."

Wounded on duty

War-diary

Even on a fresh start, you had to account for the failures of the past.

*

Tim Brewster was the second man in the queue. Sweating and smiling, he unbuttoned his jacket, hooked his thumbs over his belt, spread his fingers across his paunch, and waited his turn.

It was a long time since he had last committed all his energies to a single task, and in the intervening years he had forgotten the intensity of the rewarding sense of liberation. He had disintegrated into a series of different men—businessman, husband, father, member of the Fanling Golf Club and elder of the Presbyterian church in Nathan Road; the thematic Timothy John Brewster had been obscured by the variations. But now he had remade himself, had revitalised his one hundred and sixty-five pounds of custom-worn substance, and he had done so merely by deciding to use himself—muscles, wits, love, and the aggregate of accepted dogma and instinct that, for want of another word, he called his conscience—as an agent of death. T. J. Brewster, sometime representative of Messrs. Dunne, Makers and Stein, now representative of the Dark Angel. It was damnably queer.

Damnably queer. He had walked into the breakfast-room, with less than his usual appetite, telling himself that the arrival of the two Lins had led to over-crowding, that the house was beginning to smell of women and children; and, as Mrs. Gow was passing him a cup of coffee, and Roderick was saying that the evacuation of the mainland would shake civilian morale, he had announced— to himself as well as to the others at the table—that he was going to enlist in the Volunteers. Surprised, trying to trace the origins of his resolve and to examine its implications, he had almost yielded to Jenny's entreaties—acknowledged his responsibilities, admitted that his heart was unsound—and almost withdrawn from the venture, with his good reputation enhanced and his smooth skin intact. But the resolve had taken possession of him. And now he was second man in the long queue.

The first man in the queue—a middle-aged Eurasian—was holding things up. Eagerly apologetic and excitedly confused, he was explaining to the clerk behind the table that he had intended to enlist much earlier, even before the Japanese invasion.

Jack Finlayson, looking thinner and less nonchalant than usual, brushed his way into the office. "What the hell's holding us up?" he demanded.

The embarrassed clerk said: "I've finished with him, sir. I've got his particulars."

Finlayson stared at the Eurasian and asked: "What's your name?"

"Franco Mendes."

"Right, Mendes. Move on."

Brewster stepped forward and nodded to Finlayson. "Didn't expect to see you here."

The captain touched his ginger moustache and muttered: "Convalescent still. Got a devil of a dose of malaria during a stunt on the mainland before the balloon went up. Well, see you later, Tim. Can't hold things up, y'know."

"Name?" asked the clerk.

"Timothy John Brewster."

*

"And James?" asked Mrs. Gow, a kindly, bewildered expression on her sallow face.

"He's coming with me," claimed Mr. Gow.

"Shouldn't he have a rest?"

"Bless us, he has no intention of resting, my dear. If I don't take him with me, he'll be running after Tim Brewster."

"James? Nonsense!" said Mrs. Gow.

As he stood like a ventriloquist's doll between the Gows, James Lin was reminded of his paternal grandmother, who had enlivened the last years of her somnolently secure matriarchy by putting rebellious words into her children's mouths in order to provide herself with opportunities for eloquent reproach. The truth was that he had hoped to rest, had little enthusiasm for Mr. Gow's choice of patriotic labour, and had no enthusiasm for military service. But, grateful to the Gows for letting him shelter Anna in their house, he was ready to submit himself to their will.

"In China, morale is a matter of rice," said Mr. Gow for the third time.

"Not that you wouldn't make a good soldier," Mrs. Gow nervously assured James.

"One recruit more or less won't affect the army's morale," said her husband. "But another man on rice distribution—especially the kind of man who can thumb his nose at the Director of Medical Services—will definitely help to bolster civilian morale."

"I'm sure Roderick's right."

James smiled. "You have persuaded me."

*

Mrs. Gow sat on the end of the bed and asked, "Feeling better?"

Anna Lin smiled shyly. "It's very kind of you—"

"Nonsense! I'm terribly glad James brought you here." She touched the girl's hand, grateful for her gentle company. "You must be very proud of him."

Observing the sudden hesitancy of Anna's smile, she abandoned the topic and smoothed the bed-cover. She thought the girl's attitude rather absurd (and curiously un-Chinese), but Jenny Brewster had already made plain that others would share the attitude. There was, apparently, a moral principle involved. Mrs. Gow disdained argument about moral principles. Ethics was the sandy site that men had laboriously created as a basis for the building of their patriarchal claims. Applying the intellect to matters that were essentially intuitive was like supping soup with a fork. Mrs. Gow knew, without any rational effort, that James had done right in bringing his sister back to the island. To argue, as Jenny had done, that either *all* the nurses should have been brought across to the island or *all* the nurses should have stayed at their posts in Kowloon was not to miss the point, but to make a point that any sheep could make. And if, after the tearful scene she had made over Tim's blithe departure, Jenny had the gall to play the Roman matron and wound Anna with spiteful references to her dereliction of duty, she would go, on the instant, bag and baggage, baggage and brood. Mrs. Gow would get Roderick to issue the marching orders.

"Roderick and James have gone down to help with the rice distribution in the city, but they promised to come back as early as possible. I feel terribly isolated without Roderick these days—even although the house is crammed with people. But you'll keep me company now."

Anna looked embarrassed.

"You're not"—guessed Mrs. Gow, momentarily unable to conceal her disappointment—"wanting to go back to nursing?"

"Yes."

"You don't have to, you know. They don't need any more nurses. They don't need me. Nobody would hold it against you—" Mrs. Gow checked the false assurance—surprised, ashamed, even frightened as she recognised how desperately she wanted the young girl's placid company.

"If you would like me to stay—" Anna responded sensitively.

Mrs. Gow touched her hand again. "Mary will take you down to the hospital." She rose and started to tidy the room—two of her Chinese boys had deserted. "Tomorrow, perhaps. I don't think that she or Maud will be going down today." She could not say for certain. They had gone straight back to their bedroom after Maud had received the news of her boy-friend's death on the mainland. And Mrs. Gow could not bring herself to approach them.

*

It was the next day—Saturday—before Morris felt ready to make a fresh start, before he could look across the no-man's blue-water channel at the enemy-occupied mainland without immediately thinking of the dead lying in their little enclaves on the hills.

He slept for a few hours after dawn and wakened with a strong desire to clean himself. While Ripley went in search of water, Morris kept himself apart from Barker and his section, sat against the rear wall of the pillbox, with his feet drawn back out of the way and his head between his knees, unwilling to speak or be spoken to until he was clean. He began to doubt whether Ripley would be successful. The tenements alongside the recreation ground behind the pillbox and a good number of the small craft in Causeway Bay in front of the pillbox were still occupied, but the Chinese occupants might be unwilling to lend a bucket or to part with water. Craig had spoken about the likelihood of a water shortage: the mainland reservoirs had formerly supplied more than half of the island's piped water.

On Ripley's cheerful summons, Morris hurried outside.

"It's not 'ot," the runner apologised, setting an enamel pail on the pavement. "They say"—he jerked his thumb and his sharp nose towards the tenements—"they're short of firewood."

"Fine," said Morris gratefully. And there, on the pavement, under a clouded sky that held the rumble of distant gunfire, he made his fresh start.

He washed and shaved, brushed his teeth, combed his hair, trimmed his nails, changed his socks (the only articles of clothing in his pack), rubbed his boots with a sheet of Chinese newspaper, rinsed his dirty socks and hung them to dry inside the pillbox, on a rung of the short iron ladder to the observation-slits in the turret. And then, making him feel that he was acting in harmony with some progressive, ameliorative ordering of events, Silver and the company storeman arrived with a bundle of shirts, slacks and woollen jerseys. In a panglossian mood, Morris reproved Sime for ungraciously enquiring about underwear.

Silver was loudly welcomed. The first sure indication of the men's recovery from the shock of battle had been their grumbling about the loss of all their belongings on the mainland. Recounting the contents of their abandoned kit-bags and boxes, they had found comfort in a new kind of rivalry, in which each tried to claim the heaviest loss. On their own reckoning, Barker and his section of ten men were poorer to the extent of at least eight hundred pounds sterling: they had left behind—in addition to the usual kit of infantry soldiers—such articles as a piano-accordion, a mah-jongg set in solid ivory, two carved camphorwood chests, a silver swimming trophy, three cameras, and a pair of snakeskin shoes which Sime had had made by hand from paper patterns of his wife's feet. In contrast, Silver's offerings were paltry; but they were fresh possessions. And, except for Sime's enquiry about underwear, the C.Q.M.S. was given a welcome that plainly startled him.

Launching himself on the mood of the moment, Morris ordered the sections to borrow brushes and sweep out and air the pillboxes. There was a strong smell of the previous, Indian occupants in the concrete cells, which caused him to wonder what kind of stink the Scots made in Indian nostrils. Ignoring complaints about the lack of water-containers and toilet gear, he also insisted that every man should wash, shave and change into fresh uniform before noon. To restore general good humour and to answer his own craving for a smoke, he asked Ripley to pass the hat round the platoon and try his luck at buying cigarettes and other comforts in the densely populated area west of the bay. He gave Ripley four dollars and seventy-five cents—all the money he had in his pockets—and then, to escape the noisy activity in the pillboxes, he started to walk along the sea-front.

He did not yet have a map of the island, but he knew that he was about halfway along the north shore. Across the water lay Kowloon peninsula, foreshortened now into an unimpressive stretch of hazy godowns and wharves, concrete blocks and cranes and towers, between the deserted channel and the cloudy dragon-hills. Westwards on the island lay the city of Victoria, climbing from the narrow shore into the backbone of hills. Eastwards, the bulge of North Point—where a power station and other industrial premises stood—blocked his view. Behind him, Happy Valley cut deep into the hills, cluttered on the lower levels with buildings, cemeteries and a race-course. All in all, it seemed an improbable battlefield.

His own front typified the complexities of defence. Causeway Bay, an anchorage for small craft, was crowded with junks, sampans, yachts, launches and dinghies, and he looked seawards through a forest of masts, spars and rigging. On the junks and sampans, hundreds of Chinese continued to live quietly and calmly. Some of them watched him now. Sitting on decks, scraping vegetables, washing clothes, mending brown sails, they looked up as he walked along the road.

Their nearness disturbed him—not simply because they blocked his view, not simply because he might have to fire over their heads or into their midst when the Japanese invaded the island, but also because he might have to commit acts of war in front of witnesses. Before dawn broke on him on Golden Hill, he could have taken pleasure in the thought of fighting before spectators, could have

believed that the presence of friends beyond red firing-flags would
heighten a soldier's courage, harden his resolve. But, after Golden
Hill, it seemed to him that it would be—*indecent* for any un-
committed person to spy on battle.

A spinning shell passed overhead, caught up his attention, and
exploded his overwrought ideas in the hills. He winced and swore.

As he walked along the front, the nearness of so many people—
men, women and children—began to disturb him in another way.
He might see Anna—on her way to some hospital. Or Nell might
come to visit him—with a basket of comforts. Disturbing thoughts
—flashes of sanity weakening his helmeted will.

The air-raid sirens wailed another warning. He walked back
towards Barker's pillbox, and fixed his gaze on the timber-yard
about thirty yards to its right front, at the eastern corner of the
bay. The high board fence around the yard and the tall stacks of
weathering planks inside offered excellent cover for invaders. He
had already suggested to Craig that fence and stacks should be
removed by coolie labour, and Craig had merely promised to
consider the suggestion.

"*Cumshaw! Cumshaw!*"

Two tiny half-naked Chinese boys had appeared with outstretched hands. He was feeling inside his pocket before he remembered that he had given Ripley all his money. "Get to hell out of
here," he said impatiently. "Go home, d'you hear? *Chop-chop!*"
Grinning, they stood their ground until he made to cuff their
shaven heads; then they scampered along the front to one of the
junks.

An improbable battlefield. An intolerably small, dark and airless
pillbox.

During the raid, Ripley returned, laden with cigarettes and
pomelos. The smokers gave him a welcome that surpassed the
welcome to Silver. Sime, the only non-smoker in the section, was
less than satisfied. "This," he explained, holding his bitter fruit
before him, "is what you eat to give you an appetite. Like grape-
fruit or tomato juice."

Ripley looked round the gloomy interior, mouth and eyes wide
open. "That's the thanks you get," he exclaimed hoarsely. "That's
gratitude, like. You want to go yourself next time, George."

Sime looked sad and embarrassed. "It's just—well, we could have
done with something solid, when we're on two bare meals a day."

"George," said Barker kindly, "there's a bloody war on. The Chinks won't sell you real chow. Anything else—a rickshaw, a fourteen-year-old virgin, the pants off their own legs—but not chow. Eat up your pomelo and don't spit the pips on the floor."

Morris inhaled smoke and grinned. He was glad that he had chosen to lodge with Barker—broad face, broad mind; square in build, square in dealing.

Mollified, Ripley took a share of the comforts to the other two pillboxes, and the section settled down to wait out the raid. Sime sat on the concrete floor, the centre of attention as he cut his pomelo in halves with his bayonet, carefully wiped the bayonet with a grimy handkerchief, handed one half to Paterson and cautiously started to suck the other half. Blind to the watching eyes, he distorted his face, smacked his lips and persevered.

"Not so much noise," grumbled Lance-Corporal Arkison, wet-mouthed and envious.

Sime wiped a spirt of juice from his spectacles. "You should have a spoon," he explained, by way of apology.

"You'll get the peel, Arkison," sneered Paterson. He sat against a wall, his lean dark face almost lost in shadow.

Barker improvidently smoked one cigarette after another.

These were the men that Morris watched: Barker taking things as they came; Arkison thinking from his belly; Sime sucking a pomelo, without relish but with splendid resolve; Paterson containing his old anger in the shadow. They were his own men, and he felt towards them as he could not feel towards Torrance's men. Even Paterson's implacable enmity made a stronger claim on him than the strangers' mild friendliness.

After the raid, Craig telephoned to warn him that the C.O. and the padre were visiting the lines, that several fifth-columnists had been arrested less than half a mile west of Causeway Bay, and that the Japanese were collecting craft in Kowloon Bay. In retaliation he reminded Craig about the timber-yard.

"The odds are," said Craig, "that the Japanese will level the site for you—with a bomb or a shell."

Indignantly Morris replaced the receiver.

"He's not going to get the timber shifted?" guessed Barker.

"He's waiting for the Japs to do it—with high explosive."

Barker laughed heartily. "He's a character."

Morris stood by the telephone and began to smile. Craig was

more than a character. The very thought of him was almost as energising as an independent act of will.

At midday, Morris and Sergeant Meechan started to inspect the platoon. They had reached Macdonald's pillbox, and Meechan was testing the proficiency of the Vickers' team, when the C.O. and the padre arrived. Morris hurried to meet them as they stepped down from their truck. Mair carried his ash stick, and Ewen carried a carton of cigarettes, the pastors of the flock, with crook and comfort. Morris halted smartly before them and saluted.

"Everything all right, eh?" enquired Mair. His tone was jovial, but his bright blue eyes were restlessly watchful.

"Yes sir. We're settling in."

The C.O. inspected the pillbox, spoke cheerfully to several of the men, and led Morris back to the truck. "Good, good," he said vaguely, tapping his stick on the ground, still restless and watchful. "You saw the launch this morning?"

Considerately Ewen explained, "The Japanese came over for a peace parley—in a launch flying a white flag."

"We didn't spot it," Morris admitted reluctantly. "Our front" —he waved his hand towards the bay—"is badly obscured."

"Naturally," said Mair, looking in another direction, "we're fighting on. No surrender."

Uncertain as to what was expected of him, Morris smiled.

"I've brought some cigarettes," said Ewen. As he held out the carton, a shell screamed over their heads and fell short of the hills. When he had recovered from the shock, he asked with nervous jocularity, "Does that happen often?"

"We're getting accustomed to it," Morris replied indirectly.

The C.O. stared at him, suddenly concentrating his attention. "Good man," he said. And, speaking now with greater frankness and friendliness, he added: "Keep your chaps busy, Morris. Don't let them get pillbox jitters. You know what I mean?"

"Claustrophobic places," explained Ewen.

"We'll be all right, sir."

"I'm counting on that." He shook Morris's hand and turned slowly towards the truck, obviously searching for something more to say.

"You'll be glad to hear," said Ewen, shaking Morris's hand, "that we've got Major Guthrie's dog with us at headquarters—still alive and kicking."

The C.O. turned back. "Knew there was something else. Here," he said, thrusting a piece of paper at Morris, "a message from the Prime Minister—to be read to all troops. Not just now," he added hurriedly as Morris began to skim through the message. "You can hang on to that copy. Keep your chin up, old man."

Inside the pillbox Morris read aloud the Prime Minister's message to the Governor and Defenders of Hongkong:

"We are all watching day by day and hour by hour your stubborn defence of the port and fortress of Hongkong. You guard a link between the Far East and Europe long famous in world civilisation. We are sure that the defence of Hongkong against barbarous and unprovoked attack will add a glorious page to British annals.

"All our hearts are with you in your ordeal. Every day of your resistance brings nearer our certain final victory."

After a few moments of uneasy silence, Richardson, the South American, said, "We should send some reply—a picture-postcard at least?"

Cratchley, the convict, smiled and said softly: "Weather ideal. Wish you were here."

"That's enough," ordered Corporal Macdonald.

In the other pillboxes, Morris made the section-commanders read the message. Most of the men were visibly heartened by the bold words. But he, for his part, was stricken with a premonition of failure. Everybody—Prime Minister, C.O., Craig—expected too much.

Early in the evening, the Japanese shelled the batteries in the rear again, with heavy guns and concentrated fire. Morris and the men in Barker's pillbox, awed to silence by the noise of the shells passing over their heads, kept close to the concrete walls. The falling screech of one shell made Morris shut his eyes and clench his teeth. There was a rending crash of wood and a piping of Chinese voices, but no explosion. For a moment, Morris thought that the timber-yard had been struck. But Paterson, looking sideways through a fire-slit, said laconically: "Dud. Landed among the junks."

"Just count the bangs," urged Ripley confidently, "'alf the stuff going over is dud."

Before the bombardment ended, another shell fell short, its descending screech suddenly failing and giving way to an instant of silence that was as suddenly shattered by explosion. This time, there was a hoarse, urgent cry just outside the pillbox. Morris scrambled to his feet, finding the air thick with dust and pulsing with reverberations, and crowded with Barker and Ripley to the door. One of the sentries lay on the pavement, trembling and shock-white: one of Torrance's men, with both his legs torn and broken.

Ripley tried to telephone for an ambulance, and found that the line was dead. "Cut by the shelling," he advised Morris. "I'll get something—something on wheels, like." And he set off at the double.

Morris felt obliged to stay by the wounded sentry, but he left it to Barker to control the bleeding, to crack the jokes. It was enough to have to sit on the pavement in the failing light, passively involved in another's agony. He smoked a cigarette and counted the bangs, until the shell-fire ceased, until Ripley returned, standing in the back of an open truck. Then, loathly, he helped to lift the sentry, and inwardly cursed the wretched man for clinging to consciousness, pleading, groaning, gasping and swearing. It was not until they had managed, sweating and nervously silent, to lay him on the truck with both his legs still unsevered that he closed his eyes and sagged out of his pain.

Barker altered the sentry-roster and detailed a man to wash the blood off the pavement.

The sky was darkening, and the mood of morning could no longer be shored up by Silver, Ripley, Barker, the C.O., the padre or the Prime Minister.

Earlier than usual, Morris ordered the platoon to stand to arms. He waited with Sergeant Meechan outside Barker's pillbox, watching the dusk melt buildings, masts, and stacks of timber into the solid obscurity of night.

"Going to kip down tonight?" asked the sergeant, with heavy humour.

"Maybe," said Morris casually.

But after supper, when the off-duty members of the section stretched out on the concrete floor to sleep, he went outside again and kept watch with the sentries as he had done the night before, waiting for the darkness to take human shape in front of his guns. According to Craig, it was between dusk and dawn that the Japanese would try to make a landing.

"Not so lively tonight, sir," said Sime cheerfully in the early hours of Sunday morning. During the previous night, the last British troops had left the mainland, and a launch running across to the island with salvaged dynamite had been blown out of the water by blundering machine-gun fire from a pillbox to the west of Morris's front. "Big fire along there, though," said Sime, as if he were glad to distinguish one danger in the night's recesses.

Morris glanced at the red glow over the north-west of the island. "Don't look at it too long," he advised. "It'll blind you."

Obediently, Sime turned to his front. A little later, rather wearily, he asked, "How much longer are we going to stay in this sector, sir?"

"I don't know."

Sime pondered. "Sooner we move the better, wouldn't you say, sir?"

Morris agreed. It might be possible to make a better, fresher start elsewhere.

Chapter Two

AFTER the days of starting, the days of waiting, the days of messages.

Sunday morning.

And Ehud said, I have a message from God unto thee. And he arose out of his seat.

And Ehud put forth his left hand, and took the dagger from his right thigh, and thrust it into his belly:

And the haft also went in after the blade; and the fat closed upon the blade, so that he could not draw the dagger out of his belly; and the dirt came out.

Macdonald closed his Bible and rose to answer the telephone.

*

After he had phoned Craig's message to the other sections, Morris settled down in a corner of Barker's pillbox to sleep.

Craig had been reminding the platoon that, under the standing orders he had issued on Friday, they were—so far as bladder, bowels and the sentry roster permitted—to remain inside their pillboxes during the hours of daylight. It was one of the standing orders that Morris had wilfully failed to enforce. He had argued with himself that the enemy would either see nothing through the forest of masts in Causeway Bay or see all. Squat, loopholed buildings—even if they appeared to be deserted—were unlikely to be mistaken for harbour installations or public conveniences.

After a long night within the walls of darkness, he disliked the prospect of a long day within walls of concrete. More space was needed for a waiting game than for an active game. And there was now little to do but wait. The initiative was with the enemy: in Kowloon Bay, under cover of their air-raids and counter-battery fire, the Japanese collected craft for their invasion; on the island, Chinese fifth-columnists shone signal lights, sniped, spread false rumours and incited desertion, looting and riot. Or so, at least, Craig reported in his messages. Morris knew no more about such matters than Craig cared to tell him. In his own narrow space, little seemed to happen. He waited, with a growing sense of frustration, unable to join in the action, unable to understand the action, receiving messages that told too little, sending messages that told nothing.

There were times at night when it was difficult to believe that he might surrender to sleep and yet carry on living. It seemed then that it was only through conscious effort that he could survive, that anything could survive. He felt that he was breathing life into his world. But those times were few. His prevailing mood by night, as by day, was one of frustration. And, frustrated, he recognised how dependent he was on other people—not only on men like Craig but also on men like Sime.

He was loath to admit even to himself that he derived comfort from Sime's presence. Sime was an absurd little man, naively idealistic, ingenuously loyal: a Boy Scout in spirit, and a shop assistant in flesh. What was it in this trite-tongued, duck-bottomed little man that was so comforting? Morris pillowed his head on his hand and worried, until he began to apprehend that Sime was not so wholly Sime as to exclude everyone else. Paterson was wholly Paterson, filling his skin tight, branding everything he did or said with his name and number. But Sime was not wholly Sime: there was room inside his skin for flabby notions of patriotism and valour and obedience and God-alone-knew-how-many other selfless standards that he had cheerfully swallowed on other men's recommendations. There were so many of these borrowed notions inside him that there was little space left for the nucleus of will that was Sime, insistently Sime. His was a nondescript and, therefore, hospitable presence; an unassertive existence that belonged in part to anyone who wanted to share it. The ones who were too much themselves were inhospitable—like Paterson, like Craig—walled up.

Morris watched the boots drag across the dusty shadowed floor as two relieving sentries left the pillbox. Then he closed his eyes and, counting the distant explosions, tried to forget the pressure of the walls on his spirit, tried to sleep.

*

On Sunday night, when the Rajputs took over the defences of the north-eastern sector, and the rest of the battalion retired to Wanchai Gap to refit and reorganise in the hills, D Company moved about three-quarters of a mile westwards into positions on the Bowrington front. Craig appreciated the implied commendation of his company's morale in the message from Mair and responded with a twinge of anxiety. Given a free choice, he would have taken the company out of the line for a day or two and allowed the scattered and makeshift sections a chance to come together and regain a sense of solidarity. He doubted whether Morris had sufficient presence to make three pillbox crews feel unified under his command; and whether Anstey had sufficient interest to keep the men in his line of weapon-pits working together, preparing to support each other.

He transferred his headquarters before dusk and, leaving Holt to supervise Anstey's move in the rear, went down to the front to keep an eye on Morris. Almost at once he found himself involved in one of the misfortunes that so often fluttered dusty wings around Morris's peep of light: the simple transfer of 17 Platoon from three pillboxes on Causeway Bay to three pillboxes on the Bowrington waterfront less than a mile to the west was suddenly complicated by the arrival of only one of the three promised trucks and by the driver's report that the other trucks had broken down— one having cracked an axle in a shell-hole, and the other having ground to a halt through sabotage. "Shit and grit in the works, sir," said the driver, a cheerful Englishman, with English euphemism.

Craig sent Sergeant Meechan ahead with Barker's section in the truck, and marched with Morris and the other two sections through the moonlit streets. "Be ready for trouble," he warned them. And he was surprised when, despite the sporadic shelling and the threat of sniping, Morris and his men set off in high spirits. Instead of grumbling about the lack of transport, or falling darkly silent in face of the dangers of the streets, or sullenly murmuring about the inequity of their being the only platoon in the battalion again to be confined in pillboxes, they cheerfully expanded themselves to enjoy their brief freedom. It was an incalculable, instinctive reaction.

There could be no doubt that Morris was on easy terms with his men. He could speak to them without bending as Anstey had to bend. He did speak to them, until Craig had to call for silence. And even then the easiness between subaltern and men was apparent, Morris keeping close to the sections and using unconventional hand-signals to guide them and force their pace. Craig brought up the rear alone. The high spirits of the men encouraged him, but the easiness between Morris and the men gave him little assurance. It seemed to him that Morris had gained the easiness of relations cheaply, by allowing himself to react instinctively, by conceding a common shallowness of mind, by surrendering some of his authority. It took a seasoned soldier like Ketchen to combine barrack-room familiarity with the austere qualities of leadership.

Craig stayed with the platoon and watched them stand to arms before dawn and stand down after dawn. In the last hour of darkness, from Japanese loudspeakers in Kowloon, came the faint breeze-shaken melodies of *Home, Sweet Home* and other English songs. The music was as slackening as strong drink in its effect on the men. It made their vigil seem absurd.

Before he left, he conveyed to Morris and Barker's section two messages he received from Holt at company headquarters: in the darkness, two ferry boats full of Japanese soldiers had been sunk; and, in the morning light, a thrust across the Lyemun channel at the north-eastern shore had been repulsed.

The messages spoke for themselves. He saw that Morris and the men looked a little grimmer, and left to rejoin Holt.

*

The Bowrington front had been cleared for battle. The three pill-boxes squatted on the edge of the long promenade—the praya, according to Ripley—that stretched from the industrial premises on the west of Causeway Bay past the districts of Bowrington and red-light Wanchai to the Naval Dockyard, which lay close to the administrative centre of Victoria. The channel between the praya and the tip of Kowloon peninsula, less than a mile wide, was empty of craft. The praya itself was deserted, except for the sentries standing on the pavements under the arcades of the four-storey waterfront tenements. The only outward sign of life in the tenements was the orange peel spread along the broad balustrades of some verandahs to dry into fuel; but, when Sergeant Meechan came back from posting the two Lyon light crews on first-floor verandahs, he reported that the flats were still crawling with people.

Morris had again stationed himself with Barker, occupying the centre pillbox, which stood beside a pair of petrol pumps and a stone jetty that helped to break the concrete-and-salt-water monotony of the scene. Ripley made arrangements for the sections to use the lavatory in one of the nearest flats and then set off to reconnoitre the network of streets in the rear in search of food and cigarettes.

The shelling was heavier than on previous days, but Morris managed to ignore it—discussing with Barker the possibility of washing, shaving and exercising after dark—until a sentry reported that pillboxes to the west were under fire. Morris then climbed a few rungs of the iron ladder, until he could see through the observation-slits in the turret, and remained there for most of the forenoon, watching the enemy shells explode on the water-front in the north-western sector. The bombardment moved gradually eastwards, so gradually that—if the Japanese continued to deal with the shore defences systematically—he could count on a day of grace before the shells tried to find him. Towards noon, he spotted activity in front of the godowns at the end of Kowloon peninsula. Soon afterwards, heavy mortars opened fire from there, adding to the destruction in the north-west. He feared mortar-bombs more than he feared shells.

Rousing himself, he descended and went to the telephone. For the first time he had something significant to report to Craig, and he had been so absorbed in his own observations and reckonings that he had failed to send a message promptly. Trying to make up for lost time, he fumbled nervously with the receiver and began to panic. It was a great comfort to hear Craig's tinny voice, to answer his pointed questions and to acknowledge his permission to move the platoon to alternative positions whenever the pillboxes seemed to be in danger of bombardment.

In mid-afternoon he began to feel ill. The concrete walls leaned towards him, and the irregular bursting of bombs and shells broke the rhythm of his pulse. His head ached and his empty stomach seemed to swell; perspiration gathered on his brow and he had to swallow hard to check spasms of nausea. He held to the iron ladder and hoped that his distress was not evident to the section.

Conversation had dried up. There was a constant tremor in the air that distorted voices. The men sat or stood around the walls, waiting in silence.

He pressed his face close to a slit and sucked in fresh air. The bombardment of the shore defences was being carried out slowly and systematically. There was still no immediate threat to his own pillboxes, no excuse to quit them.

Below, two men prepared to relieve the sentries.

Sime spoke.

"Not on your life," replied one of the relief.

"I could do with a breath of fresh air," explained Sime. "I feel a bit queer."

"You're not the only one that feels like that."

Morris rubbed his sweating brow again his hand. "Not by a long chalk," he told Sime. "We'll move out for a while."

The pillboxes had been sited to block three side streets leading from the praya up to the main road. On the corners of each street-opening, right-angled blast-walls had been constructed. They were of solid concrete, without embrasures for weapons, but Craig and Morris had already agreed that they would serve well enough as alternative positions. Rapidly, cheerfully, the sections left their pillboxes and set up their guns to fire over the blast-walls.

Morris informed Craig of the move, without explanation, but with the assurance that he was leaving the door of his own pillbox open so that he would hear the telephone ringing across the praya. After a pause, Craig acknowledged the hasty message, suggested that Morris should put through a routine call every hour, and instructed him to reoccupy the pillboxes at dusk, when the danger of invasion would be greater than the danger of bombardment.

Lying on the pavement under the arcade, confined between the angled blast-wall and the tenement, but able to breathe freely and to look along the praya or up the side street without peering through a slit, Morris gained control over himself and was able to rest. Since Friday morning he had not slept for more than two or three hours at a time. It was becoming difficult to sleep. He could lie at ease, but he could not always lower himself to the depth at which he was able to surrender his conscious control.

In the evening, when he had risen to keep watch with the sentries leaning against the blast-wall, two Chinese girls in blue cotton gowns and an old amah in black tunic and trousers came down the side street.

"They're coming here," said Sime in great surprise.

"The amah's got a basket," Arkison observed.

"Leave this to me," said Barker confidently. He rose to his knees and motioned to the women to keep their heads down. The girls halted, and spoke in a sharp-toned mixture of pidgin and vernacular that Morris could not follow. "They've brought tea," Barker announced.

"No chow?" asked Arkison.

"They say chow's short." Barker waved the women forward.

The amah had two flasks of green tea. One of the girls had a bottle of aspirins. Arkison swore in disappointment, but everyone else cheerfully accepted an aspirin and a cup of hot bitter tea. The other girl, who had a slight cast in one eye, enquired after Prentice.

"Prentice of A Company?" asked Barker. "You his popsy?"

"Pricky Prentice?" said one of Torrance's men. "He was killed."

"Shut your flaming mouth," said Barker.

The girl turned her head slowly and gracefully. It was difficult to tell at whom she was looking. "P'lentice—him dead?"

Barker nodded.

The girl turned her face towards Morris and touched her chin and murmured to Barker, who interpreted: "This cheeky besom says you look Chinese, sir. You don't have much hair on your chin."

The men laughed—except Sime, who leaned forward to the girl and warned her, "Mr. Morris—officer."

"Number One," added Barker.

Morris tried to look unconcerned. The girls tittered gently and chattered together in shrill twanging tones.

"They'll bring us razor blades tomorrow," announced Barker, interpreting.

"No chow?" pleaded Arkison directly.

The girls ignored him and scolded the amah for taking so long to repack the flasks and cups.

"Good lassies," said Barker, watching them walk lightly up the street. "Their hearts are in the right places—and the rest of their works too, I dare say."

"Out for all they can get," muttered Arkison.

"She didn't waste any tears on Prentice—the squint-eyed, impudent one," said Sime.

In the dusk, while Morris watched the men carrying their equipment back to the pillbox, Barker came to his side and said: "You know, sir, your boy lives near here—not more than a quarter of a mile away."

"Ah Chan?"

The corporal nodded. "Same stair as Macdonald's wife." He looked at Morris's crumpled clothes. "He might be able to fix you up with some of the things you need. You could send Ripley up to contact him. Or you could send Macdonald. It's not more than a couple of hundred yards from his box. Smiler—Sergeant Meechan could keep an eye on the section while Macdonald was away."

"It's a queer bloody war, this," said Morris, containing his sudden excitement.

*

Corporal Macdonald carried his Tommy gun under his arm and walked warily. It looked like being another day of continuous bombardment. The first air-raid of the morning was over, but the shelling continued. One of the blocks ahead of him had been hit, and the air was still misted with concrete dust. Along the middle of the street was a great smouldering mound of uncollected household refuse, and the smoke peppered the mist. Deeply excited, he walked along the deserted pavement, sharply aware of the hidden wickedness in the crowded tenements, of the dust and smoke stinking of destruction.

He went first to his own place. Poppy's cubicle was bare except for the wooden bunk and the straw mat. He stood still, hearing his breathing. He crossed the passage to Mimi Pak's cubicle and found it, too, was empty. He stood still again, until the voices that his heavy boots had silenced resumed their murmuring; then he shouted, asking whether anybody knew where Poppy had gone. Not to be frustrated by evasive silences, he went round the flat, pushing open doors, pulling aside curtains.

Mr. Cheung and four of his children crowded together defensively. They were sorry, he said, but they could not help. They had been too taken up with their own misfortunes to notice Poppy's departure: the Joyful Prosperity hardware store had closed, their eldest son had died, Mrs. Cheung was queuing up for rice, there was no fuel to cook the rice, and the water had been turned off. Mr. Ng gave question for question: when would the dockyards take on labour again?—what would happen to the tools he had left in the little room at the end of the godown? Mrs. Bun, the ivory-carver's wife, was unintelligible.

"*Maskee,*" said Macdonald grimly, and went down to the flat below and hammered on the door. There was scuffling and whispering inside. He shouted for Ah Chan, who then opened the door cautiously, peeping round the edge, stiff-faced with fear. Macdonald pushed the door back. "Mr Morris wants to see you."

The boy made jerky, pleading gestures with his hands and tried to speak.

"Come on," ordered Macdonald roughly. "It's not far."

Chan turned away and, in an instant, disappeared. Furiously determined that he would not be frustrated again by oriental cunning, heathen elusiveness, Macdonald strode into the flat, shouting threats, kicking at and splintering frail partition walls. Then Chan appeared again, slipping into his white mess jacket. Macdonald came to an abrupt halt. He took his hand off a curtain that he had been ready to tear down. "All right," he said sourly, "Let's go."

*

On Macdonald's signal, Morris left Barker's section behind the blast-wall, to which they had retired again just before dawn, and trotted up the side-street to meet Ah Chan—an older, shabbier, sick-faced, frightened Ah Chan.

"Will I wait?" asked Macdonald.

"No," said Morris, staring uneasily at the boy. "Thanks very much, Mac. Is your wife all right?"

"She was out." Macdonald saluted and went away.

Morris said uncomfortably: "You don't look well. Sick?"

Chan grasped his arm and spoke urgently and breathlessly, apparently seeking some assurance that he had given good service.

"Ah Chan number one boy," said Morris.

"You speak?" He went through the motions of writing.

"You want references—a chitty saying Ah Chan number one boy?"

Chan nodded eagerly. So Morris tore a leaf out of his notebook and scribbled on it in pencil: *To whom it may concern, Ah Chan served me for six weeks and performed his duties willingly and efficiently.* He added his signature, rank and unit and the date,

and handed the scrap of paper to Chan, who scrutinised it carefully, betraying a conflict of hope and suspicion.

"It says you're a good boy."

Chan mumbled his gratitude and ducked his head several times.
Diffidently, feeling that he was taking an unfair advantage, Morris
pulled out his message.

*

While the police broke up the shouting crowd and tried to
reform an orderly queue, James Lin watched from a distance. This,
he was ready to explain, was the only position for a wise man:
far enough away from the crowd to avoid being struck by fists or
missiles, and close enough to the distribution point to assure Mr.
Gow and the other organisers that he was available for duty as
soon as the rice arrived. An old wise man would probably be able
to rest on that explanation, but a young wise man—particularly
one who had some understanding of western attitudes—could not
help regretting that wisdom had such a womanish look in times
of violence. He was greatly cheered when he saw approaching him
a familiar figure under a high-crowned, narrow-brimmed hat.

Sammy King stopped a few paces short of him, looked back at
the crowd and asked mildly, "What gives?"

"The rice hasn't arrived. Some of the food stores have been destroyed, and the transport has broken down."

Sammy nodded. "Things look bad."

"They put men in prison for saying things like that." James
smiled, one Chinese to another. "Old T. P. Wong was arrested
today for defeatist talk."

"So I hear. Nothing wrong with a British-built prison. Long
way safer than the basement of a newspaper office."

"You couldn't be sure they'd classify you as a defeatist. They
might decide you were a fifth-columnist and shoot you."

Sammy nodded. "I don't know what number sports columns
are."

A shell rustled overhead and exploded near by. Sammy adjusted
his hat and pulled from his pocket a folded piece of paper. "It's
for Anna. Man called Chan brought it. When I told him she
wasn't in the office, he said he'd come back tomorrow for an
answer."

Curiously, James examined the address. Another shell burst in
the vicinity. Sammy prepared to leave. "Saw the fortune-teller this

morning," he said. "Told me it was a bad day for calling on friends."

*

It had been the worst evening of the war. Only one boy and an amah remained of the staff, and, since neither was a competent cook, supper had been a thoroughly dispiriting meal, consisting of the usual frugal portions of canned food deprived of all disguise. Roderick, whose enthusiasm for rice distribution would not survive another failure of transport, had eaten in brooding silence until old Willox's malicious reference to concrete.

"Shells go through it like knives through butter. A signalman on his way up to the Peak told me. He saw it with his own eyes— like knives through butter."

"Which concrete are you talking about?" Roderick had asked sharply. "The island's covered with concrete."

"Oh, it's only the new stuff that's defective—the stuff that was used for the defences."

"Which defences? They weren't all put up at once. They weren't all put up by the same contractors."

Willox had started to wriggle. Roderick was a formidable opponent when roused. "Oh, I don't know which he had in mind."

"Then it's slanderous to peddle the gossip here. You know well enough, Willox, that I had a share in one of the contracts."

Mrs. Willox had left the table, trembling with indignation. Old Willox, flushed and twitching, had lingered only long enough to clean his plate. Soon after supper, Roderick and James Lin, pleading tiredness, had gone to bed. Peter Deveaux, without troubling to find an excuse, had limped after them. He wilted whenever he was not basking in a woman's attention, and, in the oppressive atmosphere, heavy with the echoes of Roderick's anger and the rumble of war at the curtained windows, none of the women in the house had tried to shine on him. Three had been absent in body: Mrs. Willox, who had indignantly kept to her room, his mother, who was on night-duty at the men's convalescent hospital, and Maud Granger, poor girl, who was now living at the officers' hospital, immured with her grief. The others had been absent in spirit: Jenny Brewster, who had not looked Peter's way since Tim's departure on Friday morning, Mary, who still wore the shadow of Hugh Craig on her penitent face, and Anna Lin, who had been oddly excited all

H

evening, who had touched off the last ugly display of fireworks.

Some time after Peter's departure, she had asked Mary where Hugh was stationed. Mary, warming to life, had begun to reply eagerly: "I didn't know till today. There's only one of his subalterns in the hospital—a funny little man called Williamson— and he was wounded on the mainland. But the chaplain looked in today—Ewen, an awfully shy man—and he told me that Hugh was quite close by—"

"He shouldn't have told you," Jenny had interrupted angrily.

"Why not?"

"The soldiers' positions are supposed to be secret."

"Bosh!"

"Then why hasn't Tim told me where he is?"

"What harm did the chaplain do by telling me where Hugh is? I'm not a fifth-columnist."

"But you're going around telling other people."

"You mean Anna? You mean Anna may be a fifth-columnist?"

Anna had sat as rigid as a wooden doll. Mary had twisted about in her anger. "You're a bitch in the manger, Jenny. And— and you can go to hell."

Jenny had gone to bed.

Mrs. Gow had gone to bed . . . She lay now remembering the ugly pattern of the evening and imagining how she might have intervened and shaped pleasure for everyone. A sound of sobbing distracted her, a soft, pitifully human sound audible between the claps of gun-thunder. It came from Jenny's room. And suddenly, for no reason that she could think of, Mrs. Gow was filled with terror.

*

On Stanley Peninsula, on the south coast of the island, Volunteers Franco Mendes and Timothy John Brewster stood guard on the heavy guns.

It was a long time since Mendes had last examined the shapes of night. He had watched his world too often with a camera-eye, catching the crudity of light on miraculous surfaces of skin and rock, silk and sea, leaf and metal. Now, in the dark, he remembered the earlier mysteries, which did not burn an image on a photographic plate, which were visible only to the living-and-dying eye, the believing eye.

"Damned cold," muttered Brewster.

"Yes," said Mendes, although he was warm in a way that he

could not explain. "Yes," he said, "it's damned cold." He had stopped feeling grateful for Brewster's comradeship. He could speak to Brewster as he had never been able to speak to Charles Anstey. And he was warmer now than Brewster was. "The man who was killed today—he was a friend?" he asked, suddenly impelled to find a reason for Brewster's coldness.

"No."

"It will happen again?"

"I expect so. The shells are old—made in 1918. Any one of them's liable to burst like that, right in front of the muzzle."

The sea spread every glimmer of starlight. The hills gathered shadow. Wetness and dryness.

"Soon we will fight with our little guns."

"Rifles," corrected Brewster.

"Rifles."

"And I hope they fire forwards," said Brewster.

An explosion beyond the hills, on the north shore, rumbled around the island like a wild beast. Mendes grasped his rifle more firmly, and waited.

*

When the echoes of the shell-burst had lost themselves among the dark hills, Craig looked down towards the north shore and continued his brief, reluctant summary of information: "More than half the pillboxes were knocked out today. Another day's shelling and mortaring will finish them off."

"Morris?" enquired Anstey.

"His boxes haven't been hit yet. They'll be on the list for tomorrow. But he's lying back from them in alternative positions. He should be all right."

"How is he?"

"Fine."

"Tail up?"

"Yes." He started to lead Anstey along the line of shallow weapon-pits. "You should get fair warning back here—when the invasion starts. But you'll have to see that the men are on their toes from dusk till dawn."

"Does he realise he's in for it tomorrow?" asked Anstey slowly.

"Morris? Of course he does."

There was something unpleasant about Anstey's persistent interest in Morris's reactions. Craig could not immediately put a name to the kind of unpleasantness and did not care to search for one.

*

As the light came up on Wednesday, 17th December, Morris was able to see more clearly the two shell-craters on the praya between Barker's position and Foggo's.

"Dead lucky we are," said Ripley.

"Keep your head down," said Morris cautiously.

The bombardment of the north shore had continued sporadically throughout the night, and the mortars on Kowloon peninsula were still firing across the channel. But for the two shells that had harmlessly exploded on the praya, the Bowrington and Wanchai fronts had been spared, while the defences to the west and east had been systematically destroyed.

"They're fattening us up for something," said Barker.

"Maybe not," said Morris hopefully. "Maybe they're not planning to land here."

At half past nine in the morning, there was a heavy air-raid on Victoria, followed by a short, concentrated artillery and mortar bombardment that battered the senses numb. Soon afterwards Paterson, on sentry-go, roused the shaken section to see two launches flying white flags crossing the channel towards the ferry pier west of the Naval Dockyard.

"What are they up to?" asked Sime.

"They'll be calling on us to surrender," guessed Morris.

Sime stared across the water, his pudgy face dirty, unshaven, unfamiliar. "We won't give in, will we?"

"It's only a question of time," said Arkison.

It was the first utterance of the thought in the section. Morris glanced from face to face, trying to pick out the other men who had started to contemplate defeat, but the only certainty he achieved was that the thought had not occurred to Sime.

"That's a terrible thing to say," Sime told his lance-corporal. "They won't beat us with big guns. They'll have to cross the water if they want to take the island, and then we'll show them, won't we, sir?" He looked to Morris for confirmation.

Morris nodded. "We can hold out for a long time yet." He could not see an end. His imagination could grapple neither defeat nor victory.

"We're not the only ones in this war," Barker reminded everybody. "Some day the Navy might sail in and blow Kowloon to hell."

The section eased away from the wall again and sat down on the pavement to wait. Arkison chewed a piece of bamboo to relieve his hunger. Ripley teased out the sodden tobacco from three dog-ends and rolled a cigarette.

When the telephone in the pillbox rang, Morris crossed the praya to answer the call. Craig reported that the Japanese had ceased hostilities till four o'clock in the afternoon in order to give the Governor and the G.O.C. time to consider surrender.

"Did they ask for time?" Morris's heart leapt.

"No," replied Craig deliberately and coldly. "We're not surrendering. Get that into your own head and into your men's heads."

"You don't have to worry about us," said Morris hotly. "There's nothing wrong with our morale."

As he returned to the blast-wall, his anger vanished. "Our luck holds," he said, smiling.

*

The water supply to the tenements was temporarily cut off.

"All right," said Lance-Corporal Foggo bleakly. "Try some place else."

"It'll be cut off all over the island, I expect," protested Jannelli.

Foggo spat. "You want some gumption, boy. The Chinks'll have bastarding buckets of it to keep them going. You heard what Morris said. Faces washed and shaved by noon. Get moving."

Jannelli, clutching an armful of empty water-bottles, looked at the pavement. "I'm tired," he said. "Could Punchy help me?"

Foggo was ready to lose his temper, when McGuire, lying on the pavement, made the mistake of rolling over to face the blast-wall. "All right," said Foggo, "I can still see your big bum, McGuire. Get on your feet, *chullo*!"

McGuire was poor company. He had lost his freakishness when he had lost Piggy Fraser. He was ordinary without Piggy running around him explaining his existence. He was now just an overgrown stupid man who seldom opened his mouth except to complain of hunger. He was just the man you took with you to carry the load.

The streets between the waterfront and the main road were deserted, some of them almost entirely blocked by piles of smouldering rubbish. On the main road a civilian truck was approaching in low gear, preceded by two coolies who kept up a sing-song cry as they shuffled along. When the truck went past, Jannelli saw that it was loaded with corpses, sprawling bodies of men, women and children—some of them naked—piled up into a wobbling heap. As if drawn by a magnet, he followed the truck.

A young woman with staring eyes brought a dead infant out to the coolies, and Jannelli ran forward and asked for water. She spat on him and scuttled back to her house.

At an intersection where a bomb had burst, the truck halted beside the crater, and the two coolies entered a building that had been torn open. "Dead loss, this," said Jannelli. He stood in front of McGuire and looked around, wondering where to go, bemused by the sunlight on his eyes and the silence in his ears.

A young Chinese leapt out of a doorway and ran into the road, dragging at the end of a cord a screaming monkey. The young man shouted hoarsely and, fending off the maddened monkey, pointed to the rifle slung over Jannelli's shoulder.

"He wants us to kill it," mumbled Jannelli. He stood still, listening to the young man shouting and the monkey screaming. "You do it, Punchy." He turned to McGuire, who neither moved nor spoke. "Go on, Punchy. Put your foot on it and stop its noise." Then, seeing that McGuire was trembling, he unslung his own rifle and thumbed forward the safety catch. He was wondering whether he could hit a jumping monkey, when it suddenly came to rest and sat up on its haunches and stared at him. The noise of his shot echoed off the buildings, and the monkey jerked backwards into the crater.

They all stood there, looking down at the dead monkey. "It happens so quickly," muttered Jannelli. They stood still, their contorted shadows fallen down the side of the crater. "First thing I've killed with this rifle."

He persuaded the young man to fill two bottles with water and decided to rejoin the section. "If Foggo thinks he can do any better, let him try." He scrutinised his companion with fresh interest. "Come on, tough guy."

McGuire lagged on the way back, until Jannelli had to stop

and wait for him. The big man was still trembling. "It's the bug," he mumbled. Disbelieving, Jannelli looked at him closely. "You're right, Punchy," he said flatly. "You've got another dose of malaria." It was a bitter disappointment. Malaria was ordinary. Fear was exciting.

*

When Richardson and Cratchley came stooping along from the other end of the blast-wall, Macdonald watched them, alert, suspicious. Richardson sat on his hunkers in front of the corporal. "This is a good time to go on the scrounge," he said precisely and pleasantly. "What say Cratchley and I try to get some cigarettes and chow?"

"No."

"Morris is not so strict," Richardson smiled. "He sends Ripley on the scrounge. He even sent you—"

"Shut up."

"The boys don't have any fags," said Cratchley quietly.

"We could be back before the inspection," added Richardson.

Macdonald looked from one to the other. "I know what you're after," he said contemptuously.

Richardson laughed softly. "No harm in dipping our wicks on the way."

"You're a couple of dirty goats."

The South American stopped laughing. Macdonald looked from one to the other again, from Richardson's narrow dark eyes to Cratchley's pale empty eyes. They were good fighting-men, among the best in the battalion, and he exulted in his power over them. "Get back to your places," he said. "Nobody in this section is going after whores or cigarettes or anything else."

Their boots scraped on the pavement as they went back to their places. A single Japanese plane buzzed overhead like a baffled fly on a summer window.

Poppy Macdonald—the corporal's wife with a cubicle to herself on an island where thousands of homeless people slept on the streets; with God's blessing and a registrar's certificate in a part of the world where British soldiers could license their lust in a heathen ritual under a Chinese law that dissolved like joss-stick smoke when the troopship sailed—Poppy Macdonald was dead. There remained only Poppy Wu, the Chinese taxi-dancer, the hairless body and the singing voice, the hollow of mind and spirit.

Did it matter why she had surrendered her security, her hope of salvation? Did it matter where on the island she had sought refuge for a little time?—She was on the way down to her eternal grave. He could not delay her descent, keep her alive by thinking about her, by considering whether even yet he should . . . Was it his weakness and wickedness that made him want to hold her back, or could his yearning be described as Christian compassion? It was torment trying to decide.

He felt tired and apathetic by the time Morris and Meechan came round on their tour of inspection.

"We couldn't clean up, sir. No water."

Morris was unmoved. "It's the same all along the line."

"Nobody sick?" muttered Meechan, as if he did not want the men to hear.

"Nobody."

Meechan smiled and said to Morris, "That's only McGuire, then, and he's no loss."

Morris nodded, and stepped aside to see the rest of the section. "I've got news for you," he announced self-consciously. "Chinese forces are on their way to relieve the garrison. The message came down from G.H.Q.," he added, raising his voice.

Macdonald watched the men looking at each other, searching for someone with the strength to believe and make others believe.

"They are coming by land or by sea, sir?" asked Richardson in a neat voice, sharp as a pin against a balloon.

"By land, marching down to take the Japs in the rear."

"When can we expect them, sir?"

"I don't know. You've got the message now. You can make what you like of it." Morris, reddening, turned to Macdonald and asked quietly, almost guiltily, "No news from your end? Nothing from your wife—or Ah Chan?"

"Nothing, sir."

They stood looking at each other, Macdonald aware of his own dark strength.

*

Before the end of the truce, Craig and Holt visited the platoon. They were both clean-shaven and neatly dressed, and they both spoke of the military situation in terms that made Morris's own limited experiences seem ignoble and irrelevant. To hold his own, to explain his frowsy appearance and his failure to see the battle in perspective, he had to hint at the nervous tension of duty on the waterfront and at the lack of regular communication between the platoon and the C.Q.M.S. The interest shown by Craig and Holt led him to say more than he had really wanted to say.

"We're reduced to scrounging," he complained. "Silver sends us two bare meals at any times that suit him between dusk and dawn, no cigarettes, no water, no toilet gear. And there's very little we can wheedle out of the Chinese now. They're feeling the pinch themselves."

While Holt was taking note of the platoon's requirements, the two Chinese girls and their amah came shuffling down the pavement. Craig and Holt turned to stare at them. Morris glanced at Barker, who merely grinned.

"It's the local comforts committee," said Morris, trying to introduce the subject as lightly as possible.

Holt turned to Craig. "What's Morris grumbling about? He has his own commissariat."

Craig smiled evasively. "They come regularly?"

"This is just their second visit," said Morris.

"No Molotov cocktails in that basket?" asked Holt, enjoying the occasion. "This is fifth-column territory, you know."

"I cover them, sir," said Barker, coming forward with his Tommy gun under his arm.

"Only in the military sense, I hope," murmured Holt.

In the basket there were two flasks of green tea, several cups and a packet of razor blades. The squint-eyed girl delicately pulled one blade out of the packet and handed it to Morris, saying in a shrill laughing voice, "Number One shavee."

He held the blade between thumb and forefinger, trying to shape a small smile of gratitude while Craig and Holt stared at him.

Holt turned to Craig again and said, "Nothing like this at our headquarters, Number One."

From the corner of his eye Morris saw that Craig was as embarrassed as he was.

*

The Japanese announced the end of the truce with a roar of guns and mortars. One of the first shells burst against the tene-

H*

ment across the street from Barker's post, and the shouting and screaming inside the building chilled Morris's blood.

"It's our turn now," said Barker.

"Keep your heads down," said Morris automatically.

There was nothing to cling to on the pavement, no tufts of coarse grass or stones or gnarled stems of scrub to wrap his fingers around. He clenched his fists and tried to control his breathing. Two shells landed on the praya, and the air trembled with the violence of the explosions, and the noise reverberated in the empty streets, cracking from one unyielding surface to another.

Barker took a cautious look over the blast-wall. "They're gunning for our boxes, all right."

"Sooner they get them the better," said Arkison.

Sime stared at him, without expression.

"Down!" warned Morris, as the confused rumbling in his ears sharpened to the sibilance of another falling shell. His head felt curiously square, as if he had been punched on the nose. His teeth bit on grit. His eyes and nostrils smarted. His bowels stirred uneasily as his belly pressed against the shuddering pavement.

Macdonald's pillbox was blown open; Foggo's, although hit several times, was only holed. Barker's box stood up to the first hit, and, while they waited for the Japanese gunners to reload, the corporal muttered to Morris, "They don't have to be far off target to blow us all to hell." When the next shell struck his box, buckling the rear wall and jamming the door, Barker grinned and said, "Bloody good shot!"

A few minutes later the men began to look up from the pavement. Barker shouted to them: "We've had our ration." They sat listening to the distant explosions. Arkison rose and stooped his way towards the house in which the section were allowed to use the lavatory. Before he reached the entrance, a bomb fell with sickening abruptness and burst in the street, and he doubled up with a hoarse shout. Shocked and stiff, several men moved towards him. His right thigh was deeply gashed. Once again —the telephone link with Craig lost—Ripley set off to find transport.

"Never even knew there was an air-raid on," complained Arkison breathlessly. "I've pissed in my slacks," he added later.

Barker, who was checking the bleeding, said, "You don't have to tell me that."

By the time Ripley arrived with an ambulance, Arkison was unconscious.

"Will he be all right?" asked Sime.

Barker nodded and walked to his kit and tore off a strip of four-by-two to wipe his hands. Paterson followed him and asked, "Who's going to take his place?"

Barker glanced up from his bloodstained hands. "You looking for promotion?"

Paterson sneered. "You know what you can do with promotion so far as I'm concerned."

Morris, aware that Paterson was speaking on Sime's behalf, said, "I'll have a word with the Skipper about it." He tried to catch Paterson's eye, but the Bren-gunner turned away.

                                *

When the electric supply failed, Mrs. Gresham opened the black-out curtains and allowed the starlight and the cold air to invade the room. In the dimensions of the gun-rumbling night, words withered, fell dry and broken from the lips. And the refugee-guests began to scatter to their bedrooms.

Joan and Nell shared a small room that looked out on a dark, rustling shrubbery.

"This is the end," Joan decided.

Nell stood at the window, listening to the guns and the leaves and the slicing of a zip-fastener.

"We're getting out of here." The words were wrapped in Joan's dress. "We'll take our bags with us in the morning. And I won't be sorry to leave."

Nell sighed. "You can't blame the Greshams for putting the light out."

"I'm not blaming them. But it's the last straw. There's the journey up here every night, with all these armed robbers running wild. And there's this poky little room, and the boring conversation, and the rotten food, and the shortage of water, and now—no light."

"And where do you think you'll find a better place?"

"We'll just stay in the hospital. We may not be comfier there, but we'll be safer."

"Last night you were grumbling about the hospital."

"And I'd a perfect right to grumble. I'll tell you something else I heard today. Anna Lin's working at the *officers'* hospital. How did *she* get pushed in there at the last minute?"

Nell stared at the shrubbery, looking for a better place.

The bed-springs creaked. "That's the kind of thing that makes me grumble. God knows, it's not snobbishness that makes me—"

"Oh, shut up," said Nell wearily. Guns and leaves and longing stirred and saddened her.

*

"Grim," said Ripley hoarsely, breaking a long silence.

"Worst yet," said Barker.

It was Thursday morning, 18th December, and the bombardment of the island continued. Heavy smoke from the blazing oil tanks at North Point darkened the sky above the narrow channel.

"What's happened to all our own guns?" asked Sime. After a pause Paterson said, "Blown to hell, George."

*

Macdonald watched Richardson and Cratchley cleaning and oiling the machine-gun. The South American looked up and smiled: "Last Thursday, it was we who crossed to the island. This Thursday, it will be the Japs."

"What makes you so sure?"

Richardson held up his hand and, grinning delightedly, conducted the runaway orchestra of artillery. "This is the climax. They can't play louder or faster than this."

*

Towards noon, when the noise of bombardment had diminished, a smartly dressed inspector of police strode down the pavement and asked for Mr. Morris. Morris sat up, vaguely uneasy. "I've been ordered to put myself under your command," said the inspector. He had a sharp tongue and inquisitive eyes. "I've got sixty men waiting in the back street. Where do you want us to go?"

"Sixty?" Morris rose to his feet, adjusting his equipment, trying to shake off his drowsy bewilderment. "What are you supposed to do?"

The inspector smiled unpleasantly. "I'm waiting for you to tell me."

They walked in silence to the back street where the sixty policemen, bearing an assortment of firearms, stood at ease in a body. "Don't let them hang about in a bunch like that," said Morris sourly. "You'd better cover the intersections back here, in case one of our forward posts is overrun."

After the police detachment had been spread out into a support line twice as strong in numbers as the front line, the inspector took Morris aside and showed him an envelope. "This is for you?" he asked deliberately.

The envelope, which had been slit open, bore Morris's rank, name and regiment, and the words *By hand*.

"Where did you get it?"

"It was lying in the station—taken off a fifth-columnist who was arrested yesterday."

Morris's pulse quickened. "What's his name?"

"Chan. Your boy?"

"Yes," said Morris stiffly.

The inspector nodded. "He produced a reference you wrote for him."

"How did he come to be arrested?"

"We found incriminating evidence in his house—Japanese propaganda leaflets for distribution among the Chinese."

They looked at each other. "There's no suggestion," said the inspector patronisingly, "that you or your correspondent knew anything about his treachery. But you'd be well advised to restrict your contacts with the Chinese till you know them better."

Morris's lips trembled with anger. "Did Chan admit—"

"Nothing. Tried to blame a brother who used to live with him. We haven't been able to pick the brother up. We're not sure that he ever existed."

"What'll happen to Chan?"

"It's happened. We executed him yesterday."

Morris stumbled away. Before he reached the blast-wall he halted in a doorway to read the letter. It was some time before he could exorcize the trembling image of Ah Chan and make sense of the strange words that were already known to the police.

Tuesday, 16th December
Dear Johnny,
            Your note makes me very happy. You say you wrote to make sure that I would not forget you. I remember you very well—a tall young man running down the steps of the

Peninsula Hotel, a young man who seemed stranger to me at that moment than he does now. I tell James that guns speak a universal language and that bombs may break down more than walls. He says it is an absurd simplification, this idea of mine. And perhaps you will say that it is absurd and picture me with a new, fierce face. Do you understand this nonsense?

Since I wrote the last words I have spent some minutes wondering whether I should tear up this letter and begin another. Perhaps it is only the Chinese who are afraid to speak too loudly or write too freely about their happiness.

James and I are lodging with the Gows. James is helping to distribute rice, and Mary has found me a job in the hospital where she works. You can assure Captain Craig that she is well. It is a curious place to work. Some of the girls seem to be anxiously waiting for certain young men to be wounded.

It is difficult to see how and when the fighting will end. People do not speak about it. Not even James.

Do not be too brave, Johnny. I am not waiting to see you in hospital. We will meet afterwards. You will bring Dick, and after he has looked at me carefully, he will take James away to the wine shop.

I cannot write any more.

Love,

Anna.

The battle was out of focus. The anger of the guns seemed misplaced. He wished that he could find tears to ease the constriction in his throat and bathe his aching, grimy eyes.

It was not until evening, when the Bowrington front came under heavy fire again, that he emerged, cold and shaking, from the sanctuary that Anna had created.

After the ordeal, after acknowledging the message from Foggo reporting the death of one private and the wounding of another, he leaned against the blast-wall, dazedly searching the channel. About half-past nine the noise of sustained machine-gun fire carried from the north-east sector, beyond Causeway Bay, and green Very lights burst in the dark sky.

"Stand to!" he shouted. "This is it."

He sent Ripley to inform the other sections and the inspector that the Japanese were attempting to land in the north-east, and to warn the Lyon-light crews to be ready to throw their beams in front of the platoon. He sent another man back with a message to Craig.

"Now," he said to Barker, "we'll maybe have more to do than swap messages."

Chapter Three

N o w, in the early afternoon of Friday, 19th December, there was at last a chance to thrust at the enemy. Craig had shown on Golden Hill that D Company could stand against determined assault, and in Bowrington that they could stand under heavy bombardment. Negative virtues, Chinese virtues. He wanted now to show that they could attack.

The main snag—the formidable snag—was the lack of detailed information about the enemy's numbers and dispositions. As he looked eastwards over the wide valley he had to cross, Craig fired questions that Ballantyne could not answer.

"We know as much as we need to know," argued the adjutant in an unconvincingly lazy voice, "for a quick punch at them."

"No doubt," said Holt, his voice still sharp with grief for Farquhar, "we'll pick up the details as they pick us off."

"Go down the road," Craig told him quietly. There was no time for bitterness. "See if there's any sign of the platoons yet."

Holt went down the road, and Ballantyne went up, to rejoin Mair. Left alone, Craig reviewed the facts.

During the night the Japanese had landed in the north-east sector and swiftly overrun the eastern half of the island. They had battered a hole in the coastal defences, climbed quickly into the thinly-held hills, and pushed their way westwards along the back-bone of the island as far as this wide valley. They were on Jardine's Lookout, the massive feature on the other side of the valley, and in Wong-nei-chong Gap, the cleft between Jardine's Lookout and Mount Nicholson at the head of the valley. After one night's fighting, they were holding the heights and the main reservoirs in the eastern half of the island and were blocking the only road that cut across the island from north to south, the road that humped over Wong-nei-chong Gap, the road on which Craig was standing. The immediate danger was that the two brigades of the garrison would be separated. The main body of the East Brigade were now somewhere in the south-east. The West Brigade were preparing to launch a general counter-attack with the primary object of regaining the dominating height of Jardine's Lookout.

This distant, general's-eye view of the facts did not satisfy Craig. The need for fuller information about the enemy had already been tragically demonstrated around Wong-nei-chong Gap.

In the early morning the Japanese had attacked the Canadians holding the Gap and had surrounded West Brigade headquarters near by. A party of sappers sent up from the north side to relieve the defenders had been unable to fight their way through the enemy ring. A naval party sent up from the south had been ambushed before they reached the Gap. Farquhar, the adjutant's assistant, had then taken up a party of Scots from the north; and the few, including Farquhar, who had broken through to Brigade H.Q. had died alongside the brigadier and his staff. Another party —found by the R.A.S.C.—had made a fresh attempt to reach the Gap from the south, but their fate was still unknown . . . A story of failure founded on failure, of inadequacy heaped on inadequacy, as corpse fell on corpse.

But—no time for bitterness—the bloody story of the Gap was finished. The counter-attack was to be along a wide front—Indians, Canadians and Scots advancing with the support of eight field guns. There would, at worst, be no flinging of handfuls after handfuls of men to their death in a narrow trap. There would be all the strength the West Brigade could muster, and there would be ample room for manoeuvre.

He raised his binoculars to his eyes. From the road where he stood, the road that climbed round the flanks of Mount Cameron and Mount Nicholson to Wong-nei-chong Gap, he could see most of the field for the coming battle. The British still held the valley —Happy Valley—a gape-mouthed valley blocked with houses, cemeteries and a race-course, opening out on the dust-white tenements of Bowrington. The Japanese lay in the hills opposite him, overlooking the whole valley, seeing and unseen. He had to lead D Company across the valley and up the north-west slope of Jardine's Lookout. And he would do it, imperfect as the information about the enemy was, imperfect as his instruments were.

The first of his instruments to arrive was the new man—

Second-Lieutenant Wallace, one of the Volunteers who had been commissioned by the Governor to make up the dwindling number of subalterns in the garrison. He was an older man than Craig, short and fair, with a fleshy face, an eager smile and a nervously accented voice.

"For the time being," explained Craig, "you're spare. I'm short of a platoon commander, but I'm also short of a platoon. You'll just have to tag along with one of the platoons, and learn the job. If one of the commanders is knocked out—"

Wallace interrupted. "I'm not looking for a dead man's shoes." He smiled uneasily. "I'll be content to tag along and do what I can to help."

Anstey, the next arrival, was showing signs of strain. After he had halted his silent men and left his sergeant to disperse them from the road, he approached Craig with a neat-footed and round-shouldered gait, like a sullen girl. When he lifted his head to look at them, his dark shrunken face and bloodshot eyes told the rest of his story.

"I've got a second-in-command for you," said Craig, on the spur of the moment.

Anstey looked suspiciously at the new man and shook hands. "You just tell me what to do," urged Wallace, with anxious affability.

Then the two trucks carrying 17 Platoon climbed round the bend, roaring in low gear. Holt stopped the trucks below Anstey's platoon, and Morris and his men, chattering and grinning like a pack of monkeys, scrambled down to the road and started to sort themselves out, bantering and pushing.

"Less bobbery!" shouted Craig. He watched Morris disperse his men and follow Holt up the road; then, taking care that his words would not carry to Mair and Ballantyne, he said: "Don't let that happen again, Morris. You're supposed to be commanding a platoon—not inciting a rabble."

Morris's dirty face reddened.

"You brought the Vickers guns?"

"Two of them," said Morris hoarsely. "I left the other one with the police. That's what you wanted?"

There was a rebellious inflection in the query, which Craig heard with surprise but without comment. He turned, to bring all the subalterns under his eye, and recited the bare facts of the situation as Ballantyne had described it. Holt, who had heard the original version and Craig's unanswered questions about it, listened carefully and watched closely. Anstey kept his head down and his face in the shadow of his helmet. Wallace nodded attentively. Morris developed a frown. "You forget," he broke in, "that I haven't got a map. I don't know any of these places you're talking about." Holt smiled sourly. "You don't need a map," said Craig quietly. "The Gap's at the top of this road, and there's Jardine's Lookout at the other side of the valley."

Morris stared and swore. "What are we standing about here for? They'll see all our preparations."

Craig smiled patiently. This was the kind of near-sightedness that won decorations. Morris swallowed the camel-fact of the enemy's presence halfway along the island and strained at this gnat. "We can't hide anything," he explained. "We're starting at 1500 hours in broad daylight, and we've got to go right across the valley and up the side of the Lookout."

Holt patted Morris's shoulder. "Before we've gone far enough to come under fire, they'll have the news of our counter-attack in the Tokyo evening papers."

Craig had just started to issue his orders for the counter-attack when he was interrupted by a runner, who asked him to report immediately to the C.O.

Mair and Ballantyne had moved up the road to the entrance of the house serving as battalion headquarters. When he joined them there, they were reading a map, and the adjutant was dictating hurriedly to a clerk.

"Change of orders," announced Mair harshly. He crooked his stick around the back of his neck and stared up at Craig with bright, challenging eyes. "Before the general counter-attack goes in, we've to occupy Wong-nei-chong Gap—immediately, see?"

Craig clenched his fists and inhaled sharply.

"We've to make a job of it this time," said Mair, staring steadily at Craig. "Two companies—one to sneak round the back of Mount Nicholson—the other to make a bold dash straight up the road. Got the idea? I'm sending McNaughton Smith round Nicholson— he's back at duty again. And I'm sending you up the road. All right?"

"Up the open road in broad daylight?" said Craig thickly, trying to curb his anger.

Mair nodded his head slowly. "Those are the orders I got, Hugh," he said quietly. "Those are the orders I give." He turned away and took his stick from his neck and swung it jerkily by his side. "Did Morris bring those Vickers with him? . . . Good, good. Send the trucks up ahead with one Vickers crew in each. They'll be able to give you covering fire, d'you see?" Abruptly, he reached for Craig's hand, shook it, and said, "One last thing." He stepped away from the clerks. "Morris has more spunk than Anstey. You can see them reflected in their platoons. Morris's men are ready to fight. Anstey's aren't. Put Morris into the Gap first."

*

The column started to move. First the truck carrying Richardson and Cratchley with a Vickers gun; then the truck carrying Holt, beside the driver, and Paterson and Sime in the back with the other Vickers gun; then the platoons on foot. The column started to wind up the road that climbed round the flanks of Mount Cameron and Mount Nicholson to Wong-nei-chong Gap.

Morris, marching behind the second truck, turned his head to the right and saluted as he passed battalion headquarters. Mair returned the salute, and nodded and smiled. Morris turned his head to the front again and marched on. There might be hell to pay at the top of the road, but, for the moment, climbing away from the salt-water slap and shuddering sharp-echoing concrete of Bowrington, marching between the roaring trucks and the iron-heeled company, he was invigorated by an exultant release of energy from reserves that he had imagined to be exhausted.

Sime looked over the tail of the second truck and smiled. "We'll show them now, sir."

Morris nodded. "Keep your head down," he said cheerfully.

They passed a junction, where a side road sloped down into the valley, and climbed towards a sharp right bend in the main road. Morris, wondering whether he would get his first glimpse of the Gap when he turned the bend, lengthened his stride and caught up with the second truck. But, when he followed it roun to the right, he forgot to look up for the Gap. The first truck h d halted suddenly, and the driver of the second truck now jumped on his brake. Ahead of them the road was strewn with obstacles: a burnt-out army vehicle, a mangled motor-cycle, and about a dozen dead soldiers, some of them Scots and some—in distinctively heavy greatcoats—Canadians. While he stared, he heard—even above the stuttering of the truck engines and the broken clatter of feet at his back—the urgent murmur of falling mortar bombs. "Take cover," he shouted, as he leaped off the road.

He had jumped to the left, downhill from the road, and the explosions that rocked the trucks blew their destruction over his head. He was safe and safe and safe . . . as one after another the bombs burst above him. He could hear Mair shouting, but could not disentangle the words from the noise of bombardment. Glancing over the verge, he saw the Old Horse striding up the road, brandishing his stick and yelling, driving the stragglers to cover. "Get a bloody move—" he shouted between explosions, "—understand Mr. Morris's order?"

The bombardment ceased. After a moment of ear-plugging silence Morris heard a steady hissing as of steam and a thin cry of pain. He climbed shakily to the road and—heavy-footed, stiff-legged—walked up towards the trucks.

"Stay where you are," shouted Mair.

Morris halted and looked back.

"Not you, Mr. Morris. Carry on and take a quick look round."

In the second truck Paterson and Sime lay together, shaken, dazed, but unscratched. His voice unsteady with thankfulness, Morris shouted for men to help them to cover. Holt and the driver were dead.

In the other truck Cratchley looked up with pale empty eyes and said, "Richardson's hit in the chest."

"Are you all right?"

Cratchley nodded.

Morris glanced at the driver crouched over the steering wheel, his face a mask of blood and oil. He glanced at the shattered, smoking engine and at the corpses on the road. "Come on," he said hoarsely. "We'll get Richardson out of this."

*

Like men in a dream, Mair and Ballantyne stood watching Morris and the released convict carrying a casualty down from one of the trucks.

"They were firing from Jardine's Lookout, sir," said Craig urgently. "They've got the whole road under observation, and they've got the range. If I stick to the road, I'll be sunk before I

ever get to the Gap. I want to take the company off the road,
scatter them through the scrub—"

Red-faced, shiny-eyed, Mair wheeled round to interrupt. "You'll
take your company down to the low road and hide out there till
nightfall." He was shaking with anger. "I'll tell Brigade. I'll tell
G.H.Q. No man from my battalion goes into the Gap before dark
—before those bloody field guns they promised us have softened
up the opposition." He turned aside, allowed his strained facial
muscles to relax, and called out to Morris: "Well done, lad. Take
your chaps down the hill to the road below and keep them tucked
out of sight." To Craig, he added, "See that they all get a hot meal
after dusk." And, beckoning to Ballantyne, he strode back towards
his headquarters.

Craig sagged, slightly ashamed that he should feel so relieved
. . . Good Old Horse.

*

During the long afternoon the sky clouded over and rain set in.
The cold water dripped from the branches overhead and ran in
rivulets down the steep hillside. Morris sat with his head bowed,
holding his wet shirt-collar against the back of his neck, and
letting the trickle of rain from the brim of his helmet fall between
his splayed legs. Anstey sat beside him, shivering.

"Where's the new man?" asked Morris, his jaws stiff with cold.

"W-Wallace? I don't know. I left him with the platoon. I don't
like him."

"He'll be feeling lonely."

Anstey shuddered violently. "You know why he's here? He's
waiting for one of us to be knocked out."

Morris glanced at his companion's small dark face and took a
deep breath and grinned. "I suppose he is. Well, he can have my
place right now. I've had about enough for the time being. I'll
come back when the rain stops."

Anstey did not respond, and they lapsed into silence again.

Towards evening Ripley sneaked up to the high road and
returned with three greatcoats—one on his back and two over his
arm.

"Where did you g-get them?" asked Anstey harshly.

"Just the job for you, sir," said Ripley with husky persuasion.
"Nice and warm, like."

"Where did you—"

"Oh, shut up," said Morris, remembering the corpses ahead of the trucks. "Does it matter?" He slipped out of his equipment and pulled the heavy Canadian coat over his soaked khaki drill. "Good man, Ripley. I'd give you a fag, if I had any."

Smiling and winking, Ripley produced a packet of cigarettes and a box of matches. The cigarettes, too, were Canadian.

"Want me to 'elp you, sir?" Ripley asked Anstey, holding out the spare coat.

"No," said Anstey angrily. "There's blood on it."

Ripley took the coat away, and Morris sat smoking and listening to the rain on his helmet.

Before dark he walked along the hillside to visit his platoon. Paterson and Sime had recovered. Sime, who was wearing the coat that Anstey had refused, looked rather pleased with himself. "It just shows you, sir," he said. "They couldn't hit the back of that truck, and it wasn't even moving." Paterson described himself unsmilingly as, "Fine." And Barker summed up for the rest of the section: "Nothing wrong with us that a plate of stew and a tot of rum won't cure." Morris gave them four cigarettes to share out, and moved along to the next section.

Foggo complained about the bastard rain. "In your next incarnation," said Morris, winking at Jannelli, "you'll maybe be a bastard duck and glad to see it." He gave them four cigarettes and moved on.

Cratchley was sitting by himself, and grateful for a smoke. "The two lads who carried Richardson down say he was still breathing when they left him at the hospital," he said calmly. Macdonald was more concerned; he shook his head and said: "We've lost the best gunner in the battalion." Meechan rubbed the palm of his hand across his wet face. "*Maskee*," he said. "It's mortars we need, not machine-guns." He took a cigarette and surveyed Morris. "Nice coat," he commented. "If your face was cleaner, you'd look like a bloody brass-hat."

Morris returned to Anstey and sat beside him as darkness fell with the rain.

"Pity about Holt," he said, saddened by the darkness.

"Farquhar too," said Anstey.

"Is Farquhar—?"

"This morning. They were at Oxford together, you know. I wanted to go to Oxford."

"Not me." Then Morris recognised the opening in Anstey's defences and tried to break through. "What was your subject?"

"Does it matter?"

There was a sound of suffering in the words that silenced Morris.

Later, however, when Silver waddled down the road with a party of men carrying dixies, and Morris started to ease himself to his feet, Anstey said quickly: "I suppose we'll be moving forward as soon as we've eaten?"

"I suppose so."

"Are you frightened, Morris?"

"I think so. I'm too cold and hungry to be sure."

*

The island was no longer secure. The house was no longer a comfortable refuge. The narrow bed in the dark was no longer a complete escape. Box within box within box—and in the last, the smallest one, only yourself.

James Lin lay and listened to the occasional distant explosions, the steady rattle of rain on the window, and the impatient beating of his heart.

He should not have stayed in the colony. He should not have come to the Gows' house. He should not have retired to bed until he was exhausted enough to fall immediately asleep.

He lay thinking—unable to stop thinking—of ruin. The guns outside and the broken pattern inside. Anna, Mary, and Mrs. Deveaux were living in hospitals. Peter Deveaux had left to join his mother. Mrs. Brewster and her children were staying only because Mr. Brewster might not be able to trace them if they moved. The Willoxes were staying only because they had no other place to go to. Mrs. Gow had become an ineffectual, finger-twisting, self-centred, elderly woman. Roderick Gow was like an exiled emperor, alternately tyrannising his small band of adherents and seeking their approval and applause of his old unscrupulous empery.

It was easier to contemplate the changes in the Gows than the changes in the Lins. Anna had found strength, and James had lost it. Man of two worlds, he had called himself. Man of no world, he could call himself now.

He could find neither the resignation of the East nor the decisiveness of the West. He could neither content himself to remain out of the fight nor reach the resolve to take up arms. The causes were as tangled as the fallen tram-wires down in the dirty streets.

*

Peter Deveaux wakened with a shiver, bewildered for a moment to find himself in the murmurous lobby of the Grips. There were smells of whisky and tobacco smoke in his nostrils and a thick voice in his ears: "The motor-torpedo-boats attacked the ferries this morning? All right. But that hasn't stopped the Japs, has it? They're still coming across." The lobby was crowded with armchair generals.

He seized his bag and heaved himself out of the chair. Angered by the ugliness around him and by his mother's forgetfulness, he limped quickly towards the staircase and climbed to the first floor of the hotel, where wounded soldiers were lying on mattresses on the polished boards. The dim light, the silence and the smell of antiseptic were unnerving. He saw a solitary nurse and, hobbling quietly towards her, joyfully recognised Nell Griffiths.

"Hello, Peter," she said, more surprised than pleased.

"Hello," he said. "I've been waiting downstairs for God knows how long." He watched her face. "I'm cold and hungry and tired." Still watching her expressionless face, he suddenly remembered the men lying on the floor, vying with him for her compassion. "And I twisted my leg on the way down here—tripped over some tram-wires trailing across the road."

She was still damnably cool. "What do you want?" she asked.

His anger blazed. "My mother promised to find a bed for me here. Where the hell is she?"

*

The column started to move. Craig stood on the high road and watched the first men come up—two scouts, Barker leading his section, Morris leading Foggo's section. He fell into step with Morris.

"Dead quiet," he reminded him softly.

Morris nodded.

"We've got to make a job of it—show that the C.O. was right in holding back till dark."

Morris nodded.

Awkwardly intent on inspiring the subaltern with some warmth and confidence, Craig added, "The C.O. seems to have a pretty high opinion of you."

Morris looked round, startled and suspicious.

"When he's around," said Craig, smiling, "it seems you can't put a foot wrong."

Morris responded with a shy grin. "He doesn't know how many feet I have."

Content, Craig marched with him round the bend of the high road and past the two trucks where Holt and the drivers sat waiting for burial. Then, while Barker's section cleared a lane between the corpses on the road, Craig said, "I'll wait for Anstey here. We'll be right on your heels."

"See you in the Gap," said Morris.

Craig watched him go . . . Mair had not managed to get support from the eight field guns allotted for the original counterattack . . . It was unusually quiet in the valley. But Indians, Canadians and Scots were all moving forward now.

*

Barker followed the scouts. Paterson followed Barker. Sime, hampered by his new greatcoat, sweated and panted after Paterson.

*

Foggo followed Morris, and Jannelli followed Foggo . . . Seventy-eight, seventy-nine, eighty, eighty-one . . .

*

Macdonald took long easy strides, feeling his wet clothes chafe against his skin, and the blood reinvigorate his chilled limbs; listening to Cratchley and the others at his back, willing them not to set their feet down clumsily, not to rattle their weapons and equipment; regretting that the rain had not continued to pour, to wash out the little noises of the advance, to add its violence to the occasion.

*

Morris strained his eyes, trying to distinguish dark from dark. The road climbed round the side of Mount Nicholson. On his right, he could make out wooded slopes rising towards the hazy skyline; on his left, he could rather feel than see the steep fall into the black pit of the valley. Following Barker's section round another sharp bend in the road, he suddenly discerned the head of the valley, where a shoulder of Jardine's Lookout sloped down to meet Mount Nicholson. When Barker's section halted, he stood still for a few moments, waiting for the advance to continue, before he realised that they had reached Wong-nei-chong Gap.

Heart in mouth, he went forward to join Barker in the narrow stretch of road between the shoulders of the hills. After a hasty look around, stumbling over corpses, he brought up the rest of the platoon and disposed the sections to meet attack from east, south or west.

As Craig led Anstey's platoon into the Gap, the spell of silence was broken : half-a-dozen hand-grenades burst on the road, flaming briefly on the disintegrating file. The scattering of Anstey's men among Morris's produced a sudden confusion, which was aggravated by another light shower of grenades.

"Stand fast," called Craig clearly.

Against the steep face of the cutting on the east side of the road, he spoke to his subalterns. "There's a police-station above us. The Japs are inside it." He looked at each of them in turn. "You've seen the station, Anstey?"

"From a distance," replied Anstey, defensively.

"You know it, Wallace?"

"Ye-es." The word came loathly, but Wallace then nodded his head eagerly.

"You'll go with Anstey. There's a flight of steps up the face of this cutting. It's no distance from the top to the station. Toss grenades inside, work round to the rear and try to find a way in. As soon as you're clear of the steps, Morris and I will follow and try to break in at the front."

With his men at his back, Morris watched Anstey and Wallace lead their platoon quietly up the narrow flight of steps. His throat was dry, his breathing ragged. His heart leapt at the sudden, terrifyingly close, clatter of heavy machine-guns. Anstey's platoon began to fall back in disorder.

"Stay where you are," shouted Craig. Thrusting a way for himself, he ran up the steps. "Follow me." 16 Platoon started to climb again. "All together—charge !"

Morris's stomach heaved as he watched Anstey's men scrambling up after Craig. Then the machine-guns opened fire, tracer bullets burning bright arcs across the Gap, and he saw that the assault had been checked. The last men on the steps were tumbling into the road, crowded from above, and other men were slithering and

recklessly leaping down the face of the cutting, some of them
falling on top of his own sections.

"Stand fast, 17 Platoon," he shouted. "Mr. Anstey's platoon,
rally on the other side of the road."

The guns ceased fire, and, in the whispering, scuffling silence,
he waited for Craig, Anstey and Wallace. The narrowness of his
sympathies was brought home to him when Lance-Corporal Foggo,
at his back, muttered: "Bastard massacre. Only about a half of
them's come down."

One of the casualties on the steps was still moving—a big man,
big enough to be Craig. Morris called for a couple of volunteers,
led them up to the big man, and, after a glance at his face, watched
them carry him down. On his own, cautiously, he climbed higher,
twice startled when other survivors crawled over the edge of the
cutting and fell to the road.

"Mr. Morris," came a call from below.

Morris hesitated, lying against the steps. He was almost at the
top. He could see a boot against the sky.

"Mr. Morris!" It was Ripley calling.

In a confusion of relief and frustration he hurried down to the
road, where he found McNaughton Smith waiting for him.

"Hello, Morris." The size of the man and the rich resonance of
his voice were reassuring. "I've arrived rather sooner than I
expected to, but I gather that things are already at sixes and
sevens."

"Craig's still up there. He was attacking the police-station. It's
pretty heavily defended—with two or three machine-guns."

McNaughton Smith looked at him carefully. "And what were
you planning to do?"

"To bring him down—along with any other wounded still up
there."

"On your own?"

"Of course not," said Morris touchily. "I was just making a
recce."

"I'd like to hear your report."

"Damn it, I didn't have time to reach the top. But, if you've
finished quizzing me, I'll go back now."

McNaughton Smith took a box from his greatcoat pocket. "Have
a piece of Turkish Delight, old man, and let's put our heads
together. We can't take up the offensive till my men recover their

breath. They've come a long way at forced pace. We'll get Ramsay to join us. He's the only subaltern left in my company."

"But what about Craig and the others?"

"Send someone up to look for them."

Morris turned towards Ripley, and hesitated. But the runner had heard. "You want me to 'ave a dekko, sir?" Uneasily, Morris said, "Yes—but don't stick your neck out."

C.S.M. Duncan was patiently sorting out D Company on the scrubby shoulder of Mount Nicholson. Leaving him in command, Morris followed McNaughton Smith to the southern end of the Gap and into the side road where B Company were waiting alongside the shoulder. A faint crackle of small-arms fire rose out of the darkness below.

"East Brigade in action," said McNaughton Smith approvingly. "Now, Ramsay, have a sweet and give us the benefit of your attention."

"For God's sake," said Morris, "let's get a move on!"

McNaughton Smith looked at him solemnly. Fatty Ramsay chewed Turkish Delight, and the sweet smell seemed to heighten the absurdity of the situation.

"To advance up those narrow steps," said the captain, "would be to invite a repetition of disaster. Have you reconnoitred the flank?"

"No-o," admitted Morris, suspiciously.

"There's a side road—like this one—at the end of the Gap. You haven't ventured up it?"

"No." Morris was angry. "I didn't know there was a side road."

"We'll take a look at it now."

"Craig isn't a bloody fool," said Morris hotly. "He wouldn't have taken us up the steps if there'd been an easier way round the flank."

*

With Ripley at his heels and Anstey in his arms, Craig confronted them—McNaughton Smith unctuously unreal, Ramsay chewing (a whore's cud, from the smell of it), and Morris incoherent. He laid Anstey at the side of the road, and the subaltern's helmet tipped back, revealing the small dark face stiffened by shock, the eyes bright with terror.

"He looks bad," whispered Morris nervously. "We'd better get him out of here."

Craig touched Morris's arm and led him aside. "He's not so bad as he looks. There are others worse than he is. And we can't spare a carrying party yet."

"What about Wallace?"

"He's dead." Craig hesitated. "You and I seem to have a special dispensation, Johnny," he said gently.

Morris straightened up and managed to smile.

"I was about to reconnoitre the flank," said McNaughton Smith. "It might cost less life to—"

"It's worse than the front," said Craig sharply. "There's a thick belt of wire all the way round—British wire."

McNaughton Smith nodded equably. "A job for the artillery."

Craig hesitated, wondering how long the surrendering silence would continue, if he chose not to speak first. "We can try both front and flank this time. Take your pick."

"I'll take the front," said McNaughton Smith calmly, "but I won't launch an assault until your chaps have negotiated the wire on the flank and are able to give us covering fire."

*

Morris led his platoon cautiously up the side road, while Craig waited with the survivors of Anstey's platoon. It was confusingly dark on the flank, and disconcertingly quiet. Morris spread the sections along the road and, passing by touch of hand the order to advance, climbed over the wall and up the steep grassy slope to the wire. There were two double-apron fences and, between them, an extended concertina of Dannaert wire. Ripley nudged him and swore in a husky whisper. He nodded glumly. If it had been McNaughton Smith instead of Craig waiting at the road-end, he might have withdrawn his platoon without even touching the wire.

There was only one way to approach such a breadth of barbed-wire entanglement on so steep a slope. He lay down on his back and, while Ripley helped him to raise the bottom strands of wire, he dug in his heels and thrust himself head-first under the first apron. As he did so, he was startled by a distant scream of pain.

*

Shaken by the screaming, Jannelli relaxed his grip of the taut wire.

"Watch my bastard face," hissed Foggo.

Jannelli heaved the wire up again and allowed Foggo to wriggle underneath.

*

The screaming came in short, panic-choked breaths. Paterson and Sime looked at each other.

"Who is it?" whispered Sime nervously.

"Coming from the Gap," guessed Paterson. Then he pointed towards Barker, who was signalling them to follow him under the first fence.

Sime shivered and followed.

*

Macdonald tore his arm on a barb, as he struggled impatiently upwards. Cratchley, at his side, said slyly, "That's Anstey screaming." Macdonald muttered contemptuously, "Shut your dirty mouth and keep moving."

*

A single shot like a whip-crack ended the screaming.

Breathing more easily, Morris reached up behind his head to lift the roll of Dannaert wire off the ground. He winced at the swish of falling missiles, lost himself in an explosion. Swollen-headed, ballooning up out of darkness, he became aware of the tugging at his feet, of Ripley's hoarse voice vibrating against his ears, "Let go—let go—go—let go the bloody wire—wire."

He let go. He felt the barbs tearing his clothing, knees, cheek, ear and hands. He heard a frenzied rattling of machine-gun fire.

"Are you all right, sir? Not wounded, like?"

Morris heaved a great breath, but could not speak. There seemed to be vomit in his throat.

Craig and Meechan were speaking somewhere.

"Like flies on fly-paper." Ripley's voice again. "Lucky for us we 'adn't all got under the wire. Lucky for us it was only grenades."

"You were the only lucky ones." Craig, bitter again, frustrated. "Any other casualties, Meechan?"

"Corporal Barker lost some fingers."

Morris tried to ask to see Barker, but could not make himself understood. He let go again.

When he recovered, his head was aching, his torn flesh smarting and his damp body tremulous with cold. It was still dark, and Ripley was still by his side.

"'Ave a swig of this, sir." Stale water. "We're up on the shoulder of Nicholson, sir. We're all 'ere—w'at's left of the two companies. We've called off the attack, but we're going to stay 'ere and keep the Japs on the other side of the Gap." Morris did not care. "We got off pretty light—our own platoon, like. But Mr. Ramsay 'ad bad luck. When 'e 'eard the Japs plastering us with grenades, 'e thought it was us giving 'im cover, and 'e started to attack and ran right into the machine-guns like Mr. Anstey did. 'E was almost cut in 'alf, they tell me."

Morris tried not to care. "Anstey—and the other wounded—have they been carried down yet?"

Ripley was silent for a few moments. "The wounded 'ave been carried down. Not Mr. Anstey. 'E's dead." He was silent for another few moments. "There's something else you're bound to 'ear sooner or later, sir. Remember that screaming? That was Mr. Anstey. And remember that shot? That was the Skipper."

Morris's head began to feel swollen again. His cheeks burned and his temples throbbed. "What?"

"Captain Craig shot Mr. Anstey—to stop 'im screaming, like."

"Who—" began Morris shakily, "who told you that?"

"Some of the lads in Mr. Anstey's platoon. They were waiting with Captain Craig at the road-end, and they saw 'im go back into the Gap, and then they 'eard the shot."

"Christ!" exclaimed Morris excitedly. "That's no proof."

Ripley turned his sharp-nosed face away.

"You keep your bloody mouth shut, or—or I'll have you court-martialled, see?" And, in a confusion of terror and shame, Morris fought back an impulse to batter the runner senseless.

*

The two depleted companies lay on the shoulder of Mount Nicholson, immediately above the main road, ready to halt any enemy advance across Wong-nei-chong Gap. In the dark of next morning they received a reply to the message they had sent down to battalion H.Q. McNaughton Smith was to withdraw his company down the valley to a new line. Craig was to hold the enemy at the Gap until the new line was formed.

"When you go down," said Craig forcefully, "you might impress on Mair that we can't hold out unless he sends up some food and ammunition."

"With pleasure," promised McNaughton Smith.

Before B Company withdrew, Craig walked across the shoulder to warn his platoon commanders of the movement and to extend their already thin lines. He was desperately tired. He had failed Mair, and he might fail him again. He might not be able to hold this exposed shoulder with less than half a company of shaken, exhausted men. He came first to C.S.M. Duncan, whom he had set in command of Anstey's platoon. When he came to Morris, he heard B Company starting to move out.

"Tell your men to stand fast," he ordered Sergeant Meechan. And, lying beside Morris, he forced himself to repeat what he had already told C.S.M. Duncan. But, having said what he had to say, he found himself ready for once to say more. He was ready to talk about anything—to testify to his survival, to Morris's survival.

"You still look pretty seedy," he said. "Maybe you should go down with B Company."

Morris hesitated before he muttered gruffly, "I'm all right."

The instinctive hesitation. The grudging resolve. Chinese Morris. Craig felt warmed by his understanding of the young man. "I mean it," he said, trying to put some of his warmth into the words. "If you're still feeling the concussion, you'd better go—"

"Look," interrupted Morris with harsh hostility, "I'm not going down on my own. But I'd like to know why the hell it's B Company, not Don, that's going down. Why do we always get the tarry end of the stick?"

Suddenly cold again, bewildered, Craig struggled to his feet. "Too early," he muttered, "to say which end has tar on it."

He tried to find the place where he had left his runner. On his way, he stumbled over a man and fell awkwardly to the ground, bumping his face against the damp earth. As he strove giddily to regain his feet, he accidentally laid his hand on the man, and shivered. The man was dead. Craig could not make out the face of the corpse and did not care to look closer. He stared at the shadowed bulk, the unknown, the unknowable, soldier. Tasting earth on his lips, he spat, tasting the final defeat.

He found his own place and slept for two hours. Then, after making a round of the company, he settled down to wait for food and ammunition. When the sky began to lighten, he sent his

I

runner down with a message to Mair, demanding supplies for the
coming day.

*

In the daylight, Morris lay apart, bleakly aware of his height
above sea-level, feeling the lift of the ground against his belly and
the oppression of the cloud-curdled sky on his back. The land
shaped itself to his discomfort: the hills bore against his head and
feet and fell away on either side of him; from time to time he had
to raise his helmet to counter the longitudinal pressure, and from
time to time he had to spread his arms to preserve his latitudinal
balance. He made these movements with a certain detachment—
able to observe himself with torpid interest and to criticise his
lack of resistance to the mild concussion he had suffered under the
barbed wire—but he could not break the obsessional ritual until
he heard Meechan's warning shout and the fall and slapping
explosions of mortar bombs.

This was an art of war that had been neglected in his training:
the art of defence by simple endurance. You needed no weapons,
you offered no violence. You lay on the ground, a few yards away
from your neighbours, and kept your head down, while the enemy
spent his ammunition.

When the bombardment ended, he shook crumbs of rock and soil
from his hands and looked along the scattered line of prostrate
men. He remembered the Mohammedan muleteers on their prayer-
rugs, the Chinese abasing themselves in smoky joss-houses. He
remembered Anna, and wished that he had gone down with B
Company and not stayed to press his dirty face against the earth
and wait to hear someone else cry out as hot metal tore into cold
flesh. If anyone but Craig had told him to go down, he would have
gone, rejoicing. But it was Craig who had told him, Craig, who
thought he was Lord God Almighty, who shrugged off the burden of Torrance and left him to the hawks, who shut Anstey's
pitiful mouth with a bullet. The swish of mortar bombs again.

After the second bombardment, Craig stumbled across to his side.
"They're softening us up before they attack. We'll have to get
more ammunition. I sent my runner down, but he seems to have
been knocked out. We'll have to send someone else."

Morris twisted round to face him and caught sight of Ripley
lying at their feet. He had not spoken to the man all day. He felt
uneasy in his presence.

"I'll 'ave a go, sir," Ripley said.

Stirred by a premonition, Morris wanted to protest.

Craig did not give him time. "I've got the message written out—ammunition immediately and food after dusk. Find a way down under cover and guide the ammo-carriers back."

"Right, sir," said Ripley.

"Move fast," ordered Craig. "Be back within the hour."

"Fastest man in the battalion," boasted Ripley, with an anxious, smiling glance at Morris. "Quarter-mile champion, like."

It was the first time Morris had heard of the championship. The husky boast echoed in his mind as he watched Ripley jolt downhill out of sight.

As the hours passed, Morris lay alone, separated from all his men by Ripley's shadow.

*

It was wearing towards evening when the Japanese advanced. They crossed the road suddenly and took cover before D Company could fire a shot. The forward section of C.S.M. Duncan's platoon stumbled to their feet and, stiffened by fear and cold and inaction, started to run jerkily back.

Craig heaved himself up and drew his revolver. "Get a grip of yourselves," he shouted. "Get down and prepare to fire." They stared at him, their pallid faces ugly with terror and fatigue, and lowered themselves wearily, despairingly, to the ground. He looked along the line for other signs of cracking, and his attention was held by Morris, whose sick face was turned towards him, whose red-rimmed eyes were staring fixedly, loathingly, at his revolver. He shouted: "Snap out of it. Look to your front. Have you no grenades left to throw at them?" There was a moment of silence that gave him answer; then they came under mortar fire again, and he dropped to the ground, weakened by anger at his helplessness.

A cold wet mist blew up from the valley, suddenly filling the Gap. When the bombardment ended, the Japanese climbed out of the mist and fell back under small-arms fire, suffering a few casualties. They fell back so quickly that Craig knew what would happen next. The mortars would batter his line again, would keep on battering until they had battered his few remaining men into the ground. He jerked himself to his feet and ordered the company to withdraw. "At the double," he shouted, in anguish. "Before they mortar us again."

He stood aside and watched the men scrambling past him. They were afraid of the enemy at their backs, and he was afraid of the enemy inside him. He could understand now why Anstey had shot himself.

*

Mair received Don Company with dazed sympathy and toneless encouragement, and housed them in his headquarters for the night. Morris and his platoon were allotted an upper room in which, since the windows were uncurtained, they were forbidden to strike a light. As soon as they had managed to sort themselves out on the floor, a cook stumbled noisily and peevishly into the room, dumped down a dixie, and said loudly: "Bring this back to the cookhouse when it's empty or you get no bloody breakfast, see?"

"Away and stuff yourself," said Foggo fiercely.

Without a glimmer of light to help them, Morris and Meechan attempted to share out the stew in equal portions. His cold hands slimy with grease, his head aching from the clamour of complaint, Morris wished to hell they had been allowed to go to sleep hungry. In the end he, Meechan and two privates did go hungry. He let the privates clean out the dixie with their fingers, and lay down, bitter and empty.

He could not rid his mind of the image of Craig's strained face, of the sound of Craig's cracking voice, as he shouted the order to withdraw. It had sounded like someone else shouting against Craig's will, someone who had seen that even Lord God Almighty could not make men with rifles hold out against men with mortars. The Craig who had shouted was certainly not the Craig who had brought up the rear of the withdrawal, who now lay downstairs. Downstairs-Craig would lie awake tormenting himself. Tomorrow-Craig would torment the company . . . It was time Craig was humbled . . . He should have been sent back to the Gap, as he had sent Morris back to Golden Hill . . . Or he should be wounded and have to wait in pain for someone to take pity on him and carry him down . . .

Later, when the room was quiet, Morris remembered the dixie. "One volunteer to take the dixie back," he requested. Nobody responded. He sat up and said loudly, "Somebody's got to take that bloody dixie back." Nobody—not even George Sime—volunteered.

"*Maskee*," he said. "You can whistle for your flaming breakfast."

Later, he rose and picked his way across to the dixie. "You bloody shower," he said contemptuously, but not so loudly, for he was beginning to believe that he was the only man in the room still awake.

Chapter Four

BEFORE dawn Craig mustered the company outside battalion headquarters and counted heads. There were thirty-four men left.

Mair and Ballantyne came out and took note of the number. Their boots crunched on wet gravel. Their voices sounded harsh, their words ragged, in the thin, dark, morning air. Mair detached himself from Craig and the adjutant and approached the silent ranks. "You'll be wondering," he said, "what the Old Warhorse has in store for you this time—eh?"

Morris, standing in front of his platoon, heard their responsive movements as consciousness quickened in their sleep-softened, goose-pimpled flesh.

"I've stuck Don Company out on a limb more than once—Golden Hill, the North Shore, Wong-nei-chong Gap—and you'll be wondering whether I'm going to stick you out on another limb —eh?" Briskly he tapped the gravel with his ash stick.

He paweth in the valley and rejoiceth in his strength: he goeth on to meet the armed men. Morris shivered.

"Well, you're not going out on your own this time. You're just going a couple of hundred yards up the road to join the rest of the battalion. There's a strong line up there—the Indians in the valley and our own companies on the lower slopes of Mount Nicholson. We've got the Frogs pinned down in the head of the valley, and we'll keep them pinned there. We'll all hang together this time— and hold our ground." He thumped his stick against his leg, looked up and down the ranks, and nodded to Morris, who—as a startled gesture of acknowledgement—sprang to attention. The men greeted the C.O.'s assurance with murmurs of thankful relief. Morris hoped that Sime would not, in the first flush of gratitude, call out, "Good Old Warhorse!" And in the same instant he recognised the absurdity of his own position—the only member of the company standing stiffly to attention. He hesitated uncomfortably, until

Craig came forward and, in a voice that cut through the men's complacent murmuring, took command.

Once again they marched up the road that led to Wong-nei-chong Gap, but this time they did not have far to go. They halted beside two petrol pumps perched on the outward verge of the road. Morris remembered them: ahead lay the junction of the low road —where Anstey had shivered without a greatcoat, and Wallace had sat alone—and the high road—where Holt and the two drivers sat waiting for burial. He hated this valley—on the east, the massive hills where the invisible Japanese lay, and, on the west, this road that climbed round Mount Cameron and Mount Nicholson to the narrow Gap where the corpses lay thick on the ground.

Craig called Morris and Duncan forward and pointed into the thinning darkness. "A and C Companies are below the road, linking with the Indians in the valley. B Company are straddling the road. And we've to find positions above the road." He was as cold and hard as ice. "The Canadians are up behind us, on Mount Cameron."

Duncan, still anxiously establishing himself as a platoon commander, asked, "Will there be anyone on our right flank—higher up Mount Nicholson?"

"There are Canadians on the other side of Nicholson. There won't be anyone on the crest till the enemy take it."

Duncan looked uncomfortable. "They'll be sitting right on top of us, then."

Craig turned on him. "Your men weren't very keen to block the way up to the crest last night!"

Then, mercifully, from a short driveway opposite the petrol pumps, McNaughton Smith emerged into the road and wished them all a good morning.

"If you come up this way," he said pleasantly, "you'll contact guides ready to point out the right flank of my company." To Craig, he added, "You may find it convenient to share my headquarters. I've taken possession of the garage at the top of this drive. It's cut out of the living rock, and it houses a very comfortable motor-car."

Craig responded stiffly. "I'll see how it lies in relation to my platoon positions."

"You'll find it lies closer to your positions than to mine," admitted McNaughton Smith with genial candour. "I was seduced by the car—a Bentley."

Craig turned rudely aside. "Lead on, Sergeant-Major Duncan."

McNaughton Smith laid a hand on his arm. "Before you go," he said in a deep, confidential tone, "let me say how glad I am to see you and young Morris here. When I heard that you'd withdrawn from the Gap, I didn't ask for details. Without knowing your particular reasons, I was satisfied that you'd taken the right decision."

"*I'm* not satisfied," said Craig, hollow-voiced.

"There are breaches that cannot be filled with dead." McNaughton Smith's hands made pale pleading movements in the shadows. "Our only purpose now is to delay defeat, and to do that we must stay alive."

"Follow Duncan," Craig ordered Morris.

McNaughton Smith stood erect and silent, a large man under a small helmet.

On Sergeant Meechan's suggestion, Morris decided to reorganise his platoon into two sections. Stumbling around hastily in the half-light under spindly trees, they attached Paterson and Sime to Corporal Macdonald, and the remainder of Barker's section to Lance-Corporal Foggo.

Paterson was the only complainant. "What's the idea?" he demanded.

"There aren't enough men for three sections," Morris explained.

"Two sections or three, you'll still have the same number of men."

"Chipperow," said Meechan.

But Paterson stood his ground. "You're doing Sime out of his promotion, that's all."

"I'm not forgetting Sime," said Morris. And he resolved to enquire about the procedure for promotion in the field.

For two or three hours after dawn, the company lay under cover, unmoving and unmolested. Morris drowsed, mistily aware of the men around him and of the sounds of distant battle. Broken sunlight fell on him and warmed him, and once, in a moment of miracle, a bird sat above him and sang. But by mid-morning Duncan's fears had been realised. The enemy had advanced from Jardine's Lookout, passed over the corpses in Wong-nei-chong Gap, and seized the crest of Mount Nicholson, the first height in the western half of the island. From the heights of Mount Nicholson, Japanese snipers started firing along the battalion line. Morris rolled over to his left side, peered up the hill, and kept watch for enemy movement against the bright skyline, until a runner crawled up from the rear to summon him to Craig's headquarters.

"It's in that garage, sir. Snuggest H.Q. we've ever had."

"Good," said Morris sarcastically.

As he went down, dazed by the lingering image of the bright skyline, he caught sight of the petrol pumps at the side of the road and was seized with a strong sense of pattern. Golden Hill and Torrance—the petrol pumps at Bowrington—Wong-nei-chong Gap and Anstey—the petrol pumps here. It was a pattern that seemed to have the inexplicable significance of nonsense rhyme. Craig left Torrance to die—petrol pumps—Craig shot Anstey— petrol pumps . . . By the petrol pumps at Bowrington, the girls with green tea; by the petrol pumps here, the singing bird. By the petrol pumps at Bowrington, Holt adding leaven to Craig's stodginess; by the petrol pumps here, McNaughton Smith pouring cold water on Craig's fevered resolve. A pattern that could be so varied seemed also to be validated. Excited out of his languid resentment, he descended the hill slowly, as he looked within himself for other variations.

Craig was standing in the mouth of the garage. Behind him, inside the sunless cavern, McNaughton Smith sat upright, but with closed eyes, on the back-seat of the Bentley.

"The enemy are up on Mount Nicholson already," announced Craig brusquely.

Morris's resentment revived. "I know. They've been sniping at us."

"You didn't report that."

"We're lying doggo," said Morris, on the defensive. "Anyway," he added, turning aside at the crack of a distant rifle, "you can hear them from here." He kept his head averted, pretending to look at something on the hillside.

"You don't seem to like the way I run this company."

"Eh?" To maintain his pretence of innocence, he was obliged to glance now, enquiringly, at Craig's neat pale face.

"You can speak your mind." It sounded like a challenge.

"What are you getting at?" Morris wriggled uncomfortably.

I*

"Maybe it'll help if I tell you that the C.O. has just made you a captain."

"You mean—" Morris found himself short of breath—"you mean I'm moving?"

"The C.O. didn't have that in mind but, if you want to move, I'll speak to him about it."

"No, no." Morris flushed. "I wasn't asking for a transfer. I was just wondering why he promoted me."

"For services rendered, I imagine."

Morris thought he could detect a sneer behind the words. He clenched his fists and tried to control his nervous breathing. "Did you have anything to do with this?"

"Nothing. You're under no obligation to me. So maybe you'll answer my question now. You don't like the way I run things?"

Uneasily, Morris looked up and saw the strained expression on Craig's face. He was not ready to fight with Craig, formidable Craig.

"Speak frankly, Morris." McNaughton Smith's voice echoed portentously in the sunless cavern. "It would do you both good to have a bit of what the troops call 'a barney'."

Morris smiled weakly, searching his numb mind for vestiges of reasoned complaints, trying to reach beyond the cryptic pattern of the petrol pumps.

"All right," said Craig tiredly, "let it drop."

"Tell him, Morris," came the resonant voice from the Bentley, "tell him that flesh and blood—"

Craig wheeled round angrily. "Shut up!"

McNaughton Smith closed his eyes again. "Very well. May I just offer my congratulations to Captain Morris?"

"Thank you," said Morris unhappily.

Craig led him a little way down the drive. "I've got a job for you. Our line is in the wrong place. We should be further back, with our right flank against Mount Cameron, linking with the Canadians on top."

"You want us to move back?"

Craig's anger sparked again. "No! Our orders are to stand here!" He controlled himself. "We'll have to make sure the enemy don't work their way down from Mount Nicholson and get between us and Mount Cameron. We'll have to patrol the gap between the hills and see that it's kept clear of Japanese. You'll

take the first patrol, Duncan the next . . ." Before he dismissed
Morris, he added sharply: "One other thing. Get yourself and your
men cleaned up a bit."

Morris was about to protest, when he recalled that, despite the
shortage of water, McNaughton Smith and the company runner,
as well as Craig, were clean-faced and shaven. As he climbed the
hill, his smothered resentment turned against himself. Despon-
dently he numbered his faults. But the faults that he could
enumerate—a dirty face, a servile timidity, a tendency to pity himself—appeared to him to be no more than symptoms. He could not
remake himself to his own satisfaction simply by washing his face,
adopting a swagger and counting his blessings—any more than
the M.O. could cure malaria simply by heaping blankets on a
shivering patient. These faults of his were symptomatic of some
basic defect in his character, of some larger negation. There was
something *lacking* in him.

Suddenly he stopped, tensing his muscles, stretching his fingers,
disturbingly aware that the thing he lacked was within his grasp,
that he could reach out and take it—if only he knew what the
devil it was. And this was no day-dream; this awareness was as
certain as a bird's song. He knew—as he knew sky and hills and
the percussions of battle—that he need not always feel awkward,
inadequate, ashamed.

It was a momentary enlightenment. As he set himself to the
hill again, he remembered his resolve to enquire about the possibility of promoting Sime. How the hell could he have forgotten
Sime's promotion when his own promotion was being discussed? —
Selfishness was another fault to add to the list. And how the hell
could he decently announce his own promotion and, in the next
breath, admit that Sime's promotion was still in the balance?
Maybe vanity was another fault to add to the list.

He chose Macdonald's section for the patrol and, leaving Sergeant
Meechan with Foggo's section, led the way round the back of the
isolated house that stood above the garage, and struck up into the
cleft between Mount Nicholson and Mount Cameron.

The sun was still shining, and the hills were bold with colour
and shadow. He kept the lead, taking sensuous pleasure in the
stretch of his stride, in the tightening of his thigh muscles as he
climbed, in the weight of his boots on rock. It seemed a long time
since he had last been permitted to walk in daylight. But he soon

climbed out of his strength and met his hunger and tiredness again. While he rested, Macdonald came up to him and said: "You shouldn't be taking the lead, sir. I'll send a scout ahead for the rest of the way." The corporal looked down the slope and called, "Paterson! Up here, *jildi*!"

With his eyes half-closed, Morris saw Macdonald dark against the sky, man and gun all of a piece. He wondered how men like Macdonald and Craig came by their self-assurance.

There were no Japanese in the cleft between the hills, and—since the patrol went unchallenged—there seemed to be no Japanese far enough along the crest of Mount Nicholson to overlook the cleft. Scouting ahead, Paterson made contact with Canadian troops who were being pushed back by the enemy on the other side of Mount Nicholson.

Leading the patrol downhill, Morris lost the way and brought them out in front of, instead of behind, the house above the garage.

"The door's open," he observed to Macdonald, checking his pace. "There can't be anybody in there?"

"I'm just wondering," said Macdonald, "whether a Jap sniper could have got this far forward during the night." The rest of the patrol, coming to a halt behind him, picked up his alertness and turned to stare at the house.

"Will I take a dekko inside?" Cratchley volunteered, blinking his pale eyes.

Macdonald shook his head contemptuously. "Not on your own, boy. I know you."

"There might be some water in the pipes," suggested Sime.

"There might be some chow and fags lying around," said Paterson.

"Enough of that," warned Macdonald.

Morris, his curiosity aroused, said, "We'd better make sure it's empty."

They entered cautiously. The ground floor had been thoroughly looted. There was a trickle of water left in the pipes, but the pantries were empty except for one smashed jar of marmalade swarming with insects. Upstairs, the looters had evidently not had time to complete their work; two rooms still wore some of their luxury. One had been a woman's bedroom; and a woman's ghost seemed to hang in the perfumed air. The patrol stood crowded together just inside the door and looked around. A silk cover, dragged from the bed, had caught on a cabinet and been left lying in gleaming folds across the soft-piled carpet. One drawer of a chest had been pulled out and overturned, and the contents of white linen and lace spilled on the floor.

Cratchley made for the dressing-table.

"Come back here," ordered Macdonald.

"There might be some fags."

"Come back here or I'll flatten you." The corporal's dark face was ugly with contempt. "Downstairs, all of you. The whore's gone out of business."

"She wasn't that," muttered Sime.

"Wasn't what?" demanded Macdonald.

"What you called her."

"You knew her?" sneered the corporal.

"Come on," said Morris, "let's go." They filed out, looking dirtier, clumsier, heavier, coarser than before. "And while I'm making my report, get yourselves cleaned up. You're a bloody disgrace to the company."

*

It was a dark night with a heavy dew. Standing by the petrol pumps, Craig tried to interpret the stammering and flashing of small-arms and read the course of the battle. The line was threatened on both flanks: it seemed to him that, in the valley, the Indians and A and C Companies were holding their ground against successive thrusts; but it sounded as if the enemy were still advancing on the right, behind Mount Nicholson. He had turned Morris's platoon to meet any break-through by the cleft between the hills, and he had sent a frank message down to battalion H.Q., expressing his doubt whether the line could hold through the night. There was now nothing left to do but wait—and make sure that all the men waited.

Although B and D Companies were not being attacked, they had suffered a few casualties from chance bursts fired by trigger-happy Japanese machine-gunners on top of Mount Nicholson. Already, two wounded men had passed him on their way to the rear. The first man, carried by two of his comrades, had been seriously wounded in the neck and shoulders; Craig had watched them go down, and only on the approach of the second party had he begun to wonder whether the two carriers would return. The second party had consisted of a man wounded in the upper arm and a man keeping him company, and Craig had taken note of the chaperon's name and sent him back to the line.

He stood until he began to feel giddy with fatigue and had to lean against one of the cold moisture-beaded pumps. He waited until the Japanese assaults had spent themselves and, with silence humming in his ears, he knew that the line had held and that there would be no order to withdraw. The Old Horse would clamp his jaws and close his eyes now, letting the faint-hearted message he had received from Craig stand in the war-diary as a measure of his own stubborn resolve this night. *Enemy attacks on left wing of battalion repulsed without loss of ground,* he would tell himself, like a man offering his evening prayer or counting sheep. *Enemy attacks on A and C Companies repulsed. Battalion line unbroken.*

As Craig walked stiffly across to the garage drive, he heard another footstep on the road. "Halt," he ordered. "Where are you going?" he demanded, moving up the road to confront the man.

"I've—I've been wounded, sir."

"Where?"

"In the—in the arm."

Craig felt the man's arms. "You're lying. What's your name?"

"Briggs, sir."

"B Company?"

"Yes, sir."

Weighed down with shame and anger, Craig gripped the man's shoulder. "Get back to your post—before I break every bone in your cowardly body."

This was the foretaste of defeat. The task now would be to salvage fragments of the breaking patterns of discipline, to organise fear. To make others stand fast, he would have to stand fast himself. To make himself stand fast, he would have to humble himself, narrow his thinking and feeling, shut his eyes to much and stop his mouth, accept orders impossible of achievement.

When he reached the garage, he wakened McNaughton Smith. "It's time you took a spell out there."

"What in heaven's name for?" asked the other peevishly.

"To turn back deserters."

"From *my* company?" McNaughton Smith heaved himself upright on the back seat of the Bentley.

"I've sent two men back to your company. I've got their names."

"I'll speak to them in the morning. No desertions from your company, I hope?"

"Two. They took one of the wounded down and they haven't come back." Craig's voice shook. "I'm pretty sure that Cratchley, the ex-convict, was one of them. I didn't see the other's face."

"You couldn't be on the *qui-vive* all the time," said McNaughton Smith unctuously.

"Cut out the sarcasm," said Craig. "Are you going to take over for a spell?"

"No, I'm not. You're losing your sense of proportion. It may be that a sentry should be posted, but there's no need for me—or for you—to play the angel with the flaming sword all night long."

Craig went to the back of the garage and lay down and fell asleep, without a prayer.

In the morning, the Japanese withheld their infantry and bombarded the line with heavy mortars.

*

James Lin came down the hill, carefully observing how the morning sunlight fell on scarred buildings and dirty streets.

> *Where soldiers go*
> *Bare thorns and brambles grow.*

James Lin came down the hill, down to his own level, happily observing his descent.

Good iron is not made into nails . . .

This was the way a man walked down to his ancestors.

He prepared his explanation . . . When the earth is eaten black, the locusts fly on. So it was in the house on the Peak. There was another air-raid yesterday, much more destructive than the first; the water pipes and the telephone wires were cut, and several windows were blown in and one of the Brewster children scratched about the legs by shattered glass. We saw the blackness and began to move on. Mrs. Gow, Mrs. Brewster and the children moved immediately after the raid, making for a hospital; attended by Roderick Gow and one Chinese servant, they wound their way down the hill in hurried procession. We watched them go, the Willoxes and I, and stood in silence at the broken windows long after the procession had dropped from sight. We waited, restricting our movements and guarding our tongues as if we had suddenly recognised that we were in a stranger's house, and suspending our decisions about the future as if we had suddenly found ourselves in strangers' bodies. When Roderick came back, he told us that he had decided to take up arms and sharply suggested to us that, as there was little food and less water in his house, it was time we set about looking for another refuge. He went to collect some of his possessions, but we—still withdrawn from the world of arms and possessions, conscious of neither hunger nor thirst—rested in strange bodies in a strange house. It was the deepest rest I have ever known. It was the kind of peace that must come to a dying man when he sees at last the immensity of the shadow over him and the futility of trying to drag himself back into the light. And, although we were in strange bodies, I knew the Willoxes' peace as deeply as I knew my own. We sat there—the old man, the old woman, and the young man with the old head—until Roderick was ready to leave. Impatiently, he offered to lead the Willoxes to a house lower down the hill. To me, he said: "You'll be all right, James. You must have plenty of friends to turn to." Either he had forgotten that Anna and I have few friends in Victoria, or he simply meant that I am Chinese and that there are thousands of other Chinese in the city. I watched the Willoxes follow him down the hill, and shut the door. It occurred to me that he had not expected me to accompany him to the battle, as he had once expected me to accompany Tim Brewster, and I guessed —I am certain, now, that, at this time when the Westerners are drawing close their circle of defence, he sees me outside the circle, with the other Chinese. During the night, alone in his house, I saw myself as he had seen me . . .

Walking downhill, James wondered to whom he should make his explanation—to Anna or Sammy King.

There were two obstacles between him and Anna: one, he hated hospitals, because of their smell of disinfectant—the acrid smell that Westerners regarded as the warrant of cleanliness—and because of the impression of mourning conveyed by their white appearances and their murmurous, shuffling sounds; and, one (wilfully he fell back on the Chinese method of enumeration), he was by no means sure that Anna would understand his explanation. The war had at once sharpened her perceptions and misdirected her conceptions . . .

This is the difference between us now. A bullet breaks a mirror and I pick up a fragment and look at my strange face; I remember then who I am and where I have come from, and I am able to decide where I must go. A bullet breaks a mirror, and Anna says: "Bullets break things, break flesh. Bullets break so many things, so many different kinds of flesh, that people prize more highly what cannot be broken by bullets." She is thinking of John Morris, of the intangible link between them that bullets cannot strike. She is deceived into thinking that the strength of the intangible against the tangible is a measure of its strength against the intangible. She is looking at Morris, not in the mirror. And because Morris is a man who does not cast a great shadow, is the kind of man who will always escape the headlines, she thinks that they will be left in peace together, East and West. And it is too early to undeceive her . . .

Sammy King was playing cards with a compositor, two machine-operators and a stranger. Moreover, he had removed his hat and revealed his undistinguished cranium . . . No, I don't want to play . . . Hesitating on the fringe of the group, James tried to master his disappointment and suppress the old feeling of aimlessness that threatened his new-found confidence.

"Things don't look too good," said Sammy. "Japanese navy blockading the island, British blowing up the oil depots." He paused to concentrate on the game. He looked unusually solemn, but perhaps only because he was not chewing; he seemed to have run out of seeds and gum.

James turned away. The floor at his feet was littered with cigarette-ends, spoiled paper, empty food-containers.

"Only thing to do," said Sammy, "is to pack close. Choy, here, snuck out of Blue Pool Road last night—saw the Japanese raping and bayoneting."

One of the players suggested that Sammy was unlikely to be raped.

"You don't know these monkeys," said Sammy.

James scuffled his way through the litter.

"What are you aiming to do?" asked Sammy.

Nothing . . . James spoke bitterly . . . Nothing at all.

*

"Again?" suggested Mendes. "Will we do it again?"

Brewster shook his head and rose from the Lewis gun. "I'm going to have a smoke," he explained to the instructor, Ignatief. "I think I've got the hang of it anyway."

"Bloody good," said Ignatief. He had a long face and heavy-lidded eyes, and everything he said sounded lugubrious. "One bloody lesson and you get the hang!"

A few paces to the rear, Brewster lay down and lit a cigarette-end. He was tired and nervous.

"Will we do stoppage again?" Mendes asked the White Russian. "This time I will do it right."

Brewster scowled at the bitter-tasting stub between his finger and thumb. It was easy enough to go through the motions of firing a Lewis gun and dealing with stoppages, but it was not so easy to do other things right. He could see now—although he had been as blind as a boy at the time—that he should have either stayed with Jenny and the kids or insisted on being posted to the West Brigade. Now that the East Brigade's counter-attacks had failed and the survivors had fallen back on the Stanley Peninsula, it was clear that there was no longer a chance of breaking through the Japanese wedge between the brigades, that the men cut off in Stanley could do nothing to halt the enemy's advance on the city, that their only purpose in fighting now would be to save their own skins. Here, he could do nothing for Jenny and the kids. Here, he could do nothing but stand sentry and learn to handle a Lewis gun. And, from the sounds of battle, he knew that the Japanese were already hard against the crowded city.

*

The bomber climbed into trailers of cloud, banked over the harbour, and dived back on Mount Cameron. The screaming of its engines was punctuated by the mortar-bursts on the battalion line.

"He's putting on an act," said Birse sourly. "He knows bloody well that—for all the opposition he's likely to find—he could putter over with his flaps down."

Two or three puffs of black smoke appeared in the wake of the plane.

"There's our ack-ack now," Kerr retorted, as if he felt obliged to justify his minutes-old appointment to the command of H.Q. Company.

"They'll have to do better than that," said Niven.

The pilot pulled out of his dive, and for an instant it looked as if he had been making a feint on the hill. Then the bomb that he had dropped exploded on the crest.

"He knows his job," muttered McNaughton Smith.

"He must be a German," said Birse. "The Nips don't fly like that."

Craig lay between Kerr and McNaughton Smith, watching and listening, until the mortar-fire on the battalion slackened, and Ballantyne shouted from the doorway of battalion H.Q.: "Company commanders ! We're ready for you now."

They could not, however, enter H.Q. immediately. They had to stand aside and make way for the stretcher-bearers carrying Major Ingham out. He had been wounded by the second mortar-bomb that had hit the building, a few minutes after the company commanders had assembled, and he was unconscious now, his face as white as the hair at his temples. They stood still, awkwardly bunched together, until the stretcher-party reached the road and disappeared downhill.

Inside, two clerks were clearing up debris under the supervision of the dusty and dishevelled C.O. The company commanders ranged themselves on one side of the room: Kerr, H.Q.; Birse, A; McNaughton Smith, B; Niven, C; and Craig, D. Mair wasted no time. Anxious to disperse the gathering before the Japanese mortars re-opened fire, he dismissed the clerks and issued his orders quickly.

He had been instructed to adjust the battalion line and was now ready to admit that, from the outset, he had considered that the line was too far forward. "Our right flank should be against Mount Cameron, not Mount Nicholson. We're going to pull back, but we'll have to do it damn carefully, after dark. The enemy are now within a hundred yards of our front." He looked aggressively along the row of officers, slapped dust from his arms, and turned to a wall-map. There was still a West Brigade line of sorts across the island, from north shore to south shore. The heavier pressure was against the northern half of the line, where the Japanese were obviously intent on seizing Mount Cameron and thereby over-looking the city. To resist the pressure, the northern line was to be adjusted: the English machine-gun battalion would continue to block the enemy's advance along the north shore; to link with the English, the Indians would withdraw to the mouth of Happy Valley; to link with the Indians, the Scots would withdraw to the eastern slopes of Mount Cameron; and the Canadians would continue to hold the crest and western slopes of the hill.

Craig noted that Mair had been ordered to set up his new headquarters in Wanchai Gap, to the west of Mount Cameron. It sounded suspiciously like an anticipation of the Mount's fall to the enemy and the battalion's withdrawal to the west.

"Our line will be shorter than it is at present," said Mair, "and I've decided to take one platoon with me for local defence of Wanchai Gap. Don will be on the right flank again, but on steeper ground, and could, I think, spare a platoon." He raised his eyebrows and stared at Craig.

"Morris's platoon?" guessed Craig.

The C.O. continued to stare. "No," he said. "We'll leave Morris in the line. He'll manage on his own better than Duncan would. I want you yourself in Wanchai Gap, d'you see?"

Craig kept his mouth shut, suspicious and dejected. Did Mair and Ballantyne think that, because he had pulled out of Wong-nei-chong Gap, because he had thought that the line might break last night, he was needing a rest? Did they think that Captain Morris would be more reliable on the right flank? In an instant, seeing the shrewdly confidential look in Mair's bright blue eyes, he dismissed his suspicions, guessed that the battalion were to make their last stand at Wanchai Gap and that he was being detailed to help Mair select the last positions. But he was still dejected, loath to leave the line.

There were no questions. Mair gave them permission to leave.

"One moment, please, gentlemen," said Ballantyne. To the C.O., he added in explanation, "The P.M.'s message, sir."

Mair slapped some more dust away. "All right. Get a move on. Read it out, man." And he stood with his head bowed and his dirty face wrinkled in a bemused frown while the adjutant read the message.

"P.M. to Governor, Hongkong

"We were greatly concerned to hear of the landings on Hongkong Island which have been effected by the Japanese. We cannot judge from here the conditions which rendered these landings possible or prevented effective counter-attacks upon the intruders. There must however be no thought of surrender. Every part of the island must be fought and the enemy resisted with the utmost stubbornness.

"The enemy should be compelled to expend the utmost life and equipment. There must be vigorous fighting in the inner

defences, and, if the need be, from house to house. Every day
that you are able to maintain your resistance you help the Allied
cause all over the world, and by a prolonged resistance you and
your men can win the lasting honour which we are sure will be
your due."

Chapter Five

A s soon as there was full darkness that night, battalion headquarters, escorted by C.S.M. Duncan's platoon, began their march
out of Happy Valley, making for Wanchai Gap, to the west of
Mount Cameron. An hour later, the remainder of the battalion
began their withdrawal down the valley to the eastern slopes of
Mount Cameron. Craig delayed his own departure for Wanchai
Gap in order to accompany 17 Platoon. He was unwilling to
relinquish command of the right of the battalion line until he had
seen Morris's men carefully disposed in their new dispositions, unwilling to part from Morris until he had satisfied himself that the
new captain was fully conscious of his responsibility.

Marching down the road with Morris, he remembered their
march up the road, from the junction to the mortared trucks, on
their way to Wong-nei-chong Gap. Now, as then, he was aware
of the closeness of the young man, of the ease with which they
could, in the dark of night, in face of the dark of death, open their
minds and mouths and come to some kind of understanding. But,
as the silence between them lengthened, he saw with weary clarity
that what he wanted to do—what he yearned to do in these last
dark minutes—was not to understand Morris but to change him.
He wanted to destroy the young man's awkward humility and
weakening compassion and into the void left unload some of his
own angry pride and ruthless determination. He wanted to make
Morris ready to fight—to fight like a man possessed . . . Why?
. . . It was not—*pace* the Prime Minister—because Morris and his
handful of men could compel the enemy to expend much life and
equipment, not because their resistance could be prolonged and
lasting honour their due . . . Why, then? . . . Was it not simply
because of Craig's pride, because of his determination to show the
fools who had involved him in this tragic farce that he could rise
above their folly, that he had a dignity and a worth they had not
taken into their shabby reckonings? Was it not because he would

not die—he would not let Morris die—until the fools had been
made to see how much of human strength and courage they had
thrown away?

*

Craig was silent, his gait jerkily stiff, as if he were impatient to
be off to Wanchai Gap. Several times it was on the tip of Morris's
tongue to say that he could find his own way and that Craig should
push on ahead. But he was not quite ready to let him go.

Since their exchange of words at the garage, the previous day,
he had seen little of Craig but had often thought of him. Under
heavy mortar bombardment, he had found that thinking about
Craig helped to steady him. And, now that they were to be
separated for the first time, there were two things he wanted to
say. First, he wanted to ask about Anstey—not with any vindic-
tive intention, but simply to rid his mind of the tormenting doubt,
the uneasy ghost. He believed that he was ready now to swallow
poor old Ripley's story, to accept that, in the tricky situation at the
Gap, Craig might have been obliged to shoot—to give the *coup-de-
grâce*—in order to avert panic.

The other thing he wanted to say was even more difficult to put
into words. He wanted to find some way of letting Craig know—
without embarrassment to either of them—that he recognised and
respected his—well, his soldierly qualities. He had not always welcomed Craig's orders, but that was because he himself lacked some
of the—call them 'soldierly qualities' for the time being. There
were some things—Torrance, Anstey, Ripley—that had hurt
at the time, but . . . But now, with Craig so unapproachably
silent, so jerkily impatient, some of these things started to hurt
again.

It was a cloudy night. When he reached the stones that he and
Sergeant Meechan had piled up just before dusk to mark the point
of departure from the road, Morris could barely distinguish the
scrubby buttress above, which had been selected by the C.O. himself for the battalion's right flank position.

"Let Meechan take the men up the hill," said Craig, in a rough,
constrained voice. "I'd like to have a word with you."

Morris followed Craig across the road and turned to watch
Meechan directing the first section up the side of Mount Cameron.
"Well," he said, trying to make an opening for what he had to
say, "we're on our own this time."

"That's what I want to talk about," said Craig. "If the enemy break through up here, they'll have the rest of the battalion at their mercy below." He was speaking hurriedly, as if still impatient. "It would be just as well, too, to remind your men that the city lies at their backs. When this line goes, a lot of women and children may die. Unless you get orders to withdraw, you fight it out here."

"Barring the two desertions," said Morris, and he found that his voice, too, was coarsened by constraint, "my men have always waited for the order to withdraw."

"Up till now, I've always been around to see you didn't give that order too soon."

Morris's sudden anger made his voice even thicker. "You think—"

"I think you'd like to spare your men more than is possible. Your job is to make them fight."

"We never get a chance to fight! We can't fight mortars!"

"Keep your voice down. Mortars won't take the city. So long as there's some kind of a line here after the mortaring, you'll be able to delay their infantry."

Morris lost his head. "The way we did at Wong-nei-chong?" he sneered. "It wasn't me that gave the order to withdraw up there." Immediately the words were out of his mouth, he sagged. Now, trembling with shame and anger, he sensed Craig's effort to contain himself, to support himself. Then, because Craig would not, or could not, speak, he had to say something else to ward off the wounding silence. "And what happened to Anstey up there?"

After a moment, Craig said in a new voice, an empty voice, "He shot himself."

"Anstey," said Morris, wishing he could keep his voice steady, wishing he could see Craig's face more clearly, "didn't have the nerve to shoot himself."

After another pause, Craig asked, "You think I shot him?"

"If I do," said Morris truculently, "I'm not the only one."

"No point in prolonging this. You've got your orders."

"I got my orders," muttered Morris, "from the C.O. I'm responsible to him from now on."

As Craig turned away, he revealed his pale, drawn face. It was the face of the man who had shouted the order to withdraw from Wong-nei-chong Gap.

Shaken, Morris watched him march down the road alone . . .
small neat head, erect carriage, stiff legs. Aware that he might be
watching him for the last time, he felt remorse beginning already
to eat into his anger.

*

There were only twelve men left—the platoon having suffered
since the withdrawal from Wong-nei-chong Gap three casualties as
well as two desertions—and Morris had to deploy them widely to
cover the slope from the top of the buttress down to the road.
As soon as the men were in position, Sergeant Meechan dis-
tributed hard tack and settled down beside Morris to eat his own
ration.

"Well," he said, "we're on our own this time." Then, his mouth
full of biscuit, he added jocularly, "But we've still got a captain in
command."

"Who told you?" asked Morris sharply.

"The Skipper. Congratulations, sir."

"Thank you," said Morris grudgingly.

They scanned the front in silence.

"No kip tonight," said Meechan.

"Is that a dig at me?"

The sergeant belched. "Could do with a tot of rum. Biscuits
don't take up much space."

"You seem to have got it into your head," persisted Morris, "that
I'm a real charpoy-wallah!"

Mildly, Meechan retorted, "You had a bit of a barney with the
Skipper just now?"

Morris peered at the scarred face. "So what?" he challenged.

"So you don't have to take it out of my bloody hide. He's a
queer chap. He'll never be satisfied."

Morris bowed his head. "Somebody," he muttered, trying to
relax, "once said I was like Craig—in some ways."

"He must have been looking through a bottle he'd just emptied."

"It was a girl."

"That explains it. Women never know much about men like the
Skipper. Women are easy satisfied."

It was a long time since Meechan had been so talkative. There
was no rum in him either. It was, Morris guessed, something less
palatable than rum that was slackening his tongue.

"You heard what the Skipper said—no withdrawal?"

"Aye."

"You weren't supposed to hear."

"You were supposed to tell us."

Morris hesitated. "We'll maybe not be pushed as hard as the Skipper seems to expect."

"We'll be pushed," said Meechan flatly. And the conversation died.

Morris felt a vague need to prepare himself, to orientate himself . . . Canadians on his right, on the crest and western slopes of Mount Cameron; McNaughton Smith on his left, below the road; the enemy in front; and the women and children in the rear —Anna Lin, Nell Griffiths, Joan Aitchison, Mary Gow, Torrance's whores, the green-tea girls, the two little beggars at Causeway Bay—for whom he had to be ready to die . . . Suddenly, he could hear his mother saying, *What was the sense of it, when he knew that the Japanese would get into the city anyway? What good did it do, holding them back a while longer, angering them all the more and making them all the harder on the women and children?* And he could see how his father, with one of his books of Scottish history on his knees, would be bewildered by the difference between the stirring battles for lost causes that had long ago cut off kings and the hopeless battles that now cut off penniless and unqualified students of law. And he could see his sister wearing black, like an old woman, and young Davie crying secret tears. They would never understand. Careful people, sheltered by their lack of money and their Presbyterian training from high adventure and uninhibited joy, suspicious of everyone unlike themselves, they would never understand . . . But Craig would understand.

As Morris kept vigil, the darkness began to burn on his tired eyes, and the wavering breeze to pain his cold hard ears. When the firing started, he was momentarily unable to place it.

"Other side of the hill," said Meechan.

Morris agreed. The attack was against the Canadians on the western slopes of Mount Cameron. The impatient rattling of distant automatics vibrated inside him. He had been hoping that the night would pass without incident and that he would be given an hour or two of daylight to prepare himself and his men, but his hopes were now rattled out of him. He could not for longer than a heart-beat deceive himself with the possibility that the

Japanese might be trying to by-pass Mount Cameron and force their way into the city through Wanchai Gap. He knew, from what he had been told and had seen, that the battle, where-ever it had started, would be for possession of this cold dark hill.

"Pass the word along," he said to Meechan. "No retreat." He heard the word go up the slope to Foggo's section and down the slope to Macdonald's. He peered at his wrist-watch, sud-denly anxious to mark the time. It was only ten minutes past ten—2210 hours. He spread his elbows on the damp ground and waited.

When the battle climbed to the crest of the hill, he called up to Foggo, "Watch your flank." The firing, like the breeze, was spas-modic. The noise gusted over the waiting platoon. "We could do with our Lyon lights here," he said to Meechan, aware that he was speaking only in order to keep his throat open. After every lull the guns sounded impatient to repair the breach in their death-rattle, to stitch up the holes of silence. "Ripley used to say the Japs couldn't see in the dark." His voice was almost as hoarse as Ripley's had been.

"It would take a flaming cat to see anything tonight," muttered the sergeant.

They were lying close together, and Morris could not remember which of them had made the move.

"Will I give the order to fix bayonets?" asked Meechan.

"Aye." And, as the order passed along the line, Morris rubbed his eyes, breaking the crust on the lashes, and drew his revolver. These were the only preparations that now seemed to make any sense. Nothing that he could think or feel would lighten the weight of darkness on his eyes or improve the mechanism of the weapon his his right hand. He heard the clicking of bayonets on rifles, and waited.

The bursts of distant firing seemed suddenly to take visible shape; their insistent hammering in his head seemed to create blotches of shadow in front of his eyes. He narrowed the spread of his elbows and raised himself in an effort to see more clearly. The stretching of his stomach caused him to belch wind that left a sour taste in his mouth and reminded him of his heartburn on Golden Hill.

"Enemy in front," shouted sharp-eyed Jannelli.

Morris could not see the enemy shadows now, but his tightened muscles acknowledged their approach. He kept his head up and tried to detect movement on the dark slopes and to control his fear-spiralled thoughts. Torrance—petrol pumps—Anstey—petrol pumps—Morris . . . Morris, Morris, Morris, throwing off his tiredness, quickened by the invulnerable lust for life.

At last he caught glimpses of the men coming towards him across the slopes. It was impossible to count them: there might have been half a dozen or half a hundred scattered through the scrub. It was possible only to discern particular men, now here, now there, and to sense the general approach of an extended line.

"Sights down," he ordered.

"Better not let them close in on us," warned Meechan harshly.

Morris raised himself to his knees and shouted, "Rapid—fire." And, as Brens and rifles fired, he shouted again: "Cease fire. Don't waste your ammo. They've gone to ground." He ducked as a few Japanese bullets whistled over the platoon. "D'you think we got any of them?" he asked Meechan.

"Hard to say. They flopped as soon as we opened up."

Anxiously Morris raised himself again to stare ahead. "If they come forward on their bellies, we'll have a devil of a job spotting them." Someone in Foggo's section fired, and out of the scrub in front came a hoarse cry. "That's the way," he called out excitedly. "Pick them off one by one." After an uneasy silence, the Japanese line jerked out of the scrub and charged, uttering strange, abrupt cries and throwing grenades ahead. "Fire!" he shouted.

"Now we'll show them," yelled Sime, down on the left.

The enemy line buckled and fell into cover. A few more grenades came over.

"They're withdrawing," said Meechan.

Morris felt cheated, unsatisfied. Warm now, and full-throated, he shouted to his platoon: "Don't let them get away. Shoot the arses off them."

But the Japanese kept to ground and withdrew without further casualties. For a long time one of their wounded called after them, in a shrill frightened voice, like a timid dog tied up in the dark. When at last he died—his final call falling away to a tremulous moan—the night seemed empty without him.

The sweat chilled on Morris's body. His excitement gave way to exhaustion. He lay beside Meechan, craving a smoke, staring swollen-eyed to the front, waiting.

In the early morning there was another attack on the crest. He could neither see any movement nor make any sense out of the pattern of shots. He could only lie still and wait for the next assault on his own line. Waiting, he tried to see himself as Craig at Wong-nei-chong Gap, tried to imagine how his will to stand fast might be undermined, but all that he achieved was a clearer recognition of how cruelly unfair his taunt about Craig's withdrawal from the Gap had been. Here, he stood in the West Brigade line, with Canadians above, Scots and Indians below. At the Gap, Craig had stood alone.

*

In Wanchai Gap, under the light of dawn, Mair looked very old. His sleepless eyes were heavily pouched and his cheeks were drawn. He leaned on his ash stick and spoke with jerky deliberation. "We've just been informed—the enemy captured the crest of Mount Cameron—early this morning. We've been ordered to hold them there. That means we'll have to string the battalion out—round the northern slopes of the hill."

Craig looked from Mair to Ballantyne, who had a field-dressing on his left forearm and a stolid expression on his face.

"I know, I know," muttered Mair understandingly. "It's a tall order, but we're the only troops available at the moment to stand between the hill and the city. I've ordered A, B and C Companies to withdraw to the northern slopes—as soon as they can disengage themselves from the enemy—and to await my order to fall back on the Gap here—as soon as the Brigadier has re-formed the rest of the line."

"What happens to Morris?" asked Craig stiffly.

Mair looked at him closely. "Somebody has to cover the withdrawal from the valley—somebody has to stay in the valley to block the roads for as long as possible. Morris is best placed to do both jobs."

"It won't be for long, sir," said Craig, dully, "with the enemy sitting on top of him."

"I know . . . I know. But, God help me, I've no choice." He checked himself, cleared his throat, and added, "I've sent a runner to tell him to fight it out on his own."

"You can count on him," said Craig. It was the end of Morris. He would die on Mount Cameron, as Craig should have died at Wong-nei-chong Gap, as Craig had still to die elsewhere. It was like an echo of the taunt that Morris had flung at him the night before, but this time his humiliation was mingled not with anger but with grief.

*

Looking down the crowded ward, Mary Gow caught sight of Anna Lin and another girl tucking in the new arrival. Walking towards them, she tried to remember whether she had ever met the man. She certainly could not recognise his bandaged head. "Captain Birse?" she enquired.

His bloodshot eyes turned towards her. "Hello, Mary," he mumbled.

"Feeling comfier?"

"Feel like hell."

"We'll give you something to make you sleep."

From the other side of the ward, Lieutenant Williamson called out: "Can't hear what he says. Ask him how things are going."

"Please don't shout," she said nervously. Turning back to Birse, trying to disguise her eagerness, she suggested, "Perhaps you'd rather not talk just yet?"

He looked up at her. "Hugh's all right."

She caught her breath, glanced at Anna and smiled.

"What does he say?" demanded Williamson.

Mary answered self-consciously, "He says Captain Craig's all right."

"How about Anstey and Morris?"

She felt obliged to look to Birse for an answer. But, when she caught his mumbled words, she told Williamson and the ward at large: "No more questions till he's had a rest. He says Anstey's gone and Morris is still alive and kicking."

"Good old Johnny," said Williamson excitedly.

"Morris?" repeated Captain Finlayson of the Volunteers, sitting up in bed. "I think I know Morris. Tall, thin chap?"

"That's him," said Williamson, blinking and grinning horribly.

"He was in that exercise in the Kamtin Valley?" asked Finlayson.

"That's him."

"Well, well, well," said Finlayson, smoothing his ginger moustache, "it must be true that there's a special providence for drunk men and children."

"What d'you mean, eh?" demanded Williamson aggressively. He had been fighting for his battalion ever since he was wheeled into the ward.

The breakfast trolley rattled in, briskly diverting the lieutenant's interest and reminding Mary of her duties elsewhere. Anna's helper had already gone, but Anna still stood by the bed, bright-eyed and slightly tremulous.

"You're over-tired," said Mary.

"No," said Anna, suddenly shy. "I am not tired." She picked up a bundle of soiled linen. "I am glad he was able to give you some news."

Mary glanced down at Birse's closed eyes. Already, she was waiting for the next arrival, the next few words of news, the next remote chance of getting a message from Hugh, who seemed to be slipping further and further away from her.

                                    *

It was full light now, and neither messages nor rations had reached 17 Platoon.

Sergeant Meechan spat a pebble from his mouth and swore at C.Q.M.S. Silver. "The bloody mules get better feeding than we do."

Morris was resting. "Just as well we don't have Punchy McGuire on the strength."

"Every man has a belly," said Meechan sourly, his scarred cheek twitching. Then, resignedly, he rubbed his unshaven face with his dirty hands and took a sip of water from his bottle. "Could do with a tot of rum," he muttered.

The clouds had broken up, and the sunlight fell warm on Morris's back, relaxing his taut cold flesh, loosening the coil of hunger in his stomach. He lay and let the sun stretch him out to his full size. He had no fear of falling asleep, for he seemed to have outworn his fatigue.

In the dark, he had thought of death. In the sunlight, he thought of life. His hands clutched, as they had clutched on the hillside above the petrol pumps, reaching for what he lacked. Seized with a desire to assert himself, he began to feel a nervous craving for the shuddering noise of his Bren guns, the smell of burnt cordite, and the sight of falling enemy; began to feel affronted that he was neither strengthened by messages from his own side nor challenged by the other side, that he was left in a great silence which suggested he and his dozen men had been overlooked or dismissed as insignificant. There was fighting down on the north shore, at the mouth of the valley, and there was a murmur of guns from the south of the island, but in the valley itself there was neither sound nor movement. The sun shone on bare white buildings, empty roads, deserted slopes, as it moved slowly across the sky.

In the late afternoon, a party of Japanese started to move down from Mount Nicholson into the cleft between the hills that he had patrolled with Macdonald's section. He ordered the Brens to open fire. Two of the party fell, but the remainder managed to scuttle down from rock to rock and disappeared into the cleft. He kept watch for them, his eyes tight in their sockets, his vigilance like a knot inside his head, until he began to feel uneasy. "What's happened to those Japs who went down into the *khud*?" he asked. And, when Meechan made no answer, he rose cautiously to his knees and scanned his front from flank to flank. He saw the helmets and tired streaky faces of some of his men who turned to look out of the scrub, but he saw no enemy. "They must still be in the *khud*," he said doubtfully. "If they'd gone up, the Canadians would have fired on them. If they'd gone down, B Company would have fired." And, when Meechan still made no answer, he lay down again, puzzled and uneasy, and waited for something else to happen.

He did not have long to wait. The hiss of falling mortar bombs shocked him into alertness. There were explosions and cries along the platoon line.

"They're up on top," exclaimed Meechan, wide-eyed, pointing to the crest of Mount Cameron. "They're firing down on us."

Morris peered up at the naked skyline. He could scarcely find breath to speak. "Where are the Canadians?"

"Get back in your places." Above, Lance-Corporal Foggo shouted at his men. "And keep your bastard heads down."

"We can't stay here," muttered Meechan urgently, "with them sitting right on top of us."

"Any casualties?" Morris called out.

"Two," answered Foggo. "One a goner, by the looks of him."

"One wounded," added Corporal Macdonald below.

"Spread out a bit further," ordered Morris deliberately, self-consciously. "And you, Foggo, pull back your right flank to face up to the crest." Craig couldn't have asked for more.

"We can't stay here," protested Meechan. "They've got—"

There was another hissing in the air, and Morris glimpsed a blur of the bomb that burst a few yards in front of him and Meechan. His eyes darkened and his head swelled to the roar of the explosion, and his outstretched left arm was hit as if by a hammer. The hill tilted up, and he fell into the clanging darkness, slowly turning round and round and round. Voices were shouting after him, shouting down into the darkness, and he remembered Ripley's hoarse voice reaching after him at Wong-nei-chong Gap and tried to struggle upwards. The hill swelled under him, lifting him through nausea into the light.

The air was heavy with dust and suffering noises. Meechan's face was old and grey. Above, Foggo's bow legs were sticking out of the scrub, jerking convulsively. From below, came Paterson's anguished voice: "Where are you hit, George?"

Morris struggled to raise himself, his head heavy with disaster and guilt. "Get down to the road," he shouted. " Get down to the road," he shouted, louder, "before they mortar us again."

Men stumbled out of the scrub and rushed downhill.

"Close in on B Company's flank," he gasped to Meechan, shamed and frightened by the sergeant's pallor.

Meechan, too, was trying to rise. As he rolled over, he revealed his blood-soaked back. Nervously harsh, Morris urged: "Chullo, Smiler. They've got our range." Awkwardly, with his good arm, he helped the sergeant to his feet. "How bad is it?" Meechan asked soberly. After a flinching glance at the torn cloth and blood from shoulder-blades to buttocks, Morris answered quickly: "Nothing deep. But you'll have a smile coming and going now." Gripping the sergeant's arm, he hurried him down the slope.

In the dry ditch beside the road, there were seven survivors: Corporal Macdonald, Paterson holding Sime in his arms, Jannelli, and three of Torrance's men: seven survivors out of twelve.

"Did you bring down your wounded?" he asked suspiciously.

"Couldn't move two of them," answered Macdonald with the unconcern of Craig.

Jannelli answered for the other section. "One wounded with us,

K

sir." He indicated one of Torrance's men. "Lance-Corporal Foggo and two men killed."

Poor bastard Foggo.

Morris made a nervous reckoning. Four wounded: himself, Meechan, Sime and one of Torrance's men. Only five unwounded: Macdonald, Paterson, Jannelli and two of Torrance's men. "We're not running out," he said shakily. "We're going downhill to contact B Company and find out what the hell's happening and get a better position."

He led across the road, and, as he reached the other side, a burst of machine-gun bullets whistled past his back. He jumped down into the scrub and twisted round to look back. One of Torrance's men—Hislop—was crawling painfully across the road. The other seven had fallen back into the ditch. "They're coming down the road," called Macdonald. Morris drew his revolver. "Leave it to me," cried Macdonald impatiently. He leapt out of cover, fell to his knees, and pressed the trigger of his Tommy gun. "Keep moving," he shouted. "Down to the low road."

Swallowing his resentment at the corporal's seizure of command Morris helped Hislop down through the scrub.

It looked as if the low road were also under fire. A dead man lay sprawled across it, with one hand reaching out almost to the feet of the huddled survivors of 17 Platoon. "It's one of the runners from battalion H.Q.," said Jannelli. "He must have been on his way up to us."

Morris stared at the corpse, wondering.

Macdonald jerked his hand dismissively. "He won't tell us much now." With his gun cocked, he ran across the road and squatted on the other side. "Seems to be all right," he said. "But you'd better make it snappy."

They hurried across and forced their way down through a mass of shrubbery. Stiff branches caught at Morris's left arm and made him swear aloud. Hislop, at his other side, was grimly silent. When they fought clear of the dark tangle, they found themselves on the brink of a frightening drop. They were standing on top of a concrete retaining wall—between twenty and thirty feet in height, on Morris's dizzy estimation—overlooking a cluster of houses perched on the steep hillside.

Morris looked round anxiously. "B Company must be down there somewhere."

"We can't all make that jump," said Paterson bitterly, sitting with Sime in his lap.

Morris lowered Hislop to the ground and walked over to take a look at Sime. The little man was conscious but, without his spectacles, appeared to be seeing from a distance, like a dying man. His arms were clasped around his middle, and there was blood on one of his hands. "How d'you feel, George?"

"Not too bad, sir."

"He can't make that jump," said Paterson.

Morris looked up at Meechan, who shook his bowed head. "We don't have much choice. If we follow this escarpment, we'll strike the road again."

"And we don't have much time," added Macdonald. He held up his hand for silence. There were crackling and scuffling sounds of movement on the hillside above. "Hold him tight when you jump," he advised Paterson. "I'll be down below to help you break his fall."

Macdonald and Meechan jumped. The corporal scrambled to his feet, but the sergeant lay still. Paterson, his face strained with apprehension, jumped with Sime in his arms, and Macdonald, his gun thrown aside, flung out his arms to receive them and fell under them.

Jannelli asked, "Will you manage, sir?"

Morris grunted. When he saw Meechan getting to his feet, he walked back to Hislop. "Can you jump by yourself?" he asked.

At his back, Jannelli said, "I could jump with him, the way Paterson did with Sime."

Hislop shook his head. He had difficulty in speaking. "Don't move me."

"The Japs are right on top of us," said Morris impatiently. "Go on," he added to Jannelli. "Get the hell out of here. You couldn't lift him, never mind jump with him." He turned to look for the other two men left on top and was just in time to see them leaping off with arms outspread like ugly, scraggy birds. "Bastards," he muttered. "Come on, Hislop. You can hang on to me. We'll go over together."

Hislop shook his head. "Don't move me." His face was streaked with dirt and pallor; his eyes were dull and sluggish. He might not live to feel the Japanese bayonet.

"Corporal Macdonald says to hurry, sir," announced Jannelli.

"Come on," Morris pleaded with Hislop.

Hislop shook his head, closed his eyes.

Morris ran down and sprang outwards after Jannelli. He landed awkwardly, knocking the wind out of himself, grazing his right elbow. Macdonald helped him to his feet and asked, "Where's Hislop?" Morris straightened himself up and saw that everyone was looking at him. "He's not coming. He's pretty far gone."

"The Japs'll get him," said Paterson.

"He wouldn't let us move him." Morris was almost shouting.

"That's right," said Jannelli.

And it was Jannelli's support more than anything else that made Morris recognise how completely he was losing command. "Get moving," he said roughly. "Macdonald will lead, and I'll bring up the rear. We can't have far to go. B Company can't be much further down the hill."

They went down between the houses, moving hurriedly in broken step and ragged order, glancing to right and rear for signs of pursuit. Macdonald took the most direct route he could find, and it was hard going for the wounded men at his back. Finally, to escape the maze of walls, he climbed over a low bridge and splashed down a hill-burn that spilled between boulders and eddied in frothy pools. "You stupid bastard," shouted Paterson, slithering drunkenly under his burden. Twice Morris fell and struggled to his feet gasping from the shock of the steely-cold water. "Hold it, Macdonald," he shouted. "Wait for me."

They gathered under cover of a spinney of stunted trees. "What the hell are you trying to do?" Morris demanded breathlessly of Macdonald. "You're supposed to be looking for B Company, not breaking our necks."

"Looks as if B Company's pulled out," muttered Meechan.

Morris nursed his aching arm and said angrily, "They wouldn't go without telling us."

"The runner that was knocked off," said Meechan, "—he must have been trying to reach us."

They were all silent.

Morris felt shrunken and inadequate. He had made an awful botch of things. It was time for Craig to bawl him out, to tell him what to do next. "We'll have a look further down," he said indecisively. "I'll lead."

He led them down under the trees. As he descended, he decided that Meechan must be right. There was no sign either of B Company or, further downhill, of A or C Company. The runner must have been carrying orders for a general withdrawal. It was galling to think that, if the orders had reached 17 Platoon, Foggo, Hislop and four other men might still be alive.

Still uncertain what to do, he led his party across a cemetery, and, as they followed a path between rows of headstones, a machine-gun opened fire on them from their right. He jumped behind a granite pillar and shouted, "Run for it." He drew his revolver and fired wildly in the direction of the gun. "Keep your heads down and move fast. There's plenty of cover." He watched them hurrying past him: Meechan with his eyes half-closed and his mouth open; Paterson, dark with sweat and blood, bent-kneed under the weight of Sime, whose round face was puckered with pain; Jannelli staring at him like a frightened deer; and the two survivors of Torrance's men. Macdonald was approaching less hurriedly, moving from grave to grave, giving covering fire. "Come on, Mac. Run for it." Dourly, he waited for the corporal and followed him out of the cemetery.

Meechan, bowed and unsteady, had taken up the lead, and Morris, bewildered, exhausted, tailed along wretchedly in the rear, accepting defeat. They reached the road alongside the race-track and followed it till, in the mouth of the valley, they came to a sangar manned by English machine-gunners—clean and tidy strangers, with inquisitive eyes and soft, surprised voices—who said that the only vehicle in the vicinity, a rations-truck, would soon be returning to Murray Barracks. Raising his head, trying to assert some pride in his dirty and tattered distinction as an infantryman, Morris thanked the gunners curtly. He led his party to the truck and came to an arrangement with the driver. In the fading light, they set off for the city.

At the first halt, the unwounded men climbed out to make their way on foot up to battalion H.Q. in Wanchai Gap: Macdonald, Jannelli and the two men of Torrance's. Morris looked at Paterson, expecting him to join the men on the road, then realising, with a cold and prickly sensation, that it was a wounded man who had carried Sime all the way from Mount Cameron to the truck.

"I didn't know you'd been hit," he said awkwardly.

"You want to see the hole?" asked Paterson.

"Shut up," said Meechan wearily. "It's his shoulder, sir. He's got more guts than civility."

After an uneasy silence, Morris looked down at Macdonald. "Think you can give the C.O. a full report?"

Macdonald nodded. "I think so, Mr. Morris."

"*Captain* Morris," corrected Meechan.

There was another uneasy silence. It was apparently the first time that Meechan had announced the promotion.

"Congratulations, sir," said Jannelli.

"Are you finished?" asked the driver.

Morris nodded dumbly and, as the truck moved away, watched Corporal Macdonald lead all that was left of 17 Platoon up another hill. He was finished with it all, finished, a hole in his left arm and a hollow of despair inside him.

The roads were broken with shell-holes and bomb-craters and littered with fallen masonry and wires and refuse. There was a fire down by the waterfront, and the flames seemed to attract the gathering darkness. There was a smell of ruin in the air.

When the driver halted at Murray Barracks, he looked around and said, "You'd maybe 'ave been better waitin' for an ambulance."

"You said it would be easier to get one here," Morris reminded him.

"Any ambulances?" the driver shouted to a sentry.

The sentry looked about him.

"Where's the nearest hospital?" shouted Morris angrily.

"The Grips is a hospital now," replied the sentry sourly.

Morris ordered the driver to take them to the Grips, and led his party into the lobby, where groups of civilians stood talking and drinking, and a man with a cheroot said that the military hospital was upstairs. An orderly met them at the top of the stairs, took possession of their weapons and ammunition, and showed them into a large dimly-lit place where men lay on mattresses in rows across the floor. His parting words were, "I think you've come to the wrong place."

A nurse who caught sight of them summoned a doctor, who put the matter more plainly: "This is a convalescent hospital for troops. We've no facilities for treating serious wounds, and no accommodation for officers. Let me have a look at you." With firm clean hands and brisk questions, he subdued their indignation. "You'll all live," he said, after his examination. "The little man's

in the poorest shape, but he has a good pulse and a good colour."
He ordered an ambulance, handed round his cigarettes, and said to
Morris: "There's no need for you yourself to go. I could soon
winkle the splinter out of your arm, and I dare say we could put
you up for the night—informally, you know?"

"Good," said Morris. But he felt that he had been exposed as a
fraud. It was the last straw. He was ready to weep.

"You'll get a good kip anyway," said Meechan, hoarse from
exhaustion.

The stretcher-bearers were approaching.

"Sorry I brought you to the wrong place," Morris mumbled.
"Look after yourselves. Look after George."

Paterson stared at him uneasily, lowered his gaze and said
quietly, "Cheerio."

The doctor led Morris to a platform at the top of the room,
probed the black hole in his left arm, told him that the splinter
seemed to have worked its own way out, and dressed the wound.
While he was completing the dressing, he paused to beckon and
say, "Nurse, can you find a corner for this officer?"

The nurse answered in a throaty voice, "I think so." Morris
jerked his head round to look at her. As she led him away from
the platform, they looked at each other again and smiled. It was
a smile that stretched his drawn face and expanded his tight
chest, that filled his dry throat and made it risky for him to
speak.

Nell touched his good arm. "I'm so glad to see you safe,
Johnny."

"Almost unscratched." It was a boast now.

She helped him to take off his helmet, harness, greatcoat and
boots and to settle himself in a camp-bed. She told him to sleep
and went away. Later—how much later Morris could not guess—
she returned with the doctor, who asked quietly, "Can't you sleep,
old boy?"

Thickly, Morris answered, "I seem to've forgotten the drill."

"We'll give you a jag of morphia."

Nell gave him the jag. He watched her pale face above him.
"My eyes won't shut," he muttered. Tight and crusty.

She wiped his eyes with damp cotton-wool. He could feel it
teasing out against his burnt eyelashes. She said something that
he could not catch. He thought something that he could not say,

as his jaws seemed to have slackened. She was still pressing the cotton-wool against his eyes and his brow, pressing him down and away from her, down and down, until he could hear once again the hollow noises of the depths to which he had dropped in Wong-nei-chong Gap and on Mount Cameron.

Chapter Six

CRIBBED in the sagging camp-bed, Morris wakened to the twilight of the makeshift ward. He was lying with his feet crossed and his hands resting on his stomach, after the fashion of a dead crusader. He lay still, loath to emerge from his drowsy weakness, fearing that if he moved he would suffer pain or recognition. There was only one person he wished to admit into his quiet corner of the world, and he kept his eyes half-open to watch for her.

"You like your sleep, don't you?"

Reluctantly he looked up at the big mouth and brightly inquisitive eyes. "Hello, Joan," he said lifelessly. Joan Aitchison, the scrawny blonde with whom Nell had shared the flat in Kowloon.

She twitched his blanket this way and that, bending over him, examining his face. "You were supposed to be signed off this morning, m'lad. And it's nearly three o'clock now."

"In the afternoon?" He felt pitifully weak.

She nodded, watching him with disconcerting interest.

"I suppose I'd better get up, then."

"You'll have to wait till the M.O. sees you. I'll go and fetch him." She looked away and twitched the blanket again. "I heard that Dick Torrance—" She glanced at him, her face ugly with enquiry and suppressed emotion.

"He was killed on the mainland."

She nodded quickly and went away.

It was a long time since he had last thought about Dick Torrance. *This must be the place where we drank gimlets with Fatty Ramsay. The band played on the doctor's platform under the boarded windows. The couples danced over the mattresses. Craig and Mary Gow sat over there, beside the man with the bandaged eyes. James and Anna sat over here, close to the camp-bed.*

The doctor advised: "You'd better spend another night here, Morris. You need the rest." And Morris smiled, and regretted smiling, and fell asleep.

When he next wakened, he ate a slice of bread and drank a cup of tea. He was glad that neither the nurse who brought the food nor any of the convalescents near his camp-bed tried to make him talk. There was still only one person he wished to admit into his privacy, and he lay quiet until she came.

On catching sight of her, he felt a twinge of disappointment. Nell had the white face of a tired girl and the flabby figure of a self-indulgent woman. She had dark smudges under her eyes and no lipstick on her mouth.

"If you can walk to the bathroom," she said, "I'll help you to wash."

The bath was half-full of brown well-water, and a notice on the wall gave warning: 'The Japs have captured the reservoirs. This is the last water for toilet purposes. Use carefully.' The wash-basin was ringed with scum. The lid of the pan was plastered with another notice: 'Please do not use this W.C.' Portents of ruin.

While Nell ladled water from the bath into the basin, he caught sight of himself in a mirror and stared at the small-eyed, thin-jawed, dirt-streaked, patchily bearded face. "Is that me?" It was an ugly, defiant face, which did not seem to belong to the man who had been content to lie narrowly confined in the sagging camp-bed. It soon weakened, however, when he scrubbed away the bold streaks of dirt and revealed more clearly the patchiness of the beard. "I still look like something the cat brought in," he muttered unhappily.

She made him sit on the edge of the bath and combed his hair. "I'll get you a razor," she suggested.

He slid his right arm round her waist and pressed his face against her bosom.

She smoothed his hair with her hands. "I've sent word to Anna," she said.

"I don't want Anna," he mumbled. Anna would stand before him like another mirror, like a neat reproach. "I want you, Nell." Immediate softness, unquestioning darkness.

She put her hands on his shoulders. "I've just sent the message," she said uneasily. "I should have sent it last night, but—"

"Nell—" He did not know what to say. How could he shape words to explain that he had come to grief through expecting too much of himself, that he expected nothing now, that he wanted—not to find himself in Anna—but to lose himself in softness and darkness. It was not in words that he wanted to extinguish himself. He tried to stand up, intending to kiss her.

She escaped his grasp. "I'll get a razor."

Alone, he sat on the edge of the bath, cold and angry. Everything was going to hell. The last brown water. The empty cistern above the pan with the fine mahogany-red seat. Nubile Nell carrying on like a nun.

A young man in civilian clothes appeared in the doorway. "Any news?" he asked, his thin clean face twitching with apprehension.

Morris, disliking him immediately, muttered sarcastically, "Says here the Japs have captured the reservoirs."

"It's all right for you," protested the young man shrilly. He limped forward a couple of paces. "See? I'm a cripple. I'll get short shrift if the Japs walk in here." Nettled by Morris's unconcern, he argued: "The other night they came on some of our wounded—unarmed—waiting to surrender. They didn't want to burden themselves with wounded prisoners. They bayoneted them all. One of the orderlies here has spoken to a survivor—if you want to check on the story."

"They won't go round killing off civilians—"

"They've k-killed civilians already!" exclaimed the cripple. "They've raped nurses." He hesitated, his unpleasant face betraying the switch in his thoughts. "Some of these girls here may be raped yet." He leaned forward, a lecherous gleam in his eyes. "It's on the cards, isn't it?"

"With you around it's more than likely."

The cripple stared at Morris, grinned sourly. "That seems to be the only way of getting it now."

"Oh, go to hell," said Morris.

The cripple hesitated on the verge of tears or anger, limped out, white-faced, carrion-eater, herald of ruin.

When Nell brought a razor, Morris shaved himself. She watched him, and he was shakily conscious of her nearness. But he did not touch her. When they returned to the ward, she gave him a cigarette, and, searching for a light, he found Punchy McGuire.

"How goes it, Punchy?"

"*Tik*," said the big man. But he looked at Morris as if he did not recognise him.

Everything was going to hell, all right.

*

Mary Gow stood outside the door of the officers' hospital. The sky was darkening, the air cold and tainted with smoke. There was a glow of flames above the western end of the city, a rumble of gunfire around the island.

Padre Ewen came up the drive and raised his right hand to the brim of his helmet, blessing her with a salute.

"Hello, padre." She stood aside to let him pass. She was as loath to cope with him as with her mother waiting inside.

He fingered his chin-strap. "Hugh's well. He sends his love."

She looked at him. He was like a robot, engineered to make the correct responses. "Did he say so?" She observed his surprise and discomfiture. She had broken the rules of robot-talk, and he was at a loss for an answer. "What did he really say—if anything?"

"You know what kind of a man he is."

"No." She felt compelled to torment Ewen into matching her new honesty. "When did you last see him?"

Ewen looked at her carefully. "Today. He was pretty tired, but he was still in one piece. I told him you were—well."

"And what did he say?"

The padre shook his head gently. "Nothing."

She felt the warmth of tears on her eyes and said sharply, "Thanks very much for telling me the truth this time."

"The truth?" Ewen swayed unhappily. "You're tired, Mary. Tiredness often makes us doubt."

There was a kind of tiredness that made you believe—not what you wanted to believe but what you knew you had to believe. She walked out into the open and heard him entering the hospital. She stood and thought. In front of her lay the sombre city, behind her the crowded wards and the airless little room where her pallid mother waited. There was no other place to go except inside herself, and she had been there too often already in the past few days. In a completely satisfactory world there would always be *another* place to go.

An ambulance arrived, and old Mrs. Deveaux got out and shambled up the drive, swearing at the driver until she recognised Mary. "Hello, love!" She reeked of gin. "How's Mum and Dad?"

"*He's* standing at the last barricade, waiting to shoot somebody. *She's* in bed here, ready to shoot herself."

"Jesus," said Mrs. Deveaux. "And what about yourself, girl?"

"I'm well. I must be. A padre just told me I was."

The old woman seized her arm. "Wait till I come out and we'll have a snifter together. I've got to collect some stores, and I don't want the disappointed virgins inside to smell gin on my breath. But don't go away and—oh, here, before I forget—here's a letter for that Chinese girl—Nelly Lin, is it?—no, no, it was Nelly who gave me the damn letter—"

"Anna Lin?" Mary took the letter. "She's sleeping. I'll give it to her in the morning."

"Don't go away," begged Mrs. Deveaux. "We'll have a snifter or two. It's Christmas Eve, after all."

Mary waited in the shabby twilight. The sky was rumpled with dirty clouds, and the first stars were small and weak.

*

The battle in the south was almost over. The enemy had overrun the forward positions of East Brigade and were now attacking the second line in Stanley village. On a hill south of the village, in the third and last line across the peninsula, with the sea not far from their backs, Brewster, Mendes and Ignatief waited behind their Lewis gun.

It was brighter than ever before, the battle; across the dark isthmus on which the village stood, tracer bullets cut crossing arcs, bombs blazed briefly, flame-throwers licked around pillboxes, and, now and then, a Very light hung like a new star, burning a hole in the night and revealing the sharp angles of buildings and the jerky movements of tiny men scattering into the surrounding shadows. The second line had already buckled, and the men on the hill waited for it to break or for the light of dawn to enable them to pick out the pudding-basin helmets of the enemy. Dawn was still hours away; the sky was still black and the old stars white.

There could be no doubt about it: the battle was almost over. And Brewster was able to acknowledge the certainty with a borrowed coolness.

"Just before morning," said Ignatief, "we move down the hill to that bloody big rock. You see?"

"O.K.," said Mendes.

It was from them—the White Russian and the Eurasian—that Brewster had borrowed his calm. He had come into this fight expecting too much, and, as quickly as he had discovered the nakedness of the garrison, the hopelessness of their resistance, he had lost heart. But they had come into the fight, as they went into most things, expecting little: the man without a country, and the man without a race. And he had borrowed from them a calm that was independent of hope. A few days ago, he had thought of men like Ignatief and Mendes as misfits. Now, he thought that, if they did not fit into the world, it was the world that was the wrong shape.

A Very light burst in the sky, star of Bedlam.

*

After broken sleep Morris wakened late on Christmas morning to hear the last few words of some announcement made by the doctor, in tones of polite urgency, from the band-platform. He looked out of his camp-bed and asked the man on the nearest mattress: "What was it all about?"

"Message from the General. Everybody that can fire a rifle's to get back in the line for a last stand."

They stared at each other until the man turned his head away.

"Well, m'lad, are you going?" It was Joan again—eyes, mouth, hands and accusation.

Morris flung his blanket aside. "I'd have been going anyway," he muttered.

"You'll get a chit from the M.O."

He struggled out of the bed, slipped his feet into his boots, and allowed her to tie the laces.

"Is Nell around?" he asked.

"She's off duty. She should be sleeping."

"Tell her—I didn't want to wake her."

"I wouldn't let you waken her, m'lad." She watched him stand up. "Look after yourself."

He smiled narrowly. "Just for your sake, I will."

On the platform the doctor gave him a clearance chit to present at G.H.Q. "They'll tell you where to go."

"You're not getting many customers," Morris observed.

"You're the third," said the doctor. "There may be more yet. I've got some Christmas messages to read out that may strike a spark here and there." He raised his shoulders uncomfortably. "None of these chaps is really fit for battle."

Morris returned to his camp-bed, donned his Canadian great-coat and picked up his helmet. He moved slowly, impeded not so much by the twinge of pain in his left arm as by the sensation of swelling in his limbs and head. He had lost the constrictions of fear and fatigue and now felt bloated, soft and vulnerable, sad.

From the platform, the doctor called for attention and read out the Christmas messages. There was one from the Governor: 'In pride and admiration I send my greetings this Christmas Day to all who are fighting and to all who are working so nobly and so well to sustain Hongkong against the assaults of the enemy. Fight on. Hold fast for King and Empire. God bless you all in this your finest hour.' There was a similar one, of soldierly brevity, from Fortress Headquarters. At least one man, Morris observed, rose from his mattress and walked towards the platform.

At the head of the stairs, with an orderly's help, Morris put on his harness and returned his revolver to its holster and his ammunition to the belt-pouch. He still felt sluggish, unprepared.

"Can you sell me some fags?" he asked.

The orderly shook his head. "But I'll give you a couple."

"Fine. Now I come to think of it, I don't have a brass farthing anyway." He put one cigarette in his pocket and the other in his mouth. "Any matches?" He accepted a light and put two matches in his pocket. "We're really dragging our backsides now, eh?" With the smell of tobacco in his nostrils, he was more cheerful. "I've got nothing but what I stand up in." The shamelessness of his poverty also pleased him.

The orderly asked stolidly, "You've got your chit, sir?"

Morris nodded and turned towards the stairs. On the first step he halted abruptly. Anna was coming up to him. He looked down at her small pale face, at her shyly eager expression, and was conscious of a second awakening, a stirring from open-eyed sleep, an astringent coolness on his skin. When she reached his level, they stood apart, smiling.

"We never have much time," he said.

"You are going?"

"Yes. I'm all right again." He raised his left arm a little. "Are you all right?"

"Yes."

He saw that she was trembling, and was impulsively stepping forward to take firm hold of her hand when he noticed the attentive orderly. Pausing to give the man a scowl that sent him about his business, he had time to reflect that he could be seen both from the ward and from the lobby below. He hesitated where he was and asked self-consciously, "And James?"

She betrayed anxiety. "I don't know where he is." And, as if one anxiety suggested another, she added, "Mary Gow is very unhappy. I think your Captain Craig has—jilted her."

"They weren't really suited," he said dismissively. "We're talking about other people again." He wanted to touch her. He wanted to ask how he would be able to find her after . . . but after what? The impossibility of framing a simple question about their future, the uncertainty in which they would have to leave each other, impelled him to reach out and grasp her arm.

Two men, helmeted and harnessed, with rifles slung, brushed past him and went down the stairs.

He released her arm. "I suppose I should go. I'm glad I've seen you, Anna, even for a little while. It's a pity Nell isn't here. It's through her we—"

"She's waiting," said Anna softly.

He saw Nell then, standing in the ward. She walked towards them.

"Joan said you'd be asleep and that I shouldn't waken you," he told her with defensive cheerfulness.

Nell was also on the defensive. "Sorry I didn't let you know sooner," she said to Anna. "But we looked after him well enough. He's almost as good as new."

"Better than new," he assured them. Calm, cleansed of his extravagant despair.

There was an exchange of trivialities that mocked the moment. Then, after another soldier had brushed past, he kissed Anna and Nell lightly. "See you soon," he promised. Anna smiled tremulously. "God bless," said Nell, tears in her eyes. He was on his way down the stairs before he recognised the echo of their parting on the steps of the Peninsula Hotel. He turned back and looked up at them. "Round we go again," he said, and the very words made him feel dizzy. Pattern, pattern, pattern—cheating you into thinking that your footprints were already made ahead of you, were waiting for you to step into them.

He did not look back again. He tried to hold the image of Anna in his mind—shaping her smallness, sensing her shy eagerness—as he made his way through the crowd of civilians blocking the lobby.

One man stopped him and asked, "Hear that?" Above the clamour of tongues, there were sounds of explosions. "There was supposed to be a two-hours' truce this morning to let us bring in the women and children cut off at Repulse Bay. You can hear how much of a truce the Nips are observing." The stranger's voice trembled. "Don't spare them, boy." Encouragingly, he struck Morris's wounded arm.

"You silly bugger," exclaimed Morris angrily.

He walked up the broken streets, following the directions that the doctor had given him. The sun was hot, the light crude on heavy trees and massive buildings. Sweating, nursing his arm, trying to find the calm of Anna again, he watched his elastic shadow ride over the dust.

On the gravel drive that led up to G.H.Q., a major intercepted him and took possession of the hospital chit. "Can you use that arm?" he asked morosely.

"A little."

The major looked sulkily at the arm. "You'd better go down to Murray Barracks and see what you can do about organising the members of your battalion behind the lines."

Morris made an effort to understand. "You mean the men in hospital, sir, or the non-combatants—cooks, drivers—"

"I mean what I say, damn you. There are deserters from your battalion behind the lines. Didn't you know?"

"I did not," said Morris indignantly. He was seized with anger again. It felt hard in his chest and ugly on his face.

He walked down to Murray Barracks, asked the sentry whether there were any Scots inside, and, ignoring the sentry's puzzled denial, wandered into the square. He was damned if he knew what to do next. Playing for time, he looked inside a barrack-room: iron-framed beds, kit-bags and suitcases hastily abandoned; on a bed near the door, someone's scattered belongings—clothing, toilet-gear, magazines. One of the magazines lay open—one of the kind that Birse had brought into the mess—and there, on the unknown soldier's bed, stretched a paper woman with bare breasts and frilly pants, waiting for ruin.

Morris lit his second cigarette and walked slowly across the square. He had half a mind to go back to Anna. But, hearing voices from a building ahead, he kept walking. Major Guthrie emerged, and at his heels came Willie the Boxer. Morris grinned and went forward to meet them.

Guthrie shook his hand, patted his good shoulder, and listened, with a narrowing smile, to his story. "There's a lot of fault-finding going on," he muttered. "I get to hear it while I'm dodging around on jobs like this—collecting some stores just now, d'you see? Our reputation doesn't stand very high, I'm afraid."

"Why pick on us?" Morris complained. "We're not losing this bloody war on our own."

Guthrie looked around with old discoloured eyes. "Somebody had to take the first knock. It happened to be us—at Shingmun— and that seems to make us scapegoat. There are skulkers in every unit, but folks look for the ones with the scapegoat's badges." He smiled sadly at his dog. "You can't comb through Wanchai single-handed for skulkers. You'd better come along with me in the stores-truck and rejoin the battalion."

"Good," said Morris, with a nervous quickening of pulse.

"We're all up at Wanchai Gap, except Hugh Craig. He's out with a patrol to see how things stand on Mount Cameron now. Grand soldier, Hugh." Guthrie patted Morris's shoulder again. "Your reputation's all right too, Johnny. Although you didn't get the C.O.'s message, you blocked those roads round Cameron for twice as long as we'd reckoned on."

Startled, puzzled, Morris kept his mouth shut.

*

It was after noon before the stores truck left Murray Barracks for Wanchai Gap, with Major Guthrie sitting beside the driver, and Morris sitting beside Willie the Boxer among containers of food, water and ammunition.

Morris was rested and fed, and warm enough under the winter sun to discard his Canadian greatcoat and let the breeze touch his thin shirt and slacks and his bare forearms. But he could not relax to enjoy his physical comfort . . . He was going back to ordeal by bombardment . . . He was going back to share the ordeal with strangers, now that his own platoon had—but for a corporal and three men—disintegrated into separate corpses and separate hospital cases . . . He was going back to Craig, and it would be even harder to approach Craig than to approach a stranger.

He bent towards Guthrie and asked, "Will Craig be back from his patrol yet?"

Guthrie turned his head. "He should be. But you can never tell with Hugh Craig. Least of all now. His blood is up." Daddy's face crumpled into an anxious frown. "He'll break his heart or his head before he's finished."

He had, Morris reflected uneasily, already broken five subalterns' heads and might yet break his last subaltern's heart, if not his head. Torrance, Williamson, Holt, Wallace and Anstey broken. Morris to break.

On the way up to Wanchai Gap, the truck engine failed, and they had to coast back down the road till they reached a garage. It was locked, but the driver unhesitatingly smashed a window with a spanner and crawled inside to help himself to the parts he needed. Waiting in the truck, Guthrie and his dog dozed off, and Morris began to crave a smoke.

He climbed out, taking care not to bump or jerk his left arm, and walked along a deserted side street. Soon, he remembered that he had neither any money nor anything to barter for cigarettes, and at the same time he recognised that he was still weak in the legs. He sat down on the kerb to rest, bowed his head drowsily, and did not raise it until, some minutes later, he became aware that he was being observed. When he looked up and saw an old man standing in a doorway opposite, he smiled, said "Ding hao," and, with the aid of mime, begged a cigarette. The old man held up his empty hands and ducked his head, nervously polite, but a young man came running from another doorway, holding out a packet of cigarettes. Morris rose and, with a grateful smile, stepped forward and then, startled by a noise at his back, found that he was under observation from both sides of the street. Dazed, he saw faces at doors, faces at windows, wary, inquisitive, friendly. He looked back at the young man and, holding up empty hands as the old man had done, said apologetically, "No money."

"This—Happy Christmas."

Morris reddened with pleasure. "Thanks very much."

Grinning, the young man presented his card. *Henry S. Ho. Manufacture of Choice Articles.*

Hearing Major Guthrie calling for him, Morris shook hands with Mr. Ho, shouted, *"Ding hao,"* to his public, and ran happily along the street with the sounds of strange voices and laughter in his ears.

He sobered up when he saw Guthrie's solemn face, heard his solemn words, "Over here." He walked over to Guthrie's side and looked down over rooftops and saw, between Mount Cameron and the north shore, a white flag flying. As he watched, seized now with the older man's solemnity, he saw another white flag hoisted, closer to the sea. It was a big flag and, as it caught the wind and unfurled slowly, he felt an absurd impulse to salute. Guthrie leaned against a petrol pump and muttered brokenly, "Never thought I'd live to see the day." But, watching the big flag, the clean white flag, Morris thought of it as an honest admission that should have been made before so many lives were lost.

An army motor-cycle roared up the road, and the dispatch-rider shouted as he passed them: "It's all over. Orders from G.H.Q. Rendezvous for your unit—Victoria Barracks."

Guthrie returned to the truck, threw down his helmet, took his old glengarry bonnet from his haversack, pulled it over his head, and sat with his arms folded, his face averted. The driver lay down on the steps of the garage. Morris remained by the petrol pump, wondering at the continuing noises of battle, until he could no longer stand still.

"I'll have a look for the battalion," he said. "They'll come down this road?"

Guthrie nodded.

As Morris walked up the road, an air-raid on Victoria city added to the noises of battle still echoing in the hills. He began to wonder whether the Japanese would respect the white flag, whether they would slaughter prisoners and crippled civilians and rape nurses. But he kept walking until at last he saw a column marching towards him, a column of about one hundred and fifty officers and other ranks led by Captain McNaughton Smith. He stood to the side of the road and waited for them, peering up at the dirty, tired, bewildered faces, searching for men he knew. As the column came down to him, he saw that

McNaughton Smith had no intention of halting. Hastily saluting, he shuffled into step with the portly captain and asked, "Is the rest of the battalion following?"

"This," said McNaughton Smith, "is the battalion."

"But where's the C.O.? Where's Craig?"

"The C.O. and the adjutant are behind the Japanese lines discussing the details of the capitulation. In the meantime, we have to withdraw to Victoria Barracks as quickly as possible and avoid brushes with the enemy. I suggest you fall back and join the other officers."

"But where's Craig?"

"Craig," said McNaughton Smith forbearingly, "took a patrol up Mount Cameron this morning. He and a few of his men are still there—badly wounded."

"You left them?" Morris asked incredulously.

"We got specific orders, Morris, to withdraw quickly and avoid brushes with the enemy. Evacuation of the wounded is one of the things the C.O. is discussing with the Japanese. Craig will be all right. He'll have seen the white flag and know to surrender himself if the Japanese reach him before we can send up stretcher-parties."

"The Japanese," retorted Morris excitedly, "have already slaughtered wounded who tried to surrender."

"Morris," said the large man under the small helmet, almost plaintively, "you're not helping. We got specific orders. I suggest once again you comply with them by joining the other officers in the rear."

Tremulous with unuttered protests, Morris stepped aside and watched the survivors of the battalion march past. A small group of officers brought up the rear of the column, and behind the column came a truck carrying some equipment and a few men, including Corporal Macdonald and Private Jannelli. Morris nodded hurriedly to Captain Kenny Kerr, the only officer who greeted him, and waited for the truck. Walking alongside it, he asked Macdonald apprehensively, "D'you know how badly the Skipper was wounded?"

"Both legs broken, sir."

"Were you with him?"

Macdonald nodded towards his companions in the truck. "We were all with him. We were the only ones that came back. But

we left less casualties than the Japs did," he added with grim satisfaction.

"Could you not have carried the wounded out with you?"

"Skipper's orders, sir. We'd no ammo left, and we were still under fire. We had to run for it." Macdonald's sombre gaze rested on Morris. "Were you thinking of going back for them?"

The question confused Morris. He had been trying rather to allay his fears than to consider action. "How many are there?" he parried.

"Only the Skipper and big Keith are likely to have lasted out. Four of us could carry them down." The corporal looked at his companions with an insolent, challenging smile. "Any of you game to go back?"

Jannelli, staring at Morris, nodded. The other men turned away.

Morris swallowed hard. The hills were quiet now. The only noises of battle came from somewhere along the north shore.

"There's another truck behind us," said Macdonald. "We could ask them if there's any sign of Japs on the move yet."

"We'll see what they say," decided Morris.

Macdonald and Jannelli jumped down, the corporal still holding his Tommy gun.

"You won't need that," said Morris.

"You're not going empty-handed?" protested Macdonald.

Morris watched the column and the truck disappear round a bend in the road. He inhaled quickly and said, "If we bump the Japs, we'll have a slightly better chance carrying nothing but a white flag."

Jannelli pulled a handkerchief from his pocket. "Will this do, sir?"

Morris nodded, and drew his revolver and tossed it into the ditch. Sullenly, Macdonald walked to the side of the road and hid his gun in the scrub.

Going up the road, however, the corporal soon recovered his spirits by recalling the patrol's fight on Mount Cameron. "We'd waited a long time to get them in the open. All the way from Golden Hill we'd waited. And we took more than an eye for an eye today."

They reached Wanchai Gap just as the rear party were boarding their truck. "We've not seen any Japs, and we're not waiting to see any," said the driver. "If you're going down with us, sir, you'd better jump in."

But Morris, in the uneventful climb to the Gap, had hardened his resolve. "Carry on," he told the driver.

He was going to carry Craig down, not just for Craig's sake, but also for his own sake. He too had waited a long time for this day. He was standing on his own feet now, choosing his own path. And Craig was lying on the ground, with both his stiff legs broken, unable to take a step further towards his flawless paradise.

With Macdonald in front as guide, they struck eastwards along the hills.

*

James Lin and Sammy King stood in the middle of the road and looked up at the white flag waving over Murray Barracks.

"Funeral white," said Sammy.

James glanced at his friend's moon-face bright with beer-sweat and stared at the flag again. High above the neglected streets, seen against a drift of smoke from the waterfront, its whiteness held his gaze, its easy yielding to the breeze stirred responses in his belly. "This is *su*," he said, "plain silk for plain men." He smiled broadly, belched, wiped his face on his sleeve, and wished that he had drunk less beer.

They turned and walked westwards, past the dusty deserted centre of Victoria and into the narrow streets lined with Chinese tenements. Although the air still trembled with distant explosions, people were already venturing out of their homes, standing by their doors or sauntering under the arcades. James looked at them carefully. He saw his long-dead grandfather's face under an old-fashioned buttoned hat. He saw a girl's face, long-eyed, small-mouthed, that made him think of his own seed.

"We are going back to our roots," he said, laughing at the solemnity of his thoughts.

"The simple life," said Sammy breathlessly. "A bed, a bowl of rice, and plenty time to squash bugs and pick our teeth."

"Old Shou will have room for us?"

"As long as our money lasts out."

James shook his head wisely. "*Aiyah*, how the Black-Haired People have lost their simplicity!" He looked around. Here the flags were not white: flamboyant banners boldly coloured and charactered stretched across the walls of buildings and flapped like laundry above the streets. Here the very air reeked of complexity, smelling of smoke and cooking-oil, garbage and sun-dried fish, pickles and orange peel, camphor-wood, joss-sticks, leather, tobacco, soap, tea, timber, gunpowder . . . "When our money is finished," said James tipsily, "we'll go into the hills, turn the world right side up again, find the Spirit of the Valley, the Mystic Female."

Sammy cleared his throat and spat. "And when we pass water," he said, "we'll make sure we're not facing north." And then, perhaps fearing that he had made too light of his companion's homeward, heavenward yearning, he mumbled: "It's in the old books. It was reckoned to be unlucky."

James smiled tolerantly. And they kept walking to the west of the city, to the East of their dreams.

*

Chan Kin-kwok lay fully dressed on a luxurious bed in the abandoned house he had taken over as quarters for himself and his two girls. He could take what he wanted. He was a big man now, bigger than any Westerner on the island, with a white arm-band to proclaim his authority and a ·38 revolver to prove it. His brother would still have been alive, would have been another big man, if only he had understood that the way to bigness led, not through submissive words and patient labour, but through proud words and aggressive actions. His brother should have imitated the foreign soldiers, not served them, and he would have lived to make them serve him.

When the girls burst into the bedroom, chattering like startled monkeys, Chan smiled indolently at them.

"They are coming," said Mimi Pak breathlessly.

"They are coming here," said Poppy Wu.

He swung his legs over the bed. "Why are you afraid?" he asked, touching his white arm-band. "I have worked for them. They are our friends. You should be preparing food."

"We will stay upstairs," said Poppy. Her lips were pinched, her round cheeks pale. "You go down and tell them to go away."

"You said you would protect us," Mimi reminded him.

"I have given you this house. I have brought you food and clothes and—" He broke off, hearing someone pounding on the front door.

Downstairs, he admitted five Japanese soldiers. Speaking his own language, pointing to his arm-band and smiling, he welcomed them. They pushed past him and started to search the ground floor. They were coarsely-featured, loud-voiced men, with muscular bodies and short thick legs. He followed them cautiously, fearfully. They helped themselves to food and drink, stole a few small things and, with their bayonets, destroyed a painting of a yellow-haired woman. Upstairs, they laughed at the bathroom and found Mimi and Poppy in the bedroom.

Mimi was carried screaming to the bed. Poppy was trapped between a wardrobe and wall. Sweating and trembling, Chan retreated to the door, with bowed head and inconspicuous movements. There was a time for everything: a time to be big and a time to be small. As the soldiers dragged Poppy to the floor and started to tear off her gown, she called to Chan, again and again. But he managed to reach the door without attracting the attention of the wild-voiced soldiers, and he turned and ran to safety.

*

They were climbing the north-west slope of Mount Cameron, marching, from habit, in single file: Macdonald leading, Jannelli following with his dirty handkerchief in his hand, and Morris bringing up the rear and watching the flanks.

Morris was still energised by an excitement compounded of fear and pride, which helped him to keep his tired legs moving and his doubts in check. Wilfully, he tried to look outside himself.

He looked at Macdonald. Macdonald was like Craig, a man intent on making a big mark, a man making for an exacting heaven. And, looking at Macdonald, he caught a glimpse of himself, his new self.

He looked at Jannelli. It was easy to understand Macdonald's readiness to volunteer for this last march, but not so easy to understand Jannelli's readiness.

"You all right, Jannelli?" he asked softly.

The little man glanced round, his face bright with sweat, his eyes dark with fatigue. "I'll manage, sir," he said, forcing a weary smile. "It's not far to go now."

Morris knew then that Jannelli would always be ready to march with him. And he caught another glimpse of himself, his old self.

They had not far to go. It was Morris who first caught sight of the Japanese coming round the hill. "Hold it," he warned his companions urgently, and they halted and turned to face the enemy.

There were about a dozen of them, moving in straggling formation, short-legged, splay-footed, agile. Sighting the three Scots, they uttered harsh cries, fanned out, up and down the slope, and advanced with their weapons ready. The commander carried a naked sword, and the others carried rifles and bayonets.

"Show them the flag," said Morris tensely.

Jannelli held up his handkerchief.

"Stand still and leave this to me," said Morris, intending his words for Macdonald, Craig-minded Macdonald. "Don't do anything to put their backs up." He raised his hands to show that he was unarmed, and pointed to Jannelli's handkerchief.

The Japanese formed a ring round the Scots. The commander halted in front of Morris and said loudly, *"Nanda?"* He had a broad, brown, excited face and an unpleasant smell.

"Do you speak English?" Morris asked.

The commander put his head to one side, like an ugly bird, and shouted something to his men that roused them to jeering laughter.

Sweating, shaky, Morris tried to take comfort from their laughter. "We are on our way to pick up wounded," he said. And, using Jannelli as a dummy, he tried to interpret his words in action.

In response, the Japanese commander stepped forward and, to the accompaniment of his men's laughter, went through the motions of beheading Morris.

"We're unarmed—unarmed," shouted Macdonald, showing his empty hands. "Savvy?"

Morris, patiently standing head and shoulders above his tormentor, warned, "Take it easy, Mac."

"They're not getting me without a fight," shouted the corporal, his dark face distorted with rage. "I'll take some of them with me."

"Shut up!" ordered Morris.

But it was too late. The Japanese had stopped laughing. One of the riflemen, at a word from the commander, moved forward and jabbed his bayonet at Macdonald. It would not have drawn blood. But Macdonald reached out and seized the muzzle of the rifle. He might have intended to arm himself for a last fight or simply to push back the bayonet. Before he had time to do either, the commander had leapt up and swung his two-handed sword. It struck Macdonald between neck and shoulder, and clove down through bone and flesh. Wide-eyed, open-mouthed, the corporal died as he fell.

Swollen and shaken by his kill, the Japanese commander turned to Morris and shouted at him, in hoarse, unsteady tones of indignation. It sounded as if he were complaining about Macdonald's behaviour, as if he were trying to justify the execution. His men started to chatter among themselves, and he appeared to lose the thread of his argument. He squatted on his hunkers to wipe his blade on the grass and, after a few moments of scowling silence, glanced up at Morris and Jannelli and said quietly, "Yoroshi," and made signs that they might continue their journey.

Still numb with shock, Morris could not move until the commander rose and impatiently repeated his signs. Then, grasping Jannelli's trembling arm, Morris said hoarsely: "I think they're going to let us go. Take it easy. Don't run." He nodded to the commander and, keeping hold of Jannelli's arm, turned towards the hill again.

They passed Macdonald's body and walked out of the ring of riflemen and climbed slowly and jerkily. "Oh, God," whispered Jannelli, squeezing the words from his dry throat, "what are they going to do?"

"I think," said Morris, gradually warming to life again, "they're going to let us go."

Then, in the one instant of terror, he heard the roar of rifles and felt the bullets hit his back. He fell with Jannelli and, dazed by pulsations of screaming laughter in his ears, waited for the bayonets. They did not come. The noise of the strange voices and laughter diminished and died away.

He began to emerge from his pain and find calm. He saw that Jannelli's eyes were closed, his breathing light. "Hang on," he gasped, "till the stretchers come." Jannelli did not seem to hear.

*

Jannelli was counting . . . thirty-four, thirty-five, thirty-six . . .

*

Craig lay higher up the hill, in a gully that had been washed out by rains but was now as dry as the back of his own throat. There was a merciful murmur of fatigue in his ears. He could no longer hear the accusing silence of all the men lying around him, the men who had helped him to make his last gesture, who had died to satisfy his anger and pride. He was released, for a time, from the torment of self-reproach. But only for a time. He knew that he would live. Te refused to die, to taste the final defeat.

*

. . . fifty-two, fifty-three, fifty-four, fif-

*

Morris was his old self again, cut down to size, cautiously husbanding his strength, waiting for a stretcher-party.

*

In the orderly-room at Victoria Barracks, McNaughton Smith sat erect on an iron bed-frame, took another mouthful of rum to warm his tired, hungry body, and listened patiently to the adjutant's reprimands.

"You should have kept an eye on him," said Ballantyne irately. "If anything happens to him, the Old Horse will flay you."

"It wasn't our fault," muttered Niven, sitting dejectedly on the floor. "Morris is a prize ass."

"The trouble with Morris—" began Kenny Kerr, tolerantly.

"The trouble with Morris," interrupted McNaughton Smith, suddenly, warmly, aware that he could interpret Morris more capably than Kerr or Niven or anyone else could. "The trouble with Morris is that he wears no fig-leaf to cover the flaws of his humanity. His awkwardness is so naked that it makes skill seem to be a kind of deceit." He saw, sadly, that he had already lost his audience.

Guthrie, hunched on the only chair in the room, staring at his dog, asked, "What am I going to do with Willie?"

Morris, McNaughton Smith told himself drowsily, is one of the meek—disinherited of the earth—because he does not want the earth—world with an end, amen.

"They may let me keep him," suggested Guthrie.

The dog snuffled in its sleep, breaking the uneasy silence.

*

In the failing light of Christmas Day, Craig was lifted on to a stretcher. He recognised one of the bearers—Cratchley, the convict, the deserter, driven back to the shelter of the white flag—and closed his aching eyes.

On the way down, the bearers halted, and Craig heard

Cratchley mutter: "Dekko. It's the bible-puncher. And, see, that'll be the other two up there." They started moving again, climbing across the slope. "That's the little Taliano, all right. And —sure enough, that's Boy Morris beside him."

Craig struggled to raise himself.

"It's Mr. Morris, sir."

"Dead?"

Cratchley laid down his end of the stretcher and knelt beside the bodies. "Dead. Shot in the back."

"But what—?" Craig's voice broke on the question.

"We were told to look for them too," said the other bearer solemnly. "They tried to find you earlier."

For a few moments Craig clung to the sides of the stretcher. He had asked too much of everyone he had ever known—women like Mary—men like Morris. He raised his head higher and looked at the bodies. "What's that—between them?" he asked, hoping confusedly that the paleness might be paper, a message, a last message from Morris.

"It's a hankie," said Cratchley. "For a white flag, I suppose."

Rain started to fall and roused Craig from his tormented silence. "Take me down," he muttered hoarsely.

"*Chullo*," said Cratchley to the other bearer, "before we get soaked."

They went down, leaving the dead like dark islands on the wet hillside.

For regular early information

about

FORTHCOMING NOVELS

send a postcard

giving your name and address

in block capitals

to

THE FICTION EDITOR

HODDER & STOUGHTON LTD.

1 St. Paul's House, Warwick Square

London, E.C.4